W9-BGB-663

Sullivan's Island

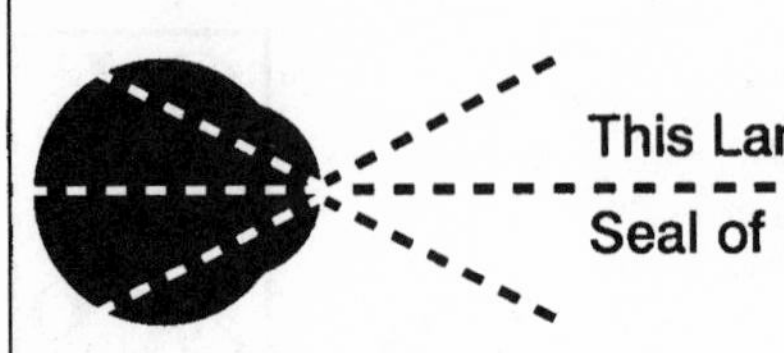

This Large Print Book carries the
Seal of Approval of N.A.V.H.

Sullivan's Island

A Lowcountry Tale

Dorothea Benton Frank

G.K. Hall & Co. • Thorndike, Maine

This is a work of fiction. Names, characters, places, and incidents are either the product of the author's imagination or are used fictitiously, and any resemblance to actual persons, living or dead, business establishments, events, or locales is entirely coincidental.

Published in 2000 by arrangement with The Berkley Publishing Group, a member of Penguin Putnam Inc.

G.K. Hall Large Print Core Series.

The text of this Large Print edition is unabridged.
Other aspects of the book may vary from the original edition.

Set in 16 pt. Plantin by Elena Picard.

Printed in the United States on permanent paper.

Library of Congress Cataloging-in-Publication Data

Frank, Dorothea Benton.
Sullivan's Island : a Lowcountry tale / Dorothea Benton Frank.
p. cm.
ISBN 0-7838-9078-8 (lg. print : hc : alk. paper)
ISBN 0-7838-9079-6 (lg. print : sc : alk. paper)
1. Sullivan's Island (S.C. : Island) — Fiction. 2. South Carolina — Fiction. 3. Sisters — Fiction. 4. Large type books.
I. Title.
PS3556.R3338 S85 2000
813′.6—dc21 00-035035

For my dear friend and mentor, Mary Kuczkir.
And for Ella Wright, who was my Livvie.

CONTENTS

Acknowledgments

I would like to thank the following wonderful people who helped me at every stage of developing this crazy tale of mine.

Special thanks to my McInerny cousins, Michael and Mary Jo and Father Larry, who helped me remember so much and set the tone with their hilarious stories of crabbing and being disciplined by the nuns of Stella Maris Grammar School. Also my Blanchard cousins, Judy Linder and Laura. I love every smart and funny bone in their bodies!

Speaking of the nuns, I'd like to acknowledge Sister Miriam, my old principal at Stella Maris; Father Kelly, my principal at Bishop England High School; and oh, Lord, Sister Rosaire, my biology teacher; all of whom told me that my sassy mouth and lack of personal discipline would bring me to no good someday. If they hadn't beaten the guilt into me, they would've been right. But it was Stephen Spade, my tenth-grade English teacher, who taught me to love the cadence of words. God bless them all.

Robert and Susan Rosen deserve a huge acknowledgment for all their legal and historic facts and research recommendations. Robert is only the funniest historian on the planet, who has written many brilliant books on Charleston. And also to my e-mail author buddy, Julie Dash. Julie, you were so much help on Gullah history, you just don't know. If you like the Gullah flavor in this book and haven't read *Daughters of the Dust*, go get it! (Okay, Julie and Robert, now y'all owe me!) I'd also like to thank author and historian Suzannah Smith Miles for answering all my questions with such grace. And to Morris Dees, of the Southern Poverty Law Center, many thanks for your help as well.

Everyone should have friends like Dan and Corky Gaby. It was their support and faith that led me to attempt this. Many thanks, y'all. I'd also like to send kisses to the members of my book group, especially Adrian Shelby, Ruth Perretti, Cherry Provost and Jean Kidd, for living through the drama and pushing me forward.

Special thanks to Dr. John F. Noonan and poet Paul Genega from Bloomfield College who put the official writer's curse on me and ruined my tennis game.

Many thanks to John McDermott of the Mount Pleasant Knights of Columbus and Billy of Billy's Back Home Restaurant. Also to my old friend Dr. George Durst, whose recollections inspired the fort scene.

To Gloria Steinem, Sean Byrne, Francesco Scavullo, Eric Dominguez, Jim Vayias, Pamela Wallace, Lynn O'Hare, Meredith Metz, Beth Grossbard, Clive and Ann Cummis and my L.A. gurus, Marvin Meyer and Joel Gotler — sincere thanks for your support. Alex Sanders, I believe you're the kindest of all southern gentlemen.

This book would be a rumor were it not for the regular beatings, guidance and faith of the most wonderful editor on earth — Gail Fortune — who helped me bring the story to life and gave me this extraordinary opportunity to be a published author. And rightfully, I bow in gratitude to Leslie Gelbman and Liz Perl. It was my mentor and dear friend — Fern Michaels to the world, Mary Kuczkir to me — who kept me going. To Pam Strickler and Russell Galen, many thanks. And let us not forget my new friend, the fabulous Matthew Rich, who helped me get my act together. To my dear friend Linda Lauren who always said this was in the cards, thank you, doll face, for your unending support. And to my wonderful and forgiving sister, Lynn Bagnal. Lynn, this is fiction, I swear it is. To my brothers, their lovely wives, and anyone else related to me or anyone I have ever known, I'd like to apologize for any embarrassment this story may cause.

Finally, to my family — my beautiful daughter, Victoria, and my gorgeous son, William, thank you for understanding why I turned the house upside down to do this. It's just your mom, trying to live her dream. And, to my magnificent husband, Peter, who practically walks on water, who ate take-out for two years and just told me to keep going: I want the world to know how grateful I am to you for believing in me. I love you all to your last freckle.

Prologue

I searched for sleep curled up in my quilt — the one made for me at my birth by my paternal grandmother's own hands. Southern women have always taken pride in the excellence of their needlework. Over the years it had been abused and then its edges rebound and its tears carefully mended. The design was my grandmother's own — so unique — a beautiful, pastel-colored garden, with a stream of gray and pale blue silk water running down its center. As a child the scene had seemed so real to me that I could imagine myself there, climbing the garden wall of stone and pale green ivy and then wading in the water.

The front was pieced together from tiny swatches of fabrics to form flowers, birds, trees and shrubs. She had probably collected those swatches for years. The back of the quilt was now ivory silk, blind-stitched over its original backing of cotton. Hundreds of tiny French knots gave the quilt texture and dimension. Its fragile state was so urgent; it should have been mounted as a wall hanging for the sake of preservation. If there was one thing that Charlestonians did it was to preserve. But, I couldn't retire it as an art object. I preferred to wrap myself in its cool folds, wondering if my grandmother — the one I had scarcely known — was trying to tell me something.

I turned in our ancient, creaking bed — my parents' bed — solid mahogany, with carved shafts of rice decorating each of its four red patina posters, a symbol of long-gone plantation crops. We had once grown the most desirable rice in the world in Charleston's rice fields — Carolina Gold. The bed was a souvenir of the past.

I remembered the day we had carried it into the house in pieces, up the steep stairs from the front hall to our bedroom — Tom and I — and together we had assembled it, fitting the neatly labeled pegs in just so. There was not a single nail in it — only handmade pegs. We had just bought our house then — an old Victorian in the historic district of downtown — and my sister had insisted that we have the bed as a housewarming gift.

My mind moved on. I tried to convince myself that the gentle, rhythmic snoring of my husband was in fact the sound of the tide coming in on Sullivan's Island. The sounds of the Island had never failed to help me fall off to deep sleep. But that night no amount of imagining or remembering brought the rest I so desperately sought.

It had been well past one o'clock when I finally got to bed and I twisted and turned until past two. Somewhere around then I kicked off the covers and opened a window. At that hour the city noises of Charleston had at long last given up to near silence, except for the occasional foghorn from the harbor or the lone car engine revving up and flying away from a red light. The car's driver — probably a college student — knew no one was around to stop him at that hour.

As I raised the sash, the night air rushed through my window, causing my curtain sheers to billow, and my bedroom air became damp all at once. Damp and slightly chilled. I should have recognized the smell of impending disaster, but I didn't. I hurried back to bed and when the alarm failed to wake me at six-thirty, I woke in a panic at seven.

The day began in a whirlwind of petty grievances. Beth didn't like the cereal I put out for her and whined about it as though I were trying to feed her poison instead of a bowl of healthy fiber. Tom couldn't find his favorite cuff links and accused me of being nosy for rearranging his jewelry tray. I had done no such thing. Who had the time for that sort of housekeeping? Rearrange his jewelry tray? What a joke that was. I had barely had time lately to remember my name. He had probably left them at the gym, I told him.

Half apologetic for his foul humor, Tom took our daughter to school so that I could get to my office at the Charleston County Library on time. Even he knew I had to make a major presentation that afternoon at work. "Good luck!" he called out on his way out the back door.

I had been up late working on a proposal for the South Carolina Electric and Gas Company. It was pretty much a done deal, but I still worried. I got paid to worry. I raced to work like a madwoman. I couldn't be late. An ugly side of government employment involved time clock punching and score keeping at an obsessive level. If you were fifteen minutes late, your salary was docked. Absurd. I had two master's degrees, but if I was fifteen minutes late for work, eyes rolled, eyebrows arched and the bookkeeper had a smug moment of glee. Where had *they* been at one in the morning? Forget it. It wasn't an argument worth the blood pressure. You see, I'd learned. Pick your battles carefully.

Anyway, I felt like a plate spinner. Remember those guys on television? *The Ed Sullivan Show*, I think — some Russian fellow who had twenty plates on flexible poles, all spinning at once over his head. That was my life. My daughter, Beth, was one plate — her academic career, her social life, her complexion and her compulsion to spend. Oh, she spun all right. My husband, Tom, was another — spinning somewhere out of my direct line of vision. The house was another — threatening to fall down around my ears. It was always something — a broken pipe, a leaking gutter — and it was my job to see about it all. Tom was too busy. Or whatever. My sex life was another plate. That one spun backwards, along with my wallet plate — slightly cracked. Don't ask. I just kept thinking that soon, things would be better — as soon as I got to the bottom of the paper on my desk, filled out all the health insurance claims, as soon as I did this or that.

I should not have been in the least surprised to discover, when I made it to the library, that I had left the support materials for the charts at home. Well, I thought, I could put a Band-Aid on that one too. Instead of lunch, I'd just fly home as fast as I could, grab the papers and fly back in time for the two o'clock meeting. It wasn't a big deal — just a mosquito bite in the scheme of things.

I gave my diskettes to our development department secretary, who swore up and down that it was no problem to print the graphs on sixteen-by-twenty paper for the easel. I blew her a kiss and ran back home at around eleven. If I got back by twelve, it would give me two solid hours to assemble everything and go over it again.

It was a gorgeous South Carolina morning. I don't know why, but I was struck by the clearness of the sky — all that blue. So beautiful. I raced down Meeting Street, passing all the tourists crossing the streets, thinking how pleasant it was to live in a place that everyone wanted to see. And Charleston is no cheesy resort. She is noble and grand. People came here to learn, to be enriched. Of course my enthusiasm was tempered by the natural reserve with which Charlestonians have the good fortune to be born. No, no. During Spoleto Festival, we do not drive down Murray Boulevard blowing our horns and swilling beers like in the football towns. Heaven forbid. We open our gardens and serve iced tea with mint sprigs to total strangers, treating them like favored friends.

I was thinking about all this graciousness and hospitality, and singing "Sixty-Minute Man" along with the radio, as I swung into my narrow driveway on Queen Street. I didn't even slam my car door, but left it open, intending to stay only long enough to get what I needed. I was already bounding up the steps to Beth's room (somehow the family word processor had migrated there) when I heard the voices. I stopped dead. Someone was in my house. Someone was in my bedroom! *"Oh, God!"* I heard a distinctly female voice cry out. *"Oh, my God!"* Was it Beth? Was someone hurting my Beth? It sounded like someone having sex! With my heartbeat loud in my ears, I sneaked back downstairs as fast as I could and grabbed the fireplace poker. I was shaking all over. I didn't know whether to call the police first or try to stop what was happening myself. I stood outside my bedroom door and listened for a minute. My box spring was creaking and groaning.

"Ride me! Yes! My tiger!"

Then an all too familiar voice said, "I'm gonna give it to you like you want it! Tell me you want it!"

"Oh! Yes! Please!"

It took me about one split second to realize I was about to confront some major bullshit. My heart sank. I could've walked out of there and maintained my dignity, but oh, no. Not me. Something made me open the door. The tiger — whose bare backside faced me — was none other than my husband, Tom. The female he rode — whose ankles he held high in the air while she clung to my headboard — was the chemically enhanced and surgically improved young woman who ran the New Age bookstore on St. Phillip's Street. I stood there in the doorway with the poker, anger rising like a geyser, waiting for them to realize they had company, thinking for a split second that a poker was a rather Freudian and humorously named weapon to have at the moment. I cleared my throat as loudly as I could when it was clear my husband and his love puppy didn't have a clue. She was the first to react.

"Tom!" she screamed. "Stop! My God!" She scrambled to cover herself with *my* sheets.

He turned around to face me and started screaming, "What are *you* doing here?"

"I live here," I said. My voice sounded weak. "I forgot some papers." I couldn't move.

"Well, go get them," he said, "and close the door!" He sounded cold and foreign. Not like the man I had shared the last sixteen years with.

His dismissal finally infuriated me beyond reason. "Get out of my house," I said, "both of you." I crossed the room and raised the fireplace tool over Tom's head. They were suddenly horrified and begged me to put it down. They scrambled to the other side of the bed to escape, caught in the sheets, knocking a lamp from the end table, sending it smashing to the ground.

"Please, Susan! I can explain! Don't do this!" Tom was pleading with me and, thank God, I heard him. I would've hit them both, bashed their brains in. I dropped the cast-iron poker to the floor and began trembling. I'd never hit anyone in my life and suddenly there was a raging murderer inside of me.

"Get out," I said to her in a low voice. My heart pounded so hard I thought I might have a stroke. She slipped out of the bed, naked and wet with perspiration, her blond hair all matted in the back from her tiger ride. Her dark pubic hair was shaved into a heart shape. "Who do you think you are?" I hissed at her. "You're not even a real blond!"

"Go downstairs, Susan," Tom said, "try to pull yourself together."

"Really?" I said. "Pull myself together? You're in

my bed with this slut and I should worry about how I *behave?* This bitch is screaming 'Ride me like a tiger!' and *I* should compose *myself?* I'll tell you what, Tom Hayes. You get that cheap whore out of my house and get your ass dressed and downstairs in five minutes. If you can't give me the apology of your life, I want you out of this house today. Is that clear?"

I didn't even know if he answered me. I slammed the door so hard behind me that it thundered all over the house. I don't remember going to the kitchen, or lighting the cigarette I found myself smoking a few minutes later. I heard the front door close. Silence. I waited for Tom to appear. Silence followed by silence. I went back to the foot of the stairs.

"Tom?"

He was gone.

I called my office after some time and apologized, saying that I had become ill, asking my boss to do the presentation. My illness wasn't a lie. The room spun around me as I fed the support material for the presentation through the fax in Tom's study. I pulled the sheets and pillowcases off our bed and flipped the mattress. I got a sponge and wiped down every square inch of my bathroom and dusted every surface in my room. It wasn't until I put the linens in the washer that I began to cry. I saw by the kitchen clock that it was afternoon — it was two-thirty. Beth had cheerleader practice and she wouldn't be home until five. What would I say to her?

I debated calling Tom's office but before I could think of what to say, I heard the front door open again. In a matter of seconds I turned to see Tom staring at me. I knew I looked horrible. My eyes were all swollen and red. Somehow the favorite dress I had chosen to wear to work now seemed frumpy and dowdy. I stood there in my stocking feet. I felt a run growing by my big toe on my left foot — it ran right up the front of my leg. I had to wear black pantyhose today? It came to me in a rush that my nails were chipped and my hair hadn't had a professional cut in six months. Needless to say, I was twenty pounds overweight.

I looked hard at Tom. He was tan and fit. He stood quietly in the doorway to the kitchen. His teeth were perfect, his stomach was as flat and hard as Formica and his loafers were shining from diligent polish. He pulled off his tie and began to roll it around his hand.

"We need to talk," he said.

"Yeah, I guess so."

"I'm sorry you found us, Susan," he said.

"Wait a minute. You're sorry *I found you?* Shouldn't the first thing you apologize for be that you betrayed me?" I began to panic all over again.

"Of course I'm sorry I betrayed you," he said quietly, looking at the floor. "We had it good together for a long time."

"What are you saying, Tom?" My breath was uneven.

"I'm saying I think we should try living apart for a while," he said.

There it was. The hideous truth. He wanted out.

"Why? Tom, why? Look, I know things haven't been great between us lately. I mean, I know we haven't been as close as we used to be, but I can change. I can try harder." I was pleading and I could see from his expression that he was embarrassed by it.

"Please, Susan, don't make this any harder than it is," he said.

"Don't make it harder? What does that mean?"

"I just need some space, some time to think," he said. "It has to be this way."

"Why?" I began to cry. "What about Beth? What about our family, Tom? What about me?"

"Look, I just came back to get some things. You know I'll take care of you and Beth. I'll talk to her. I just have to have some time, Susan."

"Look at me, Tom. Look at me in the face and tell me why this is happening, because I don't understand."

When he looked at me I knew all at once why it was happening. He didn't love me anymore. He didn't even look guilty. He looked relieved. He cleared his throat.

"Where is my black hanging bag?" he said.

"Find it yourself," I said. It began to sink in that he was really leaving. Nothing I could say or do would change that. "And while you're finding your black hanging bag that I worked overtime to buy you for Father's Day last year . . . oh, God. It's on the third floor in the hall closet." I was going to tell him to go to hell but I couldn't get the words out of my throat. What difference would it have made? Father's Day. I watched him leave the room and listened to his quiet footsteps on the stairs. I heard him walk overhead and up the steps again to the third floor. I couldn't move. I felt like someone had died and it was such a shock that I couldn't absorb it. Suddenly I started thinking about seeing him in bed with that woman and then I started getting mad again.

I went upstairs and found him lifting stacks of shirts from his drawer and putting them on the bed. His hanging bag was spread open and held several suits. I sat on the other side of the bed and tucked my feet under me.

"What's her name, Tom?" No answer. "Come on, Tom, she must have a name."

He opened his sock drawer and stopped. "Karen," he said.

"How old is she? I mean, she's obviously younger than I am. Just out of curiosity . . ."

"I don't know," he said.

"Nineteen? Twenty?" I was being a bitch but, hey, I figured, why not? "So, do you think she loves you for yourself?"

"Susan, she's twenty-three and yes, she loves me for myself."

"And you love her too. Is that right?"

"Yes, I think so," he said in a whisper.

"What was that? I couldn't hear you, Tom. Did you say she's closer to Beth's age than to yours and that you are in love with her?"

"Yes," he said.

"I see. Well, we may as well be civilized about this, to the extent that's possible for me anyway." I got up from the bed and went to the bathroom. He closed the drawer to let me pass without touching him. That act of avoidance infuriated me further. "No sense in prolonging the misery," I said, "I'll pack your shaving kit for you."

"Thanks," he said.

I closed the bathroom door behind me, locked it and looked in the mirror. I had never been so furious in my life. I ran the cold water, took off my glasses and washed my face. When had I stopped wearing contact lenses? Ten years ago? When had my teeth started turning yellow? Five years ago? I pulled his leather bag from the cabinet under the sink and opened it. Condoms? How old were they? I took his razor from his medicine cabinet and dropped it in the bag, along with his shaving cream and the Colgate. Reaching for his toothbrush, I looked at it and realized he'd been brushing his teeth for somebody else for a long time. I don't know what possessed me to do it but I dunked it in the toilet. That pleased me so much that I rubbed it around the inside rim. That seemed so pleasant I then scrubbed up under the rim, good and hard, where no toilet brush could've reached in weeks.

"Tom, do you want a hair dryer?" My heart was pounding as I put the toothbrush in its holder and dropped it in the bag.

"No, that's okay," he said.

"I'll be out in a minute," I said. I pulled off my pantyhose and threw them in the wastebasket. I took his aftershave and cologne out of the medicine cabinet. It occurred to me that he'd been wearing these for Karen. I peed in the bathroom glass, drained the Aramis and poured urine into two of his cologne bottles. "Up yours," I said quietly. I dropped the bottles in his bag and zipped it closed. Once more I looked in the mirror. I wondered what had become of the nice girl I once was.

When I went back to the bedroom, his suitcase was gone. I took the shaving kit downstairs and met him at the door.

"Where can I reach you?" I said, handing it to him.

"I'll call you," he said.

We just stood there looking at each other.

"I'm sorry, Susan, it's not you, it's me," he said. He turned and left.

"Yeah," I said. I watched him go to his car, the same way I had a million other times.

1

The Porch

1999

I began putting my life back together at the feet of my older sister and her family. She lived in Momma's house — the family shrine — on the front beach of Sullivan's Island. Every time I went over to the Island — which was frequent in the first months after Tom left — I tried to leave the harsh realities of my new life behind me.

My old station wagon rolled slowly across the causeway, liberating my daughter and me from the starched life of the peninsula to the tiny dream kingdom of Sullivan's Island. Black magic and *cunja* powder swirled invisibly in the air. The sheer mist became the milky fog of my past.

From within the pink and white branches of the overgrown oleanders, which lined both sides of the road, floated the spirits of decades long gone. The *haints* were still there, just waiting for us in the tall grasses and bushes. Suffice it to say that everything in the Lowcountry was just a-wiggling with life and it wasn't always a warm body.

The spirits urged me to roll down my windows

and breathe in the musk-laden drug of the marsh. The scents of plough mud and rotting marsh life filled my senses like a warm shower of rare perfume. Then the sirens sounded their cue and the drawbridge lifted up before us to allow passage for a tall-masted sailboat. We would be detained on the Charleston side for fifteen minutes. I left my car to stand outside and feel the air. Beth stayed in the car listening to the radio.

I walked to the edge of the marsh. The full force of the salty air washed my face and, in an instant, I was a young girl again.

I was hurrying home to my momma and Livvie, my heart already there. The sweet steam of Livvie's simmering okra soup beckoned in a long finger all the way from the back porch. In my mind I heard the voices of my brothers and my sister as we converged on the supper table, all of us bickering in Gullah over the largest piece of cornbread. Livvie ran interference, telling us to hush, warning us that Daddy was coming.

It was odd what I remembered about growing up. My first associations were tied into the smells of the marsh and the aromas of the kitchen. Maybe I should have done fragrance research instead of planning literacy programs at the county library, but I was always more inclined toward saving the world. One thing was for sure, I needed a job that would let me offer my opinions because, according to everybody I knew, that was one area where I excelled.

Livvie. God, not a day passed that I didn't remember her. She raised me — all of us, actually. Here was an old Gullah woman who put her own five children through college working as a housekeeper. Just when she should have been thinking retirement, she took on the notorious clan of Hamilton hardheaded ignoramuses. She was the captain of our destiny, redirecting our course as often as needed. With every snap of her fingers we woke up to the truths of life and our own potential a little more. It was because of her that we all loved to read. She'd shake her head and lecture. "Feast your hungry brain with a good book," she'd say. "Quit wasting time! Life's short. Humph!" Humph, indeed. Who was I kidding? It was because of her that we were not all in some treatment program. She had taught us how to think — no small feat.

She'd probably have had plenty to say if she could have seen Beth and me right now, playing instead of working. I'd told my boss I had a doctor's appointment. A tiny lie. But I had an excellent excuse for playing hooky on this particular weekday afternoon. Heat. Over one hundred degrees every day since last week. We were having a heat wave, Lowcountry style. It felt as if old-fashioned southern cooks were deep-frying us in bubbling oil like a bunch of breaded chickens. One flip of the wrist and the whole of Charleston and its barrier islands sizzled in a cast-iron skillet. We're talking hot, Bubba. Take it from an old Geechee girl. Geechee? That would be someone born in the Lowcountry, which extends from the Ogeechee River down in Georgia clear up to Georgetown, South Carolina. I was raised in the downy bosom of the Gullah culture, as opposed to a Charlestonian reared in the strictures of the Episcopal Church. Big difference. Gullah culture? Ah, Gullah. It's Lowcountry magic. That's all.

Coming to the Island made me feel younger, a little more reckless, and as I finally went back to my car and closed the door — pausing one moment to lower the audio assault of the radio — I realized the Island also made me lighthearted. I was willingly becoming re-addicted. As we arrived on the Island, I pointed out the signs of summer's early arrival to Beth, my fourteen-year-old certified volcano.

"Oh, my Lord, look! There's Mrs. Schroeder!" I said. "I can't believe she's still alive." The old woman was draped over her porch swing in her housecoat.

"Who? I mean, like, who cares, Mom? She's an old goat!"

"Well, honey, when you're an old goat like her, you will. Look at her, poor old thing with that wet rag, trying to cool her neck. Good Lord. What a life."

"Shuh! Dawg life better, iffin you ask me!"

I smiled at her. Beth's Gullah wasn't great, but we were working on it.

"This 'eah life done been plan by Gawd's hand, chile," I said.

It was a small but important blessing how the Gullah language of my youth had become a communication link to her. A budding teenager was a terrible curse for a single parent, especially given the exotic possibilities of our family's gene pool. But speaking Gullah had become a swift ramp to her soul.

Gullah was the Creole language developed by

West Africans when they were brought to the Lowcountry as slaves. While it mostly used English words in our lifetime, it had a structure and cadence all its own and most especially it had many unforgettable idiomatic expressions.

It was spoken by Livvie, taught to us, and we passed on the tradition to our own children. We used it to speak endearing words to each other, to end a small disagreement or to ignite memories of the tender time we spent with Livvie. When I was Beth's age every kid on the Island spoke Gullah to some extent, at least those lucky enough to have someone like Livvie.

I stopped at the corner for some gas at Buddy's Gulf Station, the Island institution renowned for price gouging on everything from gasoline to cigarettes. We got out of the car, I to perform the elegant task of pumping the gas and Beth to get a cold Coke. A group of old Island salts were ogling the thermometer in front of Buddy's store. One of the old men called out to Buddy.

"Jesus! If it's this hot in June, what's August gone be like?"

"Gone sell y'all a loada ice, 'eah?" Buddy said.

"Gone be hotter than the hinges on the back door of hell, that's what!" the old man shot back. "Humph!"

I smiled, listening to them. They sounded the same as Islanders had sounded for generations, same accent, same lilt in their speech. Traces of Gullah phrasing. It was my favorite music.

As we drove down the Island I decided to take Atlantic Avenue to check the horizon, watch the shrimp boats and container ships. Today's slow ride did not disappoint us. Boats were everywhere. I pointed them out to Beth. It was the whole world, these container ships, coming and going from our busy port as they had done for centuries. She nodded with me in agreement. First, that it was beautiful, second, that we were lucky to be there.

Along our drive by the water, we passed ten or so young mothers pulling their offspring home in wagons from the sweltering beaches, hopping from one bare foot to the other on the blistering asphalt roads.

"How stupid is that?" Beth said.

"What?"

"Shoot, Momma, even I know not to go to the beach without flip-flops or sandals! God, they must be dying!"

"Please. Don't use the Lord's name, unless you're in prayer. It's a hundred years in purgatory."

"You do."

"I'm an adult and personally responsible for my own immortal soul."

"Whatever." She made one of those sounds of disgust, the kind that could be confused with indigestion, used for running defense against parental dominance.

Beth. This child got the cream of our genetic smorgasbord. She inherited the Asalit blue eyes, a shade of chestnut hair with more red and wave than mine, my brains and grapefruits (bosoms), Maggie's tiny waist and when she finally stops growing she could be five feet, nine inches. She was a colt, all legs and a shiny coat, looking for a place to run. She was really beautiful to watch and she worked it too, pulling all her poor momma's chains.

"Two hundred years of Catholicism coursing in your veins is gonna make a lady out of you if it's the last thing I do," I said.

"Well, at least you're not trying to make me a nun," she said with some relief.

"Honey, I wouldn't encourage my worst enemy to the doors of a convent."

"Come on, Momma, step on it. I'm dying to go to the beach! It's so hot I could scream!"

I was just cruising along, enjoying the scene before me and looking around to see if I knew anyone. The Island had changed so much from when I was a child, but thankfully all the attempts to make it slick like Hilton Head or Kiawah had failed. Part of me depended on that. If it stayed the same I still owned it, even though my sister, Maggie, got the Island Gamble.

Maggie had laid claim to our ancestral home when our mother closed her eyes for the last time. I got the haunted mirror and that seemed like a fair trade to me. The rest of us had always known Maggie would walk those floors in adulthood. She would raise her children within the same rooms. Tradition was as much a part of her makeup as rebellion was of ours.

Digging roots off the Island had been essential to my sanity. I would have tied that house up in a bow and given it to her rather than live there. There were too many ghosts in the paneling, too many tears in the pipes. I had too much energy to stay, and back then I had no desire to reconcile the issues. No, there was no argument from me on who should get the house. If Maggie wanted it — and I would never understand why until I was well into my thirties — it was just fine with me. I had run an entire seven miles away from home to Charleston. But seven miles from this Island was another world.

At last, I pulled up in the backyard next to Maggie and Grant's boat and tooted the horn to announce our arrival. The back door swung open and Maggie called down to us from the back porch.

"Susan! Beth! Where have y'all been?" She waved, smiling at seeing us.

She looked frighteningly like a nineties version of June Cleaver, Beaver's mom, only with frosted blond hair. I hated to admit it, but she was beautiful and always had been. She had Bermuda blue eyes like all the Asalits. A natural blond toned to a perfect size six, she was pleased to no end with her life. Maggie was hopelessly lost in a Talbot's world of flowered skirts and hand-knitted sweaters. She was the president of the Garden Club and active with the Junior League. Even though we disagreed on everything from politics to the merits of duck decoy collecting, when her blue eyes met mine, we were family.

"Getting gas at Buddy's and smelling the marsh," I said, gathering up all the towels and tote bags. "Got caught by the bridge again."

"That awful old bridge! Y'all come on in! Beth, the boys are waiting. You want to go crabbing? Tide's perfect!"

"Ab! I brought my bathing suit." Beth grabbed her straw beach bag and pushed past us to find her cousins.

"In the parlance of today's young people, *ab* is short for *absolutely*," I said. "God, is it hot or what? Thanks for letting us invade your afternoon. I thought I was gone *die* in Charleston. It's so hot in the city the blacktop sinks under your feet."

"Y'all moving in? Let me help you with some of that."

"Thanks," I said.

I followed her up the steep steps into the kitchen; my eyes struggled to adjust to the low light inside.

"I hate the heat too. Well, this summer's gonna be a scorcher, I guess. You want something cold to drink?" Maggie opened the door of the refrigerator and pulled out a pitcher of iced tea.

"Please." I reached for two glasses from the cabinet and handed them to her. "No Diet Pepsi?"

"Picky, picky. No, I have to go to the store."

"Tea's fine. I'm gonna change into some shorts and hit the porch."

"Okay. Wanna go for a swim?"

"Maybe later. First I have to calm down and cool off."

"Tom?" Maggie cleared her throat with a knowing "ahem." I hated that little "ahem" thing she did.

"Who else?" I leaned against the counter as she poured, feeling embarrassed that my whole life had spun clean out of control.

"What's happened now?"

"Maggie, you should've been a shrink. I can't keep dumping stories on you about him. I'm gonna drive you crazy. Let's just say that he's still a son of a bitch." I took a long drink of the tea.

"Thanks. I'll meet you on the porch. Can you sit awhile?"

"You bet. Let me just start the dishwasher and marinate the steaks for tonight. Grant got a new grill for Father's Day and wants to break it in."

"I wish he'd break it in by putting Tom Hayes's behind on a spit," I said, thinking that I'd been muttering a lot lately. "See you on the porch."

I sprawled out in her Pawley's Island hammock, using my heel to kick off from the porch banister. The hammock, a testimony to the practical application of macramé, was like all the ones that have hung on the western end of this porch since I was a child. Hammocks were generally undervalued, except in the South and probably the Amazon. There was nothing like crawling in, stretching out and swinging away your troubles.

I closed my eyes and began daydreaming about the porch. If this porch were hanging on the side of my house in the city, it would be a veranda. But over here on the Island, it was a porch. That general lack of pretension was one more feature that made the Island so appealing.

I could be blinded and still find everything here. If I hopped out of the hammock, I could take three steps and sink into one of the two old metal frame chairs, the kind that bounced a little. There was an ancient coffee table between the chairs and the glider. If I wanted to perch in the bench swing that hangs from the other end, or park myself in a rocker, I would only have to stretch out my right arm and follow the ferns that Maggie had hung in perfect intervals above the banister.

The only differences between the porch of today

and the one of forty years ago were the ceiling fans that moved the air around, making the suffocating heat bearable, and the fresh coat of paint on the furniture and the floor. In my day, nothing much was shiny. Whatever Maggie didn't decorate, Grant painted. The porch used to be entirely screened in with doors to the outside, but Grant and Maggie took them off. The house looked wonderful without them and nobody seemed to mind an occasional yellow jacket. Even the most persnickety old-timers on the Island agreed that Maggie and Grant had done a great job with the house. You have to understand that the old Islanders were highly suspicious of any sort of change. Busybodies. After all, Grant was from Columbia, and what in the world would he know about historic beach houses? But, they crept around, one by one, with a pound cake or some fresh fish as a house gift, to see what Maggie and Grant were up to. In the end, they all said that Maggie and Grant had done all right.

Like many of the older houses on the Island, this one had its own name: the Island Gamble. Living on the edge of the Atlantic Ocean, our house had its own tide that rose, fell, foamed, swirled and, at times, went mad. Everything inside and outside was suffused with the smell of salt water and sea life. The Island Gamble was very nearly a living, breathing thing.

Our mother's parents, Sophie and Tipa Asalit, were its second owners, its first being a lady of dubious background. Legend holds that she entertained a handsome sea captain here for a prolonged period of time while her husband was in

Philadelphia on business. It must've been true, because when Tipa and our father renovated the house they found torrid love letters between the floorboards and thousands and thousands of Confederate dollars.

Island Gamble. Our grandmother had always hated the name. She said it made us sound like a bunch of hooligans. The argument was one of the few times that our grandfather ever stood up to her, that I knew of anyway. He insisted that the name not be changed, suggesting it was tampering with history to remove it. Lord knows why he picked that battle to fight, given the number of hissing matches she started, but the name remained and the Island Gamble has belonged to our family for nearly one hundred years. At first it was our family's summer house, but when Grandma Sophie became frail, Tipa moved her from the city to the beach permanently, believing the salt air would do her some good.

The Island Gamble was a sentinel; she stood tall with a commanding view of Charleston harbor and Fort Sumter. Her white clapboards made up three stories, built in the old Island style that only God could pull asunder. Her wide hips were wraparound porches and her French doors swung open for airflow. The most interesting original details were her cupola and widow's walk on the top of the house. They sat up there like a bonnet on her lovely head. When I was little, I used to climb up there to hide from everyone to write in my journals, privacy being a precious commodity in those days.

In our family, the birth of every new baby was preceded by a building frenzy. Our grandfather, with the help of our father, added rooms to the sides or off the back like a line of freight train cars. Our house was kind of crazy looking, the patchwork quilt of our family's history. She gave the impression she could withstand anything and, indeed, she had weathered scores of hurricanes, sheltered many broken hearts and played host to hundreds of people in her history. Her heart had harbored too many secrets for my blood, but I seemed to be the only one really bothered by that.

"Oh, if these walls could talk . . ." people would say.

And I'd say, If these walls started talking, the entire Island would be put under quarantine while the government moved in an army of psychiatrists.

But there were marvelous things about this place too. The hammock, for one, was extremely comforting, and Maggie was a great friend to let me come here to nurse my wounded heart. I didn't sleep too well these days with all that I'd had on my mind. I tossed and turned in my bed in the city, but the nightly visualization of this porch and hammock always helped me make headway toward some peace.

Just as I was about to drift off for a little desperately needed shut-eye, the screen door slammed.

"You want me to paint your toenails?" Maggie had arrived to cure me with a cosmetics bag and a tray of food. I looked down at my feet and shrugged in agreement.

"They look bad, 'eah? Whatcha got in that basket? Feed me, I'm starving."

'Eah. Great Gullah word, versatile like anything. It means *here, yes, right now, do you hear me, isn't it so,*

don't you agree and just about anything you want it to.

"You don't look to me like you're starving, although you do look thinner," she said.

"Okay, you can paint my toenails if it makes you feel better."

These days, if anyone told me I looked thinner, I became the most agreeable sort of woman you knew. I got up from the hammock and inspected the snacks.

"Sit 'eah and I'll pour you some more tea."

I took a stalk of celery and dipped it in fat-free ranch dressing. Maggie pointed to the glider for me to sit in and began a replay of our childhood ritual. She wadded up pieces of Kleenex and stuck them between my toes. Then she moaned in disgust about my corns and calluses, while she buffed them away. Next, she lectured me on cuticles while she clipped and finally, thank the Lord, she applied a base coat followed by two layers of some color she got as a gift with purchase from Lancôme. She always felt better when she could work on my appearance.

"I've lost twelve pounds," I told her as she applied the top coat.

"I see it in your ankles."

Of course, if she lost twelve pounds, she'd look cadaverous. "Thanks a lot," I said.

"I can see it in your face too," she said, smiling angelically, like a diet counselor from Jenny Craig. "Listen, twelve pounds is a lot, 'eah? Turkeys weigh twelve pounds! How'd you do it?"

"Swell. I've only got a few more turkeys to go. I'm counting fat grams. Can I have a tomato?"

"Well, you're looking much better!" Maggie twisted the top of the nail polish bottle back in place and offered me the Sweetgrass basket filled with raw vegetables. " 'Eah, try one. They're fabulous!"

I got up carefully, trying not to wreck my pedicure, chose a deep red one, and hobbled back to the hammock. Twisting off the stem, I chomped through its rosy skin like an apple. The juice escaped at once and ran down my chin, seeds and all. I lifted the hem of my T-shirt, exposing my hadn't-seen-the-sun-in-decades pink stomach, and wiped my face. Maggie watched, just shaking her head. What did she know? I knew I was still a bit of a femme fatale. Okay. Truth. I knew my ability to break hearts was momentarily eclipsed by my unfortunate girth. I ignored her and lost myself in the joyous simplicity of munching on a perfectly vine-ripened tomato.

"Damn! This is so good! Dee-vine! Where'd you get 'em? Are they Better Boys?"

"Yep. Mr. Andregg brought 'em over from his garden as a thank-you for ten pounds of blue mackerel the boys and Grant caught last week."

She reached for a tomato for herself, wrapped it in a napkin, and took a small bite. No drip. I ignored that too.

"Keep those boys in the river! Where's the salt shaker?"

"You don't need salt. Bad for your blood pressure and makes you retain water."

"Right. You're right. So I only have a thousand more pounds to go and I'll look like my old self. Any suggestions? I mean, I'm starving myself on twenty fat grams a day and my butt is shrinking with glacier speed . . ."

"Forget fat grams . . . just eat what you want in moderation."

"I can't forget them if I ever want to get laid again," I said under my breath.

I sat up a bit and looked out over the railing toward the ocean. The sight always took my breath away. The dark green velvet of the front yard contrasted with the radiant white of the sand dunes that separated the family's property from the beach. The white mounds cut a wavy line across the deep blue of the Atlantic, like the finger paint of a child in his first attempt to create something beautiful. Feathery sea oats grew in clumps across their tops. The water glistened and the sun danced on the phosphorus. An illusory field of diamonds.

"You know, this must be the most beautiful place on this earth," I said, realizing my voice was barely a whisper.

"I hope you don't talk like that in front of my niece."

"What? That this is gorgeous?"

"No, Susan, your reference to your sex life. Beth doesn't need to 'eah that."

"Maggie, my sex life is nonexistent. Besides, she's barely fourteen! Beth is clueless about that stuff."

"Trust me. She's not clueless. Remember when you were fourteen and had that mad crush on Simon?"

"I need a cigarette. Where'd you hide my purse?"

"It's under the hammock. I wish you wouldn't smoke. It's nasty."

I nearly fell out of the hammock trying to reach my purse and, finally having retrieved it, I dug out my Marlboro Lights and my old Zippo. I lit it and exhaled away from Maggie.

"Give it up, Maggie," I said. "You can't cure me in one day."

"I'm not trying to cure you," she said with all the indignation of an older sister, "but you should try the patch or that gum. Nobody smokes anymore, Susan, in case you haven't noticed."

"Right. Have you heard from Simon lately?"

"Not since Christmas. Let's call him. He's living in Atlanta now, you know. Who knows? Maybe his marriage is on the rocks!"

I had to giggle at the thought of calling Simon. "I've got my cell phone right 'eah! Got his number?" I said with bravado.

"No, but I've got yours. Big talker."

"Oh, well."

She raised her eyebrows at me. Maggie had been a saint since Tom left me three months ago, but with the single lift of that brow, she let me know she knew I was a chicken.

"You're right. I'm not ready for men yet, even Simon. Men still stink." I drained my glass and flicked my cigarette butt over the rail, regretting it the second I did it, knowing it landed in her roses. "Sorry. I'll get it later."

"Don't worry about it."

"Yeah, Simon. God, he was cute, 'eah? I'd love to see him again. Maybe that little girl he married ran away or something."

"Well, his card didn't say anything about her, just that he was in Atlanta to teach a course on rare viruses and fevers or something at Emory."

"Oh. Do you know that man hasn't written me in over ten years?"

"Call him."

"Yeah, right."

Simon, Simon, I thought. I wondered if he still had all his hair. When he was young he had the almighty head of silky brown hair. God, I loved him, for years and years. He must be fifty by now. I felt the heat surge again. Although the tide was coming in, there wasn't a breath of air to be had.

"Guess who did call?" I said.

"Let me guess . . ."

"Henry," I said before she could answer.

"Our dahlin' baby brother? What's up with him?"

"Well, bless his mercenary little heart, he just wanted to know if I needed anything. Is that nice, or what?"

"It's out of character, that's what," Maggie said.

"Well, normally I would be highly suspicious, but he was sincere, I think. Maybe Paula doesn't have any more plastic surgery left to do and he doesn't know what to do with his money."

"We're terrible," Maggie said.

"Yeah." The heat was paralyzing. "Maggie, was it this hot when we were kids? I don't remember it ever being this hot."

"I hate to break this to you, but you're getting older. Have you had your estrogen checked?"

I looked over at her stirring her tea like the Queen of England. I took the bait.

"Estrogen? Maggie, I'm barely forty-something."

"The first indication of menopause is a broken

thermostat. It's either that or your *weight*. In any case, if you don't do something, you could be dead by August."

"God, middle age is an unending insult."

I closed my eyes and pretended to nap. It took about two seconds for me to sense her towering over me, her and her "I'm-a-self-help-book-waiting-to-be-published" lips. I opened my weary eyes.

"What is it?" I said rather testily. "What now?"

She just stood there, feigning mild offense, waiting for me to beg her to tell me how to fix my life. Her wheels cranked and turned in her head over the gentle rustling of the palmetto fronds and the incoming waves. She drove me crazy sometimes.

"Nothing," Her Highness said, and heaved a deep sigh. She sighed the same way our mother used to. An unfair advantage.

"Come on, Maggie, spit it out. You're gonna choke if you don't." She sauntered back to the coffee table and poured me another glass of tea. She dropped a lemon in the glass and handed it to me. I pushed it in with my finger, realizing I was being a little difficult. "Okay, I'm sorry," I said. "I admit it. Nobody has ever done more for me than Livvie Singleton and you. So tell me what you're thinking, besides that it would be nice if it were eighty degrees instead of a billion."

"Susan, you have a serious opportunity here."

I just stared at her.

"You do," she said. "Come on, let's rock."

"What do you mean 'opportunity'? What I've got is a daughter with probable simmering hormones, a stack of bills you could lay end on end to

Charlotte that Tom won't help me pay, a backside that looks like thunderous Jell-O, no matter how I starve the thing. All I do is worry. Forgive me, but I'm having a hard time finding the opportunity in all this." I was prepared to mount my high horse now and she knew it. I took a seat in the rocker next to her.

"The butt's easy to fix, just walk to work instead of driving." She was perfectly calm, as though dealing with the borderline deranged.

"You're probably right . . ."

"And the exercise would do you a world of good, give you a chance to think about how to handle the rest of the stuff. Exercise is good for your brain."

"I know. You're right, you're right, you're right. But, Maggie, it's easier for you to see what I need to do than it is for me to do it!"

"Susan, listen 'eah! Do you know how many women would trade in their husbands if they had the gonads?"

"Yeah, but I never wanted to trade Tom, he traded me, remember?"

"Minor point. The fact is, what are you gonna do about it? First of all, it's been three months. Do you have a separation agreement yet?"

"No, I'm not ready for that."

"Well, if he wanted to come home, would you let him?"

I looked out at the ocean again, remembering the good things about my marriage to Tom. The way he kissed, the way it felt to be in his arms. But then, I remembered finding him in bed with his young thing and I felt my heartbeat quicken from the anxiety of his betrayal. I drained my glass. The boulder in my throat made it hard to talk about a separation agreement.

"Remember how Livvie used to say that if you rocked a chair when you weren't in it, you rocked away your life?" I said. "That always spooked me."

I avoided giving the decision and Maggie was having no part of it.

"Because you were wasting time, is what she meant. And let me tell you something else, Livvie Singleton would beat you to a pulp if she could see the time you're wasting now. She raised us to spit in the faces of those who did us wrong, not to get fat and depressed and lie around moaning. Tom Hayes is a bum and the sooner you realize it and do something about it, the sooner you can rebuild your life. If Livvie was 'eah, she'd tell you to buck up!"

"Don't mince words now. Tell me how you *really* feel."

"I'm sorry, Susan, it needs to be said. You're my closest sister and I love you. Now, for once and for all, if Tom came to you and said he was sorry, would you take him back? Please, think this through, because if you'd forgive him, so would I."

I had given hundreds of hours of thought to how it would be if Tom came home. I might forgive him but I had come to the conclusion that I'd never trust him again. A good marriage was impossible without trust, I knew that.

"No, I'd never take him back now, Maggie. No, it went too far and he's just been awful to us. He's the one who screwed another woman in our bed and walked out."

"Are you absolutely sure?"

"Yes, I'm sure. If I took him back, he'd just do it

again the first time some bubble wit lifts her Wonder Bra in his direction. Who needs it?"

"You're ready. I'll get you a list of lawyers and you can start interviewing them next week."

"Okay." I inhaled the healing salt of the beach and exhaled my soured marriage. "I just hate dealing with this, you know?"

"I know, I don't blame you for that at all." Maggie reached over, patted my arm and continued. "Look, a family breakup is a tragedy, no doubt about it, but you don't have cancer, you've got a great job and you have Beth. What's he got? Some stupid twit! Big deal! Sounds to me like he's the loser, not you."

"I hope he rots in hell."

"That's the spirit!" Maggie started cleaning up. She took our glasses and put them on the tray and, balancing it, wiped the table-top with a napkin. "You need a new haircut."

Having someone who always told me what I needed was a little exasperating, but I knew it didn't pay to call her on it.

"You're right, I need to do something about my looks. But that tightwad I need to serve with papers still has the five bucks his Aunt Helen gave him for his tenth birthday! I need another job or something."

"Or a bulldog lawyer, somebody with zero sense of humor."

"Yeah, with big teeth who's got the guts to tear a big piece out of his miserable carcass. Wait! Don't take the celery! You want a hand with that? Where are our children? It's getting late."

"You just relax, I can handle this. I guess they'll

be home soon. Listen, if they caught anything, why don't you stay for supper? Crab cocktails and grilled steaks? Not the worst meal on earth."

"Sounds good," I said. "Hey, Maggie?" I stared at her while I dug around for the right words. "I'm gonna get a lawyer. I just have to find the right person and I have to find my nerve, you know?"

"Since when have you had a problem finding nerve?"

"Very funny. What I mean to say is that I really appreciate your advice."

She smiled at me. "Well, you know your own mind. You always have. I just don't want to see you victimized again."

"I was never victimized. I just married the biggest ass in South Carolina and was too bullheaded to see it."

"Well put by the family poet!" Maggie smiled at me again. "I just want you to be yourself again, you know? Like a bad dog, chasing cars. I miss that about you. I mean, what would you do if you could do anything with your life? Like, change careers?"

She balanced the tray on her hip, held the screen door open and challenged me to come clean.

"I don't know. Maybe . . . oh, shoot, Maggie, I don't know."

"Well, think about it, little sister. There's a new world out there if you want it. Seize the day and all that. Livvie didn't raise us to wallow."

"You're right. Hey, you know, on the growing list of things I intend to do with my life is another tidbit."

"Yeah, what's that?"

"I'm gonna figure out what happened to Daddy."

She ran her fingers through her hair and looked at me like I had said something foul. "Give it up, Susan," she said. "Daddy's been dead for decades."

"That's not it, Maggie," I said. "I just have to know that I didn't cause it."

"Susan. I'm your sister. I love you. . . ."

"I know that. . . ."

"You need to concentrate on other things. Daddy died of a heart attack. Period."

I hated when she looked at me like that, taking the posture that her word was the final one on the subject. So I said, "It ain't period. It's a question I have to resolve for my own soul."

"Suit yourself. But I think your time's better spent on other avenues," she said.

"Whatever. But, I'm telling you I know in my guts that Daddy was murdered," I said.

"Susan, ain't nobody on this planet who loves you more than me but I'm telling you I can't stand to listen to this."

"Maggie," I said, "I can't stand to *think* it. I have to know that the fight didn't cause him to die. I have to believe it was the Klan."

"What is this fight you always refer to? I don't know *what* you're talking about!"

She was becoming agitated. It was suddenly clear that for some reason she didn't remember the fight. Maybe she had blocked it from her mind. I didn't know. I just wanted the waters smooth again.

"Never mind," I said, "I'll figure it out someday."

"Well, my advice is worry about the living. The

dead had their chance."

"Whoa, that's cold," I said.

"No, it's not. I care about you and Beth. That's all."

She went inside. The door slammed behind her with a loud *thwack* and the sound of wood slapping wood woke me up like a sock in the jaw. Maggie had just succinctly reduced my life to an ancient Latin maxim and some hard facts. She was right about Livvie too. Livvie would be incensed to have seen me rolling around in my despair of chocolate chip cookies and fast food for the past three months.

Maggie was always right. When all hell broke loose, Maggie was right there at my side. She'd taken Beth under her wing too. She had listened to me wail and moan ad nauseam. It was enough now. I looked defeated and that had never been a word in my vocabulary.

It's just that my head was in gridlock at the thought of a new life. I was a little afraid, you know? What if I failed? What if I couldn't take care of Beth? What if she went wild and flunked out of school and got pregnant? What if this was all there was? O Lord, I prayed, help me figure this out!

I peeled myself up from the rocker, knowing the slats had left their imprint on the back of my legs. I decided to throw one leg over the banister and straddled it like a horse, hanging on to a support beam, the same way I did when I was a child. The tide was almost high and its power was mesmerizing. I wished I could have some of it for myself.

The waves had now grown from the baby hiccups they were at low tide to crashing rollers, and washed everything in their path with silvery foam. They began down at the eastern end of the Island at Breach Inlet. Danger, danger. People drowned in whirlpools and ebb tides there every year in spite of posted warnings. Didn't people read?

I knew that attempting to investigate Daddy's death was dangerous too, but the compulsion to do so was growing each day. Of all the stones I carried in the sack tied to my heart, his death was the heaviest. I had told Maggie it was a personal guilt thing, but the guilt stemmed from being the only one who seemed to care if he had died at all, never mind *how*. Added to that was Tom's deception, which only exacerbated my thirst for truth.

The waves arrived in stacked sets of three, the current driving them in on an angle. As they reached our end of the Island, they seemed to calm in the faint, sweeping beams of the lighthouse. Turning tides were hypnotic. The water flooded the shore in anger, then turned, withdrew and renewed itself.

The beams from the lighthouse grew in intensity, spreading protection for boats at sea. It was in these moments that I was sure there was a God. He was tapping me on my stubborn shoulder, telling me the scene before me was a metaphor for my own life. Withdraw and renew; life goes on. Maybe Beth and I would stay for dinner, crack some crabs, grill steaks and shoot the breeze. Maggie was right. I needed to reinvent myself. The question was, could this old dog still hunt?

I could just see Beth and Maggie's boys now, coming down the beach in silhouette against the edge of dusk. They were swinging a basket of crabs and a bucket of bait. It could have been a photograph of our childhood, the happy days. So many days I spent with Maggie, Timmy and Henry, catching fish and crabs, throwing plough mud at each other . . . those were, I think, my happiest memories. We'd come home all sunburned and sticky and present Momma and Livvie with our catch of the day. They'd act like we were heroes for feeding the family. We were so proud.

And then there was our daddy, Big Hank.

2

THE OUTHOUSE

Summer 1963

"Don't, Daddy! Please! I'm sorry! Please stop!"

It was the unmistakable lament of my little brother Henry begging for mercy while he got a rare whipping from the old man. Henry was seldom spanked. I thought he must've blown up the church or something, because Henry was Daddy's undisputed favorite.

When Daddy took off his belt, we paid for it with the stinging disappearance of a layer of our childhood innocence. The old man had an uncontrollable temper. It simply didn't pay to draw a line in the sand with him. If you argued with him, his rage grew to such outlandish proportions that you might walk away in the right, but your backside would be covered with welts. He would never understand that these beatings changed the way we felt about him. The cracking of leather across our young skin sliced away layers of trust, and our love.

Timmy and I were on the porch, holding our breath, not moving a hair. A door slammed somewhere inside. *What now?*

"Get in the car! On the double!"

Daddy's command boomed from upstairs out to the front porch. I was sure Henry's wailing could be heard for miles. I felt very sorry for my little brother, but I wasn't sure that we weren't next. Timmy and I weren't sure if Daddy meant for *us,* or *someone else,* to get in the car. We heard Daddy stomping down the steps. Next, the screen door flung open, slammed against the back wall and he pointed his index finger at me and then Timmy.

"You children deaf?"

"No, sir," we answered together.

"Then, get in the damn car when I tell you to!"

The screen door slammed again behind him and we jumped up and followed his lead down the hall, into the kitchen, out the back door and down the steps. He was on another rampage and for whatever cryptic reason he had, he wanted us to go someplace with him. We said not one word to each other or to him.

We got in the car before he had the chance to consider boxing our ears, as he often did when his fury got the best of him. We'd unearth the details with our silence.

We were the children of a gifted and brilliant man, a World War II veteran, a civil engineer who had graduated with high honors from Georgia Tech, an adored and only son. Daddy was tall and handsome, with piercing brown eyes and straight brown hair. He wore thin wire-rimmed glasses, which wrapped tightly around the backs of his ears. On sight, he could've passed for a diplomat. His laugh and voice were loud, no, enormous. We wondered if he hadn't suffered a hearing loss during the war.

His parents, dead for nearly a decade from heart ailments, were a quiet Baptist couple who had prided themselves on refinement and doted on their son. Daddy had been accustomed to getting his way, but everything about his life with our mother's French-Irish Island family had denied him that privilege. It would have required the patience of a thousand saints to tolerate our house and there was no news of a pope traveling to Sullivan's Island to canonize our father. Daily doses of our family drama and the chaos of our grandparents' infirmities fed his rage like shovels of coal feed the furnace of a tramp steamer.

And he was having trouble at work. As an engineer, Daddy and his partner had been awarded a contract from the South Carolina Department of Education to build a new school in the country, in a colored area, which was slated to be integrated by bussing. Daddy had figured out how to heat the school, build a new gymnasium, a cafeteria and a library, all on a shoestring budget. That wasn't such a big deal; certainly there was no uprising from the colored people. But there sure was noise from the Department of Education and the local school boards. The reality was that no white family would bus their children there and it would always remain a colored school. This infuriated the authorities, who claimed that our daddy's plans would lead to having to upgrade the rural colored schools all over South Carolina. Things were happening, such as him finding his tires slashed and construction equipment destroyed, and he knew it was the work of the Ku Klux Klan.

When I thought about him like that, I had empathy for him. But when his demons bettered him, I ran for cover like everyone else.

We lowered the car windows and didn't utter a single syllable about how hot the car was as he backed out of the driveway and started down Middle Street toward the small business district. It was a sticky Saturday in the middle of June and we'd been out of school and shoes for about three weeks as another summer got under way. The United States was in the midst of the Civil Rights movement, which as far as we knew was something happening at lunch counters in Rock Hill, South Carolina, and Montgomery, Alabama. When Medgar Evers was murdered, we thought for a moment how that could happen to our daddy, but he was white and nothing like that ever happened around Charleston. We were frightened, but we were just kids and not focused on it. All the same, violence was everywhere that summer, in the newspapers and in our house.

Because of the high attrition rate of our housekeepers, we hadn't ever had a stretch of time to consider the grave injustices done to the Negro population at a close look. But the world was evolving in front of our eyes and we were changing our minds about a lot of things.

Revolutionary acts became part of our everyday existence. For example, our father, the same man who lost control of himself with the terrifying velocity of an earthquake, had taken ice water and cigarettes to some chain gang workers on the Island last week when he knew it was too hot for them to be in the sun. The same irrational man, who had just now left his eight-year-old baby son in a crumpled heap, had a heart for justice and compassion in the outside world.

"Gotta get gas," he mumbled, pulling into Buddy's Gas Station.

He got out of the car, slammed the door and went inside the store. Timmy and I stared at each other.

"It's safe to talk now," I said.

"Jesus, what in the world could've happened?" Timmy said.

"Who knows? I hope Henry's not bleeding all over the floor or he'll go crazy about that too!"

"Susan, he really *is* crazy, you know."

"Yeah, I know," I said, "but he's more unreliable than crazy."

He came out with a beer can wrapped in a small brown bag. We watched him take a long drink and heard him ask the man at the pump to check the oil. He opened the door and got in, leaving his legs hanging outside, and drained the beer. He crushed the can with his left hand and tossed it in the trash barrel.

"Two points," Daddy said.

We exhaled a small sigh of relief. He was calming down.

"Good one, Dad," Timmy said.

"Your brother, Mr. Timmy and Miss Susan, is enough to drive me right out of my skull."

"What'd he do?" I asked nonchalantly, as though this were normal behavior, which it was for him.

"Sadie quit," he answered. "I gave him the belt."

Sadie was our housekeeper. She was the third one to quit in a month.

"Because of Henry? What happened?" I asked,

even though I was sure we'd hear anyway. I knew from experience that the faster he got it out of his system, the faster he'd get over it.

"Your brother, little Mr. Henry the entrepreneur, was selling tickets for all his juvenile delinquent friends to watch poor Miss Sadie use the outhouse through one of the loose boards."

"Oh, Lord," I said, "that's not nice. Plus, it's disgusting, if you ask me." No one was asking, but Daddy sucked his teeth in agreement.

"Ah, man! I can't believe he did that! I liked Sadie! She made the best red rice I ever had!" Timmy said.

"So now, we gotta go the whole way out to Snowden and find us somebody else because your momma says she can't raise her children without help." He made another noise with his teeth and tongue that sounded like *snncck*. "I gotta pay this man. You kids want a cold Coke?" He raised his eyebrows at us, half smiled and peeled a dollar bill out of his wallet, handing it to me. "Hurry up, 'cause time's wasting."

"Yes, sir!" I said.

The money for the Cokes was his way of apologizing for beating the daylights out of Henry. I thought that was a pretty pathetic gesture, but I grabbed the money anyway. He was relaxed now, and I scampered out of the car and ran inside. Nothing like a little alcohol to improve his disposition, I thought.

The low light in the store caught me off guard and I bumped into a man coming out.

"Watch yourself, little lady!"

"Sorry!" I said, and hurried through the stench

of his beer breath and the smoke-filled room to the bar. "Two Cokes, please," I nervously asked Buddy, the proprietor of the only bar on the Island.

Every kid on the Island knew that it was *Sin City* in there, even if you were only a kid buying a Coke. There was card playing and a pool table in there. The Island men went there to escape the world and no woman, save one, that I'd ever heard of, would be caught dead inside of Buddy's. That one, Alice Simpson, happened to be our next-door neighbor. My momma said she was a disgrace to all women. I thought that was stupid; I mean, maybe she liked to play pool. And besides, why shouldn't a sinner have a place to go besides hell?

Buddy rattled around inside his cooler and put the two bottles on the counter. While he fished around for the bottle opener, he eyed me up and down. "Getting kinda grown up, ain't ya? Gone be asking for a Pabst Blue Ribbon pretty soon, isn't she, fellows?"

The two old goats at the end of the counter started laughing and I felt my face flush.

"Yeah, right, very funny," I said, not caring what they thought.

Don't you know these old buzzards started laughing and whistling real low? God, what a bunch of jerks! I grabbed the bottles, mumbled some thanks and ran out of there as fast as I could. Daddy had the car running and waiting by the curb.

"Come on, girl! It's hot as Hades in here!"

I jumped in the back with Timmy, slammed the door and we took off over the causeway to Mount

Pleasant. When we crossed the bridge, Daddy speeded up the car to sixty-five. He liked to drive fast. The marsh air came flooding through the open windows, blowing my long hair into a mass of damp tangles. Some old geezer on the radio was crooning like a sick cat. It was Daddy's favorite station and I wasn't about to ask him to lower the volume. In spite of the possibility of instantaneous death, Timmy and I couldn't resist the temptation of making faces at each other and silently imitating the singer. Daddy cut his eye at us in the rearview mirror and I could tell from his back that he was smiling by the way he shook his head. He let his arm rest on the windowsill and I knew that, for the moment, all was well.

"Y'all children!"

That was all he said until we turned down Rifle Range Road. The mood changed in an instant from the liveliness of spiky marsh, swooping birds and the deep blue of the sparkling inland waterway to the mysterious, dreamy and haunted world of the past. The Spanish moss hung in long torn pieces from the live oaks that covered the road in umbrella shade. Their long sheets looked like ghosts floating across your path when you drove this road after dark. I imagined bedraggled soldiers walking in pairs, coming home from the Revolution or the Civil War, weary and perhaps wounded, searching for home in the burned-out countryside.

I felt the spirits of freed slaves ambling along the roadside with great baskets on their heads filled with Sweetgrass and palmetto fronds for weaving more baskets to harvest rice or to hold vegetables. I saw small loads of just-picked cotton on the back of a buckboard wagon on the way to market, drawn by the slow clip-clop of a broken-down horse or mule.

When I came out here to Snowden, the hair on my arms stood up from goose bumps. Even though my family never owned a slave in all its history in the Lowcountry, my ancestors had probably condoned it. Coming here to old plantation country made me uncomfortable having white skin. In the carefree existence of Island living, I never had to think about what slavery must've been, but out here in the country reminders were everywhere.

When I really opened my eyes to the landscape, it wasn't romantic plantation life before me. It was rows of tiny clapboard houses tucked under live oaks and pines, most of them needing a paint job, some of them whitewashed. Old cars were pulled up in the side yards to rest forever. Rusted bicycles propped themselves against the steps while chickens pecked around. Hound dogs, most of them too old to bark, stood on the porches filled with unmatched upholstered chairs. But the smell of burning refuse mixed with the strong scent of pine and rich black dirt worked like a voodoo charm. It was another world.

I had made this trip with Daddy so many times I could tell how close we were to Harriet Avinger's house by the smell of the cool air and the sounds of the quiet. For as long as I could remember, Harriet had worked for Aunt Carol and Uncle Louis, Momma's brother and his wife. I had known her since I was born, I suppose. And she acted as Daddy's employment agency.

He pulled up in her front yard and turned off the

engine. She appeared suddenly on the front porch as though she had expected our arrival.

"Wait in the car," Daddy said and got out.

Timmy did, but I was in the mood to explore a little.

"You're gonna get in trouble," he said, when Daddy went inside Harriet's house.

"Bump you," I said, closing the door quietly.

Harriet had a garden in her front yard that looked like the cover of a seed catalog. Right next to the bottle tree, in an area probably thirty by sixty feet, perfect rows of lush vegetables were climbing for the sky in the summer sun. Huge melons lay like green bombs in the soft dirt.

The bottles hanging in the tree tinkled against each other in the breeze. I had always thought they were her version of a wind chime until Harriet told me they were for good luck. Some business about keeping the good spirits around and sending the bad ones away. Harriet always had some story to tell me about the things she believed and most of them were seriously weird but fascinating. I loved them all. She was a Gullah woman, and all the Gullah women had stories.

Her dogs looked up from their place under her front steps and then curled back up in their holes to sleep. They had no interest in me because they knew me pretty well.

We'd had and lost a lot of housekeepers over the years, mainly because our house was an insane asylum. If it wasn't Henry who drove them out with his hijinks, it was Grandma Sophie with her smelliness, or Grandpa Tipa with his bad attitude or Momma with her misery. She was pregnant again and that was putting it mildly. She looked like she had swallowed one of Harriet's watermelons and she wasn't due for three months! Daddy thought Momma didn't need help? Heck, she could hardly stand up!

I opened the gate of the tiny Garden of Eden and wandered between the rows. The black dirt was soft and cool under my bare feet. With soil like this to plant in, no wonder Harriet's tomatoes were as big as softballs and her melons were green and luscious. You could tell by the way the corn was so tightly attached to the stalk that it was delicious too, ready to shuck and boil. I peeled back a husk and popped out a few kernels with my thumbnail. Sweet! I hoped that this time I'd find the courage to ask for something to take home.

I could see Timmy was all nervous and jerky about me trespassing so I tortured him with a deliberately slow but perfectly timed return. Just as I got back in the car, Harriet and Daddy reappeared on the front porch of her little house, their business completed.

Like most houses in Snowden, the frame of her front door was painted a bright blue to keep out the haints. It always gave me something to think about, coming out here and seeing how Harriet lived. I mean, any fool could see she had no money to speak of, but there was a neatness and tidiness about her whole place. Her yard was raked, her porch was swept, her dogs were fed, her chickens were all fenced in and phlox and black-eyed Susans bloomed on both sides of her front steps. I jumped out of the car again.

"Daddy? Can I say hello?" I called out to them.

"Sure, come on! But we've got to hurry. I don't want you to be wasting Harriet's time."

Harriet smiled down at me and held out her arms. Harriet was a tall and thin woman with perfect white teeth. Her hair was plaited in neat, thick braids wrapped around her head. She wore a yellow print shirtwaist dress under her apron. When she hugged me, I smelled flowers.

"Hey now, Miss Susan! Lemme have a look at you!"

She held me back and looked hard in my face, smiling and teasing.

"Now, iffin I find y'all another lady to help y'all's momma — and that's a mighty big if — y'all gone let she have she privacy?"

"Harriet, I had nothing to do with it, cross my heart and hope to die! Henry pulled that one without consulting a soul! I promise!"

"Talk to them, will you, Harriet? I'm worn out from telling them how to behave," Daddy said.

The dogs stirred from their rest. Daddy walked down the steps to scratch one of the dogs behind the ears.

"I know you wasn't mixed up in this 'eah fool business, your daddy done told me it was that Mr. Henry, but you ain't always been an angel yourself, have you now?"

"No, that's true. But, shoot, Harriet, I'm thirteen now and, believe me, when the women you send us walk out on Momma, who do you think winds up having to do laundry and change beds and pull the vacuum cleaner around the house?"

"You?"

"Yeah, me! And, Maggie. If you find us somebody good, I'll make it my personal responsibility to make sure nobody messes with them. Okay?"

"Listen to you! You sure enough are growing up, Miss Susan. Soon you gone be a young lady! Getting so pretty and tall! And them blue eyes! Lawd! Y'all gone break hearts!"

"Oh, gosh, thanks." We smiled at each other for a moment. "Harriet? Can I ask you something?"

"Sure."

"How do you get your vegetables to grow so good?"

"I'll tell you a little secret." She leaned down to me and whispered in my ear, "I sing to the earth!" When she saw my suspicion, she said it again. "Yes, I do! All us women out 'eah sing to the earth. The earth is mother and mother provides for her children. Ain't that so?"

"Yes, but . . ."

"Ain't no but about it! All you be doing is singing praise to your momma and she provides for y'all. Makes sense, now don't it?"

"Whatever it is, it sure works. I've never seen watermelons like the ones you grow in my whole life!"

"Gone get yourself one for y'all to have for supper. Tell your momma I'll be finding her somebody real quick, all right? Maybe my cousin Livvie might be crazy enough to take the job. I don't know. Have to see."

"All right! Thanks! Some corn too?"

"Sure enough. Take some corn and a few tomatoes for your salad."

I heard her chuckling at my boldness. She came down the steps and stood next to my daddy. "That chile's got a quick mind," I heard her say as I put the vegetables and fruit on the floor of the backseat.

"And a hard head like a mule," he answered.

We drove home, stopping at the Piggly Wiggly for a loaf of bread and a head of lettuce. Next, he stopped at Simmon's Seafood on the causeway and bought five pounds of flounder with some hushpuppy mix.

"Reckon you and Maggie can fix hushpuppies and baked potatoes if me and the boys cook the fish? Y'all's momma likely laid up in the bed for the night."

"Sure, Daddy. No problem. And we have corn, tomatoes and watermelon!"

He just shook his head.

We were all deep in thought driving over the causeway. The gong started ringing, signaling that the bridge was going to open. We were right at the top of the bridge and could've made it across, but Daddy decided not to race the swing arm barrier like he usually did. We all got out of the car and leaned over the railing to watch the big fishing boat come down the waterway from the Isle of Palms, headed toward Charleston harbor. A man and woman waved at us from the deck and we waved back and I thought how nice it would be to float across the water, smiling to people as I passed them. I'd wear a white chiffon scarf around my neck and huge sunglasses.

Daddy was in no hurry to get home, and who could blame him? He couldn't help it if he had a trigger temper, I just wished he wouldn't pull the trigger so often. He was so nice to Harriet and all the women she sent us. It made me think about the way most white folks treated colored people.

"Daddy? Can I ask you something?"

"Sure, princess. What's on your mind?"

"How come Sadie didn't use the bathroom in the house?"

"Because your grandfather didn't want her to," he said.

"Because she's colored?" I asked.

"Yep," he answered.

"That stinks," Timmy said.

"Sure does," he said. "It's stupid. I could rebuild the outhouse and make it brand-new, but I'm not doing it."

"Why not?" I said.

"It's the principle of the thing," Daddy said.

"You mean, that you won't fix the outhouse because it shouldn't be there anyway?" I said.

"You got it," he said. "It's one of many things I can't find a way to discuss with your grandfather. There's too much wrong with this world."

He was thinking about work, I guessed. The breeze was so delicious I think we could've stood at the railing forever but the boat had gone through and the bridge would be passable in a few minutes. I wanted some more answers before Daddy got out of the mood to talk to me.

"Daddy, why do we live with them?"

He sighed a great sigh, thinking for a minute before he replied. Then, in an uncommon moment of tenderness, he put his arm around my shoulder and the short version of the story came out.

"When I was away in the war, your momma came back home to stay with them. We were just married and didn't have much money. Back then I was glad she had a place to live that didn't cost me anything. Then, when I came home I realized how feeble they had become. They needed *us* to take care of *them*. Look, some things take time to change. Your grandfather is a good man, you know? I mean, his point of view on segregation is ridiculous, but other than that he's a pretty good guy."

"I guess so, but he's so grumpy these days," I said.

"Yes, well, your grandma isn't doing well and I suppose that worries him a lot. And you children kick up such a ruckus all the time."

"Well, maybe the next one can use the bathroom inside," I said, "if you talk to him about it."

"If the outhouse fell down, she'd have to," Timmy said.

Daddy and I looked at each other, thinking the same thing, and we all started laughing.

"Don't worry, Daddy," I said, "the notorious Hamilton kids can handle the job!"

All the way home Timmy and I made crashing demolition noises and Daddy sang along with the radio. Even though I was scared to death of him half of the time, the other half of the time I adored him, at least I did on that night. There was nothing like a conspiracy to build loyalty.

I had a viable plan in place by Monday. Everyone had a role except Maggie, who said she wouldn't go near the outhouse even if it was full of money. Finally, after I called her a traitor and a priss-ass coward, she reluctantly agreed to be lookout and stood guard at the back door. I had the sledgehammer, Timmy had the crowbar and Henry had a shovel. We had to wait until Tipa went to the grocery store and old Sophie was snoring. Momma was resting. I didn't think she cared if the whole house came down, never mind the outhouse. She didn't care about anything in those days, including us. It was so hot and she was so pregnant, she was half out of her mind.

Our outhouse wasn't much by outhouse design standards. It was a two-seater and had two doors, but it was a breezy thing that had somehow withstood all the storms and weather Mother Nature had thrown at us over the decades. In the old days I imagine all the old Island houses had one in the backyard, but by 1963 most of them had been torn down. Now ours would be the next to go.

I gave the warm-up speech to my little brothers.

"Okay, y'all, when I count to three, start whacking this thing in this spot right 'eah. Don't clobber each other, don't clobber me and remember, we gotta work fast or Momma's gonna come out 'eah and cut our butts! If we all take a good hit on this side of it, and that one wall caves in, the roof might fall and then we're done. We don't want to rubbleize the thing; we want it to fall down looking natural. Got it? No screaming!"

"Okay," they said.

On three, we started swinging. As predicted, after a few good hits, the wall came down and the whole thing collapsed on an angle. I should be an engineer like Daddy, I thought. We looked at each other, covered our mouths to repress screams of delight and ran like all forty to put the tools away. We were covered in perspiration and just full of ourselves over the cleverness and success of what we had done. Henry had redeemed himself by helping and even Maggie was laughing with excitement. When we came back in the yard from the garage, Alice Simpson stepped out of the oleanders. We froze in position.

"I saw what you children did," she said in a mocking, sing-song voice.

"So what?" Henry said.

"Shut up, Henry," Timmy said, and turned to face our accuser. "What of it? We have our reasons," he added bravely.

I just looked at her. She was a washed-out blond with faded blue eyes. My momma always said she looked like the cat that swallowed the canary and I never really knew what that meant until now.

"I have my reasons too," Mrs. Simpson said with the slipperiest smile I'd ever seen. "My flower beds need weeding. If you children would be willing to pull a few weeds, Hank Hamilton will never have to hear about you destroying property. It's against the law, you know. I could call the authorities."

"Mrs. Simpson, no offense," I said, with all the courage of an admiral, "you're not calling any policeman, we ain't pulling your weeds and you go right ahead and tell Daddy. It's fine with us, right, y'all?"

"Right!"

Even Maggie had come down to join us by now. Although she was nervous about what Tipa would say, she wasn't gonna let her brothers and sister be blackmailed by this horrible woman. Old Alice was stunned that her threats didn't scare us. She stood there gasping for breath.

"Well! I never! I don't know what's come over children today! First they take a sledgehammer to the outhouse and then to be so rude!"

She spun around on the heel of her sandal and swung her behind back through the oleanders. Why a woman of her age would wear a top with no bra was incredible to me. She must've been thirty-five if she was a day! And she called herself a real estate agent! I wouldn't rent a house from her in a hurricane.

We stood there planted like a patch of asparagus for a few minutes until we heard her screen door slam.

"This calls for a celebration," Maggie said. "Come on, let's walk down to Buddy's. Timmy, if you'll go in, I'll buy everyone a Coke!"

"Deal!" he said, and off we all went.

I turned back and looked at the pile of boards, tar paper and rubble. The job was completed. It seemed as though the old outhouse got so tired it just sat down. It didn't look to me like a gang of hoodlums had done this vicious thing. No. It looked like a reasonable thing that could've happened all on its own. I was satisfied.

We were cloistered in our rooms or at friends' houses until suppertime, wanting Tipa to make his discovery without us within his reach to scream at and question. No one said anything about it at the table. We munched on fried chicken and gobbled up a mountain of stewed tomatoes over rice and butter beans as though everything was normal. We could've gotten an Academy Award for our performance: Best Liars on Sullivan's Island. We children did the dishes,

Momma went to bed, Tipa went to see about old Sophie, the Queen of Fumes, and Daddy went to the porch to read the paper. After drying a million forks and plates, my brothers, Maggie and I went out on the porch to catch the breeze. Tipa was sitting in one of the metal chairs and Daddy was lying in the glider.

"Is that a fact?" I heard Daddy say.

"What are y'all talking about?" Henry said, racing Timmy to the hammock. "I called it first!"

"Oh, move over, shrimp!" Timmy said, climbing in the other end.

"I am not a shrimp!" Henry said.

"For the love of Pete, will you boys settle down?" Daddy said, and not unpleasantly. "Sophie and y'all's momma have gone to bed!"

Maggie and I plopped in the porch swing at the other end of the porch.

"Now, I'd like to ask you a question. Do any of you rascals know anything about the outhouse?" Daddy's voice was filled with thinly disguised mirth. It was a signal to commence telling whoppers, bobbing and weaving with the facts like a prizefighter.

"Daddy, I'll be fifteen in six months. I'm hardly a rascal!" It was Maggie talking, of course, covering the sin of telling a lie by annoying everyone with her offended attitude. She never missed her chance to remind all of us that we were wet behind the ears, and that she was the great lady.

"Just answer me without any speeches, okay?"

"What happened?" I asked. Poker face.

"Well, it seems that today, I went off to the post office to collect the mail," Tipa reported like a detective, "because everybody in this family is too busy and too important to do it, and when I came back our outhouse had fallen down." He searched our faces for any slivers of guilt.

"Oh, no! Nobody's gonna blame me for this one! I was at Bubba's house and I can prove it!" Timmy was good at this lying business.

"You have an alibi too, I assume, Mr. Henry?" Daddy said.

"Yup, went crabbing with Stevie Durst. Ask his momma. She drove us to Breach Inlet."

"Girls?" Daddy said.

"Oh, please, Daddy, I wouldn't go near that nasty old thing if you paid me!"

Maggie hadn't lied. Nothing on her conscience.

"Susan?"

"I'll go with Maggie on this one. I'll bet that thing causes tuberculosis! I'd rather hold it till I died!"

"No reason to be so disgusting, Susan," Maggie said.

"Whose side are you on?" I said to her.

"TB or not TB! That's the congestion!" Timmy said and he and Henry started laughing and punching each other. "Consumption be done about it? Of cough! Of cough!"

At this point we were all giggling, even Daddy. But Grandpa Tipa was steamed. He stood up abruptly and headed for the door. He stopped to face us, took a deep breath and began to stutter. I was just about to feel some remorse for us pulling one over on him. His seersucker pants were all wrinkled and his shirt had a big spot on the front. Very unusual for a man who was fastidiously neat.

The remorse fizzled as he dropped another one of his bigot bombs on us.

"You all think you're funny, don't you? Well, let me tell y'all something, if you think your daddy is gonna bring another Negress in 'eah and that she's gonna use a bathroom in my house, y'all got another thing coming, you 'eah me? Over my dead body! This is still *my house!*"

The door slammed behind him. We all fell silent. Even we, who always had a smart answer, didn't know what to say. We looked at our old man, who was folding up his paper, obviously getting ready to call it a night.

"What are we gonna do, Daddy?" I said.

"We're gonna build a bathroom on the back of the kitchen, that's what. I checked the layout of the pipes when I got home tonight and won't be such a big deal. You boys can help me and Uncle Louis. Keep you out of trouble for a few weeks."

"Cool!" Henry said.

"No problem, Dad," Timmy chimed in.

"And you girls can keep the mess clear and keep us fed. Sound like a plan?"

"Yes, sir, sure does," I said, "but, Dad, what's Tipa gonna say?"

"Grandpa Tipa to you, young lady!"

"Yeah, Susan's right, Daddy," Maggie said, "Grandpa's gonna raise the devil over spending money on a colored woman."

"Let me worry about that. You girls lock up, okay? I'm gonna go see about your momma. She isn't feeling so great tonight." Daddy looked at us, his face satisfied for once with what he saw in us. He went inside. "See y'all in the morning," he called over his shoulder.

The door closed quietly. Maggie got up and lay down in the glider, pretending to sleep. The boys whispered and teased each other in the early evening light. Lightning bugs blinked all over the yard and the ocean rolled in. Another day was coming to a close.

I shifted my position in the swing to dream a little, rested my head on a pillow and turned away from them. I thought about visiting Harriet's house and wondered who would be the next victim she sent us.

My father's solution was a good one. He was right, about this at least. I mean he was a big s.o.b. and all that when it struck him to be one, but Tipa's point of view was just plain wrong. What possible difference did it make where somebody sat on a bus, or which water fountain somebody used? Most of all, I'd be thoroughly and permanently reviling my grandfather's guts if he pitched a fit over the soon-to-be-built bathroom being used by our soon-to-start new housekeeper. I thought that it must be hard for old people to know when they were being horrible and old-fashioned. I doubted that my father would be successful in changing my grandfather's heart.

Everyone went to bed except Timmy and me. He was still full of the devil over the outhouse crash and wanted to talk about it. In whispers, we continued talking about all that had happened that day. I was too young to solve the big problems, but I could swing a sledgehammer with the best of them.

"I went *bam!* And it caved right in!" Timmy said.

"Shhh! They'll hear you!"

"Think Daddy can build a bathroom?" he asked.

"Daddy can build anything, dog breath, he's an engineer. Plus Uncle Louis will really be the one to do it. Quit breathing on me."

"Bump you. Think Tipa's gonna have a cow over it?"

"He's gonna have a whole barnyard, but if Daddy doesn't care, we shouldn't either."

Just then we saw the police car pull up in the backyard of Alice Simpson's house. We dropped to the floor to watch. The chief of police, Albert Johnson, known as Fat Albert to the natives, got out and went up the back steps. Through the oleanders we could just make out the shine and clump of his heavy black shoes — regulation footwear for cops. Maybe she was getting us arrested. I thought, *Oh no, we're going to reform school!* But, nope, her windows were wide open and all her lights were on. The music of Peter, Paul and Mary floated across the indigo darkness. With our noses near the floorboards, we saw her and Fat Albert together in the living room, laughing. He handed her a baggie of something. She gave him something to drink and turned off a few lights. A few minutes passed and then we saw them again in the living room. We smelled a trail of the most curious odor, like burning rope and sweet spices, as they settled themselves on the sofa in her living room. They were smoking something in a pipe.

"She's not getting us arrested," Timmy said, as quietly as possible. "Just what the hell do you think they're doing over there?" We could see them dancing now, real close, sort of kissing.

"They're not doing it yet, but they will be soon. Momma was right. She is a disgrace. Everybody knows old Fat Albert is married. Hell, he's got four kids!"

"This explains what Daddy said."

"What did he say?" This was news to me.

"He said the hinges on her door need replacing every month or so."

"My God, Timmy, do you know what this means?"

"What? That we've got ringside seats for the wildest show in town?"

"No! That we live next door to a bona fide whorehouse! Holy Moly."

3

The Lawyer

1999

I specialized in small acts of defiance when I was young. The outhouse episode was only one of them. But years of Catholic school education and failed attempts at bucking the system had tempered my character and I was filled with dread at the thought of ending my marriage. I was extremely reluctant to file papers against Tom.

Several weeks had passed since that afternoon at Maggie's and I still hadn't engaged the services of an attorney. I'd spent nights thinking about what Livvie would have told me to do. I could hear her saying to get moving; the decision had been made, accept the truth, move on. But I couldn't move. Once the lawyers got involved, I knew there would be no going back.

At first, I thought it would be less painful if I used a lawyer that Tom and I both knew, that a familiar face would make it easier. I made some phone calls and had a few meetings with a few of Tom's colleagues that we'd known since law school. In all their scholarly wisdom they advised me that they'd seen a lot of men go through the "young chick thing" and that Tom would probably tire of it very soon and come home. I should wait, they said.

Sure, I'd let him have his little fling all over Charleston in my face and I'd just knit him some nice socks in the meanwhile.

"I think not, okay?" I said to them.

One particularly unevolved attorney was on the Broad Street lawyers softball team with Tom and flat out refused to hear my side, citing "the team" as a conflict of interest. This idiot ball league was so uncreative that they called themselves things like the Lawmen, the Medicine Men, the Home Boys and the Numbers Guys. You got it. Lawyers, doctors, real estate brokers and accountants. Cute.

"Well, Harold, why *did* you give me an appointment?" I leaned forward in the tufted leather chair opposite his burl walnut desk, only to notice he was bestowing on me his lackluster interpretation of the "come hither" look. Lucky me.

"I was hoping you'd just want a shoulder to lean on. I heard you were looking pretty fantastic these days and I wanted to see for myself."

"Why, Harold Small, you're married. I don't think your Marla'd be too thrilled to hear you'd loaned me her shoulder." Sarcasm dripped from my lips.

"Well, I can't represent you. It's a conflict."

"Conflict of what?" I said. "What do y'all think? That y'all are Mickey Mantle and Yogi Berra?"

"I'm sorry, I'm just not comfortable about taking your case against Tom. He's a teammate."

"Excuse me. I've been turned down by better lawyers than you, Harold." I got up and went to the door. "Have a nice life. And, by the way, I've seen you play. You couldn't bat a ball into the broadside of a barn."

My list of old friends and Grant and Maggie's list were practically the same and it was getting me nowhere. One interview was more ridiculous than the next. They did, however, fuel the fire of my courage. I needed to do my own research. On an impulse suggested from a poster at the library, I called the battered women's shelter and asked to speak to the executive director. It couldn't hurt. Somebody like her had to be much more in the loop of what a woman could do to resuscitate herself. I should have done this in the first place. She gave me the name of a splendid new attorney who'd moved to Charleston two years ago from somewhere in Vermont. Michelle Stoney was reputed to be the most skilled and intimidating feminist lawyer in the city, handling messy cases like kidnapping by parents, child and spousal abuse and deadbeat dads.

A Yankee feminist, I thought. Perfect. That should scare the hell out of him.

That night as I lay in bed, checking and recording the decline of my thighs with a tape measure, I thought about my prospective lawyer and burst into laughter. I had called Ms. Stoney and had spoken to her for a few minutes. She sounded so capable and understanding. I couldn't wait to meet her. We had made an appointment for four-thirty the following day. At last, there was hope.

I was a spastic bag of radiating raw nervous energy when I pulled into the parking lot outside her office west of the Ashley River. Miraculously, I managed to get from my car to her office without convulsions.

I loved her waiting room. It was solid establishment and reeked of success, but feminine. The overstuffed couches stood against paneled walls of gleaming mahogany. The enormous windows, swagged in salmon velvet, were flanked with bookcases filled with books that looked to be a hundred years old.

A huge arrangement of fresh flowers graced the center of a round table that offered pamphlets of information on divorce law. I guess I expected to see pictures of Gloria Steinem and Susan Faludi on the walls. There were only photos of families and dogs on a rocky shore that I assumed was Maine, or some other foreign place.

After taking my name and assuring me that Ms. Stoney would only be a minute, the smart, young receptionist offered me a cappuccino or espresso and I declined.

"I have decaf too. You sure?"

"Yes, thanks."

She's got a regular Starbuck's franchise going here, I thought and picked up a copy of *People*. The buzzer of her telephone intercom rang and she picked it up.

"Yes, Ms. Stoney. I will."

That was the moment I started coming unglued. My hands became clammy and my tongue got thick.

"Mrs. Hayes? Ms. Stoney will see you now. Please follow me."

I followed her down the short hall, our steps muffled by the thick carpet, past a research library with two paralegals working away on computers, past a powder room and a small kitchen. Her double doors opened and there she stood.

"Thanks, Donna." The receptionist turned and left. "I'm Michelle Stoney, Mrs. Hayes." She shook my hand soundly and motioned for me to enter. "Would you like something to drink? Coffee?"

She had perfect teeth, had to be laser bleached. I guessed her age to be about forty-eight. Her dark hair was pulled back at the nape of her neck and secured by one of the most beautiful tortoiseshell clasps I'd ever seen.

"Please, call me Susan," I said, voice shaking a little. "No, thanks, too hot for coffee."

I took a seat in front of the desk and she sat next to me in the matching tub chair. She wore a plain Rolex that showed from the cuff of her navy pin-stripe coatdress. She was downright pretty in a buttoned-up kind of way.

"Would you like a Diet Pepsi? I have a ton of them in my fridge."

"Yes, thanks," I said, heartened by her choice in soft drinks, "that'd be great."

I dropped my purse at my feet, and my cigarettes fell out on the Persian rug between our chairs. She saw them and her eyes brightened.

"Oh! Do you smoke?"

I blanched at my bad habit and she continued.

"I haven't had a cigarette in ages," she said,

"gave it up, but every now and then . . ."

"Please! Help yourself!" I offered her the pack and dug around for my lighter. "I'm always quitting and then I start again, and then the next thing you know . . . well, you know how it is."

She pulled out a huge crystal ashtray from her bottom drawer and we were in business. We torched two low-tar death sticks and popped open two cans of frosty chemicals. She was obviously a woman of extraordinary taste. I began to tell her the whole miserable saga. I watched her eyebrows narrow as she took notes.

"Do you remember the exact date?" she asked.

"Yes. Wednesday, April twenty-eighth. I was supposed to give a presentation at two o'clock on a literacy program with day care for unwed mothers. Stupidly, I had left the whole mess in a folder on the kitchen counter that morning. When I went through my briefcase, I couldn't believe it wasn't there. I had worked half the night on the darn thing."

"We all forget things."

"True. Anyway, it was about eleven o'clock and almost lunchtime. I told my secretary that I was going to run home and I'd be back as fast as possible. I took my car and drove down to Queen Street, where we live. I was going to grab the folder and hurry back. I came in the back door and dropped my bag on the floor by the stairs and heard somebody upstairs. I thought, Oh, God, there's a robber in the house! I reached for the poker from the fireplace, shaking all over."

"I'm sure you were terrified!"

"I was! But I listened for a moment and heard

their voices. At first I thought it was Beth with some boy, and started sneaking up the steps, thinking I'd kill whoever would dare to do something to my little girl!"

"How old is your daughter?"

"Thirteen, almost fourteen."

"Not so young, these days."

"In a pig's eye, but anyhow, when I got to the top of the stairs I heard the voices coming from my room. I couldn't believe that she'd do something like this in my room!"

"Sort of the ultimate rebellion, right?"

"Exactly. Then all of a sudden it hit me. It wasn't Beth but Tom. I could hear whoever this woman was saying stuff like 'Oh! Tom! Ride me! Yes! My tiger!' Can you imagine?"

"Dear God. What did you do?"

"The stupidest thing possible. I opened the door and caught them! Why did I do that?"

"I probably would've done the same thing. It's that unstoppable desire to disprove what you know, right?"

"I guess. Anyway, he stopped giving her what was mine long enough to turn around and see me. She sat up and saw me, then rolled over and covered her head with a pillow. I guess she thought I was gonna hit her with the poker, which I nearly did. She screamed, 'Oh, no!' And he said, 'What the hell are you doing here?' I said, 'I live here.' Right away, I started explaining what and why, and then I thought, What the hell am I doing? He's in the bed with this slut — in *our* bed, no less — and he's the one who should be apologizing, not me!"

"So what happened?"

"I went downstairs and waited for him, but he left with her."

"That probably made you feel pretty bad."

"Yeah, you could say that. I was so numb and ill that I couldn't go back to work. So I did what women do in times of trial." She looked up at me and I said, "I started cleaning everything in sight."

"Classic," she said.

"Right. About two-thirty he showed up again, probably thinking that I'd be back at work and he wouldn't have to deal with me. But I was in the kitchen, still cleaning. When I asked him how he could do this to me, to himself, to our families, do you know what he said? He told me he was sorry I had caught them. Not that he was sorry he wrecked our life! He packed some stuff and left. Just like that."

I wasn't surprised that she didn't ask about the Aramis bottle filled with eau de whiz — I had never told anyone about that. Even I knew it was over the top. But I was surprised she didn't remark on the toothbrush story because by now everyone in Charleston knew about that. I guess I bragged a little and word got out. In fact, people stopped me on the street and in the grocery store to ask me if it was true. That single peanut-sized episode of revenge had elevated me to something of a cult hero among the jilted women of Charleston. I continued to spill the family juice without even worrying about whether or not she intended to take my case.

"So then I was so upset that I started helping him pack. While he was stacking all his shirts and suits into his hanging bag, I went into the bathroom and dumped a lot of his stuff out of the medicine cabinet. I took his toothbrush and looked at it for a minute and then I scrubbed the toilet with it. Good, too, all under the rim, everywhere. Then I dropped it in his shaving kit."

Even though Michelle was grinning from ear to ear, experience made me stop.

"Ms. Stoney . . ."

"Michelle, please . . ."

"Michelle, my husband thinks he is the Perry Mason of Charleston and that no one will represent me against him. If this is a problem for you, I guess this is when you should tell me."

"Susan? I hope you'll pardon me for saying this, but your husband is a big fat skunk first, and a lawyer second. I'll handle this for you with pleasure." Michelle smiled, leaned back in her chair and exhaled a cloud of blue smoke toward the ceiling. "You have to do two things: try to the best of your ability to document all contact you have with him from this moment on. Does he show up when he's supposed to? Is he hostile? That sort of thing. Then, itemize your expenses the best you can. Keep a good journal."

"I can do that. I used to do that all the time. I like you, Michelle. I trust you."

"You can trust me better than your own mother."

"You know, I heard he's living with her. She's twenty-three and has breast implants. He's practically a pedophile."

"Good grief."

"I know I shouldn't dwell on it, but I still can't believe I found them together. Calling out his name at the top of her squeaky, insipid little lungs, and him yelling back, 'Yes! Yes!' Infuriating! Can you imagine how I felt? How will I ever get that image out of my head? I'd like to kick his butt the whole way to California."

"We can do that without even changing shoes. The question is, where are we heading here? Is there any desire on your part or his for reconciliation?"

"It's not possible."

"You're absolutely sure about that?"

"Yes. I've dissected this thing to death, and you know what I haven't even told my sister?"

"Tell me."

"Tom stopped loving me years ago. I don't know how we stayed together as long as we did. But, now I'm sure of this, I don't want the kind of marriage where my husband thinks he's stuck with me, especially given his preference for young nymphomaniacs. Part of it is surely my fault. I mean, when I look back, I remember many times when I could've tried harder. I just didn't. I don't even know why. I was probably too tired from running the house, working full-time and taking care of our daughter to cite chapter and verse from *The Joy of Sex*, you know what I mean?"

"I know exactly what you mean."

"Oddly, he never complained. I guess that's when he found Karen. I understand that a lot of men do these things when they get around fifty, but he didn't have to do it in our house, in our bed. If I hadn't come home to get my presentation papers, I never would've known, although I think men who screw their little girlfriends in their own home have a secret desire to be caught."

"Maybe. I don't know, but I've heard that said."

"Anyway, our marriage has been in rigor mortis for ages. I guess I thought that eventually things would go back to being good again. We'd been through ups and downs like everyone. But that's not what happened. I resented being expected to do everything. And he resented me resenting him. We didn't talk; we swam the River Sarcasm. And worse, our silence was the smoldering kind. He didn't like the way I looked anymore, even when I tried to change my looks. He just didn't want me anymore. I didn't fit his fantasy."

"Fit his fantasy?"

"Yeah, I have this theory that you marry your fantasy."

"How's that?"

"Well, it goes like this: He dies for women with a big bosom, you have a big bosom, he dies for you. He falls apart for big blue eyes and a wicked meat sauce, you make an incredible Bolognese and, kaboom, he looks in your blue eyes and he's yours forever, until you burn his meatballs, no pun intended."

"Of course not."

"Anyway, I don't fit his fantasy anymore and I probably never will again."

"Not fitting someone's fantasy is hardly grounds for infidelity."

She was right. It wasn't funny. It was sobering.

"My family has lived in this city for over two hundred years and he's humiliated me in front of every single person I know," I said. "Every time I turned around there was someone I've known all my life either whispering when they saw me coming or dying to tell me that they'd see Tom and Karen out and about. I don't know what I ever did to him for him to hurt me so. Maybe I wasn't the perfect wife, but I deserved better than this. And, if that's not bad enough, he refuses to give me what he should in financial support. That's really why I decided I had to get legal help."

I was babbling like the white water in the Colorado River.

"Yes, tell me about that. Has he been sending you money once a month? Or do you have to go to him?"

"At first, I guess he felt guilty about leaving, so he just left the checking account as it was and I paid the bills from money he deposited. That's over now. He hasn't made a deposit in two months. Now he's got this new idea in his head that he'll contribute to our support, but I can't live any better than he does. Is that legal? I mean, do I have to sell my house if he decides to live in a one-bedroom apartment?"

"No. Under South Carolina law, you're entitled to more than that. How long were you married?"

"Sixteen years."

"And have you contributed in any way to his business?"

"I'd say so. I supported us while he went to law school at Carolina. I've certainly grilled enough steaks for clients and partners."

"Hmm, that's good. Could I trouble you for one more cigarette?"

"Of course! Help yourself!"

I liked this woman. A lot. She was going to help

me negotiate the next twenty years of my life and Beth's future as well.

"Thanks. Have you always lived in your home on Queen Street?"

"We bought it six months after he went into a practice with three friends of his. That was soon after we moved back to Charleston. Michelle?"

"Yes?"

"I don't want to sound desperate, but I need a separation agreement that's going to guarantee support for me and for our daughter starting right away or as soon as possible. I'm running out of cash and I don't want to have to borrow money. I can't go on like this, begging him for the mortgage, begging him for Beth's tuition. Why is he doing this to us?"

The tears started to roll down my cheeks now and she handed me a Kleenex.

"This kind of thing happens more often than you'd believe. We'll get this all straightened out. Remember, time heals. It really does. I can bring him to his senses."

"Thank you. I really mean it."

"I know you do." She patted my arm. "Okay, now, tell me the famous toothbrush story in slow motion. I just love that one."

It took me three days to get the outline of a budget done. Should I charge Tom for all the over-the-counter sleeping pills I took because he robbed me of decent rest at night? Should I pad it to cover my daily dose of amusing Chardonnay that I sipped while watching the eleven o'clock news? I began keeping a diary, which was actually rather cleansing. I had done it for years as a child. It kept me sane then and it couldn't hurt now.

I sent the budget to the intrepid Ms. Stoney, who padded it by fifteen percent, saying I had neglected things like vacations, unexpected illnesses, unpaid leave from work and so on. She notified Tom that I had retained her and he was not pleased.

"If you think I'm paying the bill for Michelle Stoney, that man-hating, viper-tongued lesbian bitch from hell, y'all can both kiss my sweet ass," he screamed at me from his car phone.

"What's that? Tom, dear, there's so much static I can't 'eah you," I lied. "Did you say Michelle can kiss your ass? I'll tell her you said so. Better yet, tell her yourself."

"You're not getting one cent from me now, Susan! This really pisses me off!"

"I'm shaking in my shoes. You listen to me, and 'eah me good. I don't give two shits if you're pissed off. You're going to pay Stoney's bill and you're going to sign a fair separation agreement with me. And quick, too. If you don't, my two huge brothers would be happy to discuss it with you. That's a real option. And another thing, don't you ever speak to me this way again. It's harassment, cupcake, and the viper wouldn't like it."

"Are you threatening me?"

"Nope. I'm assuring you."

I slammed the phone down. It felt great.

I hadn't seen Maggie in several weeks. The following Sunday, I got up early and met her at Mass on the Island. I had some old newspaper articles I wanted to show her. After church, we said hello to all the old ladies from the Altar Society, our mother's surviving friends, and decided to go over the bridge to Billy's Back Home Restaurant for brunch. Billy's is just a place on the side of the road. There's always a line and the food's worth the wait. Its interiors are considerably enhanced by blinking Christmas lights, fishing pictures and a huge sled suspended from the ceiling, so they leave the decorations up all year. It's sort of festive.

Brunch is a relative term here because they're not serving up mimosas and croissants at Billy's. No, no. In the Lowcountry it's got gravy on it — the biscuits, the ham, the grits — it all swims in a puddle of "heart attack on a plate." When you eat this stuff, it slides down like wet cement and stays there for weeks, asking directions to your arteries and hips. I planned to resist. After ten minutes or so, we got a booth and menus.

"God, wouldn't you love to have just one biscuit?" Maggie licked her lips at the passing trays laden with biscuits as big as your head, juicy sausages and crisp waffles covered in whipped cream from a can.

"Not me, baby," I replied. "I'll have a dry salad and a Diet Pepsi with lemon, please," I said to the waitress.

The waitress, wearing a hairnet and, on her stretched-to-capacity T-shirt, a sticker that read DOLORES on it, sucked her teeth at me.

"How 'bout you, honey?" she said to Maggie.

"I'll have one poached egg in a cup, one piece of bacon, well done, and dry whole wheat toast, with black coffee."

"You want grits with that?"
"No, thanks."
"Home fries?"
"No, thanks."
"You girls must be starving. I'll bring it out right away."
"We're here for the ambience," I replied. "Forgive us. We're anorexic, it runs in the family."
Maggie giggled. Big Dolores stared at us and turned on the heel of her running shoe. We watched her bulbous rear waddle over to the kitchen ledge, where she attached our order to a clothespin.
"What's with her?" Maggie asked. "Doesn't she know salad dressing is fifty percent of a girl's caloric intake? I read that in a magazine."
"Dolores is intimidated 'cause we're so good-looking. Let's overtip her and really aggravate her."
"Well, I see you're feeling like your sassy old self again. God knows, you're as thin as I've seen you in years! How's it going?"
I lit a cigarette and exhaled away from her as she began to fan my smoke.
"Have I told you lately how brilliant you are?"
"No, tell me." Maggie smiled, and sat up to receive a compliment.
Dolores put my Pepsi on the table with a clunk and poured Maggie's coffee. She slid my salad across the table and Maggie's platter as well.
"I forgot your lemon. I'll be right back."
"I started walking to and from work, and seven more pounds fell off in the last three weeks. I didn't even diet. Even my shoes are loose. You are a genius! And you were right about walking being

good for my brain. I feel like a new woman! Besides, who could eat in this heat anyway?"

"See? I knew it!" She was smug but nicely so.

"I owe it all to you. God, this must be the hottest summer in a million years." I took a long drink and reached in my purse for the manila envelope of newspaper clippings from 1963. " 'Eah, look at this."

"What's this? Old newspaper articles? Does this have to do with Daddy?" I could see that she didn't have the same enthusiasm for my research that I did, but she thumbed through them politely. "What's this one about the Klan got to do with anything?"

She referred to an old article about an African-American church burning near Georgetown, about forty miles from Sullivan's Island. Huge crosses had been burned in the yard the night before the church completely burned to the ground. The Ku Klux Klan was suspected of the crime but they had no suspects. No surprise there.

"Well, I'm not sure, but I decided to see how much stuff I could dig up. Maggie, we were so young then. I just want to know as much as possible about how it was and what really happened."

"What's it going to prove?"

"Probably nothing, but certainly there was more violence going on than I remember."

"Yeah, I'm sure that's so." Her interest had shifted because the next thing she said was, "You need to come over with Beth and spend the night. I feel like I haven't seen you in an age, girl."

"You're right. Maybe next weekend." I folded the copies and put them away. It wasn't that

Maggie didn't care; she didn't have the same desire to know as I did. "Beth starts school on Wednesday, freshman orientation. God, I can't believe she's going to high school!"

"Merciful mother, where does the time go? High school! What's happening with Mr. Tom?" she said, changing the subject again.

"Well, let's see. Last week, I saw him cruising King Street in a new convertible Mustang with Miss Karen in a ponytail and halter-top. They were wearing matching Ray-Bans. Isn't that adorable? I'm so happy for them."

"If Grant ever did this to me and the boys I'd kill him. Get a lawyer yet?"

"Nope, I got *the* lawyer. Michelle Stoney."

"Michelle Stoney?" Maggie whispered. "Michelle Stoney? Jesus, Mary and Joseph! Even I know who she is! Oh, my God! I can't believe you didn't tell me!"

"I wanted to see your face." I picked at a radish. "Close ya jaw, girl, or you gone be catching flies."

"This is gonna be like squashing an ant with an anvil! Wait till Tom finds out!"

"Tom found out."

"How'd he take it?"

"Not well." I couldn't help laughing. "He little party be over now. She gone clean he clock."

"Men stink."

"Listen, I've been saying that for years, except that we love the smell. This whole thing is incredible. He's been driving me crazy. This is typical Tom: He says he's coming for Beth on Friday at four, he calls at three to say he's held up and he'll call later. He calls back at six, I can hear he's in a bar, and he lies, saying he's hung up with a client, can he pick her up in the morning. I say, 'Sure, sure,' and take Beth to a movie or something.

"The next morning he doesn't call, so I have to call him. There's no answer at his place because he's sleeping at the slut's apartment. I leave a message on voice mail and he picks it up around noon. Then, he calls to say he's taking Karen to do some errands and can he pick Beth up afterwards. I say, 'Sure,' and he arrives at five with the slut and a car full of packages from every clothing store in the mall. All stuff he's bought her, I'm sure. But just let me ask him for the money for the mortgage or something like heart surgery, he goes into this routine how he's not a rich man and what do I think and blah, blah, blah. But Michelle is gonna take care of all that, thank God. And, needless to say, these little psychodramas aren't doing much for Beth's stability or her relationship with him. 'Eah?"

"Do you need to borrow some money? I have my own stash, you know."

"No, thanks, I'm fine."

"What can I do to help?"

"There's nothing to help. Everything's actually going to be fine. At least, I feel like it is. But thanks, you're the best sister in the world."

The late afternoon sun was shining the next day as I walked home from work down King Street toward my home. Maggie called this "power walking" or something like that and she had no idea how on the money she was. The myriad benefits of this daily routine were priceless. First and foremost, I was looking not half-bad. I could wear everything in my size-ten closet, even though they were so out of style that they looked like costumes. They fit. I recycled what seemed usable and dumped the rest into the trash. And I felt so good that I had even regained my sense of humor, especially when I'd think about Big Tom and Michelle in the ring. Ha!

Second, I walked past shop windows, seeing my reflection, which reminded me to correct my posture. The displays tempted me with new things to save my money for. Shoot, I should tell Michelle to demand a clothing allowance for me, I thought. If I got married again, Tom wouldn't have to pay alimony! It made perfect sense to me.

Third, I had the time to shake off work and prepare to meet Beth. Now, this was a formidable challenge, but for the first time in months, I was up to the task. Beth, Beth, Beth. Barely fourteen years old and she wore her smorgasbord of teenage issues like a badge of honor. Beth the Contrarian. Beth the Contentious.

Hormones. There seemed to be time for hormones in everyone else's life except my own. When Beth wasn't trying to smoke something or drink something, she was trying to pierce something. Just this morning she took another six months off my life.

"Mom! Why are you always treating me like such a baby? God, Mom, every person in my entire class has a third hole in their ear! I mean, it's totally infantile not to have a third hole!"

"Someday, you'll thank me your ears don't look like Swiss cheese," I replied with practiced calm.

"I hate living in this house!" she screamed, and slammed the front door almost off its hinges as she left for school.

When possible, I tried to ignore her hysterics because I didn't have the strength to fight over everything. Then too, it was time for her to test her own judgment and make some mistakes. I couldn't be in an adversarial position with her all the time if I expected her to come to me and tell me her troubles. I thanked God I had a sister like Maggie. When Beth was possessed by the devil, I'd call her and we'd have a good hen session.

"There's no book of instructions on how to raise a teenager, and darned little to recommend the job anyway," Maggie told me this morning. "You think my boys don't give me a run for my money? Remember Bucky and his friends watching that X-rated movie in my den last year? *The Moans of Marilyn*! I still don't know where they got it!"

"Yeah, God. I love her so much, but sometimes I'd like to just start screaming, you know what I'm talking about?"

"Susan, you probably *should* scream once in a while, and you probably love her too much."

The elder sage had spoken through the prophets, and I ignored her as I had whenever possible for the last four and one-half decades.

"Well, at least you have Grant to help you with the boys."

"Oh, some big help he's ever been. The only time in twenty years he's ever stepped in is when Bucky and Mickey had that party when we were out of town. If the police hadn't been called, and if they hadn't drunk all his Wild Turkey and wrecked the Jeep, he wouldn't have said a blessed word. Never marry a cardiologist. They are incapable of focus on anything but blood work, patients and an occasional football game."

"Men. Tom has time for his midlife crisis and I gave birth to mine."

"You're right. There's no justice. Wanna have dinner this Friday? I'm having some people over for Beaufort Boil."

"Sure. Talk to Beth, will you? Give her a little religion."

"With pleasure. Tell her that her auntie on the Island wants to have a little 'come to Jesus' meeting with her. Momma always said God would get even with us and send us children like we were."

"Revenge from the grave. She's probably up there in the big cocktail lounge in the sky drinking a Diet 7-Up and bourbon, laughing her brains out."

"No doubt. Cheer up, okay?"

"Oh, I'm fine, really. It's just this teenage transition stuff. I adore Beth. I'd marry Tom all over again just to have her."

"If you tried to marry Tom Hayes all over again, I'd drag you up the side of a mountain in Tibet and leave your sorry behind there for the birds."

But there was no trip planned for Tibet, just this nice walk home, as I prepared to meet my daughter head-on. Maggie was probably right about me loving Beth too much. It's pretty classic stuff that the wronged woman goes overboard to provide the perfect nurturing environment for her helpless child. I was dealing with her separation from her father and her transition into young womanhood with all the patience, understanding and humor that I had.

On the bright side, and there was one, there were many things that Beth and I did that brought us closer together. Naturally, we shopped, we had lunch, we did homework and we cleaned closets together. But beyond those mundane amusements — and this was a particular pleasure for Charlestonians alone — we exhumed our ancestors. Not literally, of course, but we loved to indulge ourselves with a short walk through St. Mary's Cemetery, where we would offer a prayer of thanks that our forefathers had the good sense to make Charleston their home, and in turn, ours. I'd tell the stories to Beth as my father told them to me and his father before him. Being part of this continuum was as rich a legacy as a treasure chest filled with jewels.

Charleston had given us the gift of knowing who we were, what we stood for and where we belonged in this complicated world. That pride and confidence was our birthright. Even Tom Hayes, with all his legal expertise, couldn't make this community property. Charleston was ours. Tom Hayes was from Greenville, which in my estimation was just about as pitiful as being a Yankee.

The warmth of the South Carolina afternoon sun was giving me my second wind. I turned the handle on my wrought-iron gate and began the walk up my short brick path to my little girl who was waiting for me. My Beth.

4

Beth

1999

The booming sound of the front door closing behind me thundered down the hall to the kitchen. Beth's young voice rebounded, punctuated by exuberant shrieks of delight and excitement. I riffled through the pile of catalogs and bills that waited on the hall table.

"Ohmagod! Ohmagod! Did you see the way he *looked* at me? He's so freaking fine!" Short pause. "I don't know! Do you think so?" Shriek. And then, in a guttural voice, "*Oh! My! God!* I'll *die* if he does!"

I sighed with some relief that Beth was discussing a member of the opposite sex. The nonsense I'd been dealing with lately, it could have been anything. Wait! What? Opposite sex? She was hardly old enough for Midol! Calm down, I said to myself. Breathe. Visualize the beach. Breathe. It was okay then, I was fine. I announced my arrival.

"I'm home! Hello?"

"Gotta go, the parental unit is back."

"Oh! You're on the phone?"

Parental unit? Was that who I was? In any case,

my rhetorical question prompted her to hang up. As I stepped into our kitchen there was evidence of major league terrorist activity. The contents of her backpack were strewn across the counter along with an opened carton of milk, an abandoned bag of Doritos and an open container of salsa. The breakfast dishes she promised to wash were growing moss in the sink. The dishwasher hadn't been emptied from last night. It was typical.

"Mom! I met this guy!"

"Good, honey, what about this mess?"

"Mom! You're not listening! I met this totally, devastatingly fabulous guy!"

This was a test. If I made too much of the disaster area, I was a shrew. If I gave the politically correct amount of interest to the possibility that she had met the love of her life, I was cool. If I didn't stop hyperventilating over the filthy sewer that used to be my kitchen, she might never tell me anything again. That was potentially more damaging than anything else I could think of at the moment.

I dropped the mail on the kitchen counter in the only clean spot there was.

"Tell me every word," I said, kissing her on the head, closing up the various containers. "How can you drink milk with salsa? Ugh!" I smiled obliquely. "So, tell me, who's the lucky devil?"

She made her famous sucking noise and crammed her books into her backpack.

"Jonathan. Jonathan something." Beth stopped and put her hand across her chest. "Oh, God, Mom, he's so fatally gorgeous!"

"Is he a freshman? Please don't say God." I narrowed my brows into a unibrow and put an armload of food back in the refrigerator, bringing out the half-defrosted chicken to prepare for dinner.

"Sor*ry*." She was insincere at best. "No, I don't think so. He just transferred from Porter Gaud. Me and Lucy were walking . . ."

"Lucy *and I*." A minuscule correction, I thought, as I placed the boneless, skinless breasts in the Pyrex dish.

". . . by the tennis courts and we saw him hitting serves? Jesus, the ball must've been going like a hundred miles an hour!"

"Please don't say Jesus. Did he talk to you or what?"

"Sor-*ry!* Gosh, Momma, it's hard to talk to you if you keep yelling at me!"

Her hands were on her hips and I motioned for her to continue as I cleaned up.

"I'm sorry, Beth, you're right, but technically I'm not yelling. So tell me, did this Jonathan faint from your dazzling beauty when he saw you? Hand me the sponge, will you, please?"

She tossed it to me and I began scooping up the truckload of crumbs on the sticky counters as she leaned against the sink, eyes aglow and young heart palpitating in the sunrise of her newfound love.

Look at her, I thought. One hundred and ten pounds, five feet and six inches of pure, youthful, romantic fantasy. I had felt that way about Simon at exactly her age.

"I wish, but he did stop and look at me and smile this smile that, oh, my God, made my hands like totally start sweating and my throat got like all tight. I mean, if he had said anything to me I think I would've died. This is the real thing, isn't it, Mom?"

"Like, oh, my God, oh, my God, oh, my God!" Hell, I'm not such a prude!

"Mom!"

I couldn't help laughing. Bad timing. She took my delight to mean that I was laughing at her, which I wasn't.

"Sorry, sweetie. Look, it might be the real thing. Who knows? Let's put the dishes away, shall we?"

I opened the door to the dishwasher and Beth began building a temper tantrum that could be heard across town.

"We? You mean, me! Fine! I don't care. We should be planning my trousseau, but I have to do the dishes first."

"Look, Beth, I'm delighted you met a guy who makes you feel all gooey inside. When I was your age, I never even saw a member of the opposite sex except from across a ballfield."

"That's because you were imprisoned in an all-girls school run by a bunch of Nazi nuns."

"That's right. But even if I had gone to a school like yours, when I was fourteen I was so ugly, I would've had to grovel and pay big bucks for somebody to defile my virtue. I was too proud to beg." I paused to do a shag step. "In addition, I lived in a perpetual state of negative cash flow, sort of like now, so I never even thought about boys."

"You always say you were ugly. You weren't. I've seen the pictures."

"Right. The one of me in my plaid jumper and knee socks?"

"Yeah, the uniform was dorky and you looked like a refrigerator in it . . ."

"A refrigerator?"

"Well, sorry, but you did, all sort of square . . . but your face was cute! It was!"

"*Was* is the pity." I opened a can of Diet Pepsi and lit a cigarette. "But thanks, I think. So, tell me again, what does this paragon of maleness look like?"

"Paragon? What kind of nerd-word is that? Don't blow smoke in my direction. It's gross. Secondhand smoke, Mom!"

"Remind me to remind you of that when I find the ashtray in your bathroom."

"I thought we were having a conversation about Jonathan, the whatever of maleness."

"Ah! Yes. Paragon, defined in the dictionary as a model of perfection. You know, somebody who's got it all."

"Gosh, you're like the four-one-one of English!"

"Thank you."

I took a slight bow. We smiled at each other and continued the work of restoring order. She rambled on as she unloaded the dishwasher and my mind floated away. I was a tad fanatical about the kitchen. I knew that. It flashed through my head that the whole room needed a fresh coat of paint and a change of wallpaper. The kitchen looked awful when it was dirty and pretty darn bad when it was clean. Or maybe it was that the wallpaper was one that had been here since Tom and I got married. We'd hung it together. Now I'd like to hang him. Maybe I was harboring this secret desire to wipe every room clean of every trace of him so that I could get on with my life. And what did it say about my life when I had two master's degrees and couldn't afford to change the wallpaper without taking a second job? Pretty pathetic, that was what.

"Mom! Are you listening to me?"

"Sorry, honey, my brain just took a side trip to the wallpaper store. Wouldn't it be nice to do this room over in yellow and blue with lots of white? You know, cabinets with glass doors and fresh curtains?" She looked at me as though I'd just returned to consciousness from massive electric shock treatment. "You're right. Now, you were saying about the boy wonder? He transferred from Porter Gaud, plays tennis, has a great smile and looks like a god?"

"Yeah, he's about five-ten and has huge blue eyes, thick blond hair and more teeth than Antonio Banderas. Not skinny, just fit, you know?"

I began to choke on my Pepsi. She had just described her father without realizing it. Christ on the couch of life, Freud breathes and Oedipus did the CPR. She was going to get her little heart broken — I knew it. I struggled to maintain my composure, steadfast at the wheel, as we sailed into the treacherous, uncharted waters of romance.

"He sounds adorable," I answered calmly, still coughing a little, "if you'll drain the sink and give it some clean suds, I'll wash the dishes."

"He is. He makes me feel so weird." The last of the old water sucked its way down the drain with the sound of disappearing little girlhood swirling away right behind it. "I think I need a haircut. You know, something California. What do you think?"

"We'll see." I cleared my throat. California? "I could use one too. Maybe next week we'll go to the mall together."

"Well, that'd be cool if you'd take me to the mall, 'cause Lucy and I were gonna just go there next Saturday and hang and see if Jonathan shows up with this guy, Sonny, she's like totally dying for."

"Hang?" I decided to smoke another cigarette and was wondering if I had any Xanax in the bathroom upstairs.

"Yeah, you know, you go get your hair cut, Lucy and I can cruise and, you know, do the girlie-girl thing for a couple of hours."

"Girlie-girl thing?" I was having some trouble breathing and/or swallowing.

"Mom? Are you all right?"

"Yes, I'm fine."

"Your hands are shaking. Oh, great, you're upset over the idea of me meeting a boy at the mall. Am I right?"

"No, I mean, I don't even know this boy. You don't even know his last name! I mean, he could be a serial rapist, or a sociopath, or you could wind up pregnant!"

"I can't believe you! I can't believe you would say that! Pregnant? Mom, are you like totally spassing or what? Gimme a break."

"Give you a break?" My eyes glazed over. "Look, Beth, there's nothing more exhilarating than being attracted to someone else like this. Is this a marriage? Not so far. You don't even know this boy's last name!" I took a breath. "Now, why don't we just calm down, and let's see if he calls you." There, that's better, I thought. "Then, in the time-tested (and proven) tradition of my family, I'll run a criminal background check on him, a driver's license history, and we'll see if he's registered with the AIDS clinic at the health department. If he's not, I'll invite his parents over for an interview. I'm sure they can give references. And, if they're not related to Charles Manson, then you can have him come and sit in the living room while his parents and I sit in the kitchen with a glass to the wall. How's that for giving you a break?" Pave the way to better parenting through humor, I thought, patting myself on the back.

"You're not funny."

Her adolescent rage was escalating again and I floundered around to no avail trying to lighten things up a little.

"You know what the problem with boys is? They ruin your skin. You fall for some guy and the next day you get acne like a bullfrog. You know what else happens? You get trapped in the bathroom and can't get into a decent college!"

That mildly got her attention, so I continued. "Yep! Ask your Aunt Maggie! You get in there in front of that old demon mirror and then you start obsessing about your hair and your makeup and is the hair on your legs making you look like a gorilla? And are your bosoms big enough or are they too big and then you start to sweat and does it show? You have to run, change your shirt. You can't find one, you have to iron. Then, you're habitually late for class, you flunk out and wind up on-line, at the Acme Training Institute, a loser guaranteed. I don't think that's what you want, is it?"

"Are you all right, Mom? I think you're losing

it." She was not even a little bit amused. She was, in fact, as angry as I'd ever seen her.

"I'm not losing anything. I'm fine, quite fine." I was not fine. Where did my composure go, anyway?

"Mom? You know what your problem is? You're trapped in the seventies! The Brady Bunch wasn't real, for God's sake. Nobody dates anymore; they just go to the mall or the video arcade or something and hang around. You think this guy is gonna show up with a corsage! God! You treat me like such a total baby, I can't stand it!"

It was my turn to get mad.

"First of all, I don't like your tone of voice and second, it's not your job to tell me what my problems are. Third, I don't treat you like a baby at all."

"Yes, you *do!*" Beth was serving up that most unpleasant stew of teenage screaming rage. "If Jonathan whatever-the-hell-his-last-name-is calls me and wants to meet me at the mall, I'm going if I have to take the bus and there's nothing you can do about it!"

She was absolutely shrieking at me and I didn't know what to do except to pull rank.

"Nothing I can do about it? You're telling me what I can and cannot do? I don't think so, Beth, oh, no. Let me tell you something, my defiant young daughter, you're going noplace unless I give you permission. And if you want to be treated like a grown-up, try acting like one and living up to your commitments! I come home after another underpaid, unending day, working in the most excruciating, humorless, literary abyss in the world and walk right into a land mine of filthy dishes and food and trash all over the place. I don't need this, Beth, it's not fair."

"Just because I didn't run home from school and do the dishes, I'm not old enough to go to the mall with a friend? Do you remember that I'm fourteen? Hello? Fourteen!"

"I don't care how old you are; when you start acting responsibly, then you'll get all the privileges you want! And watch your mouth, Beth, because you're very close to getting a slap in the face."

She stood at the door of the kitchen, which led to the dining room, and her blue eyes flashed the hatred of a formidable woman, not my little girl.

"Go ahead. Slap me. It won't make any difference. You know what I wish? I wish I lived with Daddy. He understands me and so does Karen."

"Karen understands you because she's your peer," I stuttered. "You know the court's granted primary custody to me. Even though it may seem like a living hell at this moment to both of us, it's how it is, so get used to it."

"You're just jealous of Karen because she's young and pretty," she hissed. "Maybe if you lost some weight and bought some clothes from this decade, Daddy might come home."

"That's not why your father left!"

"Yes, it is! Why can't you face the truth? God, Mom, the way you look is embarrassing. You look like those women on Court TV!"

I couldn't believe she had spoken to me this way. I was stunned. She stormed out of the room and I followed her down the hall. She raced up the stairs and slammed the door of her room.

"This has nothing to do with you following this

Jonathan person around a mall, do you hear me? Nothing to do with it!"

I couldn't help it. I walked into the living room and stood before the huge full-length mirror with the gilt frame, my inheritance. I broke down when I saw myself — a forty-six-year-old woman, with some very tired and afraid blue eyes, wearing a dress that hung on her like a rag from fashion hell. My eyes got hot. Tears welled up and spilled over in a fury like boiled-over oatmeal and they made me mad too. Hot and thick, they rolled down my face. I hated crying. I had thought I was doing pretty well until then. That woman in the mirror was not who I was.

This should've been the time in my life when Tom and I were concentrating on finding our poetry, cherishing moments like this with Beth. Her first boyfriend, and I couldn't handle it. I should've been gracious and understanding and said, "This is great! I remember my first crush!" I could've told her about Simon, the big fish that got away and how I had loved him. I'd never told her about him. But no, I was incapable of doing that because I was so afraid. I was afraid I couldn't make it. I was afraid because I felt alone and what if I lost her too?

The next thing I knew I had lowered myself into this sitting fetal position on the floor and started to wail, not giving a damn if the world heard me. So I wept, quietly at first, pitying myself for the loss of my Tom. Okay, he might be the fastest zipper in Charleston, but dammit, he was mine. We'd planned to retire to Sullivan's Island. I had dreamed forever that we'd buy a house next door to the Island Gamble and our children would always love Maggie's! I thought we'd all grow old rocking on that front porch together, eating boiled peanuts, and take our rightful position as old-timers, being as opinionated and as eccentric as we wanted to be. Let the young folk think we were peculiar and we wouldn't care. We'd all laugh our way to the other side together. What happened to my dream? What happened?

I blew my nose and thought some more, looking at myself in the mirror. In my mind, I could see Livvie wagging her finger at me. I had always been reasonably good-looking but now I looked like I'd been rode hard and put up wet, like Daddy used to say. All at once I was infuriated that two people could bring me to the point where I sat on the floor and wept. I felt Livvie smiling. I began to talk to the mirror as though she were there, listening.

"Tom Hayes," I muttered under my breath, "he doesn't deserve me or this girl of mine who, by the way, needs her behind kicked. No, no, this isn't about my weight. This is about Tom Hayes and his withering little pecker turning fifty! So, Miss Karen thinks he's the stud of all times, huh? I wonder if she watches the digital clock like I used to. Three minutes, Big Tom! Time's almost up! Ha! Have a ball, you losers. And you think he's generous now? Just wait until you marry the son of a bitch, you can kiss the mall good-bye!

"I may go down, dammit, but I'll go down fighting. Just who the hell do they think they are? And just what do they expect from me? I look like Mrs. Court TV? Well, I guess I do! Every last dime goes to Miss Beth's constant harangue for clothes!

It's always something! Maybe I should just fly to Atlanta and blow the bank at the shops and forget the furnace repairs. Or maybe I should just skip groceries and the phone bill . . . hire a personal trainer and get a massage and a pedicure!"

At this point, my shirt started getting wet. I hadn't cried like this since we buried my mother. And where was she now, when I needed her? Gone and useless, like always. I cried for her, as I never had when she died. I couldn't stop. Maybe this was the cry I owed myself, I thought, and then, I was done. I could either continue to be defeated or I could get myself back together. Beth.

Oh, no, Miss Beth Hayes, I'm your mother and you will not treat me this way! It's bad enough that Tom left me for Karen, but who are you, at fourteen, to dare to criticize? You have no idea the sacrifices I have made for you. More than anyone ever made for me . . .

I never heard Beth come down the stairs. Suddenly, she was next to me with a box of Kleenex and she was crying too.

"I'm sorry, Momma, I'm so sorry."

"It's all right."

"I never meant to make you cry like this."

"Sweetheart, you know I love you, but if you ever speak to me that way again, I'll rip your ears off."

"And you should. I never should have said what I said about Karen. Karen's a jerk. And I don't want to live with Daddy. He's a jerk too. I just wanna be with you, right here."

She put her head on my shoulder and I looped my arm around her. I stroked her gorgeous auburn hair and in that moment peace was restored. She was my little girl again. I accepted a Kleenex from her and blew my nose so loudly that we both started to laugh.

"Daddy's not a jerk," I offer magnanimously, "he's an asshole. And Karen's not a jerk either, she's the slut of the world, that's all." I continued to stroke her hair. "Don't share that with anyone, okay? Let's keep this between us."

"Mom, I would never repeat it. I agree with you."

"If I'd met Karen under other circumstances, I'd probably find her interesting and amusing."

"No, you wouldn't. Can I have a Kleenex?" She blew her nose and leaned back into my chest, the way she had as a little girl. "She's so lame, always tossing her hair. All she talks about is karma this and retrograde that. She wears this huge crystal around her stupid neck and talks about close encounters. Maybe she thinks aliens are after her."

"Now, there's a plan to get rid of her!" I raised my eyebrows and smiled at Beth. "I like it! Yeah, can't you see the front page of the *Post & Courier*? 'Charleston Woman, Owner of Insignificant New Age Bookstore, Abducted by Aliens!' Wouldn't that be fabulous?"

"No such luck, Mom. Come on, I'll help you burn dinner."

Beth pulled me to my feet.

"Burn? I never burn the chicken. I just like it dead. Salmonella, you know."

"Whatever." Beth smiled at me. "You need to wash your face."

"Hey! Who's the mother around here, miss?" I

swatted her backside.

"Hey! Quit killing me! Listen, forget about Jonathan. If he calls, we'll figure it out."

Upstairs in my room, I realized I had won this battle unfairly. By allowing Beth to hear me cry I had tipped the scales in my favor. My mother used to do that all the time. When she couldn't argue to a win, she'd spread the guilt as thick as peanut butter on white bread. Then she'd cry, and oh, how Marie Catherine Hamilton could cry. Big MC with the champion tear ducts. She cried more tears during her life than Shem Creek holds shrimp. Her despair was the backdrop of my childhood and probably what made me the sharp-tongued wench I was today. I was terrified of weakness and sadness and made jokes about everything. Maggie, on the other hand, denied everything. Even at Momma's funeral I looked at her and said, "As usual, old MC's lying around and we're doing everything." She looked at me and responded, "What do you mean? She's fine."

Well, I hadn't used my wit fairly and I could no longer deny that Beth and I were dealing with my own adjustment to Life After Tom as well as hers. As I washed my face, I realized I held the ammunition to decimate Beth's relationship with Tom. Piece of cake for a brutally clever girl like me. After all, Tom's pants didn't fall off in a strong breeze. He was the bad guy, not me. I could let her know about the money situation, tell her the toothbrush story, tell her how I'd found them, but no, I wouldn't allow myself to sink that low. It was as if Satan was tapping me on the shoulder but, thank the Lord, I recognized the devil's evil touch.

Now, if my mother were in my position, what would she have done? Easy. She would've had a meeting at the table with all us children and stood on the Bible while she informed us that our father was a fornicating sinner and that he had chosen another woman over his own flesh and blood. Then she would've lined us up on the front porch while she threw all his clothes over the rail and forbid us to say good-bye to him. Finally, she would've gone to bed for a year and let us fend for ourselves while she drank and cried away her grief.

And if Livvie were in my shoes, what would she do? She'd take Tom aside for a little "come to Jesus" meeting and give him the tongue lashing of his life. She'd tell him how it was all gonna be, in simple English and Gullah, so nobody got confused in the future. Then she'd tell her children not to worry, that everything was gonna be fine and that Daddy still loved them just as much as yesterday and that life goes on. She would then get on with the business of raising her children and putting food on the table.

"Well, this girl is about to rise like a phoenix," I said to my bathroom mirror. "Put on some lipstick and go deal with your daughter, and this time, be fair."

I served "twice dead chicken," nuked potatoes and salad from a bag, wondering how I'd ever gained weight from my kitchen. Beth and I found our rhythm again and everything was fine.

"Want some help with the dishes, Mom?"

"No, honey, you go do your homework. This isn't a big deal. But if you'd put some soap in the washing machine, there's a load of towels in there, that'd be a help."

"Sure. No problem."

She pushed back from the table and took her dishes to the sink, rinsing them and placing them in the dishwasher. I sat staring into space and listening to the fill cycle of the washing machine begin, followed by her footsteps. She kissed me on the head, the same way I do to her, and in that moment we both grew up a little more.

As I cleaned the kitchen I found myself sighing a lot as relief spread through my body. I decided to polish the bottoms of my pots as several sitcoms on the television droned in the background. My mind was traveling. I poured myself another glass of white wine and flipped on the eleven o'clock news in time to catch the weather report.

"High tomorrow, ninety-seven, lows expected to be in the eighties tomorrow night. And if you're going out tomorrow, don't be surprised if it feels like the tropics, as the extreme humidity is gonna cause a very bad hair day all over the Lowcountry. Expect shower activity off and on throughout the day . . ."

The young, blond meteorologist smiled and tilted her pretty head as she spoke and I found myself imitating her while I poured Cascade into the dishwasher and turned it on to do the small load, amusing myself once again with the banalities of life in this information-obsessed society. Finally, I moved the towels to the dryer, turned off all the lights and made my way upstairs to Beth to say good night.

I opened the door and saw her sitting in bed,

wearing a Citadel football jersey and reading her history book with great intensity. The low light of the room was warm and the cabbage roses of her wallpaper seemed to expel a sweet fragrance. Her room was the perfect expression of a young girl balanced somewhere between childhood and womanhood. Posters of the Grateful Dead hung on the back of her bulging closet door and her old teddy bears, frayed to a nub from years of affection, were pushed in between textbooks on the shelves above her word processor. Her cheerleader pom-poms hung from her closet doorknob. Around the top of her room were Barbies, perhaps over a hundred of them, their frozen idiotic smiles and zombie limbs sticking out like twigs in a molded plastic garland. They always made me laugh to look at them. Occasionally, I would take one down and pretend to be her in a singsong voice to get Beth to talk to me when she was annoyed about something. But tonight, I just stuck my head in the door and traveled the room with my eyes, waiting for Beth to see me. She looked up at last.

"Whatcha doing, doodle bug?"

"Oh, got a test on Friday and figured I'd better get on it, you know?"

"Yeah, you're right. I forgot to ask how your French test went."

"Ninety-three."

"That's my girl." I hung on the doorjamb, waiting for an invitation.

Beth smiled at me and the light of her bedside lamp caught her profile, casting her into Botticelli's Madonna. Her blue eyes met mine and I could detect no trace of emotional damage. The primal urge to protect her washed over me. How will we rebuild our lives? Together.

"I love you, Momma."

"I love you too, Beth, I'm so proud of you."

"Do you want to talk for a few minutes?"

She moved to the other side of her bed, the same one that had been mine in my childhood, to make room for me. She patted the empty space next to her, encouraging me to join her.

"Sure, why not?"

These late night talks were my treasure.

"I hate growing up." She sighed and looked at me.

"Me too."

"Mom, you are grown up!" she reminded me affectionately.

"I am? Oh well, it's a hard business and it doesn't happen in one day, you know."

"Like Rome?'

"Yeah, like Rome. You know, it's a very uneven process. One day you get up and think you can handle anything. The next day, life deals you a joker and you're struggling to survive all over again."

"Like Daddy bailing out on us?"

"Honey, Daddy didn't bail out on you. He bailed out of our marriage."

"I guess so."

"Anyway, life takes a lot of patience and it helps when somebody loves you along the way. Love helps a lot, but patience is your best weapon. Livvie used to preach to me that I needed to slow down to think things through. Poor woman, she needed two tongues to raise me. I was so stubborn."

"Do I hear a Livvie story coming on?"

"Oh, I don't want to bore you."

"Please! Tell me what it was like in the dark ages, when you were a kid and Livvie came to work for your family . . . back when you were gonna be a writer and move to Paris," Beth said with all the drama she could muster. "I love the Livvie stories, promise!" She added a Girl Scout salute for good measure.

"Move over, then, I need a pillow. She saved our lives, you know."

"She loved you the best, didn't she?"

"Oh, I don't know about that. I think she had this amazing ability to make all of us feel like she loved us each the best. She was remarkable."

"She was like your momma, wasn't she?'

"Well, honey, you only have one momma, but if I could've had two, she would've been the other one I'd have chosen. God, she understood everything. . . ."

"Earth calling Mom!"

"Sorry, drifting again. I was just remembering what it felt like after she came."

"Well, tell me . . . I'm waiting! Tell me about how you and Aunt Maggie and Uncle Timmy met her." I settled myself between the bumps and lumps of her old goose down pillow as the stories began to surface. "Scratch my back," she pleaded.

I reached up under her top and ran my short fingernails across her skin, the way she likes, careful to avoid the tickle zones.

"It's the gospel truth, you know. Every word."

5

LIVVIE

1963

Maggie and I were shaking the sand out of our beach towels and Timmy was winding up the crabbing lines. A bushel basket full of blue crabs sat beside us.

"I have a ton of sand in my bathing suit too," Maggie said. "Do you want to rinse off with me?"

"Me too. Augh! It's so disgusting!" I pulled away the bottom of my swimsuit and turned out a lump of wet sand.

"You're gonna go to jail for indecent exposure!"

"Kiss my butt! Last one in's a rotten egg!"

From the dunes, we sprinted to the water, not stopping until the incoming waves knocked us down, thoroughly soaking us. "You're rotten!" Maggie dove under a roller and came up with me beside her.

I took a mouthful of water and spewed it at her with the force of a garden hose, hitting her square in the face.

"You are so gross! I'm gonna murder you!"

Maggie sputtered, rinsed her face and slapped water in my direction. Laughing, I dodged her retaliation and sent her a flood of water from the ocean surface, drenching her face again. Our shrieks were a call to arms for Timmy, who watched from the water's edge, shaking his head.

"Don't worry, Maggie! I'll save you from the enemy!" Timmy dropped the crabbing gear and took a heroic, flying leap over the low waves. He grabbed me around the neck, pulling me down backwards in the shallow water. I gurgled and fought, broke free and pulled Timmy back under the water and dropped him there. Coughing my brains out, I tried to escape to the safety of the shore, but Timmy dove underwater and caught me by the legs, pulling me down again. All the while, Miss Maggie floated in regal splendor, enjoying the sounds of her little brother and sister pummeling each other.

"Help! Take that, you little creep!" I grabbed a handful of mud and threw it at Timmy, stinging him on the legs.

"Wait!" Timmy stopped and pointed in the direction of Maggie. "Let's get her."

Timmy and I, with our noses skimming the water and the stealth of submarine spies, cut through the water toward an unsuspecting Maggie, whose attention appeared to be focused on the sounds of the seagulls. I came on her from underneath and Timmy from behind. I grabbed her bathing suit and pulled her to the floor of the ocean, attempting to stand on her. The current had its way with all of us as we toppled, and Maggie rose up to the surface like a sperm whale, vowing to kill us both.

"I'm telling Daddy! You know you're not supposed to do that! That's how people drown!" Maggie's hair was over her face and she washed it back to better view her attackers. "Y'all are in deep trouble now!"

"Ah, try to get me! Come on!" I challenged her good-naturedly.

"Yeah, you tell and we'll get you again!" Timmy said.

"Oh, just forget it. Come on, we gotta get home."

Maggie surrendered, all of us knowing she wouldn't tell our father. On the way out of the water we bodysurfed, riding the waves to shore.

"We really got her, Timmy!" I crowed after sending one last mouthful of water in her direction.

"Susan Hamilton," she said, "you are a gross pig, and no man is ever gonna want you. Ladies don't spit!"

"Is that a fact?" I giggled and gave Maggie the finger.

"That's it, Susan. I'm telling."

"Oh, for God's sake, Maggie, wash the starch outta y'all's underwear."

"Y'all, cut the crap! We gotta get these crabs home before they die and start stinking all to hell."

"I wish you children wouldn't cuss so! It's vulgar!"

"Children? Excuse me?"

Muttering to ourselves about Maggie's assumption that she was the national arbiter of good taste and deportment, we gathered up our towels, the basket of wiggling and twisting crabs and the bucket of bait — a bunch of old chicken necks.

We'd just throw that old chicken neck out in the water on the end of a piece of cord, and the stupid crabs jumped on like they had a reservation on a luncheon cruise. We caught them by the bushel all the time.

We were our own parade. We cast long shadows on the soft wet sand, bulked up by the towels thrown over our shoulders. Our footprints formed an irregular trail. An occasional sun worshiper would glance up from her paperback novel and remark on our passing to a friend in the beach chair next to her.

"There go the Hamilton kids again! Do you think they ever eat anything but crabs in that house?"

"No lie. Pretty soon they're gonna grow claws and start walking sideways."

People always had something to say about other people on the Island. Even children like us were fair game. Timmy led the way down the beach and over the dunes, his crab net held high like the spear of victory. Maggie and I, who for the moment had made our peace, swung the basket between us. We reached the Island Gamble in a few minutes. We dropped the basket of crabs and threw our towels across the handrail of the front steps. As we started up the stairs, we heard the booming Gullah of a deep-voiced woman.

"Don't you children be coming up 'eah bringing sand on my porch! Go round to the back and wash your feet with the hose!"

"Holy shit!" I whispered. "What was that?" We all froze.

The woman moved closer and we could see her

then. She towered over us from the porch. She looked like a bronze statue from the Civil War. She was an enormous, stately woman, nearly six feet tall. Her jaw was square but even from the shadows I could see her eyes flashing. We braced ourselves for further instructions.

"I mean what I say now, you children go on to the back!"

"Who are you?" Timmy asked politely, too stunned to budge one inch. "I'm Timmy."

"I see that. I'm Livvie Singleton and I'm here to help y'all's momma. Harriet Avinger's cousin. What you got in that basket?" She opened the screen door and came down to the yard for inspection. "You mussy be Maggie and Susan," she remarked as she passed us, our feet still cemented to the bottom step. "You best be closing your jaw or you gone be catching flies," she added under her breath.

Maggie and I snapped out of our trance and hurried to find our manners.

"I'm Maggie, Mrs. Singleton, the eldest child."

"That's fine!" Livvie took a long look at her.

"That makes me Susan, Mrs. Singleton, it's nice to meet you." I extended my hand to Livvie, who looked at me for a moment and then shook my hand soundly, smiling broadly. She had the whitest teeth I'd ever seen and dimples on both cheeks. "I love Harriet. She's so nice."

"Yeah, she's a good woman, all right," Livvie said.

"Do you have a garden like hers?" I asked.

"Bigger," she said with a grin.

"Your melons as sweet as hers?" I asked. It took her about one split second to see where I was headed. She narrowed her eyes at me and I maintained the innocence of a choirgirl.

"Miss Susan? You want some melon from my garden, child?"

"Oh, I love watermelon," I said.

"Yeah, she can spit a seed clear across the street," Timmy said and started laughing.

"Shut up, Timmy," I said.

"All right now, let's see what you got 'eah." Livvie peered in the old bushel basket and, indeed, fifty to sixty hapless crustaceans were climbing over each other in their stupor for salt water. As one would try to escape, his brother's claw would pull him back into the abyss. "Hope you got more loyalty to each other than these devils do!"

"Yeah, isn't it awful? If they had any brains, they'd get out!" Timmy said.

"Well, they ain't got none, so we may's well cook 'em! Bring them around to the back door and we give them a funeral!" Livvie turned and climbed the stairs. "Yes, sir, Lawd, gone be some good eating for this 'eah Hamilton family tonight! Gone be a feast!"

The screen door closed without its familiar slam as she disappeared from our view. We made our way to the back steps, lugging the heavy basket and dragging our towels across the ground.

Maggie threw her towel over the clothesline and said, "Here, gimme y'all's and I'll hang them up."

"Golly gee whiz, Miss Maggie, is it my birthday or what?" I tossed her the towels and turned on the water, extending the hose from its rack to rinse our feet.

"Don't be such a wise guy, Susan," Timmy said.

Maggie let the cool water run over her feet and legs while Timmy and I sat on the back steps waiting to dry.

Livvie's voice rang out from the back porch.

"You children gone bring them crabs to me or do I have to come get 'em?"

"We're coming!" we answered together, exchanging looks of exaggerated trepidation.

"This one's not gonna be easy to train," I said.

"Train, hell. Did you see her face?" Timmy said.

"Yeah, Mount Rushmore," I said. "Come on, let's get inside."

As we crossed the threshold of our back door, evidence of a new regime was everywhere. The empty sink sparkled, the floor shone from a fresh coat of wax and we spied the plate of homemade fudge like the ears of a good bird dog perk to flush out dove. A crisp clean cloth covered the table laden for us with egg salad sandwiches, cut tomatoes and cucumbers on lettuce, a platter of sliced watermelon and a pitcher of sweetened tea. On the front burner of the stove, our family's largest pot was beginning to simmer, waiting for the crabs. Livvie dropped a cut lemon into the pot and turned to face us.

"I say to myself, Livvie? (My momma call me that 'cause she say I is the livingest gal she ever did see — short for 'lizabeth.) So, I says, Livvie? Them children mussy be ready to starve when they get themselves home! So I make y'all something to eat. Bring that basket over 'eah, boy. Soon's this water set to boiling, we have us a ceremony!" Livvie laughed and clapped her hands, bending with glee as she surveyed the shock in our faces.

"Y'all like fudge?"

Mesmerized, we took a place at the table and devoured the food, licking our fingers and happily coming to the realization that life could be worse.

"Gosh, Mrs. Singleton, this is sooooo good! I never thought egg salad could taste so good," I said. It was delicious.

"Y'all call me Livvie, okay? Celery salt, a little bit of chopped onion and mustard. That's my secret. I'll teach you how to make it, iffin you behave! Y'all want some more tea?"

The ceiling fan spread peace over the room and the three of us filled our stomachs until we could no longer swallow another bite. I sighed in satisfaction and also in relief. It was the first time anyone had taken care of us like this that I could remember.

"Let's us wash up these plates and send these boys to they watery grave. 'Eah?"

Livvie turned on the faucet and squirted some liquid soap into the sink, indicating to us to put our dishes in the sudsy water. Without prodding, Maggie and I began to wash and dry the dishes. Livvie found a pair of tongs and, one by one, she dropped the crabs into the pot, apologizing to them.

"All right, Mr. Crab, I sorry I gots to do this to you, but your life ain't wasted. No, sir, you gone serve the Lawd by feeding the Hamiltons."

We began to snicker behind her back and, hearing us, she spun around on her heels.

"What you laughing at? Get over 'eah, Mr. Timmy, you tell this crab you sorry for him. And tell him thank you."

"Ah, go on, Livvie."

"Go on nothing! You come 'eah, right now! I know this seems silly to you but you have to remember to say thank you. It's important. Don't make fun of nature! Never do that! You stir up Yemalla ire and then you ain't got no crabs!"

She handed him the tongs and he took them very reluctantly. Timmy reached for a crab and held him high in the air over the pot before releasing him.

"Yemalla? What's that?" I asked.

"Humph. Oh, Lawd!" Suddenly her face was filled with a kind of despair. "Y'all children go to church every Sunday?"

"Are you kidding me?" Timmy said. "If we don't make Mass, we have to be in the hospital or in the grave!"

"That's good," Livvie said, " 'cause everybody needs to thank the Lawd for all He does for us. Ain't that right?"

We all agreed, bobbing our heads like well-behaved morons, while she began to tell us the first of the many stories we would hear about the Gullah culture and the ways of her people.

"My family come from Africa during the time of the plantation, before the war with the Yankees. We had our own customs and what we believe and such. We come 'eah, and the white people try to get us believing in what they believe. So we learn about Jesus and learn to love the Lawd. But we always remember the ways of our ancestors and elders and honor them by telling the stories they brought across the water. Don't hurt nothing to pray to everything. Iffin everything got Gawd in him, then you should pray to everything. Ain't that right?"

"Can't hurt," I said.

"Tell us more, Livvie," Maggie piped in. "Who or what is this Yemalla?"

"She plenty powerful, that's what. You see, we believe that iffin Gawd give free will to man then He mussy give it to all He create. So we give names to Mother Nature too! Yemalla is the name of a goddess. She the power of the ocean and the moon, control the tide, soothe the spirit with her song, light the way for us. She give us fish to sustain us, like them crazy crabs fixing to get in the pot. They is her little babies, so we thank them for feeding us."

"That is the weirdest thing I ever heard, Livvie," Timmy said, giggling.

"You think so, 'eah?" Livvie shot at him.

She was getting a little irked. Timmy should've known better than to make fun of her religion, but he's a jerk.

"I don't think so, Timmy! Livvie, don't listen to him, I think it's interesting!" I said, in a hurry trying to squash the fire before it started to burn.

"Lemme tell you children something. Gawd, Lawd, Yemalla, don't make no never mind to me. All the same. Whatever you believe in, that's all right. I just think it's a gift that you can drop a hook in the river and pull out your dinner! Somebody ought to be thanked!"

She stopped talking and looked at us like a bunch of sorry-ass heathens. We were. Even though the powers in our life tried to beat Christianity into our thick heads, we resisted with vigor, relegating religion to suffering for a few hours a week in church, and cramming for religion tests in school. We talked a good enough game about heaven, hell, purgatory and limbo, but privately Timmy and I thought most of it was a load of garbage. Naturally, Maggie bought the whole thing, but she was a world-class prude. I just figured I'd do the best I could and see what happened when I died. The way I saw it, God had a whole lot of butt to kick before He got to mine, like Hitler and guys like that. Maybe He'd be worn out.

But, even in my heathen state, I had to say that Livvie had a point. Somebody should be thanked. Most importantly, I liked the idea of a female god.

"Yemalla, huh?" I said.

"That's right. Yemalla," she said with dignity.

Timmy got up again and went to her side. "All right, Mr. Crab, Livvie says I gotta do this. Sorry. I'm glad it's your butt getting blistered instead of mine!"

Well, we couldn't help snickering, even Livvie joined in. But I could see her thinking about what he had said about getting whipped. Harriet had probably told her about Daddy's temper.

Timmy, pleased with his wit, saluted to Livvie, bowed to us and tossed another crab into the pot. "Sorry, buddy," he said with great drama, waving farewell to him.

Livvie just shook her head. "You children go on do something quiet now! I'll finish this up."

I turned to Livvie and held her gaze for a long while. "I'm glad you're here, Livvie," I finally said. "Thanks for the sandwiches and everything."

"Y'all are entirely welcome." She smiled at me

as she dried the last plate. "And thanks for all y'all's help."

"I call the hammock!" Timmy yelled as he ran for the porch. "Thanks, Livvie!"

"Come back 'eah!" Livvie ordered him.

Timmy turned around and ran back to the kitchen, where Maggie and I still stood with Livvie.

"What now?" Timmy whined.

"Listen to me good, all you children. Now, I know you been used to one thing and another before Livvie come 'eah. But now I's 'eah and y'all needs to understand a few things." She looked at the three of us, our belligerence shining, as we waited for her to continue. She held out her hand and began to count on her fingers.

"Number one, ain't gone be no more slamming doors. You got old people around this house and they nearly jump outta they skin from all the noise. I ain't gone have nobody dropping dead on my time. Number two, ain't gonna be no more hollering and carrying on at the top of y'all's lungs. Iffin y'all want to holler y'all's heads off, go outside. Got a baby coming soon, and we don't need no nonsense either. Now, I gots to ask y'all a question."

"Sure, Livvie," Maggie said.

"What?" I asked.

Timmy remained silent.

"Is there some reason I ain't understanding why your momma has to make up y'all's beds? Ain't you children well enough to do this to help her?"

Timmy looked at me, who turned to Maggie for an answer.

"It's just that Momma has always done it, Livvie.

It's not like we're trying to take advantage of her," Maggie explained in complete stupidity, as guilt dawned.

"I see. Well, I gone tell y'all something. When I get off that bus this morning I see a woman come to greet me. She about to drop a baby any second, with circles under her eyes and swollen ankles that could make me cry. She's plumb wore out, I say to myself. That woman was your momma. I want you children make your beds in the morning from now on. And pick up y'all's mess too. Can you do that for her?"

"Sure. No big deal," Timmy replied, with some embarrassment.

"God, Livvie, where is Momma? We didn't even see her since we've been home," I asked.

"I reckon she's still resting, and don't use the Lawd's name like that. Who wants to help me fold towels and sheets? I got crabs to watch and chickens to fry. Your granddaddy ask me to fry him some chicken and I said I glad to do it."

"Glad to help," Maggie said quietly, her eyes glancing to me and then to Timmy.

We looked at each other and sighed. In the span of time it took the sun to travel from one side of the Island to the other, our Geechee singsong world had been transformed to one of order and expectation.

Without ceremony, Livvie presented Maggie and me with a dust cloth, a can of spray wax and a psychic message that to put clean laundry on a filthy table made *no* sense whatsoever. She never uttered a sound. She merely looked at us.

In a short time, the towers of towels covered the

fresh glossy patina of the dining room table like a growing business district of skyscrapers. Maggie and I folded, folded and folded.

"God, this Livvie is gonna wear us out!" I whispered to my sister. "Got us working like dogs."

"No kidding, but I never realized how dirty this house was until Livvie cleaned it, did you? Here, bring me the corners." Maggie gathered up the contoured sheet, folded it three times and added it to the stack. "Who used all these towels?"

"Well, it ain't Henry. He's a little pig. Momma has to yank him into the shower by the hair once a week whether he needs it or not."

"Too true. And we know for certain Grandmomma doesn't use many towels," Maggie whispered, sucking her teeth in disgust.

"Please." I made my renowned gagging sound. "She smells like a locker room."

"Susan! Shush!" Maggie gave a Hollywood sigh and me one of her famous exasperated looks.

"Sorry, your majesty," I hissed, "but I'm entitled to an opinion, you know, and she does smell just like eau de Dumpster. Hey, do you think it's possible Livvie is gonna get old Sophie straightened out?"

"If she does, that will be the miracle of the century."

"If she gets Sophie's ducks in a row this joint will become a religious shrine and we'll be flooded with pilgrims coming to take the waters. I want the candle concession." Quickly, I calculated how many candles I needed to sell at fifty cents apiece. "If I sell fifty candles a day for four hundred days, that'll give me ten thousand. If I invest it at five percent for three years, I can take a Corvette to college, pay my tuition and take us all to Florida for a vacation!"

Maggie stopped and stared at me like I came from Mars. "How does your mind work? I mean, how do you come up with these wild images and ideas?"

"I dunno. Sometimes I think I've got a brain virus or something. A genetic victim of my ancestors." I widened my eyes at Maggie and snickered.

"What?" Her face was as flat as a board.

"Oh, for God's sake, Maggie, I just try to keep myself entertained. Otherwise life is too dreary to deal with." I felt my neck getting hot. Nobody around here ever understood my sense of humor.

"Oh." Maggie returned to the laundry. "Anyway, somebody around here is using way too many towels!"

"Yeah. We've already folded twenty-two bath towels, fourteen hand towels, eighteen facecloths and a ton of kitchen towels! It's probably Daddy."

"Yeah, and who's gonna tell him what to do?"

We looked at each other at the thought of our father being put in his place. Arms filled, I followed Maggie to the linen closet.

"I like Livvie," Maggie said as she shoved the laundry into the crowded shelf.

"Me too, a lot, but Timmy says we're in boot camp with her. Hey, where did that little bum Timmy run off to? He should've been helping us!"

"Livvie made him take out all the garbage and return the bottles at the Red and White for deposit money. The last I saw of him, he was loading the wagon."

"Timmy did all that? Jesus! What next?"

"Who knows? I'm going to paint my toenails in the seclusion of my room before she finds something else for us to do."

Just then Livvie passed us with the basin, a bar of soap and towels.

"Gone give y'all's grandmomma a sponge bath," she said. "Y'all got any talcum powder in this house? Took me two hours to scrub her room today, but now it smells so good!"

"Under the sink in Momma's bathroom," I said.

Maggie and I looked at each other in complete amazement for at least the third time in a few hours. Then, Maggie climbed the steps to her room. I raced up the fourteen steps behind her to the second floor. I started thinking and grew no moss getting to Maggie's room at the end of the hall. I kicked open the door and found Maggie lying across her bed flipping through the latest edition of *Hollywood Truth*.

Maggie looked up in annoyance. "Didn't you ever hear of knocking?"

"Oh, eat it, Maggie, there we were saying how wonderful Livvie is and the truth is, this is a potential disaster! This woman's gonna turn us into her personal slaves! And, dearie, if you get caught with that piece of crap newspaper, Big Hank's gonna cut your ass."

"Daddy's never touched me."

"Lucky you." My face became serious.

"So, what do you want, garbage mouth?"

"It's her. Shoot, you'd think we'd never folded towels before. Did you hear the way she told me to fold them in thirds and then thirds again? I get enough algebra in school. I'm telling you, I've been thinking about it. Timmy was right. This is Parris Island."

"Get over it, maybe *she's* right. Every time you open the linen closet everything falls on the floor. That fold fits the shelf. And we are a bunch of slobs. As long as I don't have to clean the toilet, I don't mind pitching in a little."

"Momma needs a maid and we get the Albert Einstein of towel folding. I'm going to hide in my room. I liked the crab funeral better. Felt like calling FTD."

"You're twisted, you know that? At least she can cook."

"Yeah, well, maybe, but I still say we're in big trouble."

"She's giving old Sophie a bath. I think it's wonderful."

"We'll see. Though I don't hear any screaming."

I closed Maggie's door and slipped into my own room across the hall, breathing a sigh of surrender to the upper hand of Livvie. I had to admit that what she had accomplished in a few hours was rather miraculous. It was funny to me that even Grandpa Tipa had been nice to her. All he'd done over the past three weeks was grunt while we built the bathroom. He was usually the one that caused these women to quit by calling them one of his stupid names he had for colored people. But she'd won him over too by agreeing to fry some chicken for him.

My eyes scanned my room, as I leaned back against my door. There wasn't much about my room that was remarkable, except the privacy I had when I closed the door. Next to my bed stood an old end table of forgotten origin, its white paint chipped. There was a goosenecked lamp that I would bend to shed light on my lap as I did my homework, read books or wrote in my journals. My mahogany single bed nearly filled the room. It had four posters, each with carved shafts of wheat tied in bundles, and had provided rest to some long dead relative. Tattered stuffed animals, my old best friends, sat on the only treasure I had ever had, a handmade quilt that had belonged to my father's mother.

I kept a diary, not just one diary, but a whole collection of black-and-white speckled composition notebooks. Writing took me away. When I wrote I could say what I thought. If I said what I thought out loud, Daddy would've killed me a thousand times.

Lying on my stomach across the quilt, I reached under the bed for the wicker hamper that held them all together. I examined the security knots in the bows to make sure the prying eyes of my siblings hadn't invaded my privacy. They had not and I sighed, thinking that if they ever did read them, they'd be candidates for dentures, if I let them live at all.

The ribbons that held them together had been a gift and I had saved them all these years. They reminded me of a time when I was truly a little girl, just barely seven. MC's baby girl. The only memory I had of feeling like anyone's baby. My favorite memory of motherly attention and love.

I had been playing paper dolls on the front porch when Momma opened the screen door and found me there. I guess she thought I was looking lonely. She didn't look too happy either.

"Susan? Do you want to walk down the street with me?"

"Sure! Where're you going?"

"Miss Fanny's. Maybe we'll go get us a Coke. Put your shoes on."

Miss Fanny, one of the Island's spinsters, kept a small variety store for the convenience of her friends. Her tiny inventory included milk, bread, cold drinks, penny candy, comic books, thread, ribbon and some inexpensive bolted fabrics sold by the yard.

Fanny McGuire was the nine-to-five source of the latest news. She had the biggest ears and the longest tongue on the Island. But to her credit, she was truly as good as gold. When anyone got sick, she brought them canned chicken soup and saltines. She loved children, and their progress never missed her recognition. I loved to go there, as did most of the Island children, when our pockets allowed us a sugar splurge.

Momma and I held hands as we meandered down Middle Street toward our destination. I wanted to seem grown up and decided to ask her a few questions.

"So, Momma, how are you doing?"

"Oh, all right, I suppose. Why?"

"Well, I heard you and Daddy fighting last night. Did he hit you?"

"What are you talking about, Susan? Daddy and I don't fight! And he'd never hit me!"

"Oh. Maybe I was dreaming."

"Yes, you must've been."

I knew she was lying to me and so did she. We walked quietly for a few minutes and then we stopped.

"It's okay if you don't want to talk to me about it, Momma. I understand."

Momma knelt down and put my face in her hands.

"My word, honey, I never realized you knew anything about this. Don't you worry yourself about it. Everything's all right. Sometimes grown-ups argue, but that doesn't mean they don't love each other. How did you get so grown up?"

She kissed me on both cheeks and pulled me into a motherly embrace that I've never forgotten.

I was always thinking about everything. My parents' relationship was rocky. I knew that in spite of her reassurances. The day after they'd fight, Momma would spend the morning crying. I tried to stay with my brothers and Maggie. I wasn't afraid of my mother, only my mother's sorrow.

We entered the tiny portal and Miss Fanny looked up from her ledger to greet us.

"Marie Catherine Hamilton! How're you doing? And Miss Susan? You're growing so big and pretty!"

Miss Fanny slid open the cooler and reached down for two Coca-Colas, popping off their caps on the opener permanently fixed to the cooler's side. They clinked to the bottom of the receptacle and Fanny smiled as she handed us our drinks. I could see all her fillings.

The very fact that Miss Fanny thought I was pretty was a thrill. After all, I was Maggie's sister, and Maggie was homecoming beautiful. Maggie and Henry had blond hair, thick and shining; Timmy and I had brown hair with the revolting curse of natural kinks and curls in all the wrong places.

"So, Mrs. Hamilton! Tell me everything!" said Miss Fanny. "What's happening at your house?"

Miss Fanny and Momma launched into a fevered hen session, leaving me to wander the shelves and racks. My fingers found their way to the spools of ribbons that hung on nails behind the counter. I knew I was unworthy of the embroidered flowers of the yellow and gold ribbon.

"So, here comes Marilyn Ames right into Stella Maris Church with her hair dyed, God knows, some kind of horrible color pink and old Mrs. Dorsey is in the back pew with her ancient sister, Ida, both of them without their hearing aids on."

"Oh, no! Don't tell me!"

"Oh, yes! Old Mrs. Dorsey leans over to Ida and says at the top of her lungs, 'Do, Jesus! I didn't know hair came in that color!' Well, the whole church started to snicker and Miss Fancy Pants Ames got her comeuppance!"

"Oh! I wish I'd been there!"

"I laughed so hard I thought they were going to have to take me to St. Francis."

I drained my Coke and crawled further behind the tall counter that housed the row upon row of boxes of Mary Janes, Squirrel Nuts, Sugar Daddies and so on, happily smelling all the sugar. Smelling it was almost satisfaction enough, as my family seldom had money to spend on nonnecessities. My mouth watered.

Unknown to me, all the while Miss Fanny'd had

me in the corner of her hawklike shopkeeper eye.
"You like the ribbons, don't ya, honey?"
"Yes'm," I replied, embarrassed.
"Well, now, let's just cut you some."
Miss Fanny reached for her long, black-handled shears and removed four spools, placing them on the counter next to the nailed-in-place yardstick. I held my breath as she measured out a length of the red and navy plaid ribbon shot with gold.
"You can wear this one to school," she said to me, then turned her attention back to Momma. "Hey, are you and Hank coming to the oyster roast?"
"Gosh, it's next weekend, isn't it? I have to ask Hank."
"You gotta ask him if you can walk ten blocks and eat oysters with all your friends?"
"You know how he is, Fanny."
"Y'all come on down and bring the children. Do y'all some good!"
I watched Miss Fanny cut the green and yellow flowered ribbon, the blue watermarked satin and finally the white velvet. Miss Fanny rolled them around her rough hands, shaking her head and sucking her teeth over my daddy and his horrible ways. She dropped the ribbons in a small brown paper sack, adding a Hershey's bar and a Sugar Daddy at the last moment. She leaned over the counter and handed it to me with a wink and a warning.
"Here, this is for you from your Aunt Fanny. Now, don't you be running around telling all your little friends what I gave you. I don't need all them Geechee brats coming round 'eah looking for

something for nothing, you 'eah me, girl?"

"Yes'm." I took the bag in disbelief.

Momma, who had been immersed in the social possibilities of the oyster roast, realized what had just transpired and high-dived into action.

"My word, Fanny! That's so nice of you! What do you say, Susan?"

"Thanks, Aunt Fanny, really!"

I unrolled the frayed blue ribbon and flattened it out with my hands against the journal. That had been a sweet day, my mother's arm around my shoulder, Miss Fanny's generosity.

I didn't know what was the matter with me, why I couldn't be like Maggie, Timmy and the other people on the Island. Except that they all craved sameness, and I craved adventure. That was the big difference. Maggie wanted to go to Palmer College and become a secretary. She'd get married to some good old boy and drink beer every Saturday night for the rest of her life. My brothers would probably go to the Citadel and wind up teaching school or working at the Navy Yard, married to some nice girls with frosted hair.

"I wish I could want what they want, but it would be like wearing somebody else's skin," I wrote. "God, life would be so easy if I could feel like them."

Don't misunderstand me. My life wasn't complete misery. I really liked school. Writing was fun and math was like solving little puzzles — a game. But Island society and the kids in school thought I was weird. They said behind my back that my brain was too big and it was a shame to waste it on a girl. And they said my mouth would someday be the death of me. Well, bump them.

I had my secret writing life and that had kept me sane. Every major incident in the Hamilton history was recorded in those pages, linked with one of my doodles depicting the scene. I consoled myself that someday I'd have my own life to live and I'd be all right.

Number two pencil in my hand, I curled up on my quilt and wrote.

"Someday, I'm getting the hell off this dinky island and moving to Paris to learn all about men. I'm gonna change my name to Simone. I'm gonna speak lousy French with a Gullah accent. I'll live in a tiny apartment with lots of personality, only wear black clothes, smoke cigarettes and drink whiskey as I write great books. Maybe I'll take Livvie with me. I'll bet she can handle *anything*."

I drew a picture of us in berets and sunglasses and giggled.

I heard Daddy's car door slam. A minute later I heard the screaming start. Daddy had hit Timmy. The back door slammed. A second later I looked out and saw Henry running across the backyard — knowing him, he was running away from the belt. Good move, Henry, I thought. Then I heard Livvie's voice. She was every inch as loud as the old man.

"Stop this right now! Ain't no man gone raise a hand to a child in my care, I don't care who he is!"

"Are you pretending to tell me how to raise my children? Just who in the hell do you think you are?" Daddy hollered.

"Move out of here, Timmy!" Livvie commanded.

"Now! Move when I tell you to move, boy!"

I could hear Timmy running for the front porch and, on my tiptoes, I moved down the steps to listen in the hall.

"I ain't *pretending* nothing! I'm *telling* you. Let me tell you something, Mr. Hamilton. This is just who I am! I'm Livvie Singleton, the one who cleaned your house today, fed your children, washed your clothes and gave your mother-in-law a bath that she ain't had since Gawd knows when! And iffin you think you can find somebody else to put up with your fool, you gone right on and do him 'cause I'm a God-fearing and righteous woman and I don't need no trash from you!"

"Is that so?" he said. "Why, I ought to . . ."

"You touch one hair on this head and you is a dead white man, you 'eah me?"

Was Daddy going to hit her? Was he completely crazy? Then things got quiet and in a few seconds I heard my father laughing. He was laughing like a damn fool and I used the occasion to sneak down the steps to the porch. Timmy was lying in the hammock.

"You okay?" I asked quietly.

"Yeah, I'm okay. He just hit me in the side of my head."

"Let me see."

It was all red on the side of his face.

"Susan? That Livvie is unbelievable."

"Yeah," I agreed. "You want a cold cloth?"

"Nah, I'll live."

We heard Daddy's car start and leave the backyard with a screech. A few seconds later the screen door opened and Livvie came out.

"Timmy, let me see your face, son."

Timmy sat up and showed it to her. She placed her hand on the slap mark and began to hum an old song.

"Sing the words, Livvie," I asked, "please?"

She smiled and sang low in her rich voice:

"Let them come out with Egypt's spoil,
"No more shall they in bondage toil,
Let them come out with Egypt's spoil,
Let my people go!"

She sang and hummed for a few more minutes, holding Timmy's face in her beautiful, long, dark brown hands. She looked at Timmy's face again and the red mark was gone.

"Now, son, feel better?" she asked.

"Yeah," he said. "Where's Daddy? Is he still mad?"

"You don't trouble yourself about your daddy. He ain't mad. In fact, he give me a raise. He gone up to your uncle Louis's house to invite them to come over 'eah tonight. Now, don't you be worrying about him doing this no more. Ain't gone happen, all right?"

"He gave you a raise?" I said, completely shocked.

"Humph. Told him I put the *plat eye* on him iffin he try any more fool with me and then he start to laughing. I tell him, 'I quit,' and he say, 'Don't go,' and I say, 'Give me five dollars more a week and we'll see.' "

"What's the *plat eye?*" I asked.

"Humph. Mother Nature cure for evil, that's what," she said.

I started giggling and couldn't stop, then Timmy joined in and next Livvie started laughing so hard I could see her tonsils. She slapped her legs, bending over and straightening up and bending over again. We were a sight, carrying on, celebrating her victory.

"Don't ever leave us, Livvie," I said.

"Ain't got no plans to go nowhere except back to that kitchen and get ready for company. Y'all want to help Livvie? And, Mr. Timmy?"

He looked at her, knowing some advice was coming.

"Next time you 'eah your daddy's car in the yard, run out and see iffin you can help him, all right? Makes him mad to have to ask. You understand?"

"Yeah, I get it."

"That's my boy," she said.

We started back to the kitchen together, Livvie and I, but she stopped in the living room, looking at the big mirror at the end of the room. It was as tall as the windows and filled the space between them. The gilded frame glimmered in the semidarkness. I always thought that our living room looked like a funeral home. It was always dark in there and the mirror was so big it was spooky. When I was really little I wouldn't go in the room by myself.

"What?" I said.

"Nothing. Where'd you get that mirror?"

"Um, Grandpa Tipa got it. It came from the Planters Hotel, an old hotel that used to be on the Island. Used to be flipped horizontal and it hung behind a bar. Why?"

"Ain't no good. Big mirrors ain't no good. No, sir. They hold the spirit. The spirit come out and then you got the devil to get him out of your house. No. Ain't no good."

"Livvie! What in the world are you talking about?"

"Huh? Oh, chile, don't pay Livvie no never mind. Come, we got work to do."

When Aunt Carol and Uncle Louis pulled up in front of the house that evening, I was on the front porch with Livvie arranging little bowls of nuts and pretzels with paper cocktail napkins while she arranged glasses and an ice bucket on the card table she had covered with a white cloth. An official bar on our porch was a new feature and when I asked her why she was setting it she said, "Because I got better things to do with my time than run back and forth like a puppy dog fetching them drinks all night, that's why." It made good sense to me.

When Uncle Louis opened her car door, Aunt Carol emerged from the car one leg at a time. She was in love with her own legs and so was every man on the Island who could frost a mirror. So here they came, one by one. Long, tanned and perfect. Her toenails and fingernails were a pale frosted pink and she wore a pastel pink shell sweater with a matching cardigan over expensive linen Bermudas. Her brown alligator belt had a gold buckle with her initials on it. She shook her perfect blond hair and removed her sunglasses and smiled up to me on the porch.

"Hey, Miss Susan! How are you?"

What a phony, I thought. She thought she was Marilyn Monroe or somebody. I shot a glance at Livvie, whose jaw was locked.

"Fine! I'll tell Momma y'all're 'eah!" I called back. Passing Livvie I muttered, "That's Aunt Carol."

"Humph," she said.

The grown-ups had their night and we had ours. Maggie had gone to her best friend's house to spend the night. Timmy was upstairs with Henry watching television. I hung around with Livvie in the kitchen. She had tried to shoo me off to bed several times, but I wasn't moving. Her arrival that day might have been the most important event of my life and I didn't want to miss anything. I was washing plates when she came back in with a tray of crab shells.

"Humph," she said.

"What's wrong?" I asked.

"Nothing," she said.

"Come on, let me guess."

"Humph," she said.

"Aunt Carol's playing footsie with Daddy under the table again?"

"How'd you know that, chile? You ain't supposed to be knowing about that kind of thing at your age!" She was honestly horrified.

"I know a lot more than I should," I answered.

"Lawd, Lawd. I got to do a lot of praying on this family. I can see that now."

6

First Dates

1999

The following Saturday, Beth and I took a drive out Highway 61 with a packed cooler and our camera. We planned to picnic at Magnolia Gardens and then tour the house. As a little girl, Beth would imagine herself to be a plantation belle, wearing hoop skirts and perfecting her curtsy. I loved that memory and besides, I had had enough of work for one week. My idiot boss, Mitchell Freemont, had taken a personal shine to me and was driving me crazy. As a boss he was bearable, but if I lapsed into a momentary daydream of him naked, it was so repulsive it gave me the shakes. A plantation trip was the perfect medicine after a week of Mitchell's leering.

I pulled into Magnolia Gardens's gate, paid the admission fee and rolled down the long road to the parking lot. "Lock your door, okay, honey?"

It was a perfect September day. The brilliant blue sky above was so clear — not a cloud anywhere to be seen. The air was not humid and the temperature was somewhere in the low seventies. Our feet crunched on the gravel as we ambled along to the picnic tables.

It didn't take long to unpack the sandwiches, low-fat chips and diet sodas I had brought along. Suddenly, I was starving.

"Pickle?" I said, taking a bite from a kosher dill.

"Sure, thanks!" she said. "Why is it that eating outside makes everything taste so much better?"

"Good question. I don't know. But I do know that when we cook on the grill at the beach, even hamburgers taste like heaven. Chicken or tuna or half of each?"

"Tuna salad, please, just half. When do you think was the last time they painted these tables?"

"Before the War of Yankee Aggression," I said, smiling. "Watch out for splinters."

The sun was dancing through her rich, auburn hair and once again I found myself saying a small prayer of thanksgiving that she was mine. "Beth, you are going to be a beautiful woman, do you know that?"

"I look like my momma," she said and smiled at me. "I love you, you know. A lot."

"Baby, I adore you and you know it."

"Yeah. I know. Hey, Momma?"

"What, darling child?"

"Did you and your momma ever go on picnics?"

"Well, yes we did, sort of. Once every year Stella Maris Church had a big family picnic at Alhambra Hall. Old MC — we loved to call Momma that — she'd make deviled eggs. Livvie would fry a bunch of chicken and bake brownies. Of course, every year Momma and Uncle Louis would fight about who made the best potato salad."

"Ukk. I hate potato salad."

"Yeah, me too, but that's not the point. You see, Momma put olives in hers and Uncle Louis put onions in his. I think they both added bacon fat to the mayonnaise. Can you imagine that? It's a miracle I'm alive from eating all that garbage! Maybe I should see a vascular man. What do you think? Oh, you should've seen us in those days, three-legged races, sack races, all kinds of foolishness!"

"I think you're a little bit crazy."

"No doubt about it. Lunatics abound in the family history. I am proud to continue the legacy, even if only on a part-time basis. I do the best I can given the restraints of my life. If I didn't work in a library, I'd open a drive-through body piercing and tattoo parlor and serve barbecue sandwiches to go."

"You're feeling full of beans today, aren't you, Momma?"

"Yep. No doubt about it. Who wouldn't on a gorgeous day like this?" And I was. I had decided to put everything serious out of my mind for a little while and take a well-deserved break.

"You know what? I wish I'd been a little girl when you were. It's so boring now. It seems like everything happened in the sixties."

"I think I probably romanticize the past, Beth, a lot. Old people do that, you know."

"You're not old! Hey, can I ask you a personal question?"

"By all means."

"Are you ever gonna go out on a date? I mean, are you and Daddy getting back together or what's going on?"

Wham. She had me now. I hadn't told her anything about Michelle Stoney and I had to decide then and there what she was old enough to hear and understand. I plunged ahead, hoping our good moods would soften the blow.

"Honey, Daddy and I have been separated for a while now."

"Yeah, almost seven months. I can't see him marrying Karen, you know?"

"No, I can't either. But I'm afraid I can't see us back together either."

Her eyes began to fill with tears. "I know," she said. "This is so awful."

"Yes, it is, but sweetheart, listen to me and think about this. I know I've said this to you a hundred times since Tom left, but be patient because it's the truth. Sometimes relationships run their course and lose steam. Sometimes people get middle-aged and get afraid of dying and do stupid things, not just men but women too. A marriage can't survive unless you recommit yourself to it every single day."

"You were committed," she whispered.

Once again I found myself in the position of holding all the aces. I had another opportunity to blow her relationship with Tom to smithereens. I decided to shoulder some of the guilt instead.

"I was committed, Beth, but probably didn't work at it hard enough. I mean, I saw signs and ignored them."

"Like what?"

"Oh, like Daddy was working later and later. And, when he was home, he was glued to the television or worked in the yard and we wouldn't speak for days on end. And he lost twenty pounds and started working out every day and got in shape. Then, he bought those three-hundred-dollar Italian eyeglasses and that was the beginning of the end."

"Don't you think you could've done something?"

Ah, she was going to blame me now. I took a long look at her and then at a group of tourists walking by, thinking what I would say.

"I don't know, to tell you the truth. I mean, by the time I finally faced up to what was going on it was too late, I think. And you know what? I'm the lucky one. I have you and he's got her, right?"

"Yeah, sure, and y'all are gonna fight about money till the cows come home."

"No, sweetheart, we won't. I hired someone to work all that out for us."

"A lawyer? You hired a lawyer? I can't believe you did that! You didn't tell me this! When did you do this? Why didn't you tell me?" She was very upset.

"I'm telling you now."

"Why, Momma? You don't have to sue Daddy. He swore to me he'd take care of us!"

Tears were streaming down her face. A lawyer's child knows what divorce lawyers do. They landscape the graveyards of marriages.

"Honey, I did it because I had to. Daddy has been having some difficulty accepting the fact that he has to commit to regular financial support for us. You know that. Believe me, I waited as long as I could. It was a terribly hard decision for me to make, but I don't earn enough to support us without some help from him. You don't think I'm relishing the idea of a divorce, do you?"

"No. I know you. You'd have walked through fire first."

"Right. I hate lawyers and I hate change. But they're a necessity, especially in today's world. My lawyer's name is Michelle Stoney. She's going to work it all out. I don't want to fight with your father."

Beth shook her head and sniffed. I handed her a tissue. Watching the clouds swimming by, I thought about my conversations with Michelle. I had asked her how it usually went. I wanted to know if men in general took care of their families because they knew they should or was compliance with support motivated by fear of breaking the law. She put it in a rank nutshell when she said that women who get the best support have the most obnoxious lawyers. It tells me that time marches on and men who leave their families, for whatever reason they leave, begin a new life. They have more children, they buy another house, they join another club, and they fish in a different river. They make new friends, find new restaurants, and go to new places on vacation. Pretty soon, years pass and they can't remember what it was like with their old family.

"Honey, it's important while he still cares about me, not you — this has nothing to do with you — for me and my lawyer to make sure that we are provided for in a way that's fair for everyone. Do you understand? This is something I have to do for you and for me."

"If you think Daddy still cares about you why don't you fight for him?"

"Daddy cares, but not enough for our marriage to be like it should be. Do you understand, doodle?"

"He's changed anyway, Momma. You probably wouldn't like him now. I mean, why he would rather be with Karen I don't understand. What's wrong with him?"

"Nothing, honey, it's just your classic midlife crisis along with a willing, conniving, underhanded, immoral, big-breasted, low-class blond. He was too weak to resist, I guess, and she set a mean table."

"I hate blonds."

"Jonathan is blond," I reminded her.

"Mom? Jonathan called me last night," she said sheepishly.

"What? When were you gonna tell me this? My Lord, here come all the secrets! Come on, let's dump this stuff in the trash, throw the cooler in the car and have a nice walk. We can plan your trousseau!"

"Mom!"

Her exasperated *Mom!* was what we needed to put Tom away for a while.

"Come on! Let's go in the Barbados Tropical Garden!"

We entered the small building and were immediately transported to another climate. The lush plantings and trickling water of the fountains created a tiny paradise.

"So, tell me what he said," I said.

"Nothing. It was pretty stupid, in fact. He talked about tennis and math and wanted to know if I'd done my French homework yet."

"That doesn't sound so stupid."

"Mom! He's gorgeous, but he's seriously boring to talk to."

"Well, young guys are nervous when they call girls on the phone. Just the act of dialing probably gave him a zit." Safe, I thought, he's boring. Thank God.

"Actually, it probably did! He had this major goober today, right on his chin."

"Now that's power, when you can wreck a guy's complexion," I said.

"Whatever. I know why he called me, though."

"I thought you said he called about homework."

"Nope. Homecoming."

"What about it?" Uh-oh, not safe.

"The dance. I know he wants to take me, because Lucy told me. She's going with his friend Sonny."

"Well, we'll see." I sighed, realizing we had reached another hurdle. I guessed I'd have no choice but to jump it when she pushed me. "Beth, look at this, have you ever seen anything like this orchid?"

By chance, we had the indoor garden to ourselves. We wandered slowly, looking at and smelling the blooms. I heard something and looked up. Someone had accidentally allowed a peacock in the building and there he was at the turn in the path. He spread his feathers and nearly scared us to death. We turned and practically ran from the bird and found ourselves back outside. We laughed at ourselves.

"You should've seen your face!" Beth said. "Like the thing was a gorilla or something!"

"Did you think it would bite you?" I teased. "Oh, gosh! That was funny. Come on, let's go up to the house."

"Yeah, I love the house. Can you imagine what it must've been like to live here during the Civil War?"

"You wouldn't have been too happy. The Yankees torched the original manor house. This one's a replacement."

"So what do I do?"

"About what?"

"Jonathan. If he asks me can I go?"

"If he asks you? Of course you can!" There. I cleared the hurdle like an Olympian. Piece of cake. She grabbed me around the neck and started hugging me.

"Oh, Mom, I love you so much! Thank you, thank you, thank you!"

"Wait now! Listen, it depends on a few things, like who are you going with, who's driving and when you are to be home . . . we are going to have to establish some ground rules here, okay?"

"Okay! No problem! Oh, God!"

"Don't say God, please."

"Don't worry! Oh! I'm so happy! Wait till I tell Lucy! What am I gonna wear?"

"Don't worry, we'll arm-wrestle your father for a new dress."

We walked along the path toward the main house, with her arm around my waist and mine looped over her shoulder. Such small shoulders, I thought, so far to go yet.

As we passed the slave quarters, their ghosts seemed to stop their work and wave at me. I looked at the brochure. *Antebellum cabin.* Indeed, I said to myself. *Slave shack* is more like it. I couldn't help but think for a moment about Livvie's family and wondered if they had ever lived in such a hovel. They must have at some point.

"Hey, Beth, see that little building? That was a slave house."

"Yeah, I know, come on, we've seen it a million times. I want to go to the gift shop."

"Livvie's family probably lived in one of those."

"Really? Gee, I never thought of it that way. That's totally amazing. I mean, that somebody with her character could be born in a dump like that, that's incredible!"

"Child? Whoever said that character and integrity had a single, solitary thing to do with money?"

In minutes we had joined a group of tourists on the porch and soon we were walking through the rooms, oohing and aahing over the antiques, the art collection and the proportion of the rooms.

"I love this little bedroom," Beth said. "When I get married I'm gonna have a room like this for my daughter. And a fireplace in mine!"

I smiled at her. Nothing like a dream, I thought.

"I love the quilts," I said.

"Yeah, me too."

When the tour was over we decided we'd had enough history for one day and agreed to go home and take it easy for a while. Later we'd figure out supper and what to do for the evening. Maybe we'd see a movie or maybe we'd drive over to Maggie's. It was only three o'clock. Too late to see another plantation, too early to decide what to do about the evening. We were quiet in the car. It had been a good outing. The difficult task of telling her about retaining a lawyer was done. I thought we both had handled it pretty well, given the gravity of it. And she had secured permission for her first date, should she get the invitation. She probably would.

We turned left from Lockwood Boulevard onto Beaufain Street and then right on Rutledge Avenue.

"So, you got a lawyer?" she said.

"Yep, and you got a boyfriend?"

"Yep."

"Don't worry, sugar, Momma can handle it. Someday, I'll tell you about my first romance. It was pretty hot."

"Tell me now."

"No, I'm pooped, another time."

We were curled up on the couch watching an old Fred Astaire movie when the phone rang. Beth ran to the kitchen like her hair was in flames to answer it. I couldn't help thinking that she should try out for the track team. After all, there was definitely scholarship money in sports.

"Mom!" Beth's voice called from the kitchen. "Can Lucy and Charlene spend the night?"

Well, there goes another Saturday night, I thought. "Yes! Just tell them they have to go home early in the morning! I promised Aunt Maggie we'd go to church with her."

Silence, then giggling, then whispering, then giggling followed by two shrieks of joy and then silence again. She returned to the room and pounced on me.

"God in heaven, girl! You're gonna kill me one

of these days! Who's Charlene?"

"New talent. Moved here from Atlanta. I love you, Momma," she said.

"Me too, baby."

The phone rang again.

"I'll get it!"

She always shouted like there were thirty other people who were going to block her path to the phone. She got it on the second ring. Must've been a world record. I needed to buy a stopwatch.

"It's for you! Aunt Maggie wants you."

"Okay, tell her I'll be right there." I picked my purse up from the hall floor and dug out my cigarettes and lighter. Any conversation with Maggie was call for a smoke. "What's up?" I said to my sister.

"Susan, what are you doing tonight?"

"Beth has two friends sleeping over. Why?"

"Well, Grant has a new doctor from the hospital coming for dinner. Precious! I've seen him! Can you come for dinner?"

"No way! No blind dates."

"Come on, it's not a date! I'm your sister, for heaven's sake, and this guy is a very nice, very successful, very cute, very eligible bachelor."

I thought for half a second and took a major drag on my cigarette.

"I don't think so," I said, "but thanks for thinking of me."

"Look, I've seen him. He is very cool."

"What constitutes cool these days?"

"He walks with, I don't know, a swagger or something. I'm telling you, Susan, this would be a major mistake to pass this by. You need to get out!"

"How old?" She had me.

"I hear you smoking. Fifty-four. Divorced. Two boys in college. Ex-wife remarried, and *lives in Europe,* I might add. Bring your stuff and stay over!"

"Wait a minute, what about Beth? And her friends?"

"Bring them! Heck, I have room!"

"What time?"

"Seven-thirty."

"What are you wearing?"

"Black tissue linen pants and a tunic top. Sandals. Come on, Susan, you need some fun. Where were you all day? I've been calling since noon!"

"Magnolia Gardens with Beth."

"See what I mean? How many times are you gonna go back to that place? Good grief! You could've been getting your hair blown out!"

"Right." She was annoyingly correct as usual. "Let me talk to Beth and I'll call you back. Okay?"

"Make it fast or Grant's gonna find him another dinner partner."

My first date in Life After Tom. I hung up the phone and called Beth to come into the kitchen.

"Guess what?" I said.

"What?"

"I have a date."

"Oh, my God! Oh, my God!"

"*Oh, my God* is right. Now what are we gonna do about you and your friends?"

"Don't worry! We'll go to Charlene's or Lucy's! Here, quick! Let me use the phone."

She called them and the news was grim. They couldn't stay at Lucy's because her mother was having company and they couldn't stay at

Charlene's because her little brothers had chicken pox.

"Well, you'll all have to come with me then! Aunt Maggie said you could all stay over. You can order pizza or something."

"No way. I'm not going."

"Why not?"

"This is about trust. You don't trust me and this just proves it."

One drawback of living with a volcano is that you never knew when it would erupt. She had quite clearly inherited my father's temper and showcased it at the worst possible time.

"Of course I trust you! Good grief, Beth, this isn't about you! It's about leaving three girls, underage, in my house all night! There's no way! So, get packed and call your friends and give them the drill! We're going to Maggie's!"

"Mom! Please don't make me go to Aunt Maggie's house! I don't feel like doing that! I just want to rent some movies and eat popcorn and gossip with my friends! I mean, look at me! Am I the kind of girl who'd do something stupid? I'm on the honor roll, for Pete's sake!"

She ran upstairs and slammed the door. Against my better judgment, I was going to give in. For once, I put myself first and justified my decision by adding to my list of excuses that showing up with three teenage girls couldn't make me look any younger to Dr. Wonderful.

"Beth?" No answer. "I want to talk to you."

I went upstairs and opened her door. She was finally cleaning up after a week of throwing her clothes on the floor.

"Good idea," I said, "don't want the girls to see this mess, right?"

"Oh, Momma, everybody's a slob at my age."

"Right. Listen, I've been thinking. I'll go to Aunt Maggie's early and come home early. Just remember to keep all the doors locked and I'll be home by nine. Okay?"

"Thanks, Mom. You can trust me, I swear."

"Don't swear, help me find something to wear."

We dug through my closets trying to find something to make me look independent and reluctant but highly desirable. This was a problem, as I had to be there in less than three hours and had no time for liposuction. We finally settled on a long, crinkled, pleated burgundy gauze skirt and a V-necked black silk sweater. I thought I looked like a gypsy but Beth told me I looked hip and thin. *Hip and thin.* That was the exact phrase I needed to hear.

"Okay, get out of here. I'm getting in the shower. Thanks."

It had been decades since I'd dressed for a date. I washed my hair and wrapped myself up in a huge towel. I looked in the mirror. Contact lenses, I thought, don't wear your glasses. I pulled out a trial pack of extended-wear lenses and carefully put them in, blinking like mad until they settled into place. Slowly, I applied my makeup, taking each part of my face one step at a time. I blew out my hair, thinking I needed a haircut. I sprayed Chanel No. 5 all over myself. I got dressed and slipped on a pair of sandals. Then I did the serious hair ritual: round brush, spray with heat, flip it over the head, backcomb a little and spray again. I sort of arranged it with my fingers and sprayed it again.

Downstairs I rummaged through the refrigerator to find something to take to Maggie's for an hors d'oeuvre, remembering I had cream cheese and green pepper jelly somewhere in the jumble of plastic containers and cartons. All true Charlestonians serve green pepper jelly on cream cheese on little crackers.

I went to the living room to turn off the television and caught my reflection in the huge gilt mirror. I gave myself a good look. I hadn't worn makeup in a year and I was a little worried about how I'd renovate. Not a Bond girl, but not a librarian either. In fact, pretty cool for forty-whatever, I thought. I sure liked my body better than I had six months ago.

Suddenly, I had second thoughts about leaving Beth here, but quickly pushed them away. Maybe I'll come home earlier than I told her, I said to myself. That felt better. "Beth!" I called out. "Come give me a kiss! I gotta go!"

I threw the cheese and jelly into a plastic grocery bag with a box of water crackers and waited for her by the back door.

"Mom! You look totally awesome!"

"Thanks, honey! Now remember, no funny business!"

"Don't worry! Just have fun!"

I closed the door behind me and crossed the yard to my car. It occurred to me that when your children told you not to worry, that would be the perfect time to start worrying. All the way to the beach I worried, first about Beth and her friends and then about just what the hell I was doing rushing out to meet some jackass I'd probably hate on sight anyhow.

"You're early! Good! You can help me make salad!" Maggie said when I came through the back door, giving me a peck on the cheek. "Look at you, honey chile! You look ten years younger!"

"Thanks! I'm a wreck! I can't believe I came. I must've been crazy. I'm so nervous I don't even remember driving here. Where's Grant?"

"In the shower. Honey, just relax and let Roger talk about himself. Men love to do that. You're gonna like him, I swear, he's funny as a rip. Go look at my table and tell me what you think."

"Okay, I brought pepper jelly in here." I handed her the bag. My hands were shaking.

"You need a glass of wine," she said and poured me one.

"Industrial strength," I said and took it into the dining room. Maggie had outdone herself. Her dining room table had a low and long centerpiece of Island wildflowers and Spanish moss mixed with red grapes and lemon halves. All her china was blue and yellow and matched the country French foulard printed linens. Column candles of different heights stood on little plates. I could tell even before they were lit that her balloon goblets would shine in their light. I hoped I would too. I took three big sips and felt better. Oh, what the hell, I thought and went out to the porch to look at the beach.

It wasn't long before Grant appeared and turned on some music. Eric Satie's incredible sonata floated through the air. Perfect, I thought, dreamy but not maudlin.

"How's the greatest sister-in-law in the world?" he said.

"Fine, fine, like a freaking cow on the way to slaughter." I gave the old boy a hug. He held me back.

"Well, you look really beautiful! What have you done to yourself?"

"I washed my hair. Amazing what a little soap and water will do."

"Yeah, you clean up good. Smell good too. Going hunting?"

"Bite me, Grant, I'm nervous enough as it is."

He started laughing and teasing me. "Oh, what a girl! You sure enough do know how to charm a fellow! Want me to refresh your drink?"

"God, yes. Thanks. Wait, no. I have to drive and I'd better pace myself."

"Well, make up your mind." God, he was so smug. I needed to relax. Big time.

"Grant?" Maggie was calling.

"Coming right now, my love, my turtledove! Gotta go. Big boss's calling."

Boy, they were all in some mood tonight. Grant was flitting around like a maitre d' and Maggie was setting a "Styled by Martha Stewart" ambush for this guy.

His car pulled up right below me on the gravel drive. Blue BMW. Nice. Better than Tom's Mustang. Augh! The door opened and I was trapped. Maybe it was better this way. I saw the top of his head. Hair. Another good sign. And then he got out. Not bad. Five ten, maybe, dark hair, some gray, nice jacket. He saw me and smiled.

"Hi!" he called out. "You must be Susan?"

"Yep, I'm Susan." He came up the steps with a bottle of wine in his hand. He was very handsome.

"I'm Roger Dodds." We shook hands and I realized mine was clammy.

"Roger Dodds. I used to date a guy named Roger. Dated a Dodds too."

"Yeah?" He was still smiling. Good teeth. I realized what I said sounded completely stupid, like I'd had a thousand lovers. I only wished. He smelled good.

"That didn't sound right, I meant —"

"Don't worry, I know what you meant. Where's Grant and the Great?"

The Great?

Soon we were at the table and the evening was under way. Roger was from Aiken, South Carolina; he was an oncologist, specializing in women's cancers. We talked easily about everything from opera to duck hunting. He had lots of interests. Loved to read, travel and cook.

"You cook?" I asked.

"Love to cook," Roger said. "Does that improve my résumé?"

"By a lot," I said. "I love to eat — does that help mine?"

Everyone laughed.

"Susan is murder in the kitchen," Grant said, laughing.

"Oh! You like to cook too?" Roger said to me.

"No, she murders everything," Grant said, way too amused with himself. "I'm going to open another bottle of wine. Red? White? Both?"

No one answered and he disappeared into the kitchen, returning with two bottles. He opened them and poured another glass for everyone. I was very relaxed. Very.

"So, Susan, tell me about Charleston. Your family has been here a long time, right?"

"Lord, Roger, you're only from Aiken. You could stand on this house and spit on Aiken in a good wind!" I giggled, thinking I was pretty darn funny. "You probably know more about Charleston than I do!"

Maggie cut her eye at me. True, it was not the most feminine thing I could have said.

"So, you can spit too?" Roger said. "My God, the woman is a virtual Renaissance wonder!"

Another comedian, I thought. He and Grant should go on the Comedy Channel.

"Roger," I said, "only Charlestonians should suffer with the true knowledge of our bawdy history. We prefer for foreigners to think of us as mysterious."

"Go on, this is *very intriguing*," Roger said. "All guys love bawdy history lessons."

"Lord, Roger, you'd better look out now! My sister likes nothing better than roaming the old historic plantations," Maggie said.

"She thinks I'm obsessed," I said.

"Are you? I mean, some obsessions can be very interesting," Roger said.

Now what was that supposed to mean?

"I am not obsessed with anything, y'all," I said, trying to change the subject. "Maggie, dinner's delicious!" Maggie had prepared spicy shrimp gumbo and my favorite salad with watercress and little oranges with walnut oil dressing. I was having a wonderful time. We all were. "Did you make these croutons, Maggie? This is the best salad I've ever had."

"You are the sweetest sister I've ever had," she said. "Yep. Made 'em myself."

"You're right, I am," I answered. "You know, I'm not watching the time and I have to get home early tonight. Oh, no! It's already after nine!"

"How come?" Roger said. "The night's young!"

"Young is the operative word. I left my young daughter with two of her friends at my house in the city. God knows what they're up to."

"Been there," Roger said, with that parental, knowing look.

"Beth's a good girl, Susan, I'm sure she's fine," Maggie said. "Let's have coffee and dessert on the porch, shall we? It's such a gorgeous night!"

"Call them," Grant said, "see if you hear anything in the background."

He got up and handed me a portable phone. I dialed the number and they were all quiet. The phone rang six times. Too long. Finally someone picked up.

"Hello?" It wasn't Beth.

"Hi, who's this? Lucy?"

"Um, yes, ma'am."

"Is Beth there?"

"Um, she's in the bathroom, Mrs. Hayes. Do you want me to get her?"

"No, no. Everything okay?" There was complete silence from her end. No music. No television.

"Yes, ma'am. All's well." She giggled.

"Okay, honey, just tell Beth I'll be home around eleven, okay?"

"Over and out," she said and hung up.

I thought for a minute. Over and out?

"Great! You're staying!" Roger said. "Come on, let's help Maggie clear the table."

"No, I'm going. That child was drunk! I know it!"

"Drunk? Susan, you're imagining things!" Maggie said.

"What did she say?" Grant asked.

"She said 'Over and out' when she hung up and Beth couldn't come to the phone because she was in the bathroom."

"Go get your bag. We'll take my car," Roger said. "I raised teenagers and I've seen it all. Maggie, Grant, thanks for a fabulous meal. If we can come back, we will. Otherwise, we'll call."

We left Maggie standing in the kitchen with a bowl of trifle no doubt made from homemade pound cake.

Roger opened the car door for me, I got in and before I knew it we were through Mount Pleasant and over the Cooper River Bridge. It was a good thing I had fastened my seat belt because this joker drove like a bat out of hell.

"If I get stopped, I'll tell the cops it's a medical emergency. Will you stop worrying? Roger Dodd's here!"

"Okay, okay."

"So tell me, you work at the county library? Are you a librarian? You don't look like one."

"Hey! That light was red!"

"Pink," he said. This fellow, doctor or no doctor, thought he was at the Indianapolis 500.

"Please don't kill me, Roger. You may not have any reason to live but I do."

"Just relax."

He made the right on Queen Street on two wheels and I nearly fainted from fright. Road rage strikes the middle-aged.

As I staggered up the walk, a young man of about sixteen opened my door to me.

"Just who are you and where is my daughter?" I said in my famous mother voice.

"I'm Jonathan, Mrs. Hayes, and before you go in there I want you to know this wasn't my idea. I didn't bring the vodka."

"Go sit in my living room and don't move," I said and he scampered like a mouse to the wingback in the corner. On my couch were Lucy and another boy. Beth was nowhere to be seen. Roger waited with the delinquents. I raced upstairs and opened the door to her room. Two figures were in her bed obviously having some very enthusiastic sex. I flipped on the light and a strange girl sat up naked as a jaybird.

"Just who the hell are you?" I asked.

"Charlene. Oh, God. Busted."

"Get dressed. Both of you! Where's Beth?"

I didn't wait for an answer. I slammed the door closed and went to my room. In my bathroom my little girl was hanging her head over the toilet, throwing up.

"This is less than I expected from you, Beth," I said with the quiet fury of a mother superior. "Jonathan can't possibly be impressed."

"Oh, Momma! I'm so sorry! I'm gonna die!" She was crying and gagging and leaned over the toilet bowl again.

"No, Beth, you're not going to die. Tomorrow you will *wish* that you had died, but you won't. I'll be back. I have some other business to take care of." Well, I'll bet Roger's impressed as all hell too, I thought on the way down the stairs.

"I'm driving all of these young people home," Roger said.

"Thanks, Roger. Mother of God, what a night!"

"Your daughter's okay?"

"She'll live," I said, then looked around at the scene before me. Lolita was still buttoning her shirt, smacking her chewing gum. She smirked at me and I noticed a piece of metal in her tongue.

"What is that in your mouth?" I asked. "Is that a tongue stud?"

"What of it?" she said.

"It's *your* tongue," I said, disliking her more with each passing second, "but it must be hard to chew gum with that thing in the way."

"Not really," she said, belligerently.

This was incredible to me. In my day, if you'd been caught in the sack with some fellow, your parents would've marched you either to the altar or to a convent. That would be after every relative you owned had something to say to you about the road you were paving to hell.

I looked around the room. Pizza boxes were on the floor, along with half a bowl of popcorn, the remains of a bowl of salsa and Coke bottles. No wonder Beth threw up. Jonathan stared at the floor. Lucy and the other boy, who I assumed was Sonny, stared at each other.

"You children go home. It's enough for one night."

"I'm really sorry, Mrs. Hayes," Jonathan said. "This shouldn't have happened."

"How right you are, Jonathan. Good night." At least he appeared sober. They filed out the door until the line ended with Roger.

"Hey, thanks for a wild night! We'll have to do this again soon." He was joking. "Listen, lighten up. Didn't you ever get drunk when you were a teenager?"

"Of course! But I had the brains not to get caught," I said.

"Too bad I didn't know you then," he said.

"It's a good thing you didn't," I said. "Hey, Roger, thanks a lot. I mean it."

"Sure thing. Call Grant for me, will you, and tell him I'm on a mission. I'll call you next week."

"Okay. Roger?" He turned and looked at me. "Drive safely."

I closed the door and looked at my living room. Wrecked. I looked up the stairs and heard no noise. She's probably passed out cold, I thought.

I started picking up all the plates and glasses and saw myself in the huge floor-length mirror. My eyebrows were narrowed and my jaw was set in frustration. I could see my father's face in mine and for a moment he was there. I could hear him whispering in my mind. *Give her the belt!* Never, I thought, go back to hell where you belong, old man. In the next instant I could sense Livvie and thought for a moment that I saw her in the clouded glass. *She need her momma's love. That child is a good child.*

I finished cleaning and putting away everything, called Maggie with our regrets, turned on the dishwasher and went upstairs. Beth was in her bed with her clothes on. I pulled the quilt over her and wiped her hair away from her face. She stirred and looked at me.

"I'm so sorry, Momma." She began to cry.

"Don't cry, honey. Some lessons have to be learned the hard way. I love you. Get some sleep. We'll talk tomorrow."

I rinsed a facecloth with cool water, folded it and placed it on her forehead. I was pretty wrung out too. Turning out the lights in the hall, and pulling down the covers on my bed, I wondered what horrible battle lay ahead for me with the parents of the other children. It had been a gross mistake to leave them unsupervised. So much for perfect parenting.

There was no sun when I woke up Sunday morning, but I knew it was late. I figured it to be around ten o'clock. Rolling over in bed I squinted at my clock radio. Nine-forty-five. Good guess. I washed my face, pulled my hair into a ponytail, brushed my teeth and put on a robe. I needed coffee in the worst way. Padding by Beth's room I remembered that she'd probably need coffee too. I peeked in. At the squeak of her door hinge, she rolled over.

"I feel awful," she groaned.

"As well you should," I said. "Come on. Come on down to the kitchen and I'll tell you about the night Aunt Carol got so crocked she almost fell off the porch."

"Aunt Carol? The priss?"

This mildly piqued her interest. If I couldn't make her see what a fool she looked like last night, maybe she could see it through Aunt Carol's nearly legendary escapade.

"Yup. You're not the only one in this family who ever crawled in the bag, you know. Family's filled with legions of drunks."

"Thanks a lot. Lunatics and drunks. Great. I'll be right there." She slowly sat up in her tangled covers and fell back again. "Oh, Momma, my head's splitting!"

She was the granddaughter of Marie Catherine (a.k.a. Tallulah Bankhead) Hamilton.

"Got just the thing for you. A bacon cheeseburger. You need some grease, girl. And some carbs. I'll put the coffee on."

Somehow, with all the excitement of last night, I had neglected to watch the eleven o'clock news. I switched on the coffeemaker, tightened my robe and went outside to retrieve the morning paper. The front door complained as I unlatched the ancient locks. The sky was ominously dark blue. My bones predicted the approach of a storm. Glancing at the front page, I saw a small article about a tropical disturbance in the Bahamas. Well, it was September.

The door closed behind me and I met Beth in the hall.

"Momma, I'm so sorry about last night."

"Sweetheart, every person on the planet gets at least one stab at the Knucklehead of the Year award. I'm just glad you were home, and you weren't driving in a car. You know, if anything ever happened to you I don't think I could go on living." The thought of a phone call in the middle of the night from a hospital made my insides knot.

"Never again, I swear." She leaned against my

shoulder. "Jonathan probably thinks I'm a total, complete idiot."

"Come on, let me pour you a cup of relief. Just remember, true southern ladies do not vomit on their first dates. It's bad manners to get drunk and throw up and good manners are the moisturizer of life." With my arm around her shoulder we made our way to the kitchen, crossing two thresholds at once. Another rite of passage, another day begun.

"Yeah, thanks for reminding me. I'd rather have a Coke if we have any. I'm so thirsty. And, Momma?" I looked up at her. "Please don't tell Daddy about this."

"Don't worry. Hey, it's you and me, babe. A thousand wild horses couldn't drag it out of me."

I poured a Coke and handed it to her. She drained the glass and I poured her some more. I reached in the freezer for a hamburger patty and the hydrator for a piece of cheese and some bacon. In minutes the bacon and the burger sizzled in separate pans. Beth held her forehead on the heel of her hand.

"Aspirin?" I put two before her with a small glass of orange juice. She looked positively green. "A shower would probably do you some good too."

"Yeah, as soon as I eat something. God, Momma, you know what I can't believe? I can't believe you're not furious with me."

"I'm still kind of stunned, but that doesn't mean that I won't be furious later when I've had time to think about it all." I turned the burger and the bacon, peeled the plastic wrap from the yellow impersonation of dairy product, and laid it across the meat. "Look, it could've been worse. What about their parents? I mean, I could be liable for a lawsuit, you know."

"I'll call them and see what happened."

"Good idea." I flipped on the tiny television on the counter. Across the bottom of the screen was a weather advisory bulletin. "Storm's coming," I said, "probably nothing, but you never know." She had disappeared to the living room with the portable phone. I watched as a news bulletin came on.

". . . located five hundred miles off the coast of San Juan. Winds approaching hurricane level, seventy-five miles an hour. If it continues to pick up force, this tropical storm could become a hurricane by tonight. Stay tuned to WCIV for all the latest updates. . . ."

She came back, gave me a weak hug and went upstairs. I turned back to Beth's breakfast, frying her burger in the old black cast-iron skillet, and wondered how many times I had held it in my hands. It was one from my mother's kitchen, our version of an heirloom. One that had fried probably millions of eggs, and strips of bacon, patties of sausage, battered shrimp and fish, and grilled cheese sandwiches.

When Beth returned she was practically smiling. "No biggie," she said. "Charlene's parents were asleep when she got home and Lucy just went straight to bed too. Apparently, that guy you were with took them all out for coffee and a big fat lecture on alcoholism at the Pancake House. They were all pretty straight by the time they got home."

Talking about it irritated me. She sensed it. She knew she was in trouble with me but it was a different kind of trouble from any we'd known before.

This was her first major mistake. I didn't want to make too much of it because I knew she was sorry, and I thought things had just gotten out of control. I made a mental note to call Roger and thank him.

"Storm's coming," I repeated, putting her burger on a plate and setting it before her at the counter with the bottle of ketchup.

"Big one?"

"It can't be much. Not yet anyway. The wind's only around seventy-five miles per hour and that ain't squat in hurricane history."

"Weren't Aunt Sophie and Aunt Allison born in a hurricane?" Her mouth was full as she spoke.

"Yep. Hurricane Denise. Winds over a hundred miles an hour. Very bad news. Wipe your mouth and I'll tell you all about it, although I'm sure you've heard it before."

"Doesn't matter," she said.

She wiped and we were both glad to have the subject changed. I poured myself another cup of coffee and lit a cigarette, careful not to blow my smoke in her direction. I could tell her about her drunken Aunt Carol anytime — although I was not going to tell her about Aunt Carol and Big Hank. No, she'd never hear that one from me. I put my feet up on the bar stool next to her and began the tale of my sisters' auspicious births.

"I was about your age. It was Thursday, September the twelfth, when Hurricane Denise blew through and when the twins were born. Livvie had been working for us for, oh, I don't know, maybe six weeks?"

"And, your momma didn't know she was having twins, did she?"

"Honey, in those days, they didn't know anything! But my momma was awful big, I remember that."

"Right." She giggled. "What was it like at the beach? I would've been scared to death."

"I suppose we didn't have the good sense to be scared. The first thing we always did when a storm was brewing was fight for a good position on the porch and watch the ocean. You can't imagine how the world changed as she made her way to the coast. Ever hear that old Billie Holiday song? Something about the ill wind blowing bad on me?"

"Who the heck is Billie Holiday?"

"I'd consider it a great personal favor if you wouldn't continually remind me of my advanced age." I raised my eyebrows at her. "Ah, yes. Well, everybody was getting ready for the big storm. The hardware stores were jammed with men buying plywood and the grocery stores had long lines of women pushing bulging carts of bottled water, bread, flashlight batteries and milk. Old Islanders like us grew up on tales of these storms. The warning signs were in our blood and handed down from generation to generation like family jewels. We shopped for the storm like it was any other day. Just normal battle supplies, you know?"

7

Hurricane Denise

1963

The morning Denise hit Charleston, Daddy had gone out. Momma and I were in the kitchen making breakfast for everyone. Black cast-iron skillets were lined up on every burner — bacon in one, sausage in another, bacon drippings sizzled in a third, ready to receive four eggs to fry, and the fourth bubbled butter waiting for a spoonful of pancake batter.

I could tell Momma wasn't feeling up to snuff because she kept leaning on the counter. I was so stupid I didn't realize she was in labor, but they say low pressure can cause all kinds of things. Heart attacks, suicide and babies come early.

Livvie came rushing in the back door all in a tizzy because she was late. She was going on and on about Old Reverend Mr. Sam the bus driver, and how the bus had broken down on the causeway and how they had to wait for half an hour for her nephew to come with a fan belt. All she needed was to take one look at Momma and she knew.

"Where's Mr. Hank?" she screamed. "Lawd,

Miss MC! When did your pains start? Where's Mr. Hank?" She took Momma by the arm and supported her. "Where?"

"Gone. Louis's house. Borrow some tools. Better call him," Momma said.

"Call him, chile! Be quick!" she said to me.

Mamma was breathing hard by now, and I started getting nervous. I ran to the phone but Uncle Louis's line was busy. I figured Aunt Carol was probably working her jaw with one of her friends.

"Line's busy!" I said. My heart raced.

"Get your sister! Now!" Livvie said in a quiet, firm voice.

My tail feathers were a blur as I took the steps and beat on the bathroom door for Maggie to come out.

"Momma needs you! Hurry! She's in labor!" I said.

Maggie came out the door in a flash and we raced downstairs together. Livvie had turned off the burners and put Momma in a chair with a cold cloth on her head.

"All right, Miss MC! It's all right. I gone with Miss Susan and we bring Mr. Hank here fast as we can." Momma nodded her head and took a deep breath. "Start running," she said to me. "Maggie, keep dialing the number!"

Livvie and I ran out the back door, heading for Uncle Louis's house. We must've been some sight. I still had on my pajamas and Livvie's apron was flying in the air. Even though I was barefooted I don't think I felt a single thing on the bottom of my feet. I don't even really remember running, all I know is that Aunt Carol was out front cutting roses when she saw us running toward her. She dropped the hose and ran off screaming for my daddy. Livvie screamed at her as she was running. She was provoked that she was calling for my daddy and not my uncle. She said, "I don't care who you call! Just move your bony behind quick!" It was terribly exciting.

My daddy, Uncle Louis and Livvie finally got Momma dressed, packed and into the car. Aunt Carol wanted to go with them but at Uncle Louis's insistence she agreed to stay with us. Nobody took Momma's suitcase. Finally, Uncle Louis ran back up to the porch, grabbed it, ran down and threw it in the trunk. Sophie sat silent as a stone in that rocker when Momma asked her to go with her to the hospital. Momma was scared, I guess. I was standing next to her.

"Won't you please come with me, Momma?"

Grandma Sophie just stared at Momma like she didn't know her from a bucket of green paint. Old Grandpa Tipa answered for her. "Go with God, Marie Catherine, go with God."

Finally, Livvie came and took Momma by the hand, led her down the stairs and put her in the backseat. Now, Momma's face got all funny and I knew it was because she had never sat next to a colored person in a car, but Livvie took care of that.

"I see your face, Miss MC, but let Livvie tell you something. These men don't know nothing about babies but I can deliver that chile myself iffin I have to, so move over!"

That was the end of that. Off they went, tearing down Atlantic Avenue, as they raced to Charleston to the hospital. I said a prayer that they wouldn't kill themselves before they got there. Aunt Carol went back inside. The rain was beginning to fall and I went inside behind her. I made a sandwich and watched the weather outside the window.

Bored to death, I curled up in my room with my journal and wrote predictions about the weight and sex of the baby and made a list of names. I liked Theodore Chalmers Moultrie if it was a boy and Bettina Helena Rebecca if it was a girl. I loved historic names for boys and musical names for girls, and my list got longer. Naturally the baby would have to have a saint's name for baptism. I liked Michael or Bernadette. I was fully occupied with the business of labeling my new sibling and didn't even hear the phone ring. My concentration was broken by Aunt Carol's screaming all over the house. I ran downstairs and found her on the porch.

"Twins! Uncle Louis just called! Can you believe it?" Aunt Carol was hugging Maggie.

"Did you say twins? Oh, my God!" I said, stunned. Twins? Jesus! I knew she was fat!

"Yes! Oh, glory! Twin girls! Born not ten minutes after they got to the hospital. Y'all have two, not one but two, new sisters!"

Maggie had this awful look on her face.

"What did Uncle Louis say?" I asked.

"Oh, heavenly days! Let's go make a pot of coffee! No, let's have tea! Oh, goodness, I'm so excited, I don't know what I want! Maybe I'll have a bourbon to celebrate! Yes, that's it! Now what would you girls like?"

"A new life," Maggie muttered, so that only I could hear.

Aunt Carol had left the porch and we followed her, slamming the door for the hell of it. Down the hall to the kitchen in a row, like a family of ducks, we went. Aunt Carol was so excited you'd think she'd given birth herself. But she'd never have babies. She said to everyone on the whole planet that she didn't want to wreck her figure.

She helped herself to Daddy's bourbon and Maggie and I poured ourselves a Coke. Aunt Carol made a list of people to call to deliver the news. Maggie wandered out of the room and I stayed behind because I had a few questions.

"Is Momma okay?"

"Oh, she's fine! But Louis said she was so surprised she almost passed out! And he said your father is strutting around St. Francis Hospital like a rooster!"

"I'll bet! When are they coming back to the Island?"

"Oh, right away! Uncle Louis and your daddy are bringing Livvie here right now. The storm is coming. I mean, they can't possibly expect me to stay here all night! I have to go feed my dogs and empty my porch! And your momma's safe and sound where she is."

"That's true. How about Livvie? Did she say anything?"

"Yes! I'll tell you a secret. She had to pull your momma off the curb when they got there. Your momma was fixing to deliver those babies in the gutter! Have you ever heard of such a thing? Louis said MC just got out of the car and collapsed on the curb and started panting like a dog! My word! Your momma can be so undignified sometimes!

But I suppose she couldn't help herself. You can ask Livvie all about it when they come back. They should be here any time now."

"You know, Aunt Carol, I guess that you wouldn't understand something like sitting down on the street, since you've never been pregnant like Momma. I would've been terrified if I were her today."

It was the best retort I could come up with on the spur of the moment. It wasn't clearly rude but it made her wonder if I meant to be rude. I went outside to feel the rain, letting the door slam. It was a good day for making noise. I wasn't going to let Aunt Carol spoil my good humor. Twins! I spun around in the rain. Good Lord! Pretty soon this family was gonna burst. How would we all get in one car?

I went back inside.

"Where's Maggie?" I asked Aunt Carol.

"Hush, I'm trying to hear the weather report. Don't track water on the floor."

"Sorry," I said, thinking, *Bump you.*

She was hunched over the radio trying to tune the thing to a station, but all she was getting was whining and static.

"Where are your brothers?" She looked up with panic on her face. "I forgot all about them!"

"I wouldn't know. I'm not in charge here. You are." It just slipped out of my mouth.

"Don't you speak to me like that! Shame on you! You go and find them, Susan Hamilton, or I'm going to report you to your father!"

"Fine!" I said, not caring if she did. Daddy wouldn't beat me today. He was in a good mood. I breezed by her and went toward the front porch. Maggie was out there hanging on a banister. "Where're the boys?" I asked, letting the door slam with a huge whack.

"Who cares?" she said.

"Listen, this damn storm is coming and they're not here. I haven't seen them all morning, have you?" She wouldn't look up. "Maggie, it goes like this: The boys get killed in the storm and Daddy has us shot, okay? I think we'd better find them. Aunt Carol's threatening to tell Daddy if we don't and they're gonna be back from the hospital pretty soon."

"I hate this family," she said. "I'll go get shoes. Wait here."

She, too, slammed the door. Boy, without Livvie here it didn't take us five minutes to revert back to all our bad habits, I thought. She reappeared, slammed the door again and we were on our way.

"Let's take the bikes, it's faster," I said. "I'll go to the Lockharts' and you check the Brockingtons', okay?"

After beating on doors and not finding them we decided they must've been at the forts.

"Which one?" I screamed through the rain.

"Battery Thompson. Come on! Let's hurry!"

We raced against the wind toward Battery Thompson, which was where the Island kids most liked to play — although it was forbidden by the police and worrywart mothers. It was built after the Spanish-American War as part of the coastal defense system and named for the brave man who defended Breach Inlet against the British in 1776. (I just love Island history.) The first thing we usually did when a good storm was brewing was climb the ramparts to watch the ocean. The Battery Thompson was the best place on the Island for this because it was the most secluded. Fort Moultrie was on Middle Street, where Fat Albert, the Island lawman, could spot you too easily. He was no fun.

Sullivan's Island, named for Captain Florence O'Sullivan, had always been a lookout island for Charleston harbor. In the Dark Ages of the 1670s, he was given the job of firing a cannon to warn Charleston that enemies were coming by water. The original settlers had enough to worry about with malaria, starvation and hurricanes, without dealing with surprise attacks from pirates. So this guy O'Sullivan was picked to settle the Island. They say he was terrible, awful and just mean as hell and that he didn't give a damn what anybody thought about him either. Wasn't it just perfect that it was a rabble-rouser with a loaded cannon that put this island on the map? I was sure he was somehow related to Big Hank, which would also help explain why my idiot brothers were still outside when a hurricane was coming. Maggie and I were soaked to the skin by the time we got there.

Voices traveled across the air, and when we saw the pile of bicycles, all of them collapsed in a heap on the soft sand, we knew we'd found them. Dropping our own bicycles, we heard alarm in the boys' cries, not playfulness. Without taking a breath, we ran to the nearest ladder and began to climb up to them. Battery Thompson, a decommissioned and basically abandoned fort — like all the others on the Island — was made of poured cement and the years of salt spray and peeling paint had given it a spooky personality. Perfect for playing, or for sneaking off to smoke a stolen cigarette. Or doing something stupid like what we were about to find.

"Help! Get me out!"

"Jesus! That's Henry! Maggie, come on!" I threw my hand out to Maggie, who grabbed it and pulled herself up to the platform.

"Where are they?"

"I don't know!" I looked all across the horizon of the fort and spotted a bunch of boys at the top. "Look! Up there!"

Timmy saw me and Maggie and called out to us, waving his arms. "Hurry! We need help! Henry's stuck!" His voice cracked as he screamed.

When we reached his side seconds later, we saw the feet of our baby brother sticking out of an air shaft. He was screaming at the top of his lungs.

"Get me out! My head! My head! Do something!"

"Henry! It's Susan, Maggie's here too. Don't worry, we'll have you out in a minute. Hang on, honey, it's all right." I spun on my heels to face the boys and starting cussing at them. "What the hell happened here? Just what the hell happened?"

"We told him there was pirate's treasure in there and it would take somebody real small to get in and get it!" This explanation came from the boy we all loved to hate. Stuart had white skin and thousands of brown freckles. He was allergic to everything, a chronic nose picker, a liar and an all-around troublemaker. On top of that, he picked on little kids.

"Stuart Brockington, looking at your ugly face is enough to make me puke," I said. "When I get my little brother out of here, if he has one scratch on him, I'm gonna wipe the streets of this Island with your sorry ass. Do you hear me? Now get your good-for-nothing behind on your stupid bike and get some help! Move! Go get some help!"

I screamed so loud that I frightened Henry, who started wailing. Stuart jumped down from the fort and raced to his bike followed by two other boys.

"Timmy! How could you let this happen? If Daddy finds out, he's gonna kill every one of us!" Maggie said, unnerved by the magnitude of the storm and the situation.

"Henry? It's Maggie. I'm gonna pull on your feet a little and you see if you can push yourself out, okay?"

"I can't move! I'm stuck! I can't!" Henry was blubbering now. "Help! Get me out of here!"

"I'm going to get Mr. Struthers," I said. "That stupid Stuart won't have a clue what to do."

"I'll come with you," Timmy answered. "Maggie, stay with Henry and try to calm him down."

"Henry!" I called, "listen to me! This ain't the first time this has happened, I'm sure. Just hang on and I'll be back in ten minutes with Mr. Struthers!"

"Okay," he whimpered.

We got to our bicycles and raced toward the volunteer fire department, where Marvin Struthers had his office. He was the town mayor, fire chief and Little League coach. The oddest thing about him was that he always wore sandals — except to church. No decent man wore sandals, our momma always said. She thought they were immodest or something. I just thought they were disgusting. Hairy feet. Nasty.

The wind was blowing harder and the palmetto trees bent over double. Fortunately, the wind was behind us. Timmy and I dropped our bikes in front of the town hall, and ran for Mr. Mayor, Coach Struthers. When we swung open the door, Mrs. Smith, this old lady with a big nasty wart on her chin, who has been his secretary for the last million years, was putting on her coat. She smelled like peppermint.

"What do you children want now? Y'all should be in your home with your parents! Storm's coming!"

"Yes'm. We know, but we kind of have an emergency here and need Coach Struthers. Is he here?"

"What's the matter? Maybe I can help."

I tried to be polite, because she was old and all.

"Yes'm," I said. "We don't have much time. Our little brother has his head stuck in an air vent over to the Battery Thompson, and we couldn't pull him out, and our daddy is gonna blister our behinds if he finds out."

She looked up. "Are y'all Hank Hamilton's children?"

"Yes'm."

"Mr. Marvin! Hurry! It's an emergency!"

The sound of a toilet flushing came to our attention. In a split second, Mr. Marvin came running out of the bathroom, trying to zip up his pants. He was a big man, taller than Daddy and twice of him in the gut department.

"What's the matter, Lois?" Then he turned

around to see us. "Oh, the Hamilton children, I should've known."

I narrowed my eyes at him. We weren't any worse than any of the other Island children, there were just a lot of us and we got caught all the time.

"Mr. Marvin," Mrs. Smith gasped. "They say that they brother's stuck in an air shaft down to the fort."

"Mr. Marvin, iffin we don't shake it, Henry's gone be laid out at McAlister's by tomorrow. And y'all ain't gone have us bothering y'all no more, 'cause we're gone get beat to death."

"Ain't nobody beating nobody like that on this Island while I'm at the helm. Y'all children come and get in the truck." He hiked his pants up over his stomach like men do and headed out the door. We ran after him. I looked at his feet. Sandals! Even in the rain!

I thought riding in the truck was sort of fun with the siren blaring and all, even if my little brother's life was hanging by a thread. Jesus, I thought, he's probably passed out by now, but when we got there, no such luck. You could hear everybody screaming and somehow, Aunt Carol had gotten herself on top of the fort and her skirt was blowing in the wind every which way except down. When we climbed up we could see her underwear and maybe it was my imagination, but I thought Mr. Struthers was staring at her butt.

"Afternoon, Carol," Mr. Struthers said to our aunt.

"Oh! Marvin! I'm so glad you're here!" She clutched her bosom and wiped her eyes. "Please! Get this child out!"

"Carol, everything's all right now. You boys move aside. Henry?"

"Uh-huh?" Henry sounded so pitiful to me.

"You just relax now, I've got some motor oil, and I'm gonna drip it around your head, all right, son?"

Motor oil? Anyway, Mr. Marvin started pouring and Henry started screaming again.

"It's up my nose! Help! It's in my mouth! I'm gonna barf!"

Sure enough, the next sound we heard was our little brother barfing down the air shaft. Mr. Struthers shook his head and yanked on Henry's feet. Henry popped out of that thing like a piece of toast from the toaster and continued to barf and cry for the next few minutes.

I knew one thing — I was never having children. It was too much trouble.

"Good thing Momma's in the hospital," I said to the crowd, thinking myself pretty funny, " 'cause when she hears about this, she's gonna have a heart attack."

"Now, Susan? Your momma doesn't need to 'eah about this. 'Eah me, girl? She's got enough on her plate."

"We won't say anything, Aunt Carol, I promise," Maggie piped up quickly.

Even I started to tremble a little bit. "She ain't gone hear it pass my lips," I vowed to them. "Come on, let's go home. Thank the Lord it's raining, Henry, 'cause you don't smell so hot. Don't worry, Daddy won't even notice."

"Thank you, Marvin," Aunt Carol said in a husky voice.

"You're welcome, Carol. Glad I could help. How's Louis?"

"Oh, Louis never changes."

"Well, if he does, let me know. Can I give you a ride home?"

"No, thank you, Marvin. I'll walk with the children."

He winked at her and then offered his arm to help her down the ladder. Good grief. I looked at Maggie, who had missed the whole thing, and then to Timmy, who made a face to let me know he hadn't. Henry was busy saying good-bye to his friends and I just wanted to get home.

Livvie told me later that Stuart Brockington had made it his business to stop by our house to let them know about Henry's head being stuck. Livvie was on the front porch moving the hammock to safety when she saw him drop his bike in the yard. Aunt Carol and Livvie took his message, not believing one syllable of what he said. Mission accomplished, Stuart pushed his bicycle out of the yard and was gone. In the next moment, the alarm from the fire truck rang through the air. That was when they realized Stuart had told the truth.

"Where's Mr. Hank?" Livvie had said to my aunt.

"In the shower."

"Yes'm. You want me to go down there and take care of this?"

"No. It's better if I go. Marvin Struthers is an old friend of mine. I can convince him not to tell Hank."

"Yes'm. Thank Gawd for that. It's good when a friend can be useful for something."

"Can you wait till I get back to leave?"

"Yes'm, iffin you say so. You go on now, and I'll call Harriet to have her boy come bring me home. Iffin Mr. Hank ask me, I tell him you gone for bread and milk."

When we got home, the Island Gamble looked like it was ready for anything the skies could dump on it. All the shutters were closed, the porches emptied, the lights out. We went up the back steps and my daddy was in the kitchen with Livvie. He was eating a bowl of potato salad at the table. Livvie rushed to us.

"Mr. Henry, you come with me!" She grabbed Henry and took him back down the steps. "I'm taking him in the house the other way."

We tiptoed in the house because we knew we had been out in the storm too long, or at least Daddy might think so. Lucky for us, he couldn't have cared less.

"You children go find something quiet to do until the storm passes. Hey, Carol, I thought you went for bread and milk."

"Oh, Lord! You're right! But, you have enough, don't you? The line at the Red and White was so long, I turned around and came home!"

Boy, was she a good liar.

Later, we were all upstairs playing Monopoly on the floor when Aunt Carol brought us a tray of peanut butter and jelly sandwiches, some potato chips and a carton of milk with paper cups.

"Oh! Look at y'all! Y'all are such good children!"

"Gosh, thanks, Aunt Carol!" Maggie said, and put the tray down on the floor next to us. "Nothing else to do in this storm."

"Just sit tight and stay away from the windows, okay? Call me if you need anything. I'm going on the porch with your daddy to watch the ocean."

"Okay," we said.

I looked over at Henry, who had completely recovered from scaring us all half to death. He was devouring a sandwich and stuffing potato chips into his little mouth, seeming pretty darn relaxed for somebody who almost got killed two hours ago.

Livvie had gone home and that was a good thing, because the National Guard Reserve was riding up and down the Island in Jeeps with bullhorns, telling everyone to evacuate and go to Moultrie High School in Mount Pleasant for shelter. I'd always thought that going to a shelter would be fun. They say the Red Cross came in and they gave you all the doughnuts you could eat for free. And you got to sleep on the floor in the classrooms. It would be fun to see what they do in public schools. You know, investigate the desks of Protestants and stuff like that. Anyway, we kept on playing for a little while and it started getting dark and the storm got louder. It was raining to beat the band and the wind was whooshing and howling like crazy. Just when Timmy landed on Reading Railroad — and wouldn't you know I owned them all — the lights went out.

"Go get the flashlight!" I said to Henry.

"I don't know where it is," he said.

"It's down in the kitchen," I said.

"I ain't going," he whined, "it's too dark."

"Oh, good Lord," I said, "I'll go. Stop the game, and Maggie, don't let them touch the board."

"Hurry up," she said.

"Jeesch! I'm hurrying!"

I went down the stairs, feeling along the wall because it *was* very dark. When I got to the kitchen, the flashlight wasn't under the sink where it was supposed to be. I knew there was another one in the shed outside, but I didn't want to go out in the storm. Then I thought about the great game we had going upstairs and figured, oh, what the hell, it's just water. I went out the back door, across the back porch and through the screen door. The wind caught the screen door behind me and flipped the latch when it slammed and I realized I was locked out.

"Shit!" I screamed, knowing no one would hear me in all the noise of the storm. I ran as fast as I could to the shed. Sure enough, the big flashlight was there and it worked. What a break! I thought, and decided to go around to the front of the house and go in the front door.

I saw Mrs. Simpson was standing on her porch, with her hands on her hips, looking at our house, but she didn't see me. I realized my father would give me a lot of grief for going out in the storm, so I sneaked up to the porch. I heard my father's voice and the voice of my aunt.

"Oh, Hank! We can't do this!"

"I had you first, Carol, don't ever forget it!"

"Please, Hank! Shouldn't we stop?"

I stopped dead in my tracks and the rain just poured over me. Whatever they were doing, I wasn't supposed to see and I knew that. But I had to see. I had to know. I crept around to the corner of the house and climbed on the oil tank to peek at the porch and there they were. My daddy had Aunt Carol up against the porch railing pushing her butt with his hips. Her skirt was all scrunched up around her waist. All of a sudden I knew what I was seeing and I wanted to run away. Their voices got louder as Aunt Carol started screaming, "Oh, my God! Oh, God!"

This was just too much for me. Their voices howled around my head. I heard Mrs. Simpson laughing from her front porch. She had seen it all; I knew it. I ran to the back door, punched out the screen and unlocked the door. I stood on the back porch for a few minutes, trying to calm down. My ears were pounding. There was an old beach towel on the rack. I used it to dry myself off. For the first time in my life I wanted to throw myself on the ground and cry. There was no one I could tell this to, not even Maggie. I hated my father and my aunt from that moment on.

8

Hurricane Maybelline

1999

The library closed at three the next afternoon because of the approaching storm, which was now officially classified as a hurricane and christened Maybelline. I had been spending any spare time I had going through microfilm of the *Post & Courier* stories covering the investigation of Daddy's death from 1963. There were photographs of Daddy's school building project, and of other things he had worked on, like hospitals and municipal buildings. There were photographs of the scene of the accident showing the skid marks from the bridge to the marsh. But my eyes kept going back to the blurred photograph of his car when it was pulled from the mud of the marsh. Mr. Struthers was standing by the wrecker truck and Fat Albert was standing beside the driver's door. Fat Al was wearing civilian clothes with those same regulation, police-issue, black shoes. Even in the old photograph you could see the shine. I decided to print it and blow it up to an eight-by-ten. I did and threw it in the file of other pictures I had been gathering for several months. I was anxious to get home, make sure Beth was all right and to secure the house.

My boss, the ever-optimistic-about-his-chances Mitchell Fremont, offered me a ride home and, against my better judgment, I accepted. A ride was a ride. It was raining sheets of water and if I had chosen to walk I could have drowned.

Through my office window I watched the wind dance and cavort with the palmettos, wondering if Mitchell's toupee would stay on his head when we got outside. He came by my office and gave me the signal to go, leaving a blast of freshly applied Aqua Velva in the air.

I gathered up my things, putting the day's newspapers and some folders into my L. L. Bean canvas tote bag, twisted myself into my raincoat like Houdini, and followed him out.

We were the last people to leave. I waited in the back vestibule while he set the security alarm. We fought our way through the elements to the car, him jangling his big, heavy, power-broker key chain, nervous and twitching, and me, head down, pulling my coat around me so I didn't fly away. He clicked his remote button and the locks in his Chevy popped up with the blipping sound of a tiny spaceship.

"Get in!" he hollered.

"I am!" I answered him, thinking he irritated the daylights out of me.

I threw my things on the floorboard and struggled against the wind to close the passenger door. While I was fumbling around for the seat belt, he started the car, the windshield wipers and turned on the headlights.

"You gonna be okay at your house? I mean, can I do anything?"

"No, thanks, Mitchell. We love a little hurricane in my family. If I had thought this through I probably would've gone to the beach. I love sitting on the porch and watching the ocean go crazy. You know, boil some shrimp, get some beer . . ."

"You're some kind of woman, do you know that, Susan?"

"Get over it, Mitchell."

I looked at him in profile. Scary. No sense of humor. As we got to the intersection of King Street and George Street, I watched his fat, sweaty little hand travel like a tarantula across the upholstered bench seat toward my left knee. I crossed my legs.

"If you touch me, Mitchell Fremont, I'm gonna knock your teeth out."

The hand retreated. "Susan, you couldn't possibly believe . . . I was looking for my wallet. I thought I left it under the armrest."

"Mitchell? Let's lay our cards on the table. You have me at a total disadvantage. I work for you."

"I thought you liked your job."

"I do. That's not the point. You're always staring at me during meetings and following me around the halls."

"I think you're interesting. Is that a crime?"

"No. Look, you're a nice man, I'm sure you are. But even if you were Cary Grant and single, I'm not ready for anything. You know? I've got my hands plenty full right now. I'm a single parent with an ex-husband who's trying to drive me insane. I can't take one more person coming into my life grabbing at me for something."

"I didn't grab you, Susan."

"Right, Mitchell."

I watched the windshield wipers go back and forth and tried to calm down. Had I imagined his hand? I knew I should tell him to kiss my righteous pink behind and quit. But I also realized that I should quit when it suits me, not him. "You're right, Mitchell, you didn't. Listen, I really appreciate the ride home in this weather."

"You're welcome." He sniffed with indignance.

My patience was running on dust balls and it was a blessing for my many creditors that we arrived at my home quickly. If I'd had to drive any farther with this head-tripping little weasel, I might have had to pop him one to the right jaw. I made one last attempt to be pleasant.

"Okay. Take care then." He didn't answer me; he just looked over at me with this face of his that strangely resembled strawberry yogurt. Puffy. Puffy and sagging with no distinguishing lines of character. It was a great personal struggle to wave good-bye politely, but I did it, gritting my teeth, figuring, why make an enemy out of him now? I had bills to pay. The door of his car slammed in the wind and I ran around the back bumper and up my walk. I needed a glass of wine and a new career.

I opened the front door and stood dripping water all over my floor as I double locked and bolted it against the Mitchell Fremonts of the world. A familiar voice greeted me.

"Hi!"

I turned around to see Tom standing there with Beth behind him, smiling widely.

"What's up?" I asked him and gave Beth a kiss on the cheek.

"Nothing. I just came by to see if you needed anything. They say the eye is supposed to pass over around seven-thirty tonight, so I thought maybe I'd come by, you know, bring dinner . . . I brought some steaks and a bottle of a pretty decent red wine, you know. . . ." He smiled charmingly, crinkling his blue eyes, showing off his dimples. His dimples were a weapon all on their own — never mind his perfect pearly whites.

"Yeah, I know." Any port in a storm, I thought, taking a deep breath. "Beth? Don't you have something to do upstairs? Like homework?"

"I'll go set the table."

Beth disappeared into the kitchen — to be accurate, she floated down the hall. I could feel her mind overflowing with dreams of her mom and dad getting back together. Great, just great, I thought. Nobody except me knew that there was a tentative separation agreement on Michelle Stoney's desk, waiting for Tom's review.

I faced him. Now he had this boyish, mournful puppy look on his face. Not as bad as that skank Mitchell Fremont, but one mournful face per day is my quota.

"So what happened?" I asked. "Did your little girlfriend fly off to Sedona to sit on the vortex and meditate?"

"God, I love your caustic side, Susan. Truth is, I haven't been with her for two weeks. I had some time, so I thought I'd check the third-floor windows for you. They always leaked. I taped them with masking tape all around the edges."

"Masking tape? Now there's a thrifty alternative." I burst out laughing. "God, I'll bet that's attractive! So you're not living with her?"

"No, I took a carriage house on Tradd Street last month. I just moved in actually. It had to be painted."

"And while it was being painted, you had a spat and then rushed over here as soon as you could?"

"Something like that."

The smile again. God, he was a beautiful man.

"To tape my windows."

"Well, obviously they need to be caulked, but you need dry weather for that. I could come back another time and do it if you'd like."

"Tom, bump the third-floor windows. You never expressed any particular concern about them before."

"I'm concerned about you, Susan."

"Right. What are you doing here? What really happened to Miss Close Encounter?"

I could smell my weakness. This man had broken my heart into zillions of pieces and it was lethal for me to stand in the room with him. It was just chemistry, I reminded myself. A simple matter of pheromones.

"She dumped me," he said. "She went to a New Age convention in Charlotte last month and met someone. She says he's her true soul mate."

"Good grief."

"He's twenty-one years old."

"Ouch." My face muscles were convulsing and I chewed the insides of my cheeks so I wouldn't laugh. I decided to surrender the battle and be cautiously friendly. "Want a beer?"

"Sure. Anyway, I knew a long time ago it wouldn't last forever. We're too different, Karen and I. I've done a lot of thinking. She's not half the woman you are, Susan."

"What is it today? The low-pressure system?" First Mitchell, now Tom? All of a sudden I go from being this rejected, overweight, angry woman to an object of desire? I guessed I was on a roll. Hold the mayonnaise, I'm on a diet, I thought. My mind was spinning.

"What are you talking about?" he said.

"Never mind. Come on, let's get a drink."

I sashayed down the hall to the kitchen, Tom behind me. I could sense his eyes honing in on my newly sculpted backside like a Scud missile. Let him beg for it, I thought, and the answer will still be no.

"You look incredible, Susan. Been working out?"

He adjusted himself on a bar stool like it was the seventies and he was a young phallus. I reached into the refrigerator and took out two Bud Lights, twisting off the caps.

"Yeah, got a personal trainer, thanks to your generosity." This could be fun. I hadn't sparred with him in weeks.

"Very funny. Look, things have been tight lately, but I want to take good care of you and Beth, you know that."

I poured his beer in a glass and handed it to him. I would have liked to believe him, I thought, I really would.

"We're doing okay," I said nonchalantly.

I began to search the drawer under the counter for some pretzels.

Beth came sailing back through, taking out my grandmother's sterling flatware and horn-handled steak knives. They were tarnished to a deep blue from months of neglect. She raised her eyes to me, not breaking what appeared to be a self-imposed vow of silence.

"The polish is under the sink," I muttered to her.

Wonder of the world, she laid the silver out on a towel and actually dug around in the bottom cabinet.

"Tom, why don't we go to the living room. Maybe we can catch the news. I just want to run up and change my clothes."

"Sure. No problem. I'll see what's on the tube."

I made it up to my bedroom and tore off my clothes, all the way to my bra and panties. They were soaked too. I put on the navy lace bra I was saving in case I had to go to the hospital or in case Harrison Ford's car broke down in front of my house. I put on the matching navy lace panties. Then I slipped on a pair of my old jeans, size ten, thank you very much, and battled the zipper into submission. Seeing my flesh swell, ever so slightly, over the top of the waistband, I decided to put on a big top and was glad that I had ironed my favorite blue chambray shirt yesterday. I unbuttoned it as far down as decorum would permit, hoping he'd stew in his juices over my cleavage.

"Gonna have to be a helluva storm to let him touch this again," I said with resolve to the bathroom mirror, admiring my svelte and youngish reflection. This was such classic stuff. Husband runs off with young twit, young twit dumps him for young stud, husband crawls back to wife in repentance because all men think they married their mother, or wish they'd married their mother, because Mother always forgives and loves you.

Not this mother. Oh, no. I didn't have a revolving door on my house. No, sir.

I was formulating an evil plan of revenge. Here was the plot. I'd let him get plastered with wine and beer. I'd let him beg to sleep with me, as I knew he would, and while the storm raged all around, I'd kick him out into the night. Don't tell me "Revenge is mine, sayeth the Lord!" Livvie Singleton would have said that the Lord's a little busy and if I took the revenge for Him, it would be okay. Well, maybe not. But in any case, I was going to have at it.

Maybe, maybe, I'd let him sleep on the couch, but only if the storm was really bad. If he didn't want to sleep with me, he wouldn't have shown up with a side of beef. I knew this man. Steak was always our "dinner of seduction" menu and some things were pretty darn predictable.

I took my time washing my face and reapplied my makeup with precision and care. Not too much blush, just enough to hollow my cheeks. Not too much mascara, just enough to offset my eyes, which now, a curious side benefit of losing weight, no longer needed to be lifted. I splashed a moderate amount of his favorite perfume on my throat and wrists and glossed my lips. The thin gold chain around my neck rested on my now slightly pronounced collarbones. If the light was right, I might be able to pass for late thirties. Okay, if it was very dark. I brushed my teeth twice and gargled silently.

I was prepared to face the enemy.

As naturally as possible, I descended the stairs. I could hear the television in the living room.

"What's the word?" I said casually as I stood in front of the big gilt-framed mirror that had once hung in my mother's living room.

"Storm's coming. Look's like it's gonna make landfall just above Pawley's Island."

"Do you think they're right? Shoot, these guys are wrong all the time."

"Yeah, but now they've got that Doppler radar, and they can pinpoint the storm's eye down to which street corner and what front yard."

"Big Brother. Weird, isn't it?"

I crossed my arms and we stood together in front of the old armoire that had been refitted to hold the television and stereo, listening to the report and watching the radar arm revolve around the swelling blue mass that was Hurricane Maybelline.

Suddenly there was a loud banging noise coming from the outside wall. Something was knocking against the house. We ran to the window to look out and through the rain and the bleak light we could see a shutter dangling and slapping the house in the wind.

"I'll go fix it," Tom said. "Where's the hammer?"

"Right where you left it last spring."

It was a borderline hardball thing to have said, but it just came out. Actually, I was glad at that moment he was there. I couldn't see myself taking a ladder outside in this weather and fixing a shutter. He just looked at me.

"I'm sorry, Tom. That wasn't necessary. Listen,

thanks a lot. I'll help you if you need me."

"I do need you, Susan, but not for this. I'll be right back."

His face was as sincere as any face I'd ever seen on that man. All the clever phrases I'd practiced in my mirror in recent months were suctioned from my memory like so much smoke in a honky-tonk bar when you open a window.

I watched him leave the room. He was looking very good from the back. Yes, indeedy, that tight little backside of his was begging for a grab. It seemed like his shoulders were broader. Couldn't be, but his waist was definitely thinner. I wondered for a moment if he'd feel different in bed than he used to.

I started to rationalize. Maybe I was being too hard on him. Maybe we would just sit on the couch and try to sort things through while we watched the storm. Maybe. I doubted it.

I heard the back door close and knew he was outside in the rain. I saw my neighbor's garbage cans rolling down the street and I worried about him getting knocked unconscious by some flying object. I grabbed my parka from the front closet and rushed toward the back door.

"Where're you headed, Mom? I'm making salad. You're not going outside too, are you?" Beth looked up from the refrigerator, where she was searching for a bag of prewashed lettuce — the only kind I ever buy these days.

"Be right back, just want to grab our garbage cans before they take off for Myrtle Beach."

The door closed behind me and I stood on the back porch assessing the weather. It was raining like it would never stop. The light of sunset had surrendered to the dark mask of Maybelline. Her wind was howling like a wild beast.

"Build an ark," I said to myself, "repent, the end is near."

An enormous branch fell from an ancient oak tree at the edge of our property, missing my old car by inches, but slamming into the hood of Tom's new midlife crisis Mustang. There it lay, like a sign from God, waiting for a claims adjuster. Tom would now stay the night.

The storm reminded me of all the legendary hurricanes of my childhood and, of course, the memory of my father and aunt's front porch rendition of "Singing in the Rain." As soon as I visualized them, I pushed the image away.

"Hurry yourself," I said out loud. "This ain't no time for dragging feet."

The screen door slammed behind me and I raced toward the garbage cans by the storage house. One of the can's rubber tops sailed off into the wind like a Frisbee. A branch from my next-door neighbor's tea olive came crashing down into my rhododendrons. Good thing I quit pruning them years ago or the wind could've carried that branch right through a window like a javelin.

I opened the shed and grabbed a handful of bungee cords and a top from another can. It was not easy to fasten them to the cans but I finally did and in haste I began rolling the cart that held them back toward the house. Finally I reached the porch, after struggling over every single hole in the yard, and with great effort I got them up the steps. Beth came out to help.

"Go back inside, honey, you'll just get soaked!"

"Mom, Dad's closing the shutters! I could see him through the kitchen window. Why don't I do this and you go help him?"

"The shutters? Now?"

"Don't ask me! He's got the big ladder out!"

"Oh, dear Lord! Okay, I'll go help him. Just pull this into the laundry room."

"Okay!"

Although we stood next to each other, we had to shout to be heard. I ran around the side of the house and found Tom climbing up to the second-floor windows. On our old house, it wasn't much effort to close shutters. But it ought to have been done several hours ago. My aluminum ladder was not the sturdiest so I decided to be his anchor.

"The wind's pretty fierce so I decided to close up this side of the house. Too many trees next door. Can't get the third floor though."

"That's okay. They're taped."

"Right!"

I could see him laughing to himself as he climbed down to move the ladder to the next window. "You're beginning to drip, Susan. You can go back in if you want to. This won't take too long."

"What? And leave you out here to kill yourself in the yard? Honey, I need my alimony checks and I'm staying right here."

He smiled and jammed the ladder against the ground to secure it. "The irrepressible Susan Hamilton Hayes," he said.

He was so close I could smell his breath. He had brushed his teeth before making this house call.

Brushed his teeth and bought steaks.

"Yeah. Irrepressible. That's me. Get on up this ladder before we make Beth an orphan."

He climbed back up and unhooked one shutter from the side of the house. He climbed down, moved the ladder, climbed back up and unlocked the other. Then, as I held my breath, he reached over and, leaning into the wind, grabbed the first shutter and flipped the latch across both of them.

Finally the job was completed; we were drenched to the skin. Tom collapsed the ladder and slid it under the house, which took considerable effort as the ground was puddled everywhere. I waited for him on the back porch. Hearing us, Beth came to the door with an armful of towels and handed them to me.

"Get back inside, honey, I'm just waiting for your father."

"Oh, my God, it's awful out here!"

"Go back in!" The door slammed. "And don't say 'Oh, my God,' please," I said to the door.

I kicked off my squishing Keds, threw Tom a towel and dried my face.

"Tom, thanks a lot. Of course, if the wind changes direction on the back side of the storm, we'll need to do the other side."

"No way. Besides, the trees next door aren't so bad. I checked."

"Did you see your car?"

"Yeah, bummer."

My shirt was sticking to me and in the porch light Tom could see the color of my bra through the wet fabric.

"Black?"

"Navy, and let's go inside, I'm getting chilled."

"Navy?"

"Get in the house, you old dog."

Suddenly my kitchen seemed alive. Beth was smiling and rushing all around putting supper together. A huge salad waited in my mother's hand-carved wooden bowl. Potatoes were baking in the microwave and the broiler was hot. The seasoned steaks waited in a Pyrex dish. Thick-cut filet mignon. He meant business. The table was set with my best everything. Beth's hopes unnerved me.

"Um, I'm pretty wet," Tom said. "I didn't leave any clothes here, did I?"

"Nope, not a stitch. Come on, I'll give you a bathrobe and put your wet stuff in the dryer."

"Great. Thanks."

He unlaced his shoes and put them on a newspaper on top of the washing machine.

"Table looks great, Beth," I said. "Thanks a lot. We'll be right back."

"Oh, that's all right! Y'all take your time." She wiggled her eyebrows at us. I cleared my throat.

"We'll be right back, Beth," I said in my best parent voice.

Upstairs, he followed me to the bedroom door and just stood there as I searched the closet for two bathrobes, finding one terry cloth and one plaid flannel with ruffles. He chose the pink terry cloth.

"Here you go. Go on in the bathroom and just hand me your things through the door."

"What? After fifteen years you can't watch me undress?" He was laughing at me and I knew it.

"Spare me the pain of your gorgeous body, okay?

You belong to yourself now, not me, remember?" I opened the bathroom door, switched on the light and stood aside to allow him to enter.

"As you wish, madame. I won't be a moment."

"Just give me your clothes, alright?"

In a minute or so, out came his naked arm from around the door with wet khakis, Izod shirt and socks. No underwear? Then his fingers extended slowly from the door as he dangled his orange Calvin Klein jockey shorts in midair. Orange? He never wore anything but white when he lived here!

"Thanks."

"Oh, no, thank you!" He replied from behind the door.

I took off all my clothes — so much for the temptress in navy lace — wrapped the flannel robe around myself, gathered up all the wet laundry and made a quick trip to the laundry room. Passing through the kitchen, Beth perked up.

"What are you gonna put on now?" she asked as though she was witnessing a soap opera in real life. "Your mascara is running."

"Great." I wiped under my eyes and glanced down at the black streaks on my hands. "I dunno. Something dry. Be right back."

Having set the dryer humming, I hurried back upstairs, towel-drying my hair for the second time in two hours. Tom was still in the bathroom, singing "Stormy Weather" loud enough to wake the dead. My hands were shaking. I needed to calm down, and try to find the humor in this scenario. I realized everyone around me seemed to be the happiest they'd been in months. Including me. O Lord help me.

What was I going to put on? Going through my closet, I realized that almost everything was two sizes too big. I remembered the black T-shirt dress I'd found on a markdown rack at Loehman's last month. It was a medium, and I'd bought it when I was still a large, intending to lose weight into it. It was loose-fitting, not exactly what you'd wear to make a man drool, but it had a deep V-neck and Tom was a breast man. Pulling it out of the bag, I slipped it over my head and, bingo, it fit! Let's face it, with a body of depreciating assets, I had to use what I had.

I went to Beth's bathroom to use her cosmetics rather than share the other bathroom with Tom.

This time I decided to let my hair just fall around my shoulders and dry on its own. I couldn't help but wonder, as I finger-crimped my hair, what Livvie Singleton would have said about all this. She'd probably have listened to me tell the story and then she would have given me a piece of her mind in Gullah. I could almost see her. She'd tell me, "Men ain't what but old alley cats looking for to spray they scent." She'd hold up three fingers to me and say, "Only have three things on they mind. One, they stomach. Gotta fill him up. Two, they talliwacker. Got to let him have he way. Three, they money. Don't want to give nothin' 'less they's getting something back. That's all, chile, that's all. Don't expect much and you ain't gone be disappoint."

But how could I go through the night not expecting much? I wanted him to tell me he was wrong.

"I'm going down to open the wine!" Tom called from the hall.

"Okay! I'll be down in a minute."

Dinner had an element of absurdity to it. For openers, Tom dined in my bathrobe, swaddled in pink terry cloth with appliquéd chenille flowers. Just when I had him in the cross hairs, everything conspired to a stay of execution.

We gathered at the table, which my ebullient daughter had set as though Pope John Paul II were coming for dinner. Maybelline was screeching outside like an undulating King Kong of carnal desire, trying to blow down my front door. I was chewing a steak for the first time in months while sucking up a large glass of merlot and the object of all my pain, humiliation and anxiety was sitting across from me looking like a refugee from a transvestite after-hours club.

"So, Beth, how's school?" Tom asked.

"Awesome," she replied while passing the salad bowl.

"Translation?" he asked.

"All A's on every test," I interpreted.

"Fabulous! So you like high school, I take it?"

"Oh, yeah, it's like I totally feel like, well, you know, a person? I mean grammar school was so lame and in high school you're totally on your own. Like even my homeroom teacher, Mr. Bond, tells me I'm extremely mature for my age."

"How mature are you?" he asked, looking at me, probably wondering if he should give her a lecture on birth control. "Bond?"

"Oh, Dad! Please! Shaken, not stirred in the ninth grade? I don't think so. No, no. I think he means it's good that I actually do my assignments, show up for class on time and study for tests and stuff."

"As you should," he said and added, "and as you always have."

"Right, Dad."

"And as you always will."

"Yes, Daddy, as I always will, unless I want to go to college with America Online and wind up on welfare."

"That's my Beth! No member of the Hayes family ever accepted public assistance. Do your homework every day like a good girl."

Tom breathed a clandestine sigh of relief and the sides of my mouth turned up. This was rich. In a mere six months, Beth had gracefully transformed herself from little girl to young woman. He had missed it all. I had hoped reward would taste sweeter than it did. I felt sorry for Tom for what he had lost.

"It's like this all the time," I said to him.

"Like what, Mom? What does that mean?"

Uh-oh. I had mistakenly pressed the wrong button. I had forgotten not to refer to her in a way that required clairvoyance for her full participation.

"Beth, my angel of perfection, each day you surprise me with how truly wonderful you are. Just when I decide I'm failing you as a parent over something or other, you do something to remind me how responsible you are. It's a surprise to your daddy too. That's all. Part of us has you fixed in our mind as a little girl and you're a young lady now."

The awkward moment passed.

"And that makes you feel really old and decrepit, huh? Anybody want some sour cream? Metamucil, maybe?"

"Old? Decrepit?" Tom was horrified at the thought.

"Not too decrepit to wash your mouth out with soap, young lady!" I said.

"Like Livvie did to you and your brothers?"

"Honey, she scrubbed our mouths until we spit bubbles. God, I'll never use Ivory soap again. I can still taste it when I think about it."

"Oh, Mommy! Tell us that story!"

"It was the day I called Aunt Carol a bitch. She had done something, O Lord, I don't even remember. Probably told me to correct my posture or something. Well, I was hanging clothes on the line with Livvie and I said the evil word under my breath. Livvie grabbed me by the hand and had me up the steps in two seconds and my head in the kitchen sink. She turned on the water, grabbed the soap and with my ponytail in one hand and the soap in the other, I got religion!

"She said, 'Ain't no chile — I don't care who — ain't no chile gone use that kind of talk in this house while I'm here!'

"God, I cried and spit and cried, but I never said 'bitch' in front of her again."

"She gave it to everyone, didn't she?"

"Yep, Uncle Henry ate soap, Uncle Timmy ate soap. Yep, when she nailed us, here came the suds!"

Beth and Tom were laughing. We were all enjoying ourselves so much it made me wish for a moment that the dinner could last forever. Tom refilled my glass with the theatrical flourish of a French sommelier in drag. I toasted him and looked around the table at the faces before me. We had been a great family once. A perfect family. Had Tom's one indiscreet episode really destroyed that?

Beth insisted on doing the dishes. She filled the sink with suds while Tom and I cleared the table.

"She's really great, Susan. I owe all that to you. You've given me a truly magnificent daughter. How can I ever thank you?"

"Oh, I don't know. A sack of fifties would help. Here, give me the napkins. They need to soak. Seriously, you've always been pretty solid behind me in whatever I did with her. I'll share the credit with you."

It was the truth, in all fairness to him. I blew out the candles and the smoke from the wicks traveled, spiraling through the darkened room. Now what? I took an arm filled with plates, flatware and soiled linen to the kitchen.

"How's it going? Is the spark still there?" Beth whispered to me over the din of the running water and the ruckus of the storm.

"What kind of spark? Let's just clean up and we'll see what tomorrow brings."

I dropped the plates into the water, then turned to take the linens to soak in a tub in the laundry room and to check Tom's clothes. She followed me, hissing like the snake tempting Eve.

"Mom! You're always so impossibly philosophical!"

"No, I'm not. I'm realistic."

"No, you aren't! You're blind! Can't you see that you have a perfect opportunity here to snag Dad? Look, I'm going upstairs after the dishes are done. Whatever, okay? I'm not coming downstairs unless the roof does. Got the message?"

"Yeah, I got it. Look, let your father and me try to work things out. I don't want you to get your hopes up, Beth. Things aren't always as simple as they appear on the surface."

"There you go again. Just try, Mom. Try for me. For us."

She gave me a hug and hurried back to the dishes. I needed to talk to Maggie and fast. I couldn't trust my reserve and judgment after half a bottle of red wine. I picked up the cordless wall phone in the kitchen and dialed her number. Then I buried myself in the laundry room, pulling the louvered door tight.

"Maggie?" I whispered.

"Who's this?"

"It's me. Susan."

"What's wrong? Why are you talking like this? Are y'all all right?"

"Yes! No! I mean, yes, we're fine! I don't want to be overheard. Listen, I need your advice." I remembered I was calling her in the middle of a hurricane. "Y'all okay? The storm, I mean."

"Oh, yeah, we're fine. The lights flickered a little while ago but the power's still holding. What's going on?"

"Good, good. Tom's here."

"What? How did he get in?"

"Beth let him in. I come home, after another episode with that good-for-nothing cur Mitchell, and find him 'eah, waiting on me, in my own house."

"Have you had anything to drink? You sound a little tipsy."

"Yeah, Gawd. Been nursing a bottle of grapes with that man. Listen up, now. First he shows up 'eah with a bag of fulla filet mignons from Harris Teeter and an '82 merlot."

"Go on! Tom? Tom Hayes? That cheap sumbitch? You lie."

"I swear on Saint Peter's holy ring. Then he close up all the shutters to the south side of the house, up on a ladder in the pouring rain."

"Better check he head for scarlet fever."

"Oh, do chile, that ain't de only fever he got. He hot for ya sister now! Red hot! I got Don Juan 'eah. Tell me what!"

"I can't be telling you nothing. You is grown! But, iffin I was you, I'd be mighty careful."

"What you mean, careful? He out there in my pink bathrobe, strutting like the NBC peacock!"

"What you say? Bathrobe? Oh, Lord, my sister done lose she mind! Y'all? Mind done left she head."

I started giggling and couldn't stop.

"I thinking you be taking a little nip of Oh Be Joyful youself, 'eah?"

"What you gone do in a storm, 'eah? Jack Daniel be on the front porch, rocking with my husband and Maybelline, but I'm in 'eah talking fool with you! What you gone do? Give 'im back he pant or put him in the bed?"

"I ain't be for know."

"Then don't be asking me," she said. She paused and I heard the ice tinkle against her crystal glass.

"Iffin that man was mine, first, I beat he behind good. Then when he real sorry, I mean, sorry for true, I might let him, you know, get he wish."

"Oh, do chile, you is bad and you ain't no help, 'eah? I gots to hang up. Y'all all right?"

"Oh, yeah. I'll call you tomorrow."

I was sitting on the floor at this point. I pushed the disconnect button and sighed in complete confusion. Suddenly, Tom's hand opened the door, and there I was. Busted. He was biting his hand to keep from laughing. He'd heard every word.

"My pants dry yet?"

"Do you want them right now?" I was thoroughly embarrassed.

"Well, actually, maybe not. Maybe never. I like this robe. New image, all that. How's Maggie?"

"Fine. Great. Fine."

He offered me a hand and helped me up. It was the first time we had touched in months. It felt like the hand of a friend, which made it impossible to resist him when he pulled me against his chest. Then, he kissed me. In the midst of this reunion, we heard a thunderous crash, and the lights went out.

"What the hell was that?" I mumbled.

"Who cares? Did you feel the house move?"

"I'm not sure. Better check Beth."

"Right."

We dropped our arms from around each other and took a breath. It was as black as pitch and we couldn't see a thing.

"Flashlight?"

"Yeah, right here in this drawer."

"Pants?"

"Hold on a minute." I reached in the dryer for his damp clothes and he put them on in a hurry. I handed him a flashlight and took another for myself. We hurried down the dark hall to the steps.

"Beth?" I yelled up the stairs.

"What was that?" she called back. "Did you hear that?"

"Dunno. Stay there, I'll bring you a flashlight!" Tom called up to her. "You all right?"

"I'm fine."

He took my light and gave it to her.

"Come on down, honey, until we can see what that was," I said.

"Y'all go sit in the living room," Tom said, "and I'll have a look around."

"Tom?"

"Yeah?"

I reached out for his arm. "Be careful."

"Don't worry. I think the damage has already been done."

The understatement of the night.

A few minutes passed. By then I realized the house had been hit by something and I began guessing how much damage there was while at the same time thanking God that none of us were hurt. Beth sat close to me on the couch. We could see flashes of lightning through the shutters and the thunder continued to boom all around.

At last we heard Tom coming down the stairs.

"We've got company on the third floor. I need a mop, some towels and some big garbage bags."

"What happened?"

"Branch came through a window into the guest room. There's a helluva mess up there, but it's too dark to clean it all up. I'm gonna run for the saw and cut the limb, then just cover the window with plastic so the rain won't keep coming in. It's not fatal."

"You were right, we should've closed the third-floor shutters."

"Who knew? I'll be right back."

I held the flashlight and Beth followed me upstairs with the mop, towels and bags. When I opened the door to the room I couldn't believe what I was seeing. A live oak branch, six feet long, complete with Spanish moss, had invaded our house. The curtains, their swag and the rod were ripped from the wall and hanging from the branch. The window and its frame were destroyed. It would be tomorrow before I could assess the damage, but under my feet I felt pieces of bark, small twigs and soaking wet carpet. The wind and rain just kept coming through the hole in the wall.

"Some mess, huh?" Tom was behind me now.

"I never imagined one branch could cause so much damage," I said quietly.

"That's not the half of it; the rest of the tree is lying against the house. Too much rain this summer, probably loosened the roots. Better have the foundation checked and the support beams. Here, you hold the light and I'll saw the branches away. Beth, try to pick up what you can, I know it's dark, but let's try, okay?"

"But, Daddy, this is terrible! We could've been killed if we'd been in here!" She began to cry. I put my arm around her for a moment. I had to admit I felt like crying myself.

"Beth, this is no time to start crying. Buck up,

baby. Let's help Daddy, okay? Later we can all have a good cry together."

When silence came we knew the eye of the storm had arrived. We stopped our work for a moment to go outside and look at Queen Street. The three of us — the Wise Men, the Holy Family, the Three Stooges, the Ricardos — to think "the three of us" made me giddy with pleasure. The three of us opened the front door and held our breath. Our front yard was covered with limbs. To the left we saw the top of the oak tree peeking around the edge of our house. Clouds swept across the new moon, which would surely bring flooding. Tom and I stepped out onto the walkway.

"Stay there for a moment, Beth. Let us just see that it's safe to come out."

She nodded her head and rubbed her arms as though chilled. In a flash I wondered if she was dramatizing to make Tom see that she needed him. But, admitting the fallen tree had frightened me as well, I linked my arm through Tom's and cautiously, in the light rain, we went to do a quick investigation before the back side of the storm arrived.

The street was littered with every kind of article you could imagine, from garbage cans smashed into windshields, to a rocking chair hanging precariously from a tree. Palmettos lay across the flooded roads. Wires hung down from every building in sight. The silence was eerie.

Carefully, we made our way around the house to see the tree. There it was — huge, uprooted and lying on the side of our house. I could only guess what the cost of repairs would be.

"Good thing I closed the shutters. Can you imagine if I hadn't done anything?"

"Next time use duct tape instead." Gallows humor.

"Very funny. Like it would've made a difference. Let's go finish up."

Tom finally cut away enough of the branch so that we could cover the window with garbage bags to keep the rain out. I took the spreads off the twin beds and pulled the curtains all into bags to take to the cleaners in the morning. Beth had disappeared downstairs. It seemed that the strength of the storm was finally dissipating.

"I've gotta wash my hands," Tom said. "Think there's anything else around here for me to put on besides your bathrobe? I'm soaked again."

"Yeah, me too. I think I've got some old sweats that might do the trick. I'll bring them to you."

We were curiously quiet, the two of us. As we changed this time I didn't think about what I was putting on. We made our way downstairs to find the living room lit with twenty candles, using every candleholder I owned. A bottle of white wine was on a tray with two glasses and a bowl of salted nuts.

"I'm going to bed," Beth said, kissing me on the cheek and then Tom. "Call me if the house falls down."

We watched her follow the light of her flashlight up the stairs, not saying a word. It was a powerful demonstration of her love for both of us.

"Now what?" I said.

"Would you like a glass of wine?"

"Sure."

He poured the wine and handed me the glass,

looking into my face. His eyes told me everything I wanted to know but still I needed to hear the words.

"It appears that our daughter has plans for us," he said.

"Yes. Apparently she does."

"You're nervous, aren't you?"

"Yes, I am."

"Well, if it makes you feel any better, so am I."

We were still standing, not knowing what to do, where to sit, whether to launch the long overdue discussion, or to let the past slide and just come together again. "Tom, we have to talk," I began.

"I know we do. I'm a no-good bastard."

I was the injured party and the injuries still stung. "That's good for openers, but that's not really what I want to hear."

"I've done a lot of thinking, Susan. I was a fool, a complete fool to leave you. I got swept away with a young woman and I made the biggest mistake of my life."

"It's common."

"So they tell me. But now I see what an idiot I was and I'm begging you to forgive me and take me back. I want to come home."

"Oh, God," I said and immediately choked up.

He put his glass down and took mine, placing it next to his on the coffee table. He took my arms and draped them around his neck, putting his arms around my waist. I didn't know what to say. Tears began to slide down my face. Then he was kissing me, wiping my face with his fingers, pushing back my hair. I needed to be kissed. I realized how much desire I had and how many eons it had been since I'd been held. I returned every kiss, gesture, and touch with a surprising, growing passion. I began to grow hot, perspiring a little. He pulled me to the couch and I did not resist.

Who was this? It wasn't the Tom I remembered, the one who groped for me in the dark and then before I could spell my last name was in the bathroom washing up. No, this man, this slow, tender Cassanova, was all new to me.

We began the slow waltz of serious lovemaking. He undressed me and took a long look at me, saying I was beautiful. He was beautiful too. But unfamiliar. We were new partners, breathing together, moving together, following the lead of the other's pleasure. I could feel the quickened beat of his heart against my chest as he held me tighter. Over and over, he said he loved me in a pleading whisper that begged me to love him too. I could feel it. He thrilled me, as I never had been thrilled in all our years of marriage. He had obviously learned more than a thing or two in his absence, and while that was a stunning reminder of his infidelity, he made me want him like I never had. At last, we rested. We were too tired to move.

"Damn!" he said. "So I really do love you, you know."

"Really, really?" I said, feeling more than a little wicked.

"Yeah, really really. A lot." I could feel him smiling against my shoulder.

"I love you too," I whispered into his neck and kissed him there, ever so softly, branding him with a kind of tenderness that I hoped he'd never forget.

9

THE AFTERMATH

1963

The Lowcountry had been trampled. I knew it even before I opened my eyes. My father's cries from the yard and the cries of our neighbors reached up through our bedroom windows. "Oh, my God! Look at this! . . . You got power? Lights went out last night about seven and that was all she wrote, bubba! In all my days . . . How'd this boat get in my yard? . . . Can't find my dog! . . . Where'd the porch go?"

I listened to them as sleep dissolved into morning light. I squeezed my eyes tight. I remembered the night before as if it were a terrifying nightmare. I wasn't getting out of bed. I never wanted to see my father or my aunt again. I thought about my mother lying in the maternity ward and wondered if she had any inkling of what my father was up to. My heart was splitting for her. She deserved a parade in her honor for delivering twins, but I knew that she would return home to more lies and deception.

Momma would be in the hospital for a week and I was glad of that. She needed the rest. In the meantime, I would organize my brothers, Maggie and myself to help her. When we were in school, Livvie would be in charge of the twins. When we got home, we would rotate their care. Then Momma could rest, lose some weight, regain her sense of humor, make herself pretty and Daddy would fall in love with her all over again.

I rolled over to my night table and picked up the photograph of Momma and Daddy taken on the day of their engagement. My mother had been a beautiful woman when she was young. Her chestnut hair was carefully curled, her lips full, turned up in a smile of mischief, and those fabulous Bermuda blue eyes were filled with a love for anything life would throw her way. She was fine-boned and graceful, like a Dresden figurine, but quick and lively, like a sprite.

I ran my finger around the photograph, staring at her young face. She had wanted to go to college, but it was right after the Depression and there was only enough money to educate Uncle Louis. To this very day my grandparents thought it was a waste of money to educate women. That was not what women did. They made a good marriage and had a pack of children and settled down. *As God intended they should,* Grandpa Tipa would say, like the refrain of an old song. It was obvious to me that they had discouraged my mother from college because she might have left them, moved to Philadelphia or someplace, and married a Yankee. She had become their caretaker, and they were not grateful in the least. They were entitled to her servitude, or so they thought.

That would never happen to me. Somehow I

would get to college. But, before that, I would try to help her dig her way back to life.

From my bed I could hear Daddy moving planks of wood. I couldn't imagine why but at that moment I didn't care. The sounds of dragging branches across the yard, interspersed with my father's obscenities, drifted up to my window. Finally, I heard the brakes of Livvie's bus. I heard her voice from the yard and I jumped up, ran to the window and had a look down.

The boards I had heard were laid across concrete cinder blocks to form a bridge over the small lake in our yard. Daddy was wearing waders and he sloshed through the water to help Livvie. We would have frogs in the millions. Normally I would've run to Timmy and Henry's room, dragged them out of bed, gone and jumped in the water. No doubt Daddy would've lost his temper and screamed at us to quit goofing off, get into dry clothes and help him. But today everything that had been normal was falling away by what I had seen the night before. I wondered if Daddy knew that I knew. Maybe I would use it against him. No, I wasn't that brave. There would be nothing on my face that he would be able to identify or trace. I felt sick inside, faint. I had to gather myself and go downstairs to face everyone.

I dressed and went to the kitchen. Livvie was there, pouring out cereal for everyone. Aunt Carol was having a glass of juice. She had spent the night in our house because the storm had started to kick up something terrible and Uncle Louis had thought it would be better for her to be with us, Momma being gone and all.

"So I said to Louis, I said, 'Louis? Don't forget to feed the babies,' that's what I call my dogs, 'and let them in the bed with you because they're gonna miss their momma.' Do you know what he said?"

"No'm," Livvie said. Livvie was staring at her so funny that I thought for a moment that she knew.

"Morning," I said.

"Morning, Susan. Well, he said, 'Carol, honey? Your babies can stand one night away from you, but what am I gonna do?' Isn't that just like a man? Can't live without us! I swear, he loves me so! Well, I guess I'd better end this tea party and get on home to my Louis."

"Yes'm, you do that. I imagine he's missing you something terrible."

Then Aunt Carol picked up her pocketbook to leave and turned to us to say good-bye, and there was Livvie drinking a Coke from Momma's best crystal goblet. No one was allowed to use her crystal, especially a colored woman. Momma saved that crystal in case President Kennedy decided to come for dinner. Aunt Carol turned purple, puffed up like a blowfish and stormed out of the back door. I was stunned, but I didn't say a word.

The morning gathering of our tribe was getting under way at the same moment of Aunt Carol's departure. First came Maggie in shorts and a T-shirt and her hair up in a ponytail. She looked more like she was going out to a beach party than getting ready to clean a yard. She always looked like that. Perfect.

One by one, they swung into action, doing their parts to help. Maggie stirred powdered juice into a pitcher and the boys set the table with paper plates. I kept my face straight, hiding under the mask of just waking up. They expected me to be crabby in the morning. But I was just plain shocked and, I thought, hiding it pretty well.

"Can't be wasting no water washing dishes, y'all 'eah me?" Livvie was giving orders and handing out paper cups. "Yemoja done dump all the water in the sky on us yesterday."

"Who?" I said.

"Yemoja, Obatala and Oya. Yes, sir, they done they worst to Charleston. Nearly blow us all to kingdom come."

She was talking about her African gods again. I decided they must have something to do with storms. We knew that when there was a big storm we had to wait a day or two to be sure the water came back on and was all right to drink. We'd fill the sinks and tubs before a storm to drink, wash dishes or flush the toilets. Naturally, my brothers and my father would use the occasion as an excuse to use the yard as a toilet. Maggie and I would hold it until we turned blue. On Sullivan's Island, we were proud to have our own water supply — a combination of deep wells from which blended water was pumped by electricity. But when the lights went out, drinking water went with it. Truth told, the water reeked of sulfur but made the creamiest grits. Anyway, in a day or so we would have water and lights again. In the meanwhile we would put orange juice on cereal and laugh about it. We were professionals in the aftermath business. At least no one would have to fight about taking baths tonight. Until the power came back on we had a holiday from all that.

"No electricity. Sophie's going to have a fit that she can't have her toast and egg," Grandpa Tipa said, coming in the kitchen. "Can't you children say good morning?"

We were busy stuffing our mouths with Frosted Flakes and Tang at this point.

"Good morning, Grandpa," I said. "Did you sleep okay?"

"Of course I did. Said the rosary, you know. It's what good Catholics do when we need protection," he said. "Mrs. Singleton, I nearly ran myself ragged protecting my property yesterday! Thank you for clearing the porch for us. We certainly have a lot of electrical plugs in this house. I must've unplugged one hundred things."

"Think his Hail Marys saved the Island?" I whispered to Maggie.

"No, it was the plugs," she replied.

"Well, I'd better go deal with Sophie," he said. "Oh! Mrs. Singleton! I forgot to ask, how did you and all the Africans make out last night?"

"Me and *the Africans* made out just fine, thank you, sir. Just fine," Livvie said, narrowing her eyes at him.

I could see she wasn't pleased but she decided to let the remark pass. He had to let her know that she came from a tribal world of dark skin. He was such a big pain in the butt. He embarrassed me all the time when he said things like that.

Tipa fixed a plate of bread and a bowl of cereal and carried it off to Sophie's room. A few minutes later we heard a plate crash. Everybody stopped moving, waiting for the screaming to start. Either it was dropped by accident, or old Sophie had thrown it against the wall. I darn well knew it was the latter and I was glad Daddy was still in the yard. He didn't support Grandma Sophie's theatrics.

"Usually she only eats one piece of toast, no crust, light butter, not margarine, and a poached egg for breakfast," I offered as an explanation, meeting the surprised look on Livvie's face. "Same thing every day and only Tipa can fix it. If I fix it, she knows if somebody else fixed it and don't ask me how. Then she pitches a huge fit. Lunch is tomato soup, with one piece of toast cut in nine squares floating in it, and plain tea. It's because she's a genius."

"What kind of fool you talking, girl?" Livvie said.

"Momma says Grandma Sophie is a genius and geniuses have weird little habits. Grandma Sophie has more than her share, if you ask me," I said, thinking that if she could tell Aunt Carol to kiss off by drinking out of Momma's best glass, then I could throw a little dirt on old Sophie and Tipa.

"A genius? How is she a genius?" Livvie stood now drying her hands on a dish towel.

"She does trigonometry in her head while she sleeps," Maggie said.

"I heard tell of that, but do y'all think she threw that plate?" Livvie asked.

"Yep," said Timmy.

"She does it all the time," said Henry. "I'd get my butt whipped for sure if I did that."

"It's how it is around here, Livvie," Maggie said. "It's so embarrassing I don't ever bring my friends here. Excuse me, I'm going to get busy putting the porch back together."

"I'll come and help you in a minute," I said to Maggie and turned back to Livvie. "Yep, and she eats only Cream of Wheat for supper. Same bowl, same spoon and if you switch it she can tell."

"Think she's peculiar?" Timmy asked.

"Well, I don't know," said Henry, "I'd like to have pancakes every day and spaghetti every night."

"Yeah, sure, squirt, so would I but I don't have a temper tantrum if I don't get it!" Timmy said.

"Don't call me squirt or I'll sock you one," Henry said.

Maggie got up and left the room. We were all quiet. Livvie just kept standing there looking at us like we were a bunch of escapees from the nuthouse. Finally she said, "Humph," and began fixing some food. She handed Timmy a banana and a sandwich of bread and butter, then reached in the dark refrigerator for a Coke and gave it to Henry.

"Go on, now, take this to y'all's Daddy. See iffin y'all can help him clean up the yard," Livvie said. "Don't be opening the refrigerator and especially the freezer until the power comes back on!"

"Okay! Okay!" they said, slamming the back screen door nearly off the hinges. A few seconds later we heard, "Sorry!" Then a lot of giggling as they ran down the back steps.

"Them boys," Livvie said.

She sat down at the table next to me. It was unusual for a Negro housekeeper to sit next to anyone in the family, except a baby. I didn't mind a bit but at the same time I hoped no one would catch us.

"You all right, Susan?" she asked.

"Yeah, I'm fine."

"Humph. You's a terrible liar. You ain't fine. That's all right. Iffin you want to talk to Livvie, I'm 'eah. I just want to know one thing and it ain't about your aunt."

"What's that?"

"You think your grandmomma be right in the head?"

"I think she thinks she can do whatever she wants. I mean, Daddy raises the devil about her sometimes, but then Momma cries and Tipa gets mad and says it's still his house and have some respect for your elders and all that junk. Then Daddy goes over to Uncle Louis's, they drink a bunch of beer and Daddy comes home and it's okay for a while."

"Humph," she said. "Got a bad spirit in her. I gone fix it too. All right, enough of this long talk. I got to go clean up Mrs. Asalit's floor. I gone talk to her, don't you worry."

I didn't tell her about how Daddy would give Momma the back of his hand and I didn't tell her how Uncle Louis never did anything to help Momma with Grandmomma. I watched her take the paper towels, a grocery bag for the broken dish and the container of salt. She probably already knew everything about us anyway.

"What do you need salt for?" I asked.

"Humph," she said, "*buckra* children don't know nothing. Come on, Livvie will show you."

I went with her out of curiosity. Their room was

empty. Grandpa Tipa had taken Grandma out to the front porch to calm her down. We could hear their voices through the open French doors of their bedroom. Their bed was unmade only on one side. Tipa had slept on top of the covers, probably dressed. Sure enough, broken china covered the floor by the closet door. Livvie began to pick it up and I helped her.

"Watch your feet, child. Why don't you go put on shoes?"

I had a sudden thought that it had been ages since anybody had cared whether or not I got hurt. The tears came rolling down my cheeks and Livvie stood up and pulled me into her arms.

"There, there now. It's all right, chile, just cry it all out," she said softly to me.

I could feel my chest heaving with sobs but no noise came out, just great sighs.

"I know," she said quietly.

"How?" I said.

"Honey chile, when you're an old woman like me, you'll be amazed at what you can know just by looking at someone, especially when they don't want you to! Why don't we pray together about this a little bit?"

"Pray? Are you kidding me? I'd pray that they both go right to hell," I said.

"Susan, iffin you don't want to pray, that's all right, but sooner or later, you got to give it over to the Lawd. It's His business to punish, not our business. And, honey, listen up to Livvie, I gone tell you something. It don't pay to hate nobody, 'cause the only person who gets hurt is you. The person you hate, half the time don't know about it and the other half they don't care. So don't hate them, just know they is stupid. Grown up don't mean you can't be stupid."

"Boy, that's for sure."

"Ain't got nothing to do with you. Don't mean because they is bad that you is bad. Just means they is stupid. They make a crazy decision and didn't expect to get caught."

"How did you know?"

"Chile, all I had to do was look at your Aunt Carol and she start to run her mouth a mile a minute, looking every which way except at me. And your daddy? Normally he'd be cussing up a blue streak. But he's out there smiling and cleaning up he yard. How did you get in their business anyway?"

"Went out to the shed to get a flashlight. Got locked out and had to go to the front door. First, I heard them. Then I saw Mrs. Simpson on her porch watching them and laughing. I had to peek. I wish I hadn't."

"Yeah, I expect you do, but it's natural to peek. That don't make you bad, just normal. Too bad that woman saw them. Harriet say she something terrible."

"Yeah, you know she'll tell the immediate world and then Momma's gonna die from the shame of it."

"She ain't gone tell a living soul nothing. I see to that."

"What are you gonna do? Cut off her tongue?"

She giggled like I loved to hear.

"Yeah, Gawd. I gone to her house with your momma's big scissors hid in my apron and when she start yapping, I gone grab it and snip!"

"That would be great! You'd be famous! Gosh, Livvie, when I talk to you I feel normal."

"You are normal. You is all normal. Your brothers is just boys, that's all. And Maggie's a young lady trying to grow up and dignify herself. Can't blame her for that, can we? Now, your grandmomma and granddaddy, they is old, honey, and old folks got their ways. Can't change them. Be a mistake to try. In fact, it's a mistake to try and change anybody."

"Doesn't work anyhow," I said.

She looked at me, picked up the remaining pieces of ceramic and put them in the bag.

"Umm-hmm," she hummed, "no, we can't change them, but we can move they spirit! Yes, sir, we can do that sure enough!"

What was she talking about? The next thing I knew she was sweeping the floor. Then she stopped and opened the container of salt, poured some in her hand and started humming "Go Tell It on the Mountain." She sprinkled some in each of the four corners of the room and turned to me.

"What?" she said.

"Nothing," I said, "nothing at all."

"Gone clean up the spirits in this room, that's all. You watch, you'll see. Gone cut me some roots and make a little cunja bag and pin it to they mattress too. They don't have to know, do they?"

"Ain't gonna hear it from me," I said.

"Good. Humph. All this fool in this house is just that. I gone take care of it. You watch. Gone fix that mirror too. You believe me?"

"Yeah, I believe you."

I did believe her and I didn't know why. Except that since she'd been here, things had, in fact, started to change. The house was a lot cleaner, I always had underwear in my drawer, Sophie didn't stink anymore and Daddy hadn't whipped anybody lately. But it was more than that and her fried chicken. Her passion for righteousness was stronger than our frenzy.

We went back to the kitchen to clean up the remains of our makeshift breakfast.

"Where do you get your strength, Livvie?"

"What do you mean? Ain't you heard nothing I ever say?"

"Yeah, of course, I listen to you, but still . . ."

"Ain't no but. You wipe off the table and I gone tell you my story. 'eah, take this cloth and get busy."

"Okay."

She looked out the window remembering, shook her head and started to talk.

"When I was a little girl we didn't have nothing. I mean, we was so poor that my momma lined my shoes in cardboard when they got holes. I only had one pair and they was my treasure. She stuffed the walls with newspaper when it got cold, and Lawd, it got cold. But me and my brother knew we had love and that was the most important thing to us. And we always had plenty to eat. Cornbread, milk, field peas . . . something always on the table.

"My daddy, he was born after the Yankees came, in about 1875, and oh, how he loved to tell the stories about the Yankees. He was scared to death of them bluebellies because he believed they would come and kill you or carry you off. Maybe he told us that so's we wouldn't wander off down the road, like we liked to do.

"His daddy and mammy was still living on the plantation when he was born, even though they was free to go. His daddy had been a slave and when Mr. Lincoln freed everybody, he say where he gone go to? So, they stay and tend they own patch and work for Mr. Archibald Barnes.

"My family lived in a little cabin on the plantation, the same one where my daddy was born. All his life, my daddy was a sharecropper to the same man's family his daddy had belonged to. The Barnses they owned a big plantation out on the Wando River called Oakwood. My brother, Leroy, and me, there wasn't no school around there, so they put us in the field to work picking cotton. But I was a right smart little girl and in fact I can read a little and do some numbers, but yes, ma'am, I was put out in the field when I was only nine years old. Makes you grow up quick. Hard work makes you strong. I work hard every day; that's where I get my strength. That and knowing who I am. You children think you got it so bad, you wouldn't know what trouble looked like if he walked right up to you and shook your hand!"

Livvie sighed and waited for me to say something.

"I know that, I mean, somebody's always got it worse," I said.

"That's exactly right."

"I know, I agree, but Livvie, sometimes it's so crazy around here I think about running away. I mean, I'd never do it because where would I go? But it's too much, you know?"

"Yeah, chile, I know better than you can think I do, but you belong right 'eah. You is a Hamilton and this is where they call home. I know something else you ain't learned yet."

"You probably know plenty more than I ever will."

She laughed a little at that and shook her head. "Mm-hm, chile, these old eyes have seen it all, but what I want to tell you is this. When folks around you do crazy things, it's the devil trying to distract you from your purpose."

I just stared at her.

"That's right. Old Beelzebub himself. That's how the devil works. He ain't no fool with a red suit and a tail. No, he works on your mind. When you let your mind dwell on trouble, you can't be doing what you needs to be doing. Then he wins, you see? He can't win unless you let him because he ain't got no power on his own."

"So, basically, what you're saying is that worrying about Daddy and Aunt Carol or Grandma Sophie diverts my attention from other things, better things?"

"That's it! That's my girl!"

"Yeah, but Livvie, I don't think I'm ever gonna forget what I saw."

"I know that, chile, but listen up, every time that picture comes back in your head, ask the Lawd to help it go away. He will."

"Livvie?"

"Mm-hm?"

"Your grandfather was a slave?"

"Yes, chile, he was. They carried him off from Africa when he was a young man and he nearly died on the way 'eah. The old people didn't like to talk about slavery. It was a terrible time."

"It must've been horrible."

"It ain't over, Susan. We still got our troubles, but I just keep to myself and don't get all messed up with all this fool talk about integration and such. I don't want to eat at the lunch counter in Woolworth's over to the city. I'd rather eat in my own house!"

"Well, I ain't got the money to eat there. It's probably greasy anyway."

"Yes, but you *could* eat there. I can't. You *could* use the bathroom there. I can't. It ain't ever gone change and iffin it does, gone be a miracle for sure. Wait till all these old buckra narrow minds die and find heaven full of colored folks! Won't that be the day!"

"I don't know, Livvie, I'm not gonna even be thirteen until next month. I don't know about all this stuff."

I was embarrassed. I knew what she said was right but there wasn't anything I could do about it. Suddenly I was very glad that Daddy had built the new bathroom. If Livvie had ever been told to use the outhouse, she would have quit on the spot.

Maggie says that when colored people die and go to heaven, their skin turns white. I used to believe that when I was little, but now I knew that it was another dumb lie made up by white people.

For a long time I had always thought plantation life must've been full of music. Long days and hard work, and somehow in my mind, all of it was set to music. Slaves singing, ladies dancing, beautiful carriages and horses bringing people to parties at night with lanterns all over the yard — that sort of thing. How stupid and naive could I have been? Their music was born of pain, pain caused by people of my race.

"Well, I'm gonna go help Maggie put the porch back together, okay?"

"Susan, come back 'eah, chile."

I turned to face her.

"Listen to Livvie, I tell you what's on my mind, not to make you feel bad. I want you to *think*. Gawd got His special purpose for you, just like He does for every one of us. He done give you a very good mind. The world you have when you grow up is gonna be the one you make. You use your mind and make it better."

"I will, Livvie, I promise."

By Sunday morning it seemed that the entire Island knew that my momma had twins. Every hour somebody came over with a gift for my new sisters. Most people brought two pairs of booties — in fact, we had fifteen sets of two already — and every last one of them wanted to know what the twins' names were. They didn't have names yet. But, in the tradition of the family reputation of lying through our teeth, Timmy and I decided to quit explaining.

"I'll get it," I screamed when I heard the knock.

It was Mrs. Wilson, the red-headed schoolteacher from Sullivan's Island Elementary School. She was divorced but since talking to her was only a venial sin, I launched right in.

"Hi!" I said.

"Oh! Susan, I'm so glad I caught y'all at home! I

thought you might be at church."

"No, ma'am. We went to Mass at eight o'clock this morning. Timmy and Henry had to serve on the altar, so we all just got up and went."

"Well, that's nice, dear. Listen, this is for your new sisters."

"Thank you. Booties?"

"Yes, I made them myself! How's your momma?"

Make that sixteen pairs of two and still counting. The day was young.

"Good. Coming home Tuesday. We're going to see her in a few minutes."

"Well, please send her my best. Did she name the girls?"

"Yes, ma'am. Posie Sue and Rosie Sue. Momma likes flowers, you know, and she named them Sue in my honor. Isn't that nice?"

Her face went blank. "Well, I always say people should name their babies whatever they want," she said.

"Yes, ma'am, I think so too."

By the time we left for Charleston, my sisters had some of the craziest names you can imagine. Itchy and Scratchy, Timmy told Mrs. Fisher, because Daddy said the twins were all bumpy and rashy. Sneezy and Wheezy, I told Mrs. Mosner, because their noses were runny, but don't worry, it's not on the birth certificate, I told her. Daphne and Delilah, Tara and Scarlet, and Lucy and Ethel were some of our favorites. We were laughing so much in the car Daddy started screaming at us.

"Shut the hell up! I'm trying to drive!"

Silence prevailed and we spent the rest of the

ride looking at the damage from the storm. Trees were still down everywhere; the roads were covered in a wash of sand. The water was still high on the causeway. It was incredible how much damage could happen in just a few hours. Unfortunately Mount Pleasant had electricity again, which meant school would be open Monday.

When we reached the parking lot at the hospital, Daddy gave us a talk on our manners. We gave our word not to behave like a bunch of banshees. I had avoided talking to him and was wondering how I could avoid it for the rest of my life.

We took the elevator up to the maternity ward and waited outside Momma's room until Daddy said we could go in.

"Momma?" I said. "Hey! You alright?"

"I'm tired but I'm fine! Come give your momma a kiss," she said, "and meet your new sisters."

We bombarded her with homemade cards and signs, crawling over her to see the twins. They were in the bed with her and when I saw them I started crying. So did Maggie. They were so beautiful. Momma was so moved that she started to cry. Then Daddy grabbed the Kleenex box and started passing them out. That made us laugh. He pretended to cry, making fun of us, but he was so loud he scared the babies and they really started crying. The more they screamed the redder they got. Maggie picked up the blond and I picked up the brunette. I couldn't believe they calmed down.

"You girls are going to have to help me when I come home, you know," Momma said.

"Oh, don't worry about it, Momma. I love babies," I said, thinking of my plan.

"They look like Susan and me," Maggie said.

"Yeah, that one doesn't have any eyebrows," Henry said.

"She'll get them later, bird brain," Maggie said.

"Boy, she's got some grip!" Timmy said. The baby I held had her tiny hand wrapped around his finger. "Gonna be a wrestler!"

"I hope not!" Momma said.

"All right, you kids go wait in the waiting area and I'll be along soon," Daddy said. He was so pleasant it made me forgive him for the moment, making me hope things would be better. We lined up like good little soldiers, kissed Momma on the cheek and the twins on their heads and filed out. There was something magical about the moment. Maybe the twins would bring us good luck. Maybe Daddy would go back to loving Momma. Momma looked pretty good, I thought, considering what she'd been through. Remembering the babies' names, I giggled to myself.

The great joy of my sisters' birth and the plans to tell it all over school were dwarfed by the terrible news of the following Monday morning. When my brothers and I arrived at school we were told by our teachers to go directly to chapel for a special Mass. We were told that somebody had bombed a church in Birmingham, Alabama, killing four little girls. Many others were seriously hurt. It was a Negro church. We were absolutely stunned. The nuns were crying and there was a mood of despair that crept through the pews like poison gas, rising up from a dark place. The hideous news changed us forever.

Until then, I had no clue whatsoever that the Civil Rights movement was so dangerous. It had always just seemed so far away, like Vietnam. And I couldn't imagine who would kill children because they were colored. If grown-ups wanted to fight each other, they would, but what kind of a person bombed a church? And how deep must be the hatred that drove the person to commit such an unforgivable crime? Who would kill people while they prayed? I had a hard time trying to concentrate in my classes. I kept seeing the grief-stricken faces from the newspaper that someone was passing around. Visions of children lying in coffins tormented me all day. For some inexplicable reason, I didn't want to face Livvie when I got home. I knew she would be angry.

She was grieving as though those children had been her own. She wiped her eyes with the back of her hand, humming a church song. I found her ironing when I came in the back door with Timmy and Henry after school.

The boys each grabbed a cookie from the plate on the table she had set out for us and ran upstairs.

"Chocolate chip! Thanks, Livvie!" Timmy said.

"My favorite!" Henry squealed.

I put my books on the table and reached for a glass to pour some milk for myself.

"Want some milk?" I said.

"No, chile, I don't want nothing today. No, nothing today." She looked long at me and went back to her ironing, humming a little, but her eyes were incredibly sad.

"We had a special Mass in school for those girls in Alabama," I said quietly.

"It just don't make no sense," she said. "People killing like this. Bombing the Lawd's house. Lucifer got to be stopped! Somebody got to stop him."

"You're right," I said. "What can we do?"

"Beg Gawd to help," she said. "Gone take the mighty power of all His angels to stop this kind of thing. I'm fearing it's gone come this way. Hatred is a terrible thing. Like cancer. Eats you up."

"You're right," I repeated, at a loss for words for once in my stupid life.

"My cousin Harriet come to my house this morning with the paper. When I see them faces of them mommas and daddies crying for they children, make me cry. That's all."

"Me too."

She looked at me and realized my eyes were red too, but she was suspicious of my honesty. Couldn't she see that I was frightened by what had happened in Alabama? It meant the trouble could come here and children here might get blown up too.

"This 'eah is trouble for my people, not yours, Susan. We gone fight the fight, because every back is fitted to the burden," she said, slamming the iron on the board for emphasis. "We done carry burden since we come to this country in chains. Ain't much different now."

The last thing I'd let her do was shut me out.

"You're wrong about that, Livvie. I mean, I don't usually disagree with grown-ups and I never thought I'd disagree with you, and I'm sorry to say so, but you're wrong."

"Oh, yeah? Let me 'eah this now. Now they burning babies!"

"I know that, but I didn't do it! Listen, God made all of us, right?"

"Yeah, that's right."

"And the only difference between you and me is our skin color, right?"

"Yeah, I reckon so."

"And kids are kids, right?"

"They sure enough are." She was patiently watching me bumble my way through this and giving me all the rope I needed to hang myself.

"Well, if a colored man blew up a white church and killed some white kids, that wouldn't mean all colored people are bad, would it?"

"No, it wouldn't."

"It would mean that there was one crazy sumbitch out there, or maybe a bunch of them, but not every colored person was crazy, right?"

"You may be right, but please don't say that curse word. Ain't fitting."

"Okay, so this means that there are a bunch or maybe even a lot of bad guys in Alabama who don't want integration, but not everybody feels like that."

"I already told you. I don't care about integration. I just want peace, that's all. Just want to live my life in peace and serve the Lawd."

"Me too. But, Livvie, a lot of people do care about integration. I mean, Sister Amelia, my teacher, said plenty today that made a lot of sense to me. I think that colored kids should have the same opportunity that white kids do. Then it would be more fair. I mean, if they have the same schoolbooks and the same chances at the same tests, then colored kids can grow up and do more.

I'm not talking about you and me, here — after all, you sent all your kids to college, right?"

"Yes, I certainly did. And it wasn't easy. I cleaned toilets to buy textbooks. Think about that."

"Right, I'm sure you're right. But I'm talking about kids that probably aren't even born yet. And kids from families who don't value education."

"Even iffin they gone let all the colored children in Charleston in the white schools tomorrow, it ain't gone bring them four little girls back to life, Susan. Four little girls died yesterday because white people will always hate black people," she said. "That's just how it is. They want to hold us down."

"It's true, those little girls are gone. There will always be rednecks and bad guys. Can't change that either. But we can change education, Livvie; it's a step. Equal education could be a big step."

"Maybe, but it ain't the answer," she said, and pointed to her chest. "The answer got to come from 'eah. In the heart."

I took a big gulp of my milk and nodded at her. She was right about the solution coming from the heart. I knew that you could pass all the laws you wanted to but if somebody didn't want to obey them, they wouldn't. She got up from her ironing board to hang the shirt she had been pressing. "Momma's coming home tomorrow," I said.

This made her smile again. We really didn't want to argue with each other. "I know. Spent all morning getting they room fix up. Can't wait to hold them babies! When I told Harriet I had two new brand babies, she got so jealous I thought she'd pop! Oh, Lawd! You should've seen her face! Yes, ma'am, thought she would pop."

We began to talk about the twins and how I would help her with them and then, our discussion about integration finished for the moment, I left her and went out for a bike ride with Timmy and Henry.

The water had receded somewhat from our yard and the Island was beginning to dry up from Hurricane Denise. We rode our bikes all over Sullivan's Island looking at the damage. Seemed like every house had something happen to it, especially those on the oceanfront. We had merely lost shingles and screens and had some fallen branches plus a lot of beach sand in our yard. The old Island Gamble had another notch on her belt.

We came home late in the afternoon to do homework and have supper. I could smell the okra soup and the sweet cornbread as I climbed the back steps. Livvie was putting her coat on to catch the five o'clock bus. "See y'all on the morning train!" she said. She was leaving early and coming in early tomorrow. She smiled sadly at me and patted my arm before she went out the back door. Things had changed a little. A tiny line of color had been drawn. It broke my heart.

10

Write Away

1999

A week had passed since Hurricane Maybelline had ripped through the Southeast. Damage was in the millions of dollars and everywhere you went you heard stories, stories and more stories. I ventured out to buy paint for the guest room. I knew it was all covered by my insurance policy, but I thought I'd get estimates, do the work myself and save the money for something else. Everybody does this, don't they?

I joined the throngs of ersatz interior and exterior decorators on line at the Home Depot. Customers staggered under their armloads of screening, two-by-fours, boxes of shingles and cans of house paint. I stood on the shortest checkout line — twenty people — and while I waited, the comedy hour was free.

"Found a dog in my yard! Tag was from Pawley's Island! Dog was fine. Can you believe it?"

"Came home from my mother-in-law's house and my curtains were sucked right through the windows! Not a rip in them! Have you ever?"

"Got drunk, went to bed like usual with my old

lady, everything was fine. Never heard a thing all night! Got up and half my roof was gone!"

I had been dealing all week with claims adjusters, tree surgeons, carpenters, window guys, the carpet store. Roger hadn't called. Big shock. But he'd probably turn up at some point. And Mr. Tom hadn't called once. So much for his passionate concern. But embittered I'm not. Dumb dates and failed marriages make you either a boozehound or a philosopher. I was not even particularly surprised that Tom hadn't called. Leaving someone is a process, not just an impulsive decision. It takes a long time to let go. In some peculiar way, I was relieved that I hadn't heard from him. When I finally got home, I called Maggie.

"Hey! You want to go grab some lunch with me? I'm dying for fried shrimp, haven't had 'em in months. I'm in the mood to eat neurotically."

"Why not? Sounds good as long as you don't look at my fingernails. Cleaning up after that hussy Maybelline wrecked my manicure."

"Now there's a tragic story if I ever heard one. I'll pick you up in thirty minutes. Wanna go to the Yellow Dog on the Isle of Palms?"

"I'll be ready."

As my car swung around East Bay Street to take the bridge east of the Cooper, I found my heartbeat slowing down. I was on my way to the beach — the cure-all for whatever ails me. I mean, I was feeling philosophical because it was Saturday. Up until now, I'd been cussing like a sailor every time I passed the silent phone. And I'd been giving myself lectures ninety ways to hell and back for sleeping with Tom.

I lowered all my windows to let the air in. The air felt so good. It was a gorgeous September day and I was going to have lunch with my sister, the good egg of all times. I sneaked through Mount Pleasant (a notorious speed trap) like a drug lord with a trunk full of contraband, vigilant for redneck policemen hiding behind billboards with their shaved heads, beady eyes and radar. It was a game I played. I'd never had a speeding ticket, and I was determined never to get one. In fact, I thought, the only flawless thing in my life just might have been my driving record.

The Island looked like a wreck, the same way it always did after a storm. The million-dollar new houses on the oceanfront had taken a terrible beating, but the old shacks still stood. The tire swings in their front yards hadn't even gotten tangled in the trees. One thing I had to say for Maybelline, she had taste. And, true to her history, the Island Gamble was waving the victorious flag of survival after one more bout with Mother Nature.

"House looks good!" I called out to Maggie, who came down the back steps with her purse, ready to go. "Where's my brother-in-law and my nephews?"

"Gone fishing early this morning — out to the Gulf Stream." She got in the car, slammed the door and looked at me with one of her martyr faces. "Shoot, my house should look good! I nearly broke my back this week cleaning this yard and then we power-washed the whole house!"

"You're a good woman, Maggie. A good woman." I started to back out of the yard. "I'm sick of Maybelline and her mess too. You should see my third floor."

"Under control now?"

"Yeah, God, but only after eighty million phone calls and this incessant waiting for a human being to talk to. By the time they pick up the line, I forget who I called! I hate automated phone systems." I started toward the Isle of Palms. "I hate workmen too. You could spend your whole day waiting and they still don't come."

"How 'bout Tom? Hate him too?"

"Nah, he's just an asshole who can't help himself. I could put him on one of those daytime talk shows and a thousand angry women could tell him what a jerk he is and it wouldn't make a bit of difference."

"Didn't call, right?"

"Right. Didn't call." We drove past the gas station, Station 22 Restaurant and Dunleavey's Pub. "Bump him. It's okay with me, and it doesn't matter anyway." What a liar. "As soon as I've stuffed my face with fried food," I continued, "I've got an idea I want you to think through with me, okay?"

"I'd be grateful for any excuse to use my mind, and besides, you know how I love telling you what to do."

"Well, this time I'm inviting it. Show me no mercy."

The young waitress showed us to a booth that faced the ocean. We slid across the leather benches opposite each other and, driven by some shared genetic compulsion, we wiped the crumbs from our respective sides of the Formica-topped table.

Knowing the menu by heart, we ordered without it. The waitress brought us our drinks and we settled in for the next hour or so, watching the beach and fishing through the mayonnaise seafood dip with Club crackers, looking for pieces of crab-meat or anything that resembled seafood.

"Think this is worth the calories?" Maggie asked as I popped a fat gram-laden cracker into my mouth, washing it down with Diet Pepsi and lemon.

"Nope, but I'm tired of dieting and today is a day for celebrating."

"It is? Tell me why."

"Do you know what the total damage was to my house?"

"I'm afraid to ask."

"Sixty thousand."

Maggie let out a low whistle. She couldn't whistle for beans.

"The insurance company is only paying fifty thousand. I had a five-hundred-dollar cap in my policy on landscaping."

"Bunch of thieves, they are, the whole bunch of them, Yankee carpetbaggers."

"Yep, worse than lawyers. But I have a plan." I drained my glass and motioned to the tiny waitress in cutoffs, T-shirt and platform sandals. The waitress teetered over, smiling.

"Can I he'p you?" She smiled a wide, self-medicated smile. Prozac, I imagined.

"Just some more Diet Pepsi," I said, "thanks."

"Sure 'nough!"

"There but for the grace of God go I," I whispered to Maggie.

"In a pig's eye, honey. You and I would've dug

ditches before we wound up doing this for a living. Besides, we're at least two decades on the back side of cutoffs and platforms."

"Backside is the operative word." I giggled.

"Okay, okay. Tell me what the plan is!"

"Remember when I was a kid and I used to keep all those diaries? I found them in a big trunk in the attic when I was up there with the workmen checking the support beams."

"What's that got to do with the insurance money?"

"Just hang on, I'm gonna tell you."

The waitress returned with our baskets of fried shrimp, potatoes, a small plastic tub of coleslaw and hush puppies.

"Kin I git y'all anything else? Ketchup? Some more Pepsi?"

"No, thanks, we're fine."

She tottered away and I bit into a hushpuppy, burning the skin on the roof of my mouth. I gulped my drink to put out the fire.

"Hot, huh?"

"Yeah, bu' good. Whew! So listen, here's the deal. I've figured out that if I hang the wallpaper myself and do all the repainting myself, I can save ten thousand dollars out of the insurance settlement. My neighbor, in a fit of guilt, is replacing my shrubs."

"No kidding? That's a break. So what are you gonna do with the money? Run away to Paris and be a writer like you always said you would?"

"No, no. I wish. But nothing that exotic. I'm buying a computer for myself. I decided, and tell me what you think about this, to try to put together some essays with cartoons!"

"What? For who?"

"For the newspaper. A column about being a single mother in the nineties, about growing up in the sixties, about being Geechee children, about dealing with a husband with the zipper problem, you know, about sexual harassment . . ."

"Sweet Mary, Mother of God. You're serious!"

"Yeah, I'm dead serious. Look, Maggie, I never have two nickels extra to rub together. Beth wants to shop, and God forbid I should ever get my wardrobe together and look like something attractive to the opposite sex. What kind of money am I ever gonna make working at the Charleston County Library? I can write at night; it's bound to pay something!"

Maggie got very quiet and I waited for her to say something. She picked up a fried shrimp, squeezed a lemon over it, ran it around in her tartar sauce and finally bit into the thing. I watched her chew as she stared at me.

"Well, say something," I said. "Christmas is coming."

"Are you doing this for an excuse to get on-line in those chat rooms and meet some stud muffin?" Her face was serious.

"Gimme a break, will you? I leave the chat rooms to Beth. Would you believe I caught her talking to some guy, saying she was a twenty-three-year-old blond aerobics instructor from Malibu who loved Mexican food?"

"Good Lord, Susan. But, hey, it's another story you could write!"

"See what I mean?"

"Susan? Are you going to use your real name?"

"I don't know, probably not. Because if nobody knows who I am then I think it would be easier to really say what I think, you know what I mean?"

"I wouldn't use anybody's name in the column either. You'll get your butt sued for libel."

"Yeah, I thought of that, unless it's a politician."

"I could help you with lots of stories from when we were kids." She liked the idea. I could see it.

"I have a trunk full of them! The journals, remember?"

"Right! Well, when you run out of stuff to say, let me know."

"Maggie, people will be spending the weekend on the moon before I run out of things to say."

We started to laugh and our laughter grew. Pretty soon, tears were running down our cheeks as we were remembering all the crazy things we had done as children.

"Remember that kid Stuart?"

"Oh, God! What a little creep he was!"

That was how it all began. I spent the next two weeks writing like a maniac. I wrote a piece about going crabbing with an illustration of kids on the beach attached to it. I wrote a piece about sibling rivalry with a cartoon of kids choking each other. I particularly loved the one I wrote about Livvie. That one had a picture of a little white girl on the lap of a black woman. There was something to be said about single parenting, a lot, in fact, so I burned up the keyboard of Beth's word processor on that. I wrote about the sexual revolution and how it had passed Charleston by. They were all very tongue-in-cheek and some of them were damn funny, if I said so myself. And the cartoons set the tone. They were eaten alive with cuteness.

Beth thought I'd gone mad. She was letting me use her computer, because I couldn't make up my mind which one I wanted to buy, and she'd sacrificed her privacy. She moved to the dining room to study, saying that my laughing out loud, not to mention my pacing and smoking, broke her concentration. No doubt.

When I had twenty-five essays together, I was ready to try to sell them. But first somebody had to read them for me. Catch the goobers, fine-tune the language, gauge the rhythm, veracity and wit. I called Maggie.

"Whatcha doing?" I lit a cigarette. "Do you love me?"

"Of course I love you. What choice do I have? Where the heck have you been?"

"I've been impersonating Anna Quindlen for the last ten days. My fingers are worn down to little nubs from spilling my guts on paper. My thumbs are callused from the space bar. I need your help."

"Name it."

"Do you think you could pretend you don't know me and read what I've written and then tell me the truth? I need to have all this stuff proofread."

"You're not really seriously asking me if I like to criticize, are you? Get your bones in the car and come on over. I've been dying to see what you're up to! I'll make supper for y'all tonight."

True to form, my sister helped me once again. She found tons of errors that the spell-check feature on the word processor didn't pick up and had some good suggestions for tightening up some of the essays. It took another week to get them polished and another three days to work up my nerve to call the newspaper. I just kept telling myself that if they didn't want to run my essays, I'd try another paper. No big deal. In fact, I expected rejection.

Finally, on Friday, I looked up the number and dialed. The computerized voice that answered the phone had me so confused, I wasn't even sure who I wanted to talk to when the human voice finally came on the line.

"Hello? Can I help you?" The voice, female sounded mature and pleasantly professional.

"Um, I hope so. My name is Susan Hayes and I'm in charge of literacy outreach programs at the county library."

"Yes, Ms. Hayes, how may I direct your call?"

"Well, I'm not sure. I've written some essays about living in these hard, fast times we're in and I was hoping I might speak to someone about buying them for the paper."

"Ah, so you're a journalist too?"

"Well, an aspiring one, I mean, I've done a lot of writing —"

She cut me off in midsentence. "Just bring them to the front desk, any weekday between nine and five, and we'll have a look at them. Make sure you have your résumé and phone number attached to your portfolio and we'll call you."

"Okay. Fine. Thank you."

I wasn't used to being dismissed and it felt terrible. But then I realized I was talking to the receptionist and she probably got fifty calls a week from people who are sure they're the next Dave Barry or

Molly Ivens. Can't blame her, I thought, and then I realized: Portfolio? Don't have one! Résumé? Haven't updated it in years! I spent all Friday evening composing a new résumé and successfully resisted the urge to include any wisecracks.

Maybe I should send a copy to Roger Dodds too, I thought. He *still* hadn't called either. I could've died in the hurricane for all he knew.

The next morning I bought a black leather portfolio, to hold my essays, from Huguley's on Wentworth Street. I prayed that I'd bought the right kind and that it didn't look pretentious. I decided to beat it up a little to make me look experienced, so I threw it on the asphalt a few times and walked on it. Then I damp-wiped it and Pledged it. The end result was convincing enough to me.

On my way to work Monday, I dropped the whole kit and caboodle off at the *Post & Courier*, held my breath and began a novena to the Blessed Mother. O most gracious Virgin Mary, never was it known that anyone who fled to thy protection, implored thy help or sought thy intercession was left unaided . . .

It was in the blood. I would be a card-carrying, fish-eating, bead-pushing, candle-lighting, altar-making, incense-sniffing, genuflecting, saint-venerating Catholic until the day I died. I figured the Blessed Mother was my best bet in the Roman Catholic pantheon of possibilities. After all, she was a woman. Maybe I would resort to daily Mass in case I'd used up all my heavenly favors.

Tuesday and Wednesday went by and no one called. Not Roger, not Tom and not the newspaper. I had indulged in a thousand fantasies by late Wednesday afternoon. Ones where crowds roared at my jokes and held their breath while I spoke.

I was making a meat loaf for supper and had my hands in the bowl of chopped meat and ketchup when the phone rang. I was so deep in thought that I jumped at the loud noise.

"Beth! Can you get that? If it's Oprah, tell her there's no fee for me to appear, but I only fly first class!" I had been having a marvelous time imagining fame and fortune and how cool I'd be.

"It's for you, Mom!" Beth screamed from upstairs. "It's some man, probably wants to sell you something!"

Oh, good Lord, I thought, just when I'm up to my elbows in gook. I wiped off my hands and picked up the receiver.

"Ms. Hayes?"

"Yes?"

"This is Max Hall calling. I'm the publisher of the *Post & Courier.*" He paused.

"Oh! Yes! How nice of you to call." My heart was beating against the wall of my chest.

"I've read your essays." He took a very long pause again. Did he hate them? Did he love them? Tell me already and stop the pain!

"And?"

"Well, it happens that one of our writers who does a column on Thursdays is leaving us and I might be able to use some of your work. I'd like to meet with you and discuss it."

"Fine! When?"

"Well, would Friday around four o'clock be all right with you?"

I would've gone at three in the morning if he had wanted me to.

I marched myself into Berlin's the next afternoon like I shop there every day. I bought a pair of black Calvin Klein trousers with a jacket and a black silk T-shirt and paid the full retail price for it all. Then, full of beans, I walked down to Bob Ellis Shoes and bought a pair of black Prada pumps to match and a black knock-off Chanel bag. Thank you, Jesus, and all those good people at Metropolitan Insurance! Friday, I picked up the trousers from the alteration woman and hurried home to try on my new image. As I stood in front of the mirror on the back of my door, I liked what I saw. I was tall, thin and very cool. No, I was dignified. I went to Beth's room for the ultimate test.

"If I pull my hair back in a clamp, what do you think? Do I look like a writer or an Italian widow?"

"Groovy, baby. Shagadelic!"

"Thanks, I think."

All the way to Max Hall's office I tortured myself. What if he hated me? This was not a romance, I told myself, it was business. What if he laughed at me and thought my work was idiotic? What if he bought it, it was published and everybody knew it was me and *they* laughed at me?

"Ms. Hayes?"

His door had swung open, and a pimple-faced young man in shirtsleeves scooted out past me. I marveled that he was old enough to be a journalist. I was feeling old, but the face on Max Hall was a lot older than mine. I took a deep breath and jumped in the deep end.

"Hi!" I shook his hand. Firm grip. That was good. "Mr. Hall?"

"Call me Max." He closed the door behind us. "Everyone does."

His office was exactly what I expected. Behind his old leather-topped desk was a computer screen on a credenza, flashing news with a stock tape running across the bottom. His desk was huge and had several pencil cups and neat piles of paper stacked on both ends. He took his seat in the leather swivel chair and indicated that I should sit opposite him.

"Then call me Susan, please."

"Sure. You want coffee?"

"Sure. Black's fine."

He spoke into his intercom, asking the female outside to bring in two cups of coffee. Then he leaned back and looked at me.

"So, you want to write a column for the *Post & Courier*, do you? What kind of experience have you got?"

"Jack," I said.

"Excuse me? You worked for someone named Jack? Do I know him?"

I cleared my throat and my face got hot. I should've watched a video on how to interview.

"Um, no, Max, I mean I have a lot of experience, but not in journalism. But I do a lot of writing for my regular job at the county library. Grant proposals, brochures, that sort of thing."

"Ah! I see." He leaned across the desk and said in a low voice as his secretary left the office, closing the door behind her, "What you're telling me is that you don't know jack about journalism, is that right?"

The son of a bitch had no sense of humor.

"Well, yes and no. I mean, everyone tells me I write like a journalist and that I should write professionally and that I'm funny. Well, they think so, I'm not so sure."

"Let me be the judge of that."

"Ah, Jesus." I had spilled the coffee down my arm.

"Don't be so nervous. Here." He handed me a wad of tissues.

"Right. Max, can I be real straight with you?"

"Please. I'm about as good at mind reading as you are on interviews." He smiled and leaned back. This wasn't going as I had visualized it.

"Look. If you like the twenty-five stories you've seen, I have more. I've been keeping a journal since I was knee-high. Here's the thing. I need this job. I'm a single parent, my ex-husband is so tight he squeaks and I need to prove something."

"Now you've got my attention. What've you got to prove?"

"I need to prove to my daughter that the human spirit can overcome any trial life throws your way. These stories are for women around my age, the boomers. They're to remind them that raising kids today ought to be a breeze next to the issues we faced during segregation and the Vietnam war and all the stuff that went on thirty years ago that changed the world forever."

"You think your generation changed the world?"

"You bet we did. This planet's never been safer than it is today. The air's cleaner, the water's cleaner and the risk of nuclear war is practically nil." You go, honey, I said to myself. I wondered if the old codger had a soapbox in the closet I could use.

"So we may assume you have other opinions about other things?"

"Yeah, I guess you could say that." Why was I so out of control? This was no way to charm a guy, even I knew that. "I tend to get carried away."

"Carried away can be a good thing. I have two more writers to interview and I'll let you know by Monday. Okay?"

"Really?"

"Yeah, really. Fair enough?"

"Oh, God, yes, that's more than fair enough! Thanks, Max, listen, this is all just draft, you know, I could polish it up —"

"Quit apologizing for your writing. God, all writers are the same." He got up from his desk and opened the door for me to leave. The interview was over. I had spent eight hundred and fifty dollars on this black widow's outfit for a five-minute interview.

"Max?" I extended my hand to him and he took it. "Thanks. I really mean it."

"Sure thing, Susan Hayes, with opinions galore! I'll call you either way by the end of the weekend."

I called Maggie as soon as I got home.

"Let's get drunk," I said.

"Love to oblige, but I have to take the boys to football practice tonight. My turn to carpool. How'd it go?"

"Then can I borrow a Valium?" I twisted the phone cord around my elbow and hand, knotting the whole thing up.

"God, I wish you'd get your own. Ask your

doctor. Tell me how it went. Was it a disaster?" Why was she so cranky? Get my own Valium?

"No, I don't think so, I mean, I don't really know. It was so fast."

"Has he got your portfolio?"

"Yeah, he had read the stuff already. I guess he just wanted to see my face. I'm gonna be a wreck until he calls. Can I come over?"

"Sure."

I don't remember driving to the Island, but I came out of my trance in Maggie's kitchen as she put a bottle of peach-flavored Snapple in my hands.

"Peach-flavored tea? How can you drink this stuff?"

"It's better for you than all those nitrates you guzzle."

"Maybe. Maggie? Is something wrong?"

"I haven't seen my husband in two days." She leaned back against the sink and she had the strangest expression on her face. "Susan, Grant's having an affair," she said.

"What in the hell are you telling me?"

"I'm telling you Grant is putting away some little nurse at the hospital."

She burst into tears. I knew she sounded funny on the phone! No wonder she told me to get my own drugs. I put my arms around her.

"Come on, now. How do you know this is true? I mean, are you sure?"

"I found a matchbook with a phone number written on it in his jacket pocket."

"Call the number?"

"Yeah. Answering machine. 'Sheila and Debbie

aren't home right now . . .' What would you think?"

"I'd think what you think, but you know what? You should ask him. Just ask him."

"Here I am in this perfect life, in my clean house, and my husband is screwing around and I didn't even suspect it. But, lately, he's gone so much, I don't know, I just started getting this rotten feeling in the pit of my stomach, you know what I mean?"

"Do I know? Yeah, I know. I just can't believe Grant would do that, Maggie. He's a Eucharistic Minister, for Christ's sake, no pun intended. I mean, guys who dispense Communion every Sunday are unlikely to have affairs! I think you need more facts. Just ask him straight out. Say, 'Grant? Are you having an affair?' Just as he's about to bite into dinner, you know, catch him off guard."

"Oh, I couldn't do that, Susan, I don't have the nerve."

"Yes, you do. Then he'll say, 'Why no, honey, whyever in the world would you think that?' Then you say, 'Because I found these matches in your pocket from the White Horse Saloon with a phone number, so I called it and a girl named Debbie answered. I told her I was your wife and you're HIV positive and on a mission to infect all the sluts of the world, that's all.' That's what you say. Then you look at his face to see if he's choking or turning red or whatever."

She cracked up. I cracked up. Humor. It never fails.

"You're the best, Susan. I'm gonna do it." She paced around the kitchen table. "What do you think? Should I wash my hair?"

"Definitely. I don't want to put pressure on you, but pretend you're getting your picture taken for *Town & Country*, know what I mean? Put on the dog and when he takes the bait, whammo!"

"Whammo, huh? At this moment, I'd like to whammo him straight to McAlister's Funeral Parlor. The son of a bitch."

"Maggie! Such language! Honey, get the facts first. I have the feeling this is all a big misunderstanding. I can't for the life of me see Grant sneaking around. He loves you, first of all, and second, he's not the type."

"Livvie used to say all men were the type."

"Yeah, well, Gawd rest she soul, I'm sure that even she would've been wrong this time."

I drove back to the city with a heavy heart. Grant was fifty-one. Prime target for a nurse and an affair. It was true, he hadn't been around much, only to take the boys fishing and Sundays he'd take everyone to church and then to do something else, like see a movie. I thought about it some more and wondered what indeed would Maggie do if she were right. I knew I'd better prepare myself to step in and help her like she had helped me.

The house was quiet that night. I was watching television and Beth was reading in her room. I had decided to give myself a break in the writing business that night and just catch up on sitcoms and paying bills. At eleven o'clock, I turned off the lights and went upstairs. Beth's light was still on.

"Night, sweetie!" I blew her a kiss through the door.

"Hey, Mom! Wanna see something outrageous?"

"Why not? Today's been a day for the outrageous."

"Look at this catalog! This is what I'm gonna wear on my wedding night."

I sat on her side of the bed and she showed me a picture in a lingerie catalog of an emaciated blond with enormous breasts and big, pouty, slippery lips, wearing a white, sheer, nylon, poor excuse for a gown and robe trimmed in feathers. For a moment, I didn't know what to say. It was the worst thing I could imagine she would want to wear in front of anyone. It bordered on pornography.

"Where did you get this catalog?"

"Cool, huh? Jennifer gave it to me."

"Who's Jennifer?"

"A girl in my biology class."

"That figures. Listen, sweetie, throw that in the trash. When the time comes for you to get married, we'll go to Atlanta to shop."

"You swear?"

"Mother never swears, Beth, you know that."

Monday after work I was coming through the door with groceries for dinner and Beth was on the phone, as usual, and animated like a lunatic, waving her arms at me. The kitchen was a wreck, also as usual, but I was so stressed out that I didn't even start yelling at her.

"Sure, she's right here." She handed the phone to me. *It's him!* she mouthed, pointing to the phone. *The guy from the* Post & Courier!

"Hello?"

"Susan? Max Hall here. Nice girl you've got, nice girl."

"Thanks."

"Well, if you still want the job, it's yours. I know I shouldn't say this, but I saw those other two people and I swear to God, what some people think passes for entertainment, you wouldn't believe."

"Right. Well, I still want the job. Very much!"

"Well then, we need to settle a few things. First, we will use a number of the essays you've given me, but not all of them. So why don't you come by and we can talk about them? I have a list of possible topics for you too. You know, education, the arts, local sports, that kind of thing."

"Sure! No problem."

"Then there's the ugly business of money."

"Right, money," I repeated like a parrot.

"I'm afraid it's not much, ten cents a word, but it's something anyway."

"That's fine, I'll take it!" Tough negotiator, I thought.

"First column runs this Thursday, Living section. I have a question for you."

"Sure, what's that?"

"Do you want to use your name or a nom de plume?"

"Nom de plume, please, too many living relatives."

"All right. Oh, and one other thing . . ."

"Yes?"

"Tell Jack he's a helluva guy!"

"Right!" Oh, shit, this beast won't ever let me forget that one.

"Be in my office tomorrow at four?"

"You bet! Max, thanks, I mean it."

"Quit thanking me, you deserve a chance, Susan. You've done a lot of living and these stories will give a lot of people something to think about."

I hung up the phone and leaned against the wall. Beth grabbed me and we jumped up and down for a minute, whooping and hollering.

"My mom! The famous columnist!"

"Oh, God! I can't believe he called! He's a little bit of a stiff, I think, but who cares?"

"Right!"

Beth opened the refrigerator and found a can of Coke and I poured myself a glass of Chardonnay. We clinked aluminum and glass and I toasted myself and her.

"To the future!"

"To the future," she said and gave me a hug.

"Hey, Mom, not to change the subject, but have you heard from Dad?"

"No, why?"

"Just wondering." She sat up straight on her bar stool. "Okay, here's the dirt. I saw him with *her*."

"Oh, so what? Look, Beth, you're old enough to understand this. People should live where they want and do what they want. If he wants to come back and he's serious, you'll be the first person I tell."

"I guess. I wasn't gonna tell you but now that you have some good news, I figured it was okay."

"Right. Let them have each other. Come on!" I opened the refrigerator. "Let's make spaghetti. Tell me what happened in school today."

"Jonathan finally started speaking to me again."

"Tell him not to do you any favors. Don't we have a bell pepper?"

"Right. In the bottom drawer. So, Momma?"

I loved when she called me Momma.

"Is it hard to write?"

"Nah, it's sort of like dancing. You find a rhythm and go to town with it. Know what I mean?"

"Sort of. I mean, it's easy to write about good stuff, but what are you gonna do if they ask you to write about bad stuff?"

"Let's hope they ask. Like what?"

"I don't know, death maybe?"

"That may possibly be the toughest question I've had to answer all day, but even death has humor, wakes and funerals especially. I guess I'd advise people not to take hams to the bereaved. Did I ever tell you about the mountain of hams we always got?"

"You're weird, Mom."

11

TIPA

1963

It was a bright October morning. The last vestige of Indian summer before the gray months. I was waiting outside for the school bus with Maggie, Timmy and Henry. The twins had been home for about a month. Momma had named them Allison (after June Allison, the actress) and Sophie (after her mother) and when we took them down to Stella Maris to wash the devil out of them, they were baptized Allison Marie and Sophie Ann. They had screamed all the way through the ceremony, but from the minute they came home from the church they settled into a routine under Livvie's care. They were good babies, Livvie said.

Momma didn't get out of bed to cook breakfast for us anymore. Somehow we managed. Daddy was leaving earlier than ever for work. His construction of the county high school was well under way and there were problems all the time. Just the day before, someone had hung him in effigy from a tree by the construction site. I heard him tell Uncle Louis that there was a sign around the dummy's neck that read HANK HAMILTON LOVES NIGGERS. Just last night old Fat Albert and Mr. Struthers came by to see Daddy. They sat out on the porch talking about the danger of the threats. I thought they had frightened Daddy. But, no. They had just made him more determined to finish his project. But Daddy seemed worried and he was in extremely foul humor. Needless to say, I was scared by the whole business but knew better than to bring it up with him.

The next morning, I stood in the driveway looking for the bus. It was late. Not one of us felt like going to school. The boys kicked dirt into little clouds that covered the spit shine on Maggie's and my Wagons. We complained in our whiny voices and they imitated us, irking us to no end.

Finally, the noisy yellow bus rolled to its screechy halt, the door was opened with the flexed muscles of Miss Fanny's forearm coming toward us like Popeye's. The same lady who ran the Island's little store was our sainted chauffeur. She leaned her head sideways to greet us.

"Good morning! Come on now, let's hurry up. You kids settle down! Hey, Billy and Teddy! If y'all don't settle down, I'm gonna tell Father O'Brien!" She was yelling at the boys in the back of the bus, who were knocking each other with their lunch bags. "I swear to Gawd, them boys."

I was the last to get on.

"Hey, Miss Fanny, how're you?" I said.

"I'll tell you how I am! Them crazy Blanchard boys gone make me an old woman before my time!"

"Don't let them bug you," I said, "they're jerks."

They were still carrying on and one of the boys screamed. In the next instant Miss Fanny was pissed off in purple.

"All right, that's it! Teddy, Billy! Up to the front of the bus, on the double," Miss Fanny said. "You boys can lead the bus in the rosary and if you even so much as twitch, you're going right to Father O'Brien when we get to school!"

Taking the bus to school was an exercise in working off years in purgatory. Every day, Miss Fanny led us in a decade of the rosary as soon as we got over the Ben Sawyer Bridge. Every decade of the rosary said is the equivalent of one hundred years off in purgatory. If you say the Sorrowful Mysteries with the correct fervor, you get a thousand years off. At least that's what we thought.

"Let's be quiet, y'all! Come on, let's be quiet!" Miss Fanny hollered.

We kept laughing and carrying on like a bunch of lunatics, buoyed by the sugar of our morning dosage of Alphabits and juice. I thought we prayed enough in school. But she was insistent and she got madder and, like always, she started cussing.

"Y'all children! Dammit! If y'all don't shut the hell up, I'm gonna tell Father! Teddy! Billy! Y'all stand right there . . . in the name of the Father, and of the Son, and of the . . ."

The prayers began at the top of her voice, and instantly we all got quiet and prayed with her, snickering among ourselves that prayer began with threats and curses. Today we said the Sorrowful Mysteries.

"Think about our dear Lawd, His momma at the foot of His cross. Hail Mary, the Lawd is with thee, blessed art thou among women and blessed is the fruit of thy womb, Jesus."

Miss Fanny led us, and the Blanchard boys stood there looking pious enough to sprout halos. We knew they were trying to make us all laugh. But we didn't need them. All we had to do was hear the word *womb* and it caused a surge of giggling. In her fervor, she ignored us every time and continued.

"Holy Mary, mother of Gawd, pray for us sinners, now and at the hour of our death. Amen."

We said the fifty required Hail Marys, the four Glory Be's and were putting the serious hurt on a synchronized Apostles' Creed when the bus rolled into the dirt parking lot under the big live oak tree, dripping moss — with red bugs — and we scampered out to go pray and study for the day.

Maggie was a big-shot tenth grader at Bishop England High School and the rest of us were still sniveling runts at Stella Maris Grammar School in Mount Pleasant. Still, she was forced to ride the grammar school bus and another bus would take her to the city. Although she was my best friend at home, on the bus she sat as far away from the rest of us, with other high school students, and spent the ride silently looking out the window, rolling her eyes and being serious.

It was my last year at Stella Maris and I couldn't wait to get out. At about ten o'clock, I had just begun a math test when Father O'Brien came quietly into my classroom and whispered to Sister Martha, my teacher.

"Susan Hamilton?"

"Yes, Sister?"

"You'll go with Father O'Brien. Take your things with you."

I fumbled around and gathered up my books. Nothing was worse than being sent to Father O'Brien. He was all business and had no tolerance for children. Why somebody like him was the principal of a grammar school was merely another mystery of the Catholic Church. The scuttlebutt on him was that he had once studied with the Jesuits. That alone says it all.

"What about my test?" I asked.

"You can take it later."

"Come along now," Father O'Brien said.

"Thank you, Sister," I said.

Every eye in my class watched me leave. What had I done? Or was it Henry? Timmy? Did Maggie's bus get in a wreck? I worried all the way down the hall and to his office, where Timmy and Henry were seated on a bench in the outer office, terrified. They got up and we all went inside. We stood in front of his desk and he sat in his chair.

"Children, I'm afraid I have some very sad news to tell y'all. Your grandfather Mr. Asalit passed on this morning."

"You mean he's dead?" Henry asked.

"Son, only his body is dead; his soul now radiates with the full glory of the risen Christ. Surely you remember your catechism."

Timmy and Henry started to cry and I stood stunned, just staring at Father O'Brien. Then I put my arms around them and reached for the tissues on Father's desk.

"This is no time to indulge yourselves with tears. Pray that his soul makes a swift journey to the

Lord's bosom and save your strength to support your mother and grandmother. Remember, this is your momma who's lost her daddy and your grandmother has lost her husband."

Tears rolled down my face without a sound. I didn't know what to do, none of us did. We just stood there, time not passing, waiting for some comfort. Shaking, scared and crying.

"Can I call my momma?" I asked.

"No, let's not bother her. Your Aunt Carol is on the way here to bring y'all home. She's going to pick up Maggie first. You may make a visit to the chapel to pray for your grandfather and then you can wait on the bench outside if you'd like."

"In the school yard?"

"Yes."

Permission to wait in the school yard unsupervised was a monumental event. I grabbed a fistful of tissues and led my little brothers out.

First we peeked in the chapel and no one was there, except for the light on the altar indicating the presence of the Eucharist in the tabernacle. As fast as we could, we scampered to the front, did a bounce genuflect in front of the altar and hurried to the statue of the Blessed Mother. Her empty plaster eyes stared at me and her half smile seemed like a smirk. It gave me chills. As the oldest, I reached under the tray of candles for the matches and lit three candles, one for each of us. I made the Sign of the Cross and knocked Timmy and Henry in the ribs, encouraging them to do the same.

"Dear God," I said, "please take Grandpa Tipa straight to heaven and not anyplace else. He was a good grandpa and a good man. And he had plenty of reasons to be such a grouch. Also, please help Grandma Sophie and our momma not to go crazy from this. Amen."

"Amen," my little brothers said.

We got up and hightailed it out of there. Empty churches gave me the creeps.

The ride with Aunt Carol was like a disjointed dream. She yammered on in a nervous monologue about what we should wear and who would be coming and that we had to be quiet when we got home. As we passed people on the street, going about their lives, I wondered if they could tell our lives had just been blown open by death. Could they see it on our faces? Henry continued to cry and all Aunt Carol would say was, "There, there now."

When we reached the Island Gamble, Livvie was standing on the back steps in the sunshine waiting for us. She took one look at us and opened her arms. "Come 'eah to Livvie. He gone be all right. Everything gone be all right."

Each one of us hugged her with all our might. The strength of her arms healed me on the spot. When she saw the fear in our faces transform from fright to calm, she released us, one by one.

"Go on now and kiss your momma and grandmomma and then y'all come back 'eah to me. Maggie, see about them twins, all right, chile?"

"Sure," Maggie said.

We went inside and left Livvie with Aunt Carol on the back steps. Aunt Carol was still talking, Livvie was shaking her head.

I found Momma in her bed with old Sophie sitting in a chair beside her. Momma acted drunk but

Grandma Sophie, like the eighth wonder of the world, spoke.

"The doctor gave her a shot for her nerves," she said.

Under the circumstances, Grandma Sophie seemed fine, better than she had in my whole life. "Go and tell your aunt that I want to speak with her, child, would you please do that for me?"

Timmy ran off for Aunt Carol and Henry and I followed Sophie, who walked slowly back to her own room and crawled up on her bed.

"Come in! Come in! I won't bite you!" We took baby steps closer.

"I'm sorry you lost your husband, Grandma Sophie," Henry said, still crying.

"Well, somebody had to go first. Do you want a tissue? Go get yourself one and blow your nose. I'm just sorry I wasn't with him in the end, that's all."

"What happened, Grandma? Is it okay to ask that?" I asked.

"He dropped dead on the floor of the post office, poor thing. Had a heart attack and dropped dead. He'd gone to get the mail, just like he always does. One minute you're here, and the next, poof! Deader than Kelsey's cow. Somebody pulled his plug. I expect your father's gonna throw me out now that I don't have Tipa to protect me. Susan, look in the top drawer and see if you can find a pair of stockings for me."

"Sure!" I opened the drawer and the stale scent of old perfume escaped. "Gosh, Daddy wouldn't do that! Don't even think like that!" I found her stockings and gave them to her.

"Put them on the bed and find my robe. Oh, yes,

he would! Your father's a hard man! How am I going to manage without Tipa? He did everything for me! Where's your aunt? I need to talk to her about the funeral. Tried to talk to y'all's momma, but she's in her bed, acting like she's the only one who ever carried a cross." She cleared her throat with a terrible noise and spat in a tissue. "Get me some water too," she rasped.

"I'll go find Aunt Carol," I volunteered, anxious to get away.

"Be quick. We have a lot to do!"

"Yes'm." I gave Henry a look, he shrugged his shoulders and I took off to the kitchen. This had the earmarks of an interesting saga.

In the kitchen, Livvie was talking to Timmy.

"This day we gone be busy as bees!" she said. "Susan! I want you to come with me and we gone lay out clothes for all y'all children to wear to the funeral home. Where the masking tape is?"

"What do we need masking tape for?" I asked.

"You mussy be joking with Livvie now. Don't you know you can't be having no kinda funeral without masking tape? Come on, girl. Let's get a move on."

I asked Timmy to take the water to Sophie and left the room with her.

"Sophie's talking," I said to Livvie.

"It's shock," she said.

"Probably," I said.

"I gots to tell you a little something."

I opened the door of the boys' closet and pulled out two shirts.

"What's up? How about these?"

"I seen something with my own eyes."

"What do you mean? 'Eah's two ties. This one has a spot."

"Sit down 'eah for a minute," she said, pointing to the bed.

"What?"

Livvie had the most peculiar look on her face.

"This morning when I came to work I was on the way out to the porch to sweep. Mr. Tipa done gone to the post office. Anyway, I seen something in the living room. It was a man."

"Who?"

"I didn't know at the time, but I'll tell you this much, you could pass your hand right through him!"

"What? A ghost?"

"Yes, ma'am. It was a haint as sure as any haint I ever seen in my whole life."

"Go on, Livvie, you're putting me on."

"No, ma'am, I am not! I was passing in the hall and I seen this cloud in the big mirror. Cloud grew, took the shape of a man and stepped out to greet me."

"Are you serious?"

"As serious as I can be."

"Tell me exactly what you saw," I said, not believing a word.

"This man come out the big mirror and he wearing a hat and a suit. I told him to go back to hell or wherever he came from and don't be bothering me or anybody in this family. I tell him we ain't throwing no party and what does he want anyhow? Then he point to a picture of your grandparents and I know exactly what he up to. He didn't come for no party, he come to snuff out your granddaddy's breath! That's what! I gots to do something about that mirror. Ain't no good. Ain't gone let another sun pass till I get some cunja on that thing."

"Livvie? I know you wouldn't lie to me, but I've never seen anything like that in my life."

"Humph. I seen all kind of fool thing in my day. Come on, get your dress and let's go on downstairs."

By four o'clock the day Tipa died, we had over fifty Corningware dishes in the kitchen filled with the specialties of every housewife on the Island. Livvie was in the kitchen and I was taking turns answering the door with Maggie.

"Oh! Mrs. Dufour! A ham! That's so nice of you!"

"How's your momma, honey?"

"She's all right, I guess, haven't seen her in a while."

"Well, let's not bother her. Listen, sweetie, that's my best platter, so please tell your momma I'll be needing it back next week."

"No problem, Mrs. Dufour. I'll put your name on the bottom on a piece of masking tape."

"That's a good girl."

I carried the ten pounds of pink meat down the hall past the big mirror in the living room and stopped to give it a look. Nothing. I didn't see a ripping thing.

"Another ham," I announced as I entered the kitchen.

"Do Jesus! That's ten hams now, twenty-two bowl of potato salad, six Jell-O molds with little marshmallows and chop pecan, three chocolate cake, seven pound cake, nine dish of red rice, four dish of chicken pilau and Lawd knows how many casseroles." Livvie shook her head as she took inventory. "Tape that dish and add she name to the list. Your momma gotta thank all these women. Gimme that thing and I cut the meat off the bone. Shuh. Gone get this family a dog, that's what. All these bone."

Livvie began to hum another church song. I pushed aside some of the dishes of food and put down the ham. The table threatened to collapse under the weight of all the food. Who was going to eat it all I couldn't figure out for the life of me.

"What's that song, Livvie?" Maggie asked.

"Oh, chile, it's my favorite, well, one of my favorites anyhow. It's 'Amazing Grace.' Listen up to these words," she said and began to sing in her rich voice.

"When we've been there ten thousand years,
Bright shining as the sun,
We've no less days to sing Gawd's praise,
Than when we'd first begun.

"Ain't them pretty words?" Livvie asked.

"Beautiful," I said. The same voice that hollered at us so loud, and hushed and composed us so sweetly, was one of the most wonderful and soulful singing voices I imagined I'd ever hear. Everything stood still while she sang.

"Makes me think about Mr. Tipa and how he be singing with Gawd's angels now," Livvie said. "I love that song 'cause it remind me that Gawd's grace is saving grace. It's for everybody, y'all know what I mean?"

Maggie said, "I don't know anybody who sings like you!"

"Oh, now do child, don't be filling my head with that fool. Honey, there's so many women who sing in my church you can't be counting them all."

"Sing something else!" I said.

"Honey, I sing all day long when y'all in school," Livvie said. "Makes the time go quick and I get to praise the Lawd with song. Not so bad, 'eah? Now, Miss Maggie, that's enough yabber about me. Let me see that list."

Maggie handed her the legal pad where she was noting who had brought what in her perfect Catholic school handwriting. I hated that she got to do all the writing, even keeping score in gin rummy or canasta.

"Where're the boys?" I asked.

"I send Timmy to the Asalits for the big cooler and Mr. Henry done gone off to the Red & White to get us some paper cups and ice. Gone be people coming tonight and tomorrow and unless you girls want to wash glasses and plates, we using the throw-away kind."

"Good idea," Maggie said.

"Yeah," I said. "Is Momma still in bed?"

"The doctor pay she a call earlier and he gone come back to check on her," Livvie said.

The translation of that was that the doctor had given her a shot for her nerves. We had two doctors who served the Island. One was Dr. Whicket, who mainly gave MC bazooka shots to induce coma, and the other was Dr. Duggan, who gave her pills that dilated her eyes and put her in a trance. We called them Stick-'em Whicket and Dose-'em Duggan.

"Stick-'em was here," Maggie said. "She's zonked."

The twins were napping and apparently Sophie the Stink Bomb was taking a real shower. Daddy and Uncle Louis were in Charleston, at the funeral home I guessed, probably picking out the box. And Livvie just kept cutting ham and making aluminum foil packages, stacking them up like silver bricks on a shelf in the refrigerator. We had four dozen deviled eggs. Two dozen from the postmaster's wife, Mary Burbage, along with a lemon meringue pie, and the others were from some old biddy who went to the same church that we did.

My real interest in all this was, of course, the wake and the funeral. "So, Livvie? Ever been to a wake?"

"Oh, do Lawd! More than I can remember, chile!"

"What's a dead person look like? I mean, when they're in the box and all, is it scary?"

"They look waxy to me. And, iffin you do look, you gone see your granddaddy ain't there nohow. Just he shell, that's all. Spirit gone. But remember you don't have to look iffin you don't want to. My cousin Harriet ain't never fix her eye on a dead man yet, and she done bury both she parent and one husband."

She stopped to demonstrate how to avoid contact with a dead body. "You juss fix your eye over that coffin when you goes up to pay your respect," she said, "and don't look down."

God, I love Livvie, she's such a rock, I thought. Somebody was knocking on the back door and I stepped outside to see who it was. Lo and behold, it was Alice Simpson, standing there with a jelly roll cake from the Red & White grocery store and six bottles of Coca-Cola.

"How's y'all's momma doing, honey?"

"She's fine, Mrs. Simpson. Thanks for the cake and the Cokes. Would you like some ham?"

"No thanks. When's the wake?"

"Dunno. Daddy's in the city making all the plans with Uncle Louis."

"Well, when you find out, let me know."

"Sure. Thanks again."

I watched her go down the back steps and through the oleanders, and somehow, she seemed sad to me. Maybe she didn't have any family. If she showed up at the funeral, though, there would be plenty of tongue-wagging. That would be reason to go early and stay late.

The next morning Maggie made ham biscuits, ham omelets, and ham and eggs. It was gonna be a while before we worked our way through the mountain of meat. I had changed the twins, given them bottles and brought them downstairs to their playpen. Too bad they didn't have teeth, I thought.

Daddy, Timmy and Henry were eating and talking. Momma had been in bed since the day before and Grandma Sophie still hadn't emerged from her room. I don't know if she was expecting room service, but we weren't waiting on her. A knocking preceded Uncle Louis's appearance at the back door.

"Hey, Bubba! You up?" he yelled through the screen.

"Yeah, God, Louis, come help us eat some of this. I swear to God, it's like an ancient Hawaiian ritual. One of the elders dies and a hundred pigs are slaughtered as an offering," Daddy said. "Get up, son, and let your uncle have your seat."

Timmy jumped up and put his plate in the sink, then poured a cup of coffee for Uncle Louis.

"Yeah, old Tipa gone on the layaway plan now," Uncle Louis said. "Gone to God. Sure seems odd, you know? How's my momma this morning? Where's the sugar bowl?"

"Here." Daddy slid the bowl across the table. "Shocked, of course, but actually rallying. She didn't stop talking yesterday."

Everything was slow motion and it was the unspoken that mattered. That Uncle Louis's sense of humor was out of place, that Daddy was comparing Tipa's death to Hawaii, that Momma was in hiding — all these things built a mountain of nervous anxiety. We children acted like Indians in the forest, quietly putting one foot in front of the other, moving in the shadows.

Livvie arrived, Henry disappeared with Timmy, and Daddy and Uncle Louis continued to talk.

"Where's your momma?" Livvie whispered to me as she tied her apron.

"Don't know. Haven't seen her yet," I said.

"Hm. 'Eah." She poured a cup of coffee. "You girls take this to her. Lemme do these dish and I come join you in a minute. Gotta get her up and moving. This ain't right a-tall. Been in that bed long enough."

The hall had never seemed so dark. Maggie led and I carried the cup, the fragile porcelain tinkling against the saucer. We opened the door carefully. Momma's curtains were drawn and we could see the silhouette of her figure under the covers of her bed. I had a bad feeling and Maggie's face didn't look very hopeful either.

"Momma?" I said. "I brought you some coffee."

No answer.

"Momma?" Maggie said. "It's time to get up."

I put the coffee down on her nightstand and began opening the curtains.

"Oh, God!" she wailed. "My daddy's dead! I can't!"

She scared the bejesus out of both of us.

Livvie entered the room. "Miss MC? Come on, now, you gots to rise up and face the day!"

"Can't!" came the mournful cry from under the tangled sheets. "Let me sleep!"

Livvie opened the rest of the curtains, flooding the room with light.

"Why couldn't it have been me instead of my daddy?" Momma cried.

"You girls go on now and leave me be with your momma. Bring me a wet washcloth, Maggie. Hurry up."

My numb legs couldn't follow Livvie's order to leave the room. I couldn't believe what my mother had just said, that she wanted to be dead. We were too much for her and I knew it. Six children, a mean husband, a crazy momma, a dead daddy, and only a Gullah woman to piece her back together. My heart sank.

Maggie returned with the cloth, handed it to Livvie and left the room, not seeing me.

"Miss MC, you 'eah me and 'eah me good. The Lawd never sends us nothing we can't handle. Every back fits the burden. You gots to buck up! 'Eah." She ran the washcloth across my mother's face. " 'Eah now. I knows you sad. We's all sad. Gone miss Mr. Tipa. He was a fine man, but Gawd call him and it ain't fitting for us to be asking Gawd why. No, ma'am, can't quizzit Gawd. Come on, now, drink your coffee and I get you a dress to put on. People been bringing food since yesterday and you need to pull yourself together. This house been crawling with neighbors bring cake and such. And so many hams! Oh, do Lawd! We could feed the army!"

"How many hams?" my mother said.

"The better part of twenty by now!"

I watched my mother raise herself up to a sitting position and reach for the coffee. Like my daddy said, she looked like something from the House of Horrors. "When Carol's daddy died, they got thirty," she said. "Coffee's cold."

"Day ain't over yet," Livvie said. "I gone make another pot."

"Susan! I didn't even see you there! Come give your momma a kiss."

She put her cup on the night table, extended her arms to me and sighed a sigh that sucked in the whole room and then blew it all away. Shakily, I leaned over her bed and kissed her on the cheek. She smelled like sweat and old perfume.

"Do you really wish you were dead, Momma?"

Livvie stopped moving and must have given her one of her famous looks because I saw my mother's eyes dart in her direction.

"No, honey. I'm just upset," she said.

I left the room and knew with every cell of my thirteen-and-one-half-year-old self that she was lying.

When anybody died on Sullivan's Island, the immediate world went to the wake, viewed the body, kissed the family, waited for the Knights of Columbus honor guards to come do their thing and then said the rosary with the family priest.

I had never been to one but I'd heard the stories about them for years. Everybody said what a good job the funeral home did on the deceased and how he looked just like he or she could just sit right up and talk to you. They went to wakes to wake the dead. Very funny.

Around nine o'clock, all the grown-ups would start twitching for a cocktail, and they'd go back to the house of the person who died and party until the wee hours, eating, drinking and telling hilarious stories about the deceased.

At four o'clock on the day of Tipa's wake, Livvie lined us up in the kitchen, fussed over our appearance and wet-combed Timmy's and Henry's cowlicks into obedience. She tucked in their shirts, pressed rosaries into their hands and straightened their neckties. Then she gave us all a good lecture on protocol.

"All right. 'Eah me good. I ain't gone be hearing no stories about y'all carrying on at the funeral home, am I? Y'all be dignify and keep yourself straight! Remember, this is for y'all's granddaddy, and every eye gone be on he grandchildren, watching to see iffin y'all behaving! Iffin y'all feels like crying, try to hold on till y'all get home. Then y'all come to me and we let it all go. Iffin y'all don't want look, don't do him. Just stare over the casket like Livvie showed y'all. Now, y'all ready?"

As far as the boys were concerned, she may as well have been talking to a pile of lumber, because within five minutes of arriving at the funeral home, they had their shirttails flying, and their sweaty faces were overheated and red. The boys ran the halls with the other children who were there. The poor man who ran the place, Mr. Wilbur, I think, kept asking them to quiet down, to respect the dead, but he didn't know who he was dealing with. The boys never even came in the viewing room, which was freezing cold to keep Tipa from melting, I figured.

I was in the back of the room with Maggie, talking to Mr. Struthers and half of the Island, just yakking my head off about school and things like that, enjoying the macabre celebrity that death brought, when I spotted Mrs. Alice Simpson signing the "Book of the Dead" at the door. She looked downright respectable, in a blazer and skirt, unlike anything I'd ever seen her in.

Every head turned when she came in, and she refused to make eye contact with anyone and she went directly to my mother's side.

I could hear the old guard sucking their breath in. I knew that if somebody didn't exhale soon every flower in the room would be wilted. I wasn't about to miss one bit of this, so I followed on her heels.

Mrs. Simpson knelt by my mother.

"MC, your daddy was such a nice man," she said. "I'm so sorry for your loss."

"Thank you, Alice. Thank you for coming."

"My daddy died when I was sixteen. Suicide."

Silence from Momma.

"You've been very lucky to have had your daddy for so long," Alice said, her face starting to quiver.

"You're right, yes, you're right."

"My momma left my little brother and me the next year and I never saw her again. Then my brother died in Vietnam last year."

Finally, my mother looked at her square in the face.

"Alice! I never knew that. I'm so sorry."

To the complete astonishment of the entire universe, Momma and Alice started hugging each other and the next thing you knew, Momma invited her over later for a drink. Holy moly, I thought, holy moly. Sullivan's Island would be there in droves tonight when this got around. Poor Mrs. Simpson. Who knew?

Alice stood up, squeezed my mother's hand, blotted the corners of her eyes with a tissue and walked out.

The din in the room gradually grew back to such a level that you'd have thought they *would* wake up Tipa. The Knights of Columbus honor guards had arrived. It was the parting of the Red Sea as the crowd allowed them in. Six men wearing solemn black tuxedos, chapeaux with enormous plumage (which looked to me like Napoleon's hat), capes, gloves and swords approached the casket. I could almost hear my own heartbeat it was so quiet. I had worked my way to the back of the room. I wasn't too thrilled about getting stuck next to the casket with Tipa in it and my mother acting like the leading actress from *The Night of the Living Dead.* Momma seemed to be luxuriating in her bath of tears, tremors and grief, her chair faced away from the casket, as she had adamantly refused to look at her father's corpse.

I followed the lead of the others as they made the Sign of the Cross and began to say the rosary. It seemed like we said two thousand Hail Marys and then it was over. The honor guard filed out and people began saying good night to Momma and Grandma Sophie.

"Now, MC honey, if there's anything we can do, just call me, okay?"

"Mrs. Asalit, I knew Tipa all my life. I'm gonna miss him. Such a lovely man."

"Thank you. Thank you for coming."

The crowd had dwindled down to the twenty or thirty diehards who would no doubt follow us home. I hoped there was a doctor or a bartender among them because Momma needed a shot of something.

"Time to go, MC," my father said to my mother. Her face showed total bewilderment. "Do you want to say good-bye to your daddy? I'll help you, MC, come on, I'll stand with you."

It was the single most decent thing I'd ever seen my father do. He knew that Momma couldn't accept her father's death, but if she'd see it, maybe it would help her come to terms with it.

He helped her to her feet and she was shaking all over. I held my breath as she turned. She knelt on the white leather prie-dieu and Daddy stood behind her. My mother began to weep and wail like nothing I'd ever heard. I could see that Grandma Sophie was furious. Momma just kept going on and on, weeping like a baby. It was horrible and endless. Finally, she slowed to gulping sobs and I realized I was crying too. I looked around to find Maggie, Timmy and Henry, and all of them were crying. The remaining guests waited in sympathy at a distance.

Grandma Sophie stood up from her chair and went to Momma's side. "It's time to go now, Marie Catherine," she said, not very nicely.

Daddy stepped to Momma's other side and together they helped her get up. Momma leaned over the casket and kissed her father tenderly on the forehead.

"Good-bye, Daddy," she said.

Daddy put his arm around her and led her out, with Grandma Sophie on his other arm. She'll never get over this, I thought, never. I was getting plenty upset.

"Can you believe Mrs. Simpson showed up?" Maggie whispered to me on the way home in Aunt Carol and Uncle Louis's car. "Everybody said she had some nerve coming in there like she belonged with decent people."

"Shut up, Maggie," I said, loud enough for the grown-ups to hear me, "you don't know what the hell you're talking about."

No one said a word after that. We rode over the bridge in silence.

Morning light brought the sound of Livvie's voice raised in yet another song I'd never heard.

From down in the yard the deep velvety sound grew like the glow of a warm fire as she approached the house.

"Free at last! Free at last!
Thank Gawd I free at last!
Way down yonder in the graveyard walk,
gone meet my Jesus and we gone talk,
On my knees when the light pass by,
thought my soul would rise and fly!"

I hurried out of bed, grabbed a robe and checked the alarm clock. Seven-thirty. She was very early. When I got to the kitchen I found her decked out in what I imagined to be her Sunday best, including a felt hat with a feather on the side.

"Morning, Miss Susan. Everybody still sleeping?"

"Yeah, I guess so. Gosh, Livvie, you look so nice! You're so early!"

"Yeah, chile. What you think, that I ain't got no nice clothes? Humph."

"No, I didn't mean that."

"Good thing I slice up all that ham yesterday," she said. "Now we all organized for after the cemetery. Had my nephew drive me today. Figure this family gone need all the hands they can get today."

"Yeah," I said, looking in the cabinet for the corn flakes. I dumped some in a bowl and listened to her go on.

"Yeah, Gawd, Mr. Tipa done rise and fly. You know, I figure it ain't so bad to die. When I go I get to be with my Nelson and be with Jesus, my king.

Humph, someday this old woman gone get she reward for all the dishes she wash for the white people. Shuh, so many dish!"

I was crunching away at spoonfuls of banana and cereal. God only knew what the day would bring. This was my first funeral.

"No, sir, got to put on my good church clothes and help this family," Livvie continued. "They got trouble today. I think, everybody in this house might be crazy but I sure do love y'all children."

"I love you too, Livvie. This whole family would go to hell in a handbasket if it weren't for you."

"True enough. When I think back on the wake yesterday I says to myself, Livvie? There ain't nothing wrong with them children, it's them grown-ups. Did you see your grandmomma all dressed up and talking like she ain't got nothing wrong with her? Well, I tells you a little something, she ain't got nothing wrong. We can't be catering to her iffin we want her to get back to living. Your momma either. Shuh! No, sir, no more catering."

"You're right," I said.

"Yeah, Gawd, old Mr. Tipa done rise up and fly!"

Over the next few minutes, the Island Gamble came alive with people coming downstairs. Livvie was scrambling a dozen eggs with chopped ham and onions. She had the apron on over her dress and her hat was still on too. Coffee was perking, dishes rattled and the day began.

Daddy, Timmy and Henry each took a plate from her and went to the porch to eat. The kitchen table and the dining room table were still covered in cakes and platters. Uncle Louis and Aunt Carol showed up like they had a reservation for two and Livvie turned to greet them.

"Morning!" she said. "Y'all want some coffee?"

Aunt Carol sized up Livvie in her dress and hat and said, "Why, Livvie. Are you going somewhere?"

"Sure enough, I figure that Miss MC gone be needing a hand with them twins in the church so I put on my best dress for Mr. Tipa," she said. "I stay at home with the babies last night, but today I gone pay my respect."

"Really?" Aunt Carol said, as though the word had five syllables.

"I'm sure my sister will appreciate it," Uncle Louis said, and tried to change the subject. "Where's my brother-in-law?"

"He gone to the porch with the boys to eat. Y'all want some eggs?"

"No, thanks, come on, Carol," he said and left the room with her in tow.

"I'm going to get dressed," Maggie said.

Silence.

"Aunt Carol stuffs her bra," I said to Livvie.

Another silence.

"She does. And you should see how she acts around Mr. Struthers. She talks to him like they're naked." It was the best I had to offer.

I saw Livvie's shoulders shaking and thought she was crying. To my complete surprise, she turned to me laughing, slapping her thighs. The most dignified woman I knew dissolved into an old country girl when she laughed.

"Honey chile, when a body been colored as long as me, you get used to all kind of fool. I know I shouldn't gossip with you, but what you think? Think she trying to set all the cock to crowing in the church today? Oh, Lawsy, chile, that woman ain't nothing but goat-meat buckra! Buckra is low-class white folks, honey, and she don't bother me! I gone to feed and dress them babies now. We gots to get a move on today."

"I'll come help you," I said. I got two bottles from the refrigerator. "I'll warm these up and be there in a minute."

"Thanks, Susan."

While I waited for the water to simmer in the pot, warming the formula for my little sisters, I thought about my aunt. What a sorry-ass excuse of a woman she was. I could tell she stuffed her bra by the way she moved. I tested the milk on my arm, decided it was warm enough and went to find Livvie. I followed the sound of her voice to Momma's room and bumped smack-dab into them arguing.

"But Livvie! You're . . . you're not Catholic! You want to come to my church?"

"You mean I'm colored."

"Well, yes. I mean, I don't want you to be embarrassed, that's all," Momma said.

"You mean *you* don't want to be embarrassed. You worry what people gone say, right?"

"Livvie!" Momma said.

"Well, they might say that Gawd made my skin and He knows what He's doing, that's what! Miss MC, I quit. I gone work for today, but that's all. I sorry for you today, but I can't be working no more for somebody who don't welcome me in Gawd's house. Jesus died for everyone, not just you."

She pushed by me and almost ran to the twins' room. I chased her to the stairs and passed Daddy at the front door.

"What's up?" he said.

"Livvie quit," I whispered.

"Oh, no!" he said and for the second time in two minutes, I almost got knocked off my feet by a grown-up. When I got to the twins' room, Daddy closed the door in my face. I could hear Livvie's angry tears and I wanted to kill my mother for making her cry like that. She sounded like her heart was breaking. I pressed my ear to the door and heard almost every word.

"That's right," I heard her say.

"Please, don't . . ." Daddy said.

"Only if . . ." she said.

"How much?"

"That's right," she replied.

Silence.

The door opened.

"Women!" Daddy said, shaking his head, passing me unnoticed.

I went into the room and Livvie had my twin sisters' dresses standing up on the bed. She must've spent hours starching and ironing every ruffle.

"Ain't they cute?" Livvie said, smiling at me.

"Yeah. What happened?" I asked.

"Just a little 'come to Jesus' meeting with your daddy, that's all. Everything is fine. I gone go to the church with y'all and then we gone have a party for Mr. Tipa to beat the band!"

"But I thought you said that you were quitting."

"Listen up to me, chile, your momma and your aunt might be narrow-minded old buckra bigots, but I am the richest housekeeper and nurse on this Island!"

"Another raise?"

"Yes, ma'am! Ten dollars a week! I make them *pay* for they sins!"

12

Hank

1963

It was a Sunday and Livvie's day off, two weeks before Thanksgiving. There was a dance at the CYO club down the Island in the church hall and we all wanted to go — Maggie, Timmy and I. Henry was still too little. We asked Momma for permission and she answered through her haze of antidepressants that she guessed so. She practically lived in her bed, with frequent visits from Dose-'em and Stick-'em.

Maggie had washed her hair and I was covering my pimples with tiny dabs of makeup, which I was forbidden to wear. Maggie was meeting Lucius Pettigrew at the dance, her new boyfriend from Charleston, and she was out of her mind with excitement. I only hoped somebody would look at me. Maybe ask me to dance? I loved to dance and I'd dance with almost anybody, except my brothers, of course.

"Just what in the hell do you think you're doing?" Daddy's angry words bombed the house. He'd been in a foul mood all day, grumbling and complaining about everything. Spoiling for a fight.

Maggie and I just looked at each other. We became very quiet and the next thing we heard was Timmy screaming in terror from the bathroom down the hall.

"Please, Daddy! Don't beat me! Please, Daddy!"

I felt like I was going to throw up. I could hear Timmy crying as the belt cracked across his back. Daddy hit him five times with all his might and then stormed downstairs. I went to Timmy right away, Maggie in my trail. I passed the top of the steps and saw my mother sitting at the bottom, whimpering. She would do nothing about it. I looked at her and she looked away. She was terrified of Daddy when he was like this. I was too furious to be terrified.

Timmy was slumped over, sitting on the toilet, head in his hands, crying. His nose was running and his face was flaming red. I started crying, covering my mouth. Maggie was frozen at the door.

"Please don't cry, Timmy," I said. "Oh, please don't cry. I'll help you."

"He really hurt me, Susan. It really hurts."

I lifted the hem of his shirt and his back had wide welts all over it, rising in blisters.

"Maggie, go get some ice," I said.

Speechless, Maggie quickly went down to the kitchen. I took a hand towel and soaked it in cold water.

"Take off your shirt," I told him, "it's not that bad. If we put some ice on it, it'll feel a lot better."

"I hate his stinking guts."

I twisted out the towel and as he leaned over the sink I spread the cool cloth across his bony back. "I hate his stinking guts too," I said.

"I'd like to kill him."

"Me too. Timmy, I swear to God, one of these days we'll get even with him. And one of these days we'll get out of here." I wet another cloth and twisted it out. "I know we will. We just have to stick together and not let Daddy catch us doing anything to make him mad." Though that answer didn't seem right to me.

Maggie came back with a bowl of ice and a linen towel.

"Come on, Timmy, you can lie down on my bed and we'll fix you up," I said.

We went into my room and Timmy laid himself across my quilt. I took the towel and wrapped some cubes in it and then decided to make ice water and soak the towels in the bowl. Maggie brought some water in the bathroom glass. Timmy began to cry again, this time quietly, hopelessly.

"I love you, Timmy," Maggie said.

"I love you too, Timmy," I said. "It doesn't matter, Timmy, we'll take care of you." And we wrung out the towels again in the ice water and spread them on his back.

"Why doesn't Momma stop him?" he whispered.

"I don't know," I said, "I guess she figures that if she gets involved, it'll be worse."

"Get down here, all of you!" It was Daddy screaming from the bottom of the stairs. Quickly, Timmy jumped up and dried his eyes. Maggie and I just looked at each other but we knew we had to be quick or there could be more trouble. Daddy was standing alone on the porch, waiting for us, holding three empty brown grocery bags.

"So, your mother tells me she gave y'all permission to go out tonight. Is that true?"

"Yes, sir," we all answered together.

"Pardon me! I thought I was the head of this house!"

We said nothing. I wisely looked at the floor. Timmy cleared his throat.

"Did you have something to say about that, Mr. Timmy? Would you like the belt again?"

"No, Daddy, no. I was just clearing my throat. Honest. You're the head of the house, Daddy. We all know that."

Thick silence — like low pressure before a storm.

"Well, as long as that's understood for the moment, I'd like y'all to do something to prove y'all won't forget."

"Sure," I said.

"No problem," Maggie said.

"I won't forget, Daddy," Timmy said.

Daddy looked at Timmy and for a moment I thought he was going to hit him. But, in spite of the sarcasm and anger in his voice, he held his temper.

"The yard's full of nut grass. Do y'all know what nut grass is?"

"No, sir," I said.

"I don't think so," Maggie said.

"Yes, sir, I think I know what it is."

"Oh! Albert Einstein! Why don't you tell your sisters what it is?"

Timmy began to stutter. He hadn't done that since he was really little. "It's that skinny green gr-gr-gr-grass that has a r-r-root on the b-b-b-bottom of it that looks like a n-n-nut."

"That's r-r-r-r-ight, s-s-s-on," he said. "And here's a bag for you, and a bag for you, and a bag for you. When you've filled them all with nut grass, connected to its r-r-r-roots, come see me and *I'll* decide who's going out! Not your mother! Is that clear?"

We all nodded our heads.

"I can't *hear* you!" He put his hand to the side of his head and cupped an ear.

"Yes, sir!" we all said.

"Then get moving, on the double!" he screamed.

They can hear you in Goose Creek, I thought. God, he had a big mouth. We went down to the yard and began the impossible job of filling a bag with nut grass. It was five o'clock in the afternoon and getting chilly. We picked for a while, but it wasn't long before we realized it would be dark before we could fill our bags. Timmy started crying again. Next, Maggie started crying. Her hopes of meeting Lucius were shattered. I just got madder and madder.

"He's a no-good son of a bitch," I said to Timmy.

"No shit," he answered.

"It's not right," Maggie said.

"That's the understatement of the year," I said. "One of these days, he'll get his, and the sooner the better."

"Why not today?" Timmy said. "Why don't we just hold him down and beat the shit out of him? Let him see how it feels!"

"Oh, sure! Daddy weighs about two hundred

pounds. He'd rip off my arm and beat me to a pulp with it," I said.

"Don't even talk about that kind of thing. Y'all scare me," Maggie said.

"I've had it," Timmy said, "I'd like to kill him. I'll spend the next twenty years in a jail. I don't care! 'cause you know what? If I don't kill him, he's gonna kill me!"

He might be right, I thought. Daddy seemed capable of anything. Then we heard the screen door slam and stopped talking. Mr. Horrible came down the steps with a Budweiser in his hand and a big smirk on his face. He kept cracking the sides of the can. He looked in Maggie's bag and then in mine.

"Nice job, Maggie, you make your daddy proud. Hope you don't ruin your manicure."

She said nothing, but fought back a second brimming burst of angry tears.

"Oh, Susan! What have we here! Half full! Maybe when you grow up you can get a job picking tomatoes with the migrant workers! A natural talent!"

It didn't matter what he said. He was a stranger, an imposter. There had been a horrible mistake made at the hospital when each of us was born. It was obvious to me that we'd been switched with Satan's children.

"And how's my sissy boy doing picking weeds?" Daddy said, leaping from sarcasm to poison.

My stomach lurched and Timmy's face went from the white paste of hopelessness to a young warrior. He flew at Daddy's face with his fists clenched. Daddy dropped his beer and lost his balance. He recovered and turned to Timmy.

"Come on, you little queer! If you think you can take your old man, come on and try. You're nothing but a girl anyway."

"You suck, do you know that? You've got no right and no reason to call me that."

Timmy began to fight for his life. He was not Daddy's equal. Daddy threw him to the ground and in one great whirling motion sat on Timmy's stomach, pinning his arms.

"No!" I screamed. "No!"

Daddy slapped Timmy hard and then backhanded him, jerking Timmy's head from side to side like a rag doll again and again. Timmy got one arm free from under Daddy's legs, and he balled his fist and landed a weak punch in Daddy's stomach. Maggie started screaming and screaming, and tried to pull Daddy off. He swung around and knocked her off her feet. She landed on the ground with a thud.

I couldn't bear another minute. I couldn't stand there and let him kill my brother. It had to stop. I saw a low branch, dangling by a thread from a tree. I don't know where I found the strength, but I pulled it free from the vines that covered it, swung it around and cracked Daddy but good. Blood gushed from the wound in the side of Daddy's head. He fell sideways to the ground and just lay there, still. Inanimate. I felt the breeze cool the heat of my face. I heard my breath as my heart raced. I dropped the branch.

It took a moment to realize what I had just done. I looked from Maggie to Timmy. We were all terrified that he was dead, or, worse, that he wasn't.

"Oh, my God!" Maggie screamed.

"Shut up and think! Is he breathing?" I said.

Timmy's lip was split and his shirt was covered in blood. He rolled over the grass and checked Daddy's breath.

"He's alive."

"What are we gonna do?" Maggie said.

"We'd better get the hell out of here," I said.

"Where?" Timmy said.

"Aunt Carol, let's go to her house," Maggie said. "If we tell her and Uncle Louis, maybe they can make it right for us."

"No way in hell I'm going there," I said.

"Why not?" Maggie asked.

"Because! That's why!"

"Then *where,* Miss Genius! Do you realize what Daddy's going to do to you when he wakes up?"

Maggie was scared out of her wits. So was I. She was right. This whole incident was beyond reason. Unless we got help, we were all as good as dead. We were already in enough trouble.

"Marvin Struthers. I'm going down to Mr. Struthers. He'll help."

"He thinks we're awful! He won't help us!" Timmy said.

"Look, he's the mayor and all this bullshit has got to stop!"

I don't know where I found the words, but they were true. We left our father lying on the ground and sprinted toward the Struthers's house.

When Mrs. Struthers opened the door and saw us, she nearly fainted. Mr. Struthers called the police to check on Daddy and haul him over to the emergency room if he needed it. I thought it odd that he told the policeman not to disturb Momma but just to get Hank away from the house. He sat us down with a Coca-Cola each. He cleaned up Timmy and put ice on his swollen face and eye. Like a grandfather, he listened to the story of what drove us to do this to our father.

"I couldn't take it anymore, Mr. Struthers," Timmy said.

"I understand, son. But y'all know a child should never raise a hand against their parents, don't you?"

"Yes, sir, I know that, but you don't know what it's like for us, for me especially."

"He's not lying, Mr. Struthers. Look at his back," I said.

Timmy stood up and raised the back of his shirt. The welts were deep red now and Mr. Struthers let out a low whistle.

"Why'd he do this to you, Timmy?"

"I was using one of his deodorant pads to shine my shoes," Timmy answered. "We were going to the dance at the church and my shoes needed shining. I know I shouldn't have done it."

"That's all you did?"

"Yes, sir."

"I was there, Mr. Struthers, so was Susan. He's telling the truth," Maggie said. "It's always like this for Timmy, and not much better for us."

Mr. Struthers raised his eyebrows and sighed again. I understood the expulsion of so much breath to be an expression of his understanding and vindication for us.

"If we go home and he's there, he's gonna finish us off like a tomato sandwich!" I said this as emphatically as I could so he'd comprehend the depth of our trouble.

"Does y'all's momma know y'all're 'eah?"

"No, sir. We just took off running once we knew Daddy wasn't dead," Timmy said.

"Momma's in bed anyhow. Sleeps all the time," I said.

"Why's that?" Mr. Struthers asked.

"Guess she's tired or something," I said.

I wasn't about to tell the world that both of our parents were crazy. Besides, I didn't want to embarrass Momma.

"Well, let's get y'all home. I'll stay there and talk to y'all's daddy. Don't worry, nobody gonna hurt y'all chillrun ever again or I'm not the mayor of this Island. Let's go now."

We didn't budge an inch.

"What's wrong?" he asked.

Silence from the choir.

"I'm telling y'all, it's gonna be all right! Now, trust me, okay? I've been knowing y'all's daddy since before y'all were born. I *know* him! If I tell him to keep his hands off of y'all, he *will!* Understand?"

We nodded.

"All right, then, let's go. It's getting late and y'all's momma is gonna be worried sick about y'all."

I rolled my eyes at Maggie and, for once, she rolled hers back in agreement.

Mr. Struthers led the way up our back steps. Maybe Daddy was afraid of Mr. Struthers; after all, he was the biggest man on the Island. That was a comforting thought, the first one I'd had in a while.

"Go tell y'all's momma I'm here."

Maggie went to tell Momma, Timmy sank into a chair at the kitchen table and I opened the refrigerator. My first inclination was to stay with Timmy and Mr. Struthers. I'd do my duty and feed them.

"Mr. Struthers? Would you like a beer or some tea? Timmy? Do y'all want a sandwich?"

"Sure. Whatever you have is fine, Susan. Thanks."

Mr. Struthers took a chair at the table. He was preoccupied with what he would say to Momma and, most likely, to Daddy when he got back from the emergency room. The whole situation had to be stunning to him. It was to me. I felt like Jell-O inside. I wondered if I could get arrested for attempted murder or assault and battery. It didn't matter because there was nothing I could do about it. The deed was done. I had knocked my own father out cold with the branch of a tree. Jesus Christ. I still couldn't believe I had done it. My life could be over, I thought, it could be over and I could wind up in some horrible juvenile detention center until I'm old enough to go to the state penitentiary. At least Timmy would be there with me, but probably in a boys' center. I'd never even see him.

I took out some boiled ham, iceberg lettuce, half a tomato and the mayonnaise and began making sandwiches. If I kept busy I didn't have to think so much and maybe I could show Mr. Struthers that I had promise beyond the jailhouse.

Timmy fixed his eyes on the sugar bowl in the center of the table and he just kept shaking his head back and forth.

I put two plates in front of them and made a new

ice pack for Timmy's eye. My mind wasn't screaming but plotting the next move, trying to guess how this game would play itself out. Maggie returned with Momma. Momma took one look at Timmy, whimpered and the automatic tears flowed like the Cooper River.

"What's happened? Oh, my God, what's happened to you, Timmy? Tell me!"

She leaned over Timmy and kissed the top of his head. He resisted her attempt to remove the ice pack. She stood back with some indignation and realized the mayor was sitting at her kitchen table eating a ham sandwich and drinking tea. The fog in her eyes seemed to clear.

"Marvin! What's going on here?" she said.

Over the next few minutes the details of the incident were laid before our mother. She claimed not to have heard a blessed thing. She never heard Daddy beat Timmy. She said she didn't know. She never heard him order us out to the yard. She never heard Daddy, Timmy, Maggie and me screaming. She said this was highly unusual. She never heard the patrol car arrive and take Daddy away. She had no knowledge that Daddy was at the emergency room.

Momma seemed shocked and surprised by what she was hearing. At first I thought she was lying to Mr. Struthers. But I realized that the truth about her husband was so terrible that she couldn't hear it or make sense of it. If she never told anyone or interfered with our father's violence, perhaps it didn't exist. And Mr. Struthers's presence violated her perfect imaginary world. Now Mr. Struthers knew the truth.

Mr. Struthers went on saying, as nicely as possible, that taking care of her children and her mother were probably too much for her, but that she still had a responsibility to us. Even though the burden, on such a delicate and refined lady, was overwhelming.

"What are you telling me, Marvin?"

"I'm telling you that Hank can't do this to his children. In the least case, it ain't right. In the eyes of the law, it's criminal behavior."

"Criminal!"

"Yes, MC, criminal. Child abuse. It's against the law."

She reached in the drawer and took out a pack of cigarettes. I'd never seen my mother smoke.

"What am I supposed to do, Marvin? Tell me that!"

"That's why I'm here, MC. I've been knowing you all my life. I know what you can face up to and what you can't. I'm gonna talk to him."

She inhaled and exhaled a billowing cloud from her Salem 100. The smoke was sucked up to the ceiling fan, dispersing itself into nothingness. She had to choose. Either she would take Daddy's side or ours. In her classic bob-and-weave fashion, she chose neither.

She told Timmy to go lie down. She sent Maggie to get Henry and the twins from Aunt Carol's, where they had been for the day, playing with her pack of dogs. She ignored me, probably furious that I had had the nerve to protect her child against her husband. Or maybe she was glad. I couldn't tell.

I poured her some tea and refilled Mr.

Struthers's glass. He asked for the newspaper and began to read while Momma fidgeted, finally announcing she was going upstairs to change from her bathrobe into a dress or something. She had at least realized that it was unusual for a normal person to be in her nightgown at seven in the evening.

Soon Maggie came back with the twins and Henry, who immediately ran for his room. Maggie heated up two bottles for Sophie and Allie, announced she was going to put the twins to bed and said she was going to bed herself. I stayed in the background until I heard Daddy coming up the back steps. As fast as I could, I hid myself in the hall closet.

It was hard to hear from behind all the coats, which muffled their voices, but I heard enough to know that Mr. Struthers bought us some time. He explained the difference between normal discipline and child abuse to Daddy and Momma. Every time Daddy raised his voice to object, Mr. Struthers would calmly ask Daddy if he'd prefer to settle this dispute in court. Every time Momma would try to defend Daddy, probably out of fear for her own safety, Marvin would remind her of the definition of negligence. I was too young to understand the implications of all that he said, but I was old enough to know we would all be safer for a while. The most frightening thing of all was that I had to be protected from my momma and daddy. It filled me with shame.

As the house became quiet, I must've fallen asleep in the warmth of the closet. I didn't know how I got to my bed that night until I found one of my grandmother's hairpins in my bed. Bless her heart, I remember thinking, how did that poor old skinny bag of bones get me up the stairs and how had she found me?

After school on Monday, I ran from the school bus ahead of everyone and told Livvie what Daddy had done to Timmy and what we did to Daddy and how he got twenty-seven stitches in his head. I'd never seen her so angry. She began to iron with a vengeance, pushing the flat bottom of the iron into the clothes with all her strength, her lips set in a straight, hard line.

"Are you angry with me, Livvie?"

"Not one bit. Go on get Timmy in 'eah to me," she said.

Something in the back of her voice prompted me to drop my books on the table and run for Timmy. I brought him back, she put the iron on the resting plate and stood up from her stool. First, she stared at his black eye and bruised face.

"Pull up your shirt, boy," she said and he did it at once.

He turned around and she saw the welts.

"Ain't right. My granddaddy died with whipping scars on he back. This ain't right." The sight of his back kindled a powerful feeling down deep inside of her. Her breathing wasn't regular. Her nostrils flared as she stared at my brother's back. She let go of an enormous breath and, gently, she reached out and laid her hand across his skin. Her hand traveled each red mark, registering its length and width. Timmy didn't flinch. She moved her hand on Timmy's eye and jaw.

"Still hurt, son?" she said to him.

"Not now. It's alright now, Livvie."
"Ain't alright. Ain't alright nohow."
The wipe of her beautiful, long, dark fingers had taken away Timmy's pain. Timmy was healed, but now Livvie carried the wound. She hardened toward my father in a declaration of war.
She was very serious about protecting us. "Chillrun be Gawd's gift, ain't no doubt about that, no sir," she'd say to us over and over. We'd never know for sure, but I thought she would've done anything to shield us from Daddy. And, in a karmic twist of fate, within days Daddy needed shielding himself.
Daddy caught the devil from the president of the board of education for Charleston County. I heard Big Hank telling Momma that he'd been called in and told to scratch the cafeteria and heating in the school he was building and that the basketball courts and library were a waste of energy and money.
Daddy was disgusted. He took a lot of pride in his work. He may have been horrible to us, but he believed in education and equal opportunity for everyone. Just because no other black school in the state had those things, did that mean they never should? Daddy said that maybe it was time for them to raise the standard of facilities anyway. And apparently this guy told Daddy to mind his own business and do what he was told. But you couldn't tell Hank Hamilton something like that. Oh, no.
He and his crew continued the building his way, not altering one thumbtack of the plans. Although I had every reason to despise him, I had to give him

some due for having the courage to match his convictions. I wished he cared half as much about us.

Monday of that week, he went to work in the morning and found crosses burned into the grass and equipment smashed to pieces. It was the trademark of the Klan and the worst damage done to his work site so far. He continued anyway. On Tuesday, he was nearly run off the road into the marsh coming home late from work. He seemed to be coming home later and later, but that was of no concern to us. When he wasn't around, our home was almost a normal home. At least we felt the antics of Sophie and Momma were tolerable.

Unafraid and determined, he returned to work. Two days later, someone fired gunshots from the beach through our front windows in the middle of the night. By the grace of God, we were all asleep or someone could've easily been killed. The morning after that, Daddy tried to reassure us by saying that if they had really intended to kill somebody, they would've fired the shots at suppertime. That opinion did little to calm Momma's nerves and, as usual, she went to bed, leaving us to care for Sophie and the twins and leaving Livvie to plan our Thanksgiving meal.

That Friday morning President Kennedy was assassinated in Texas. Sister Angela, my history teacher, was called out of our class by Father O'Brien. When she returned she was crying.

"The president has been shot," she said.

The janitor rolled in a television and the sixth and seventh graders came in the room to watch the news with us. Then an announcement came over the public-address system for us to pack our things for the day and report to chapel. The whole student body filed in the little church and Father O'Brien led a special Mass for our slain president and his family and for the sins of the world. After that, school was called off for the day. We were put on buses and taken home.

We rode in silence, Miss Fanny leading us in the rosary and for once, we all prayed with her. There was no laughing, teasing or cutting of any kind of fool. We were children who could no longer believe that good always triumphed over evil. Sometimes evil won.

Livvie was in the kitchen when we came in. Her eyes were red and I could see that she'd been crying too. Momma and Grandma Sophie were in bed, overcome with grief. It was a terrible day. The only excitement came from the newspapers and the evening news as we all tried to understand why someone would want to kill our president. We decided it was the Communists.

I heard Uncle Louis and Daddy that night discussing the Bay of Pigs fiasco and the Cuban Missile Crisis. They were sitting in the kitchen when the lawman of the Island arrived. Fat Albert's car pulled up in our backyard. I hemmed and hawed, wiping the counters down over and over, hanging around to try to find out why he was there, but no such luck.

"Go see if your momma wants anything, Susan," Daddy said.

"Yes, sir," I said.

I waited until Fat Albert's patrol car left and went back to the kitchen to make Momma some hot tea. Daddy and Uncle Louis looked up at me and stopped talking.

"She wants hot tea. I'll be out of here in a moment."

They looked at each other and then at me.

"Are we in trouble?" I said.

"No, Albert just wanted to warn me again about my building project, that's all. He's afraid that there might be more trouble, with the president being shot and all," Daddy said. "He was just here out of friendly concern."

I knew Daddy was lying to me about that but I didn't know why.

It was the day before Thanksgiving, and we had a half-day of school. At Livvie's urging, Maggie and I planned to go window-shopping on King Street in Charleston. She said we needed to have some fun. We appreciated time off from the "slice-and-dice club" that preceded an elaborate holiday meal.

Ever since the incident with Timmy, and the death of the president, Livvie had been very quiet. It was as though she preferred to be left alone just to do her work. She had barely spoken to Daddy since then either, just giving him the hairy eyeball if he passed her.

In any case, Maggie and I looked forward to a day of no chores. I took the bus from Mount Pleasant over to the city and met her. We had no homework because of the holiday, so we were able to enjoy the walk without our usual load of books. We passed by all the windows on King Street, pretending to buy whatever we wanted with imaginary money. It was great fun. Maggie had a wonderful innate sense about fashion. She began to choose things for me, and after the first dozen or so dresses she pointed out, I began to see why certain things would flatter my telephone pole figure and others wouldn't.

"Accentuate what you've got going for yourself," she said. "See that blue sweater? It's the same color as your eyes."

"I know you're right. God, I wish we had some money and could go into a store and buy something."

"Yeah. I'm gonna start baby-sitting more. You should do that too. I've got fifty-seven dollars in my Band-Aid box."

"Shoot! You're rich! Let's spend it!" I was thrilled.

"I didn't bring it with me for exactly that reason. I'm gonna save up to one hundred and then spend half."

"You're so damn practical, Maggie."

"Susan, please! That mouth of yours!"

"Forget my mouth, will ya? You're right! I should start babysitting! I'm old enough!"

"Listen to your big sister, sweet pea. If you're old enough to knock the daylights out of Daddy, you'd have no problem handling a bunch of toddlers."

We started laughing. It was such a relief to laugh. The first few chortles sounded rusty, but then we got on key.

"Hey, you want to go get an ice-cream cone?"

We had a couple of dollars and decided to go to Woolworth's lunch counter and give ourselves a small treat. We pushed open the large glass doors and right in front of us was a huge display of hundreds of boxes of Whitman's Samplers. We stopped in our tracks.

"What do you think?" I asked. "Should we buy a box and eat the whole thing ourselves?"

"Susan Hamilton, we'd be sick as dogs. Hey, you know what?"

"What?"

"We should buy a box for Livvie to have for her Thanksgiving."

"Boy! She'd love that! Maybe that'll cheer her up. How much are they?"

We looked at the price stickers. The large box was seven dollars and the small box was three dollars. We calculated that we could buy her the large box, if we skipped the ice cream and used our bus fare. We'd have to walk to Daddy's office down on Broad Street and ask for a ride home with him. No doubt it would aggravate him if we showed up, but we decided it would be worth it, given all that Livvie had done for us.

"This was a great idea," I said to Maggie, leaving the store.

"Thanks," she said. "I guarantee you this will snap Livvie out of that mood of hers. I mean, what if she got so sick of the craziness in our family that she quit? What would happen to us?"

"Don't even think it."

We made our way down the street, passing the dozens of small antique stores, the Riviera movie theater and the boarded-up, vacant buildings. We reached the corner of King and Broad Streets and turned left to reach Daddy's office.

"You know," Maggie said, "he hasn't hardly spoken a word to us since the fight. We didn't call him or anything, Susan. He might not even be there. Then what would we do? We don't have bus fare!"

"Stop worrying. If he's not there we can hitch-hike home."

"One of these days you're gonna get yourself killed."

"Seriously, we can call Aunt Carol. She'll come get us."

"I don't know."

We opened the door to Daddy's office and began to climb the stairs, quietly, listening for his voice. His secretary wasn't at her desk. The door to his office was closed. Maggie knocked. There was some shuffling and then we heard Daddy shout. "We don't want any!"

"Daddy? It's us. Maggie and me," I said.

"Jesus H. Christ on a crutch! What the hell do you want?"

"We need a ride home."

It was very strange that he didn't open the door. I think we knew, big shots that we were, that he and his little secretary, Cheryl Stikes, were in there fooling around. But we didn't have the nerve to turn the handle to find out. We'd had enough trouble lately. So we waited and listened to the whispering and the shuffling. Sounded like they were getting dressed as shoes clumped the floor and zippers zipped. We'd caught him red-handed. Finally, we heard him coming to the door.

We figured he'd just go ahead and kill us when he opened the door. He was surprisingly nice. He just asked, "Okay. What's the problem?"

He looked at us with no guilt on his face. Cheryl stood behind him, running her hand through her hair, trying to restore order to her nasty teased hair.

"We need a ride home," I said. "When are you coming home?"

"I have to work late. Gotta go back out to the country to secure the equipment for the night. Could be eight, nine o'clock before I get free. I can't take you out there with me, it's not safe right now."

"Right. Shoot. Now what?" Maggie said.

"Daddy, will you lend us the money to take the bus?" I asked as sweetly as I could under the circumstances.

"Sure." He opened his wallet and gave us each ten dollars.

"You think we'll keep our mouths shut, don't you?" I couldn't help it, it just flew off my tongue like a plane leaving an aircraft carrier. Ten dollars was a stunning amount of money.

"Susan! Shut up!" Maggie said.

"I know my girls are mature enough to understand that some things are better left unsaid, that's all."

I took the ten dollars and stuffed it in my pocket and gave Daddy the worst look of hate I'd ever given anybody.

"Hey, Cheryl!" I said.

She looked up from Daddy's desk, where she was now making herself busy stacking papers. She had this fake innocent smile that made me want to puke.

"Why don't you sit on this and spin!" I gave her the finger, turned on my heels and ran down the stairs to the street. I heard Maggie's feet behind me, and Daddy's burst of laughter, booming laughter when there should have been shame.

"God almighty, Susan!" Maggie gasped. "Have you lost your mind?"

"What does he care? He's laughing like a damn idiot!"

"You're right, but he's crazy and you never know when he'll turn on us."

"He's done with us," I said and it was true.

We waited for the bus as the weather turned raw and damp. Winter was coming, a Lowcountry winter. We got on the bus and rarely spoke the whole way home, over one and a half hours.

Even though there was a change in the law, Maggie and I sat in the front of the slow, rattling bus and all the colored people sat in the back. This embarrassed me. These were the people who had given the world the woman who cherished us. I wanted to tell them that the box of chocolates we carried was for Livvie. Instead I stared out the window and thought about how much I hated my father. I swore to myself that I'd never have a husband like him, if I ever got one.

Finally, the bus stopped at our corner. Dr. Duggan's car was in the driveway. We walked through our backyard to the house.

"Dose-'em's car," Maggie remarked.

"Yup. Big shock."

"Maybe Daddy wasn't really doing anything," she said suddenly.

"Maggie, you know I love you, don't you?" I said, feeling older.

"Of course I do."

"Maggie, I'll bet that lots of families have

screwed-up parents like we do."

"Probably, but that doesn't make me feel better."

I put my arm around her shoulder. It was cold enough now for our breath to blow frost.

"No, I guess not," I said. "But look on the bright side. In three years you'll be in college, and I'll be out of here in four. We need to plan our escape, and make sure nothing happens to mess it up. For my part, I plan to study my butt off and pray to skip my senior year. Then we can share a dorm room at some learned institution and you can tell me what to do all the time."

In the pale light of early night I could see her smile. "Let's go inside. It's cold."

"Yeah, you're right."

The golden light of the kitchen shone through the windows. We climbed the steps as coconspirators. We would say nothing about what happened at Daddy's office. Our faces would reveal nothing. There was no reason to ruin everyone's holiday and no reason to give Livvie another reason to dislike Big Hank. We opened the door and faced Livvie. Henry was at the table with Timmy, both of them sitting there staring at the sugar bowl again. The hair on the back of my neck stood up.

"What's wrong?" I said.

"Get on in 'eah." She closed the door behind us. "It's y'all's grandmomma. She done had sheself a stroke not ten minutes ago, or something terrible. Timmy find she on the floor when he go to take she supper and Miss MC call the doctor. They is in there now. Your uncle is on the way."

"Oh, God. Did anybody call Daddy?" Maggie asked.

"He ain't there. We done call him."

"Probably out in the country at the construction site," I said.

We heard Uncle Louis's car door slam and the running of his shoes up the back steps.

"Where's my momma?" he asked, nearly out of breath.

"In she room," Livvie said quietly.

All at once I realized that this could mean Sophie was going to die. Shoot, we had just buried Tipa. I wasn't sure what a stroke was, but I knew they killed people all the time or, worse, left them alive in very bad shape.

"Can we go in?" I asked, not really wanting to see anything.

"Y'all bess be waiting 'eah with me for now. Go wash your hands and help me chop celery for the stuffing tomorrow. No matter what happen, still gotta eat. I don't think she gone tonight. I don't feel like that's so."

"Anything from the guy in the mirror?" I asked flippantly. This was going to be some holiday.

"Nothing, but I check on him directly. Maybe he got a ticket for Mizz Asalit to board the train to glory, but I don't think so. Not tonight, nohow."

"How do you know this stuff, Livvie?" Timmy asked.

"In my bones, son, in my bones."

We heard the doctor on the hall phone ordering an ambulance. I crept out and stood by him. He ignored me until he'd made the call.

"What is it, child?"

"I'm Susan, Dr. Duggan. Remember me? How's our grandmother?"

"Grave situation, Susan. Miss Sophie's unconscious. I've given your mother something to help her rest and I'm taking your grandmother over to St. Francis. We'll know a lot more after we see how she does tonight."

"Golly. Tomorrow's Thanksgiving. She can't die now!"

I worried that Sophie would be snatched from us like Tipa was. After his funeral, Sophie had reverted to her former behavior. She no longer spoke. She wouldn't bathe, except when Livvie took charge. She rarely left her room. Still, she was my grandmother and I wasn't ready for this. And she had helped me to my room in the dark that horrible night.

The ambulance arrived quickly. Maggie was upstairs giving the twins a bottle; Timmy and Henry were changing into their pajamas. I was entrenched in the kitchen, making a platter of sandwiches for a quick supper. When I saw the medical team come in I stopped slapping ham on mayonnaise to see what was going on.

I peeked in Grandma Sophie's room. They were lifting her onto a stretcher. They buckled big straps around her tiny body and covered her with a white blanket. She seemed so small. I thought she might get cold and hurried around them to her closet to get her bathrobe and slippers. I pressed them into Uncle Louis's hands.

"She'll need these," I said.

"You're a good girl, Susan," he said. "Tell MC that I'll call her later. Your Aunt Carol and I are going to spend the night at the hospital. Ask your daddy, when he gets home, to call over there too."

"Okay."

I followed them out the front door and down the steps. A terrible fog was rolling in. It was awful to see an ambulance parked in front of our house in the mist. *Nightmarish.* I stood on the porch for a few minutes after they left, listening to the siren wail. It became faint and then finally I could hear it no more. I leaned on the banister and listened to the ocean. Mrs. Simpson's porch light went out. She'd probably seen the whole thing.

The screen door closed behind me and I knew without looking that Livvie had come to make sure I was all right. She put her hand on my shoulder.

"Gone be all right, chile, gone be all right."

"Yeah, I know."

"Come on back inside now, this porch is a pneumonia hole tonight."

"Think she's gonna get well, Livvie?"

"Chile, we can't see what's in Gawd's mind, and you know your grandmomma ain't been right since Mr. Tipa gone. Might be she time, but only Gawd knows that."

"Livvie, Maggie and I got you something for Thanksgiving."

"What you talking about?"

"Well, we got you a big box of chocolate candy. I hope it cheers you up. You've been so, I don't know, different lately."

"Oh, chile." She heaved a great sigh. "I guess I been carrying the world. Don't you worry. Livvie's alright and you gone be alright too, 'eah?"

"We could open it and look at it. If you want to, I mean."

"Let's do that, 'eah? We could all use some sweetening up." She smiled at me and latched the screen door.

We went into the living room to turn out the lights and Livvie gave the mirror a hard look. It was irresistible, the temptation to peer into the future, I supposed. I knew that if I could've seen anything in the darn mirror, I'd have been looking all the time. She rubbed her eyes and looked again.

"Can't be," she said.

"What? What'd ya see? Tell me!"

Ignoring me, she went to the old round mahogany table, which held old family photos by the dozens. She picked up a picture of Daddy's momma, who had died before I was born. She lifted another one of Grandma Sophie and Grandpa Tipa on their wedding day.

Livvie clenched her jaw and replaced the photograph, wiping her fingerprints away from the silver frame with her apron. She started to sing.

"Livvie, talk to me!" I was becoming frightened.

"Chile, listen to these words," she said and started to sing.

"Sometimes I feel discourage,
and think my work's in vain,
but then the Holy Spirit
revive my soul again!"

"What's that supposed to mean?"

"It means when trouble come knocking on your

door, you turn your mind to the Lawd, that's what."

"You saying trouble coming 'eah?"

"Mizz Susan, I'm saying that Gawd put me 'eah in this house for a reason. Iffin trouble does come knocking, I gone hold you together. You 'eah me?"

"That's it? That's all you gonna tell me?"

"That's it. Now, let's finish that stuffing for the bird, and get a little bite of chocolate."

"Good idea!" I was suspicious. "Gosh, it's late! Are you sleeping here tonight?"

"I hadn't plan for that, but seeing how Mizz Asalit done gone off and all, maybe I bess stick around for the night."

"Yeah, that'd be good."

We chopped in silence, popping Jordan almonds and chocolate-covered caramels, except for when Livvie would sing. Rutabagas, potatoes, onions, celery, carrots, parsley. Collard greens, stripped of their spiny stems, soaked in a tub of salted water with vinegar to tenderize them. Ham bones pulled from the freezer to thaw to flavor the turnips and greens.

When Maggie came down, we added leaves to the dining room table and we got out Momma's best cloth. The snowy damask covered the table just right. It was beautiful. We set the table with a centerpiece of fruit and nuts in my grandmother's Waterford bowl. We put smilax leaves all around the bottom and thought it looked fine.

Livvie put the twins to bed. Momma was sleeping. The phone didn't ring. Daddy still wasn't home. Uncle Louis didn't call.

"Eleven-thirty! You girls bess get on to bed and

rest," Livvie said. "I'll just sleep on the cot in the twins' room."

"Where's Daddy?"

"Chile, that ain't for y'all to worry about. Be plenty of time tomorrow to find out. Now go on to bed. Thank you very much for the beautiful chocolate. It means a lot to me."

"Livvie, you mean a lot to us," I said.

"That's right," Maggie said quietly, "you do."

Just knowing Livvie was two doors away, I fell asleep like a stone sinking to the bottom of a river.

13

TAKING CONTROL

1999

I was coping with my new life very well, I thought. Basically, I gave the devil to those who needed it (that would be Beth) and kissed those deserving a kiss (that would be Beth, too). It wasn't easy, but I was putting one foot in front of the other and, like Livvie used to say, I was thanking God for my chance.

Tom was still withholding information needed to finalize our divorce settlement. Last week he had sent Beth home with an envelope containing a thousand dollars in cash. I knew it was guilt money — his guilt over the night of the storm and Beth's disappointment. I also knew he was being paid in cash by more than a few clients and not reporting it as income. I needed the thousand but I knew we'd go through it in a hurry. I stashed the bills in my old tennis shoes and tried not to feel like a hooker for the moment.

Why Tom was dragging his feet on finalizing our separation agreement I didn't understand. It baffled me, given the fact that Karen, the New Age Nympho, was once again living with him, or at least she was there every time Beth went for weekend visitation. I called Michelle Stoney and asked her to rattle his cage.

When Michelle asked him why he hadn't turned in all the tax documents she had requested, he said, "I have to call the accountant."

"That's ridiculous," I said, "what does he think? That I have an automatic money machine in the living room? Hasn't this gone on long enough?"

"I know. Give me twenty-four hours. I'll threaten a lien. That'll put a fire under his fanny. It doesn't sit well with the bar association, either, for lawyers to be sued for nonsupport. I'll call you tomorrow," she said.

That conversation taught me that even Michelle Stoney, great feminist advocate, needed gentle reminders to keep the ball rolling. I had to look out for myself.

The list went on. I still had the pleasure of Tom's bimbo, Karen, and her mouth to deal with. She had told Beth that her sex life with Tom was so fabulous that she didn't care if they ever got out of bed! I left a message on her machine.

"Tiger Woman?" I said, "this is Susan Hayes calling. Kindly confine the bells and whistles of your sex life with *my* husband to conversations with other adults. Do not, under any circumstances, attempt to educate my daughter about the joys of illegal cohabitation. My daughter is a minor and does not need to hear about how her father and his concubine thrill each other. The minute descriptions of your repugnant gymnastics are of no interest to either one of us. If this message needs any clarification, you may call me. If this continues to be an issue, my lawyer will call you. You'll find *concubine* and *repugnant* in the dictionary — if you own one — which I seriously doubt."

As long as I was telling her off, I figured an extra drive-by shooting couldn't hurt.

And I could never overlook Mitchell Freemont, the most irksome man in the galaxy. He was like one of those Bop 'em Bob dolls. My brother Timmy had one when he was little. He'd punch its red nose and it would keel over and pop back up for another punch. Whenever I caught Mitchell eyeing me in the office, I'd shoot him a Warrior Princess death ray, then watch him keel over and pop back up. Mitchell had evolved to comic relief of a sort.

On the happier side of things, my first column ran on Thursday as Max Hall had said it would. We had entitled it "Geechee Girl Remembers," which seemed clever enough. I thought the column and the cartoon looked pretty good, but it had been edited without anyone telling me. That upset me because I would've been happy to make changes but I wouldn't have made the same changes. In any case, it would earn me a hundred or so dollars and that was good. Beth's feet were still growing and I was still shrinking. Journalism was a new universe and I'd just learned my first lesson there too.

It turned out that Maggie was wrong about Grant, thank God. He did indeed have a pack of matches but said he had picked them up from the boys' room, worrying that they were smoking. Their son Bucky apparently admitted they were his and, yes, he had been smoking and, yes, he was grounded for two weeks. That was a huge relief. One divorce in the family at a time, thank you very much.

Maggie had called me to congratulate me on the column and we were talking about trusting men when my other phone line beeped. I put her on hold, thinking that call waiting was a fiendish device. I should cancel it and give Beth her own line as soon as I could afford it. It was Roger Dodds.

"Hi, remember me?" he asked.

"Roger Dodds? Roger Dodds? Aren't you a doctor or something?"

"Ah, the brutal Ms. Hayes. Yes, I'm the foreign physician from Aiken who put the kabosh on your daughter's nightclub and den of iniquity three weeks ago."

"Oh, I remember you! How are you?"

"Good, thanks. Um, I'm sorry I haven't called sooner. When the storm hit I had to go up to Aiken for a few days to help my old aunt and uncle. Their house was completely demolished."

"Oh. That's awful. Sure you weren't at the Indianapolis 500?" I didn't yawn in his ear, but I didn't quite swallow the story either.

"Very funny. No, I've given up car racing. Anyway, Uncle Richard's eighty-two and Aunt Frieda's eighty-something also. You know how it is with old people, they get scared and confused," he said.

"Yeah, well, I'm twenty-seven and I get scared and confused too," I joked, figuring maybe it wasn't a total line of bologna. "Can you hold on a minute? I'm on the line with Maggie. I'll tell her

I'll call her back." I clicked and reclicked and finally found Roger.

"Anyway, I'd like to see you again," he said. "What're you up to this weekend?"

"Oh, the usual list of household stuff. Not much."

"Want to have dinner?"

"Sure, sure. In fact, I'd love it. What night?"

"This Saturday?"

"Great. What time?"

"Eight, no, seven-thirty. I'll pick you up?"

"Why don't I drive this time?"

"Women. Why are you all always worrying?"

"Preservation of the species. Hey, I know what! I'll have Beth make cocktails."

"What a night that was for you. Did everything work out okay?"

"Well, aside from the fact that they trashed my house and my daughter sullied her pristine reputation with the entire student body, things worked out fine."

"Kids."

"Yeah, I'll see you Saturday. Hey, Roger?"

"Yeah?"

"I can't wait to see you. It'll be fun."

I called Maggie back right away.

"Hey! Guess what?" I said. "That was Roger Dodds. We have a date Saturday night."

"No kidding, that's great!"

"Yeah, I guess my life is finally moving on," I said.

"Listen, Susan, if he wants to go to bed with you, do it," she said.

"What? Are you crazy? I hardly know the man!"

Sometimes Maggie was a little cracked. Seriously.

"No, listen, I read this article that said the first sexual encounter after a marriage is the most nerve-wracking. The sooner you get it over with, the better."

"This might be the most hair-brained thing you've ever said to me."

"It's the truth! I mean, if Grant and I got divorced, it would be very hard for me to undress in front of someone else, let alone get in the bed!"

"First of all, I haven't used any birth control in a million years. Secondly, oh, good grief, Maggie! I can't think about this!"

"Well, think about it. He could be a good transition person. But you're right, you need to think about protection from disease. Who knows where he's been?"

"Jesus," I said, "thanks for the thought."

I had two days to transform myself for my second date. Beth and I decided to get new haircuts and manicures. We went out to the Citadel Mall and found a new salon that had just opened. A tiny, young, beautiful blond with an angular haircut and without one freckle, wrinkle or chipped nail was at the front desk. One look at her makeup and her pierced eyebrow and I knew I was at least a thousand years old. Great.

"Can I help you?" she said. Her voice was pleasant and professional.

"Yes, I'd like to make an appointment for a haircut and a manicure for my daughter and the works for me," I said.

"When would you like to come in?" she said.

"Well, we can shop until someone is free."

She checked the schedule book while I worried that — in this excellent adventure into beauty — they would give me a haircut like hers.

"Um," I said, "do you have someone on your staff who cuts hair for the aging?"

At least she had the intelligence to giggle. "Yes, ma'am. Kim. From New York and very good. He's also the owner. His fee is a little higher than the other stylists, but I think you'd be happy with him."

I just loved when they called me "ma'am." It reminded me to eat roughage.

"We need this, don't we?" I said to Beth.

"Oh, Mommy, in the worst way!"

"Okay, sign us up."

"Manicure and pedicure for you?"

"Yes, please."

"Wax?"

"What do you wax?" I asked.

"Legs, eyebrows, bikini line, just about anything that has hair." She giggled again.

Was I ever that silly? Sillier. "Sure, you can wax me too. Why not?"

She told us to come back in an hour and we agreed.

We ambled into Dillard's to shop for makeup. I roamed around the counters until someone from my decade at the Chanel counter asked if she could help me. Her black jacket had a tag that said her name was Eva.

"Yes, you can," I said, "I'd like a lipstick that will change my life." I was only half joking.

"Got just the thing," she said. "Why don't you sit right here?"

I climbed up in the chrome bar stool and she

looked at my face and then at my naked hands.

"Honey? You've got dry skin. Do you have about ten minutes?"

"Sure. Yeah, I know, my skin's sensitive."

"I'm gonna give you a new face. You ready?"

Eva held several different colors of makeup base next to my skin and tried one on my chin.

"This looks good," she said. "Good coverage. Do you sit in the sun?"

"Not anymore, but I grew up on the beach. I'm from the baby oil and iodine generation."

"Me too." She leaned back and looked at my face and said, "Oh, yes, this is perfect for you."

I stopped and looked in the mirror. All the little lines around my mouth seemed to have disappeared. The crow's-feet around my eyes weren't as noticeable. This was miraculous!

"Contact lenses?" she asked.

I nodded and she said, "Okay, I'll be careful. Just look down for me."

I'd been wearing them full-time. Beth came wandering over with her mouth hanging open.

"Wow, Mom! You look like a total babe!"

"You got a pretty momma," Eva said. "Now let's figure out what you have to have here."

I stared at my reflection. I had enough makeup on to be in a Mardi Gras parade, but if I toned it down a little, it wasn't all that bad.

"Here, honey, I wrote down everything for you so you can remember what to do with all this stuff. You look great, you really do," Eva said, taking my MasterCard. She reached under the counter and put handfuls of samples in my shopping bag. "I gave you some perfume samples too."

"Thanks, Eva," I said, "really. Thanks for all your help."

It was time for our salon appointments so we hurried back. I changed into a robe and was led to the waxing room.

When I came out of the room — hairless — twenty minutes later, Beth was reading a magazine, with her hair in a towel, waiting for her haircut. I must've been white as a sheet because she got up and took my elbow to lead me to a seat.

"You okay?" she said. "You want a glass of water?"

"I'm fine. Just a little sore."

"It hurt? I can't believe that, Momma. I mean, like, they say it stings a little, but shoot, you look *reeeeealllly* bad."

"Think about it. First they spread warm wax over your bikini line and cover it with a strip of cotton and then, in a single movement, they rip it off, pulling a patch of pubic hair out by the roots. I almost fainted."

"I don't want to think about it," Beth said.

"The legs weren't bad and the eyebrows were nothing, but the bikini line was a virtual religious experience. I saw Jesus, Elvis and Jimmy Hoffa."

"Man, what we women have to go through," she said.

I was thoroughly amused that she classified herself as a woman. She was growing up so quickly.

"See you later," I said and left to get my pedicure.

The girl who did my pedicure was a heavenly creature who massaged my feet until I was so happy and relaxed I forgot about the waxing experience. After she was finished I hobbled to a waiting area thinking that my toes looked like ten perfect strawberries.

A very handsome man approached me. "Hi! Ms. Hayes? I'm Kim."

I got up, shook his hand and followed him. He was about fifty, gray hair cut very short, diamond stud earring. He wore a black cashmere turtleneck pushed up over his elbows and perfectly creased black wool trousers. This was a very cool guy. Elegant, in fact. I sat in the chair and looked at him in the mirror's reflection.

"Great belt," I said, "where'd you get it?"

"Thanks. Bergdorf's in New York — it's Kieselstein," he said.

"Well, no wonder!" I said, pretending to know who Kieselstein was. The ornate silver buckle was molded in the shape of a dog's head.

"So, what are we looking for today?" he said.

I looked at his eyes and with the straightest face I could muster, I said, "I'm a woman of realistic expectations. If you could make me look like Catherine Deneuve, that would be fine."

"By the time I'm finished with you," he said, "Catherine Deneuve will want to go hide in a dark closet!" He picked through my thick head of hair and walked all around the chair fingering his chin. "Low lights," he said.

"Well, at this stage, we all look better in low lights," I said.

"No, no, no! You're funny! What I meant was that your hair needs low lights. We're going to foil the frame of your face. It's a very subtle process, and it takes a little time, but the result is a soft glow that will bring your face to life."

"Oh."

"Then we're going to take away about three inches from the bottom of your hair, give you a few layers to use the advantage of all this fabulous body you have, and round brush the devil out of it. You're going to shine like patent leather!"

I began to fret. How much was this transformation going to cost? He saw the concern on my face.

"Don't worry," he said, "just go with Fran and get shampooed."

Not worry? Okay, I wouldn't worry about it. I'd send the bill to Tom. Fran massaged my head so beautifully that I almost fell asleep. I had forgotten how good it felt to have someone work my scalp. In minutes, I was back in Kim's chair and having my hair combed out.

"Are you from Charleston?" Kim said. He sectioned my hair with the long end of a fine-tooth comb and pinned it up.

"Yep, for about a zillion years."

"Married? Lean your head down a little, okay?"

"Okay. No, getting a divorce."

"I just moved here," he said.

At least four inches of hair from the nape of my neck fell to the floor. "Oh, where are you from?" I said.

"New York. Used to manage the Sassoon Salon, finally tucked away enough money to open a salon of my own. My friend is an architect and has been nursing this insane dream of owning a plantation forever. We found a perfectly grand plantation out Highway 17, almost in Walterboro, and snapped it up! Of course, it needs everything done to it, but

Jeremy, that's my friend, is so talented. Next thing you know *Architectural Digest* will be in there with cameras!"

"Gosh, it sounds wonderful."

"Oh, it is, or it will be. So do you live in the city?"

"Yes, I have an old Victorian on Queen Street."

"Aren't you smart? That certainly makes life convenient."

"Yes, I can walk to work. But I grew up on the beach. My sister lives in that house."

"Oh? And what does she do? Ms. Hayes, you need to keep your head straight."

"Sorry. Maggie does what a surgeon's wife is supposed to do. Manages the house, runs the Garden Club, volunteers her brains out. She runs events for the wives at the Medical University. In between all that, she has two teenage sons who keep her pretty busy."

"I'll bet so. Oh, this is looking good. When's the last time you had a haircut?"

"When Nixon was president."

"You are too funny."

He looked at me and smiled. He had perfect teeth and two dimples on either side of his mouth. Precious.

"Ms. Hayes?"

"Call me Susan."

"Susan? I'm going to make you a proposition."

"How wonderful!" I said.

"No, no," he threw his head back and laughed. In a friendly gesture he rested his hands on my shoulders and spoke to my reflection. "Here's my proposal: I am going to cut and color your hair on the house. If you like it, I want you to tell your sister to come see me and I'll cut and color her hair and all the wives of the doctors at the Medical University for twenty-five percent off. The offer's good until Christmas. How does that sound?"

"I think you are going to be a very busy man."

"You know what? It's much cheaper than advertising. I'll give you a stack of business cards to take with you, okay?"

"Consider it a done deal."

I was thrilled. Maggie couldn't resist a bargain and neither could any woman I knew. Beth was finished and she came over with the cutest haircut I'd ever seen. It was swinging and shining.

"Mom! I totally love my hair! What do you think?"

"I think your hair looks beautiful but the concept of lime green nail polish escapes me. Say hello to Kim."

"Hi," she said. "Mom, I'm gonna go cruise the mall and I'll be back in an hour, okay?"

"Sure, have fun."

"Cruise the mall?" Kim said, watching her leave.

"Don't ask."

For the next two hours, he spun me around and foiled my head, rinsed my hair, conditioned it, glazed it, trimmed a little more and at last he was ready to blow it out. A gal on a low stool manicured my fingernails on a lap pillow while he worked. I felt like the queen of a lovely kingdom.

Finally, he spun me around to face the mirror and I barely recognized myself.

"Lord have mercy!"

"Like yourself?" Kim said and started to laugh.

"I should've taken a 'before' picture, don't you think?"

"Amazing," I said. "You know, I'm not an arrogant woman, but I think this is the best I've ever looked in maybe my whole life! How can I thank you?"

"Tell your friends and your sister. Don't forget we have our agreement."

Kim stood there smiling. I wanted to be his friend forever.

"Well, I suppose there is a big difference between professional care and cutting my bangs with the same scissors I use to cut cardboard, right? Kim?"

"Yes?"

"Don't ever leave me."

He wouldn't let me pay for Beth either but I tipped the shampoo girl heavily and the manicurist too. I was floating on air.

Out in the mall, Beth came toward me with a shopping bag from Record World.

"Whoa! Do I know you?"

"Very funny!"

"Seriously, Mom. That old codger did a number on you! You rock! I bet you could pass for thirty-something!"

"Thanks." Her compliment made me actually blush, something I hadn't done in a long time.

"Got some new tunes," she said, "want to see?"

"Sure. Come on, let's get a cappuccino."

What a cheery little monster I turned into with a little effort. All I had done was starve myself for six months and accidentally hustle a free makeover! Not a bad day's work at all. God, it was all so shallow.

Saturday night arrived and I wondered why I was so nervous. I was dressing for dinner with a man, that's why. Given my relationships with men, I should break out in a rash. Maggie may have been right, he might try to seduce me and I wasn't ready for that at all.

Beth was in her room packing a duffel bag to take to Tom's apartment to spend the night. I worried that she would let it slip to Tom or Karen that I was on a date. Not that they would care, but it was only a few days until the papers for our divorce would finally, at long last, be signed. I zipped the back of my dress on the way down the hall to Beth's room.

"Hi, doodle!" I said.

"Hi! Mom! You look great!"

She had the look of someone who had reconciled the facts of her life. I had a date, her father had a girlfriend and it was normal for her.

"Thanks, honey. Listen, do me a small favor, will you?"

"Sure, anything."

"If your dad or Karen mentions my social life just tell them I don't have one, okay?"

"No problem. None of their business, right?"

"Right. And don't mention my column in the paper either, all right?"

"Sure. How come?" She pulled on a pair of jeans that were ripped out at the knees and a faded Gap sweatshirt.

"Are you gonna wear that outfit to go out to dinner with your dad?"

"We're just going to Pizza Hut."

"Oh, okay. Fine. Look, it's not a huge deal if he

found out, but we are supposed to sign our papers very soon and I don't want him to think that we don't need his support. Understand?"

"Right. He'd think that, like, this doctor is moving in and paying all our bills. And that you're getting totally rich from your second job. Am I a genius or what?" She zipped her bag and gave me a crooked smile of mature knowing.

"Honey chile, baby heart, you are a certified rocket scientist. Just be cool."

"Hey, Mom. I'm a teenager. It's my job to be cool."

The doorbell rang.

"I'll get it," she said. "It's probably Daddy and if he sees you looking like that he'll be way suspicious."

"Thanks, honey. I'll see you tomorrow night." I kissed her head and she stopped and turned to me.

"Try to get home at a decent hour, Mom. You want me to call you? You know, bed check? Then, if you want him to leave, you can use me for an excuse."

"Great idea, but I think I can handle it. Go on now, Daddy's waiting."

"Love you!"

The front door opened and closed and she was gone. How priceless was that, I thought. I went downstairs to the living room to turn on some music. I caught a glance of myself in my mother's huge mirror and, for the briefest moment, didn't know it was myself. I stopped and gave myself a full appraisal. Not bad. I had on a deep brown, short, sleeveless dress that had a coat to match. My arms weren't too flabby. My hair looked really good with its auburn "low lights" and my face seemed to have less stress. My new makeup was doing its job. I looked like a woman who was perhaps going out to do the town, not like the one who, just a few months ago, had sunk to the floor and wept.

I flipped on an old favorite CD, *Clifford Brown with Strings*, and relaxed as his music warmed the room. I poured myself a glass of wine from the cooler on the coffee table and lit some candles on the mantel. The candles were sandalwood, my absolute favorite. Maggie had given me a box of them for my birthday. Old houses like mine would take on musty smells but sandalwood perfumed the rooms with the perfect amount of richness.

I hoped Roger would like Brie baked in puff pastry with peach jam. It was a recipe I clipped from the newspaper and hadn't burned beyond recognition. Hopefully he'd think that I possessed some domestic skills. At least my house looked clean. Beth and I had spent the better part of the day cleaning and waxing. She was a good girl, I thought. The doorbell rang and my date began.

"Hi! Come in!" I said.

"Hi! God, what did you do to your hair? Here, I brought you these. You look great!"

"Thanks, you don't look so bad yourself." I ran my hand through the side of my hair. "Just cut it a little, that's all. Gosh, these are so pretty! I love freesias!"

We went in the living room and I added them to the vase of grocery store flowers on the end table next to the sofa. I poured Roger a glass of wine. He touched the side of my glass with his and took a large sip.

"That's some mirror," he said.

"You don't know the half of it."

"Educate me," he said, running his hand around the side of the mirror's wide gold frame. "It looks old. Historical significance?"

"Well, this may seem hard to imagine, but way, way back in time, before the War of Yankee Aggression, over on Sullivan's Island there were resort hotels. People went there to escape the summer fevers. This mirror hung behind the bar of the Planters Hotel until 1830. Later, it was installed in the Moultrie House on the Island in 1850. The Moultrie House was a hotel and a legendary spot for summer dances. It was built right down the street from my family's beach house, right on the harbor. It even had a ballroom! Would you like a bit of this?"

I put some warm Brie on a cracker and offered it to him.

"I've never heard that. Thanks."

"Yeah, seems hard to believe, doesn't it? You can only imagine how much bourbon and whiskey has been poured out in front of this mirror. How many men twirled the tips of their handlebar mustaches, how many ladies adjusted their bonnets? God, I love history. My grandfather got his hands on it somehow and it was in our house on the Island for years."

"What a great story!"

"Anyway, there's an old Gullah belief that the mirror holds your soul. Same thing with photographs — that a little bit of your spirit becomes trapped in the mirror or on the film."

"Incredible what some people believe, isn't it?"

"Well, who knows? They might've been right. I mean, there have definitely been times when this old mirror gave me the creeps."

"So what happened to the Moultrie House? Do you want some more wine?"

"No, thanks. I'm all set. Well, it seems there was this Yankee soldier during the beginning of the war who fired a cannonball on it. It was filled with guests and they all ran outside in a fit of terror with their bloomers on fire. When they asked the Yankee why he fired on a civilian building, do you know what he said?"

"I can only venture a guess."

"Go ahead, guess."

"Because the last time he stayed there he got a bad room?"

"God, you are so smart. Do you know that?"

"Come on, let's go to dinner," he said. "I read that somewhere."

"You rascal! You let me tell you that whole story!"

"Madam, I am neither a rascal nor a rogue. And, in the style of the true southern gentleman, I have left my *Beamer* in the garage so that I could stroll the *boulevard* with your *beautiousness*."

His little speech made me giggle. "I'm not sure *beautiousness* is a word."

"Poetic license. Shall we go?"

We walked to a small restaurant in the historic area, up an old alley that I had never even known was there. We had steaks, beautiful things, thick and rare with a wonderful mustard sauce and an incredible bottle of cabernet sauvignon from the Napa Valley. We shared a Caesar salad and discovered neither one of us liked anchovies, but we loved garlic and croutons. For dessert we had something decadent in flames, cherries jubilee.

After dinner we walked arm in arm and under the marquee at the Dock Street Theater he told me I was beautiful. I thought he meant it. It must've been the wine or the streetlight. Whatever. It was nice to hear.

"That was a wonderful dinner, Roger. Thank you."

"Oh, you're welcome, it wasn't anything really. I wanted to cook for you, but another time. I had so much stuff going on today I couldn't figure out how to make dinner."

"I have a lot of days like that," I said.

"Well, I thought it might be nice to go back to my place and have a cognac or some coffee."

"Sure. I'd love to see where you live."

We walked by the old cemetery and heard the voices of teenagers deep inside the rows of tombstones. They were probably in an open mausoleum, drinking beer and fooling around. It was all terribly romantic. He held my hand and talked about growing up in Aiken and how he had married a girl he met in medical school.

"Was she a medical student?"

"No, no. She was the sister of a friend of mine. Family was from Boston, old-line and very particular about everything. She was like the Holy Grail to me. I always wanted what I couldn't have."

"I know how that is," I said.

"Well, she got pregnant and we got married and it was downhill from there. Her parents hated me. I was southern and no matter what, even when our second son was born and even though we stayed together for almost twenty years, I wasn't the man they wanted for their daughter."

"God, that's awful. People are so stupid."

"Well, it was a lot of years ago and I did my best for Adelle — that's my ex-wife's name. She was okay, I guess. Anyway, I have two great sons, and she's remarried — to a Brahmin — and living in Boston during the winter and the south of France in the summer, as they always intended she would. All's well that ends well, right?"

"I suppose so," I said.

"Here we are. Come on, I'll make us some coffee. I have a new espresso machine."

"Ah, the gadget king!"

"Yep, that's me!"

Pink stucco? His town house opened right on the street and we stepped onto his long narrow porch. The door concealed a lit private garden with a center fountain. The porch had rocking chairs and a joggling board, that most traditional of Lowcountry toys. Joggling boards are found all over Charleston — a long plank of wood pegged into two rockers that moves sideways. Immediately, I went to the center of it and sat down, bouncing.

"I used to play for hours on one of these when I was a kid," I said.

"You had one?" He was fumbling with his keys.

"No, but there was a house on the Island that had one and I'd sneak up on their porch and use it," I said.

"I'll bet you were hell on wheels," he said.

"Suh! Please! Southern Catholic ladies are perhaps purgatory on wheels, but that is all."

"I see," he said. He was pretty cute when he smiled. Finally he found the key and opened the side door. His alarm sounded. Four monotone beeps followed by another one disarmed the system and we went inside. Stepping in, I was surprised at what I found. His living room looked like something from *Southern Living* magazine. I guess I had expected a bachelor pad, thrown together-type room.

"God, Roger, this is beautiful!"

"Yeah, thanks, I went out with a decorator for a while. It was incredible what she could spend just on fabric. Pretty, though, huh?"

"Yeah."

"Make yourself comfortable, I'll put the coffee on."

"Okay."

I wandered around the room. From the picture molding to the chair rail, the walls were covered in padded red silk with embroidered gold bumblebees. The paneling below the chair rail was solid cherry and looked to be two hundred years old. The floor was covered in a Persian carpet — navy, red and ivory swirls and birds. One sofa was red and gold stripe and the other was a soft taupe velvet. On the walls hung paintings of ships, dating to the early part of the century or earlier. Over the fireplace was a nineteenth century portrait of a man.

Roger returned and caught me staring at the painting. The man in the portrait had the saddest eyes but the most beautiful face. His brown eyes looked at me, his lips were full and sullen.

"My great-grandfather," he said, "painted by John Singer Sargent at the end of his life. A good one, hey?"

"Beautiful."

He handed me a small cup and motioned for me to sit on the sofa. I took the cup, tasted the espresso and inhaled the richness of it.

"I know you're worried about drinking espresso and sleeping, but don't. I have something to take care of that," he said.

"Oh?"

With that he leaned over to a box on the coffee table and opened it. It was an antique wooden box, inlaid with jade, an old tea box. It was filled with a greenish brown dried herb, something that resembled marijuana. He pulled a pack of rolling papers from another box and began to roll a joint.

"You're kidding," I said and started to laugh.

"Oh, don't tell me you never got high in your life," he said.

"Um, yeah, but not since Woodstock."

"Excuse me, but during Woodstock, you would've been about fifteen."

"Seventeen. But I was a sympathizer."

"Well, you'll be delighted to know that the quality of drugs has vastly improved." He lit the cigarette and took a long pull.

"Oh, that's great news. Listen, Roger, I don't want to seem like a prude, but I don't do this shit anymore."

He laughed and handed it to me. I hesitated and then, in a moment of wild abandon, took a small drag and passed it back. "Holy smoke," I said.

"Yep!" He coughed and laughed and handed the joint back to me.

Now, ordinarily, I would have said, "Gee, this is cool but I gotta go." Somehow, for some reason, those words weren't coming. I was a little bit tired of doing the right thing all the time and I figured, what the hell, this guy was a responsible doctor. What was the harm? I'd get a little high, I'd probably love it and then I'd go home and sleep like a baby. Sure. I took another toke and all of a sudden I felt myself rising from my body. "Whoa! What *is* this?"

"Be cool! It's Colombian and very strong. Just relax. It's okay."

I was paralyzed. I watched him get up and put a CD on and every movement of his seemed to be under a strobe light. Jerk. Jerk. Jerk. It was so weird. I didn't remember pot being like this in the seventies. No, this was a new kind of pot. Pot? Pot? Did someone say pot? Teflon? Calphalon? Cast iron? I started to giggle. Oh, my God! My ass was flying. The music he played was mostly bass and the thumping of it reminded me of sex.

Roger came back to the couch and stood in front of me, holding out his hand. "Want to see the rest of the house?"

"Sure," I heard someone say and then realized it was myself.

Lamb to the slaughter, lamb to the slaughter. No, no. I can handle it, I told myself. He led me through a series of rooms. The dining room, a kitchen, a study then back out to the foyer. We went up the steps to the second floor.

"Nice!" I managed with no small struggle.

"Don't you think it would be nice to sit on the porch and rock?"

He started to laugh.

"Sit on the porch and rock!" He laughed again and again. "Come on!"

So we walked through two bedrooms, an office, two bathrooms and up to the third floor where there were two more bedrooms and a cedar closet with one giant bathroom in the hall. One of the bedrooms held exercise equipment.

"Well, this is handy," I said, getting on the stair stepper and beginning a fevered workout.

"Come on, now, you're gonna hurt something!"

He pulled me down from the stair stepper and into his arms. In the next instant his mouth was on mine. I thought for a second he was going to Hoover my lips. It was a curious thing to be so stoned and be kissed so heavily by someone I barely knew.

"Roger? What's happening here?"

"Come on," he said, taking me by the hand.

He led me down one flight to his bedroom. The moment Maggie predicted had arrived. I was stunned that it could happen so quickly without any real discussion and I wasn't quite mentally ready for all this action. We walked in the room and I took a good look at his bed. It looked harmless enough for a king-size bed with pillows all over it. It had an upholstered headboard and a matching spread in brown and rust paisley velvet. It certainly looked comfortable and suddenly I was very sleepy.

I stood there while he went to his closet and pulled out a wrapped box. A present! For me? I was so tired, all I wanted to do was have a nap for an hour or so and then I knew I'd be fine. My head was spinning and his voice seemed to come from another place.

"I saw this and all I could think about was you," Roger said. "Open it."

I removed the paper and found a box from Victoria's Secret. Oh, oh, I thought, what the hell is this? I undid the tissue paper and pulled out an ivory lace corset, matching thong panties and stockings. Try as I did to suppress them, I was choking on giggles. He mistook them for nerves.

"Will you put it on for me?" he asked.

"Sure! What do you think? That I'm a nun?"

Shit. He was serious. Now what? If he wants to see me in this, no problem, I thought. Maggie's right. The first time would be the worst. I would've been a wreck except for the fact that it all seemed so hilarious. He cracked up and I started laughing too.

In the bathroom, I flipped on the light and studied my face in the mirror for a minute. My eyes were bloodshot from the pot. I became fixated on that and couldn't stop staring at them.

"You all right, Susan?"

"Yes! I'll be right out."

With a boldness that came from the most remote rampart of my loose-cannon brain, I undressed and sort of tossed my bra over his shower curtain rod. I had a hard time with all the hooks and eyes of the corset and finally decided to put it on backward and then spin it around. That worked but while I was pulling and twisting, I was getting an aerobic workout. I started giggling again. Good Lord, I thought, when was the last time I laughed this much? It was a darn good thing I had waxed. *It's a good thing, Martha!* The panties were indecent! I laughed again, realizing I'd better get a grip on myself if I was going to be this dude's fantasy. Dude? I hadn't even thought of that word in twenty years! Okay, thirty.

After I had the stockings hooked up I had to decide whether or not I was going to parade back into the bedroom with or without shoes. I decided to wear the shoes, thinking I'd look taller and thinner. I used his hairbrush and ate a little bit of his toothpaste.

Suddenly, I completely lost my nerve and sat down on the lid of his toilet. Why was I doing this? If this guy asked me to run naked in his living room would I have said yes? No, I told myself, this was different. Roger had thought this out and this was what he wanted, badly enough to ask me.

I saw his robe hanging on the back of the door and put it on. It was black silk. One more look in his mirror and I saw that my face was frozen in worry. My head was still spinning a little and I couldn't remember if I'd been in the bathroom for an hour or for ten minutes. He knocked on the door again.

"It's okay, Susan, I'm not going to jump on you," he said.

"Oh! I'm coming out!"

"I just want to see you, that's all."

"I know." My voice quivered a little like a six-year-old's.

"Haven't ever done anything like this, have you?"

"No."

"It's okay. I understand. Want me to come in and get you?"

I tightened his robe around my waist. "Yeah, okay. I mean, if you want to."

The door opened and there he was. Cute, thoughtful and harmless. He held out his hand to me.

"Come on, I don't bite, unless you want me to, that is."

I took his hand but his last remark sent a tiny chill up my spine. We walked into his room and stood before the sliding mirrored doors of his closets. He stood behind me with his arms around my waist. Slowly, he untied the sash of the robe. The sash hung by my sides. He moved my hair and kissed me on the back of my neck. His breath was hot. With his right hand he opened the robe and pulled it back over my shoulder. The entire robe slipped to the floor between us. I couldn't look at myself or at him. I flushed with embarrassment.

"You are magnificent," he said.

He took me by the hand and led me to the bed.

"All I want to do is kiss you," he said.

I didn't believe that for a minute, but I had already resigned myself to the fact that this train would be very hard to stop once it got moving. He undid his tie and slipped it off. He unbuttoned his shirt and pulled his shirttail out and finally threw it on a chair. He pulled down the covers and I sat on the side of the bed while he folded his trousers neatly and put them on the chair too. Although I was preoccupied with holding in my stomach, I couldn't help but notice that he was wearing tight white briefs that told me everything else about him that I was shamelessly curious to know.

"Move over," he said.

Like a good little girl, I did. By this time I was thinking some pretty wicked thoughts. I had to admit that dressing up in this costume made me feel pretty sexy. I wanted to kiss him and the thought of making love was exciting. He began kissing me and it wasn't like the hard kiss he had given me upstairs but more like someone who was conserving his energy. I loved it and I'd be a liar to say I didn't. He moved his lips all across my throat and down the middle of my chest, never touching my breasts. This frustrated me, but he was in control here and I was eager to see how long his kisses could last. I wiggled backward, up into the pillows, as his mouth traveled my legs. From one leg to the other he went, every now and then a little nibble on the inside of my thigh. My breathing became deeper and desire took over. In fact, I was becoming rather wanton, to my complete surprise.

He unsnapped my stockings and began to remove them ever so slowly. Now I was tortured. If this man didn't crawl on me pretty soon I was going to scream. He removed my shoes, flipping them across the room over his shoulder. Now he was on the floor, kneeling at the bottom of his bed, kissing and licking my feet. Thank God I had a pedicure, I thought. I heard someone moaning and it was him. Finally! I thought, finally!

"Roger? Come back here," I said.

He began sucking my toes and they were incredibly ticklish. One of his hands disappeared, his moaning became louder and he sucked harder on my second toe.

"Roger?"

"Not now." He moaned and moaned and moaned, and stopped, rested his head on the end of the bed and dropped my right foot.

He looked up at me with the most bizarre sheepish look and said, "You were fabulous!"

"I was?"

"Yeah, do you want to spend the night or can I drive you home?"

I didn't know what to say. Was that all? I mean, no romp in the sheets for me, just clean feet? Suddenly, I wasn't stoned anymore. "Gosh, it's getting late, you know? Why don't I just call a cab?"

"Don't do anything. I'll be right back," he said and disappeared into the bathroom.

The sounds of water running were background music for what was one of the strangest moments I'd ever had in all my adult life. No, I thought again and added my childhood too. Here I was, lying on the bed of a man I'd met only twice, wearing a corset and thong panties. I had been wined, dined, and had a little smokey thrown in for good measure and my desire had died on the vine like an overlooked ripe grape. It was such a waste.

The bathroom door opened and he came out in a towel. He picked up his robe from the floor, put it on and, in the cheeriest voice I'd ever heard him use, he said, "I'm going to pour a cognac. I'll meet you downstairs."

He was getting all snuggy for the night. Now that my toes were spent he didn't need me anymore. Suddenly, I found this funny.

I rolled out of bed and wondered what Maggie would say if I told her this. As I put on my clothes in the bathroom, I practiced my lines. *Oh, yes,*

Maggie, Roger is a wonderful guy, no doubt about it. No, he's a man of his word! He said all he wanted to do was kiss me. Okay, he left out the part about wanting to get off while sucking my toes, but hey! You can't expect a man to tell you everything, right?

This was too good to drop on the phone. I'd have to drive out to the Island so that I could see her face when I told her. This would freak her right out of her Talboted, duck-motiffed, monogrammed, Junior-Leagued gourd. Yes, this was a classic dating story of industrial strength.

I invited myself over to Maggie's for brunch, promising to bring fresh bagels. I threw on an old pair of khakis, my Weejuns with no socks and a paint-stained sweatshirt with some feminist political statement on it. I drove over to the Island as fast as I could. When I pulled up in the backyard, Grant was pulling out with the boys and the boat.

"Hey! Y'all gone fishing?"

"Hey yourself! How's Roger?" Grant called out.

"Well, Roger's a *very* interesting guy," I said. "Want a bagel?"

"See? I knew you'd like him! Got pumpernickel?"

"Sure, here's two for my little baby nephews too."

The boys groaned and I smiled. They were huge — hardly babies anymore.

"Thanks. See you later," Grant said.

If Grant knew the truth about his pal Roger, he'd flat drop dead, I thought. I went in the house and helped myself to a cup of coffee. I put two bagels on a plate, got a knife out of the drawer and some cream cheese from the refrigerator. I brought it all out to the porch, where Maggie was reading the Sunday paper. The sun was shining and it was a beautiful morning. Sweater weather.

"Hey, sister," I said, "hungry?"

"Fresh bagels! Sure, gimme one. Hey, you look great — your hair, that is, not the outfit. What did you do?"

"I spent two hours with Svengali last week. He wants to meet you." She was wearing a turtleneck and a new neon green running suit — the kind that cost twice my mortgage payment. I split a bagel with the knife and spread a thin layer of low-fat cream cheese across it. "You got some helluva nerve insulting my clothes. Go look in the mirror, baby, Halloween's over."

She leaned over, took the bagel and gave me a sisterly peck on the cheek. "Kiss my fanny, honey chile, but not before you sign me up for a makeover! I just bought it. Wild, huh? 'Eah, let me see the back! Great cut!"

I just shook my head and told her all about Eva at the Chanel counter with her cache of samples and about Kim. She got very excited about the discount, as I knew she would.

"Now tell me all about Roger," she said. "How was your date? Did you do the deed?"

"Are you comfortable? Do you have any blood pressure medication in the house?"

I told her the tale, every single thing I could remember. We screamed and laughed until we had tears streaming down our faces.

"Tell me you're lying!" she said, over and over.

"Honey, I ain't lying, 'eah? This is the gospel!" I said at least ten times.

"Lord have mercy!"

"I tell you, Maggie, I ain't cut out for this singles business. I'm too straight and I'm too old to change."

"I'm glad you're straight. I like you just the way you are."

"Thanks. Hey, did I tell you that Tom's back with Karen?"

"Bump them."

"Yeah, that's what I say. I can't keep track of him and his love life and frankly, I could finally care less. I sign the papers this week."

"It's about time," she said.

"Yeah, Tom finally agreed to the money I wanted. In fact, after weeks of holding us up, he suddenly called Michelle and said that he'd give me whatever I want."

"Why would he do that? That's not like him at all."

"I have no idea. Maybe he's afraid of the Millennium."

"Which reminds me, what are we going to do on New Year's Eve?" she asked.

"I don't know. Have you spoken to the twins and the boys?"

"No, but I figured I'd invite them all for Christmas and let them stay until New Year's Day if they wanted to. I mean, the year 2000 — it's a big deal. I thought it would be special if we were all together. I could even rent another house, you know? What do you think?"

"I think that's a great idea. What's the Island doing to celebrate?"

"I don't know, but I imagine there will be fireworks and so forth. Probably a special service at Stella Maris, don't you think?"

"Yeah. God — 2000. Amazing, huh? I can't believe it's almost 'eah."

"Yeah," she said. "Grab a jacket and let's sit on the beach."

I put on one of the boys' windbreakers and off we went. We kicked off our shoes and crossed the yard, climbing the walkover that protected the dunes. On the other side, we sat on the bottom step and at the same moment, we dug our toes deep into white sand to stay warm. Its touch was cool to my skin but soothing. This burying of feet was another insignificant or maybe not so insignificant tradition that tied us together. Despite our many differences, we were sisters to the bone, locked into little habits and special words that bound us together. More importantly, we searched each other to build new similarities and to stay relevant to each other.

"Susan? I gotta tell you something," Maggie said. "I really thought that Grant was having an affair. Thank God I was wrong. I was so happy that the matches were Bucky's I didn't even want to punish him."

"I don't blame you," I said. "I would've kissed Bucky."

"Right. But I know that infidelity's possible, 'eah? That hospital's crawling with young, beautiful nurses and others who spend two hours getting all spiffed up for work in the morning. Their sole purpose in life is to trap a doctor — married or not. Grant leaves me in my nightgown looking like I'm crawling out of a train wreck and comes home late to find me looking like a tired old bag."

"You're too hard on yourself, and I told you Grant wasn't screwing around. He just wouldn't do it, Maggie."

"Listen, remember Livvie? She said, 'Trust 'em and they throw you!' She always said that."

"Well, it can't hurt to keep your eyes open, but I seriously doubt you have anything to worry about. It's not like Tom's disease is contagious."

"I don't know about that. Grant could've found another pack of matches in Bucky's room and just lied to me."

"Jesus, Maggie. What is this, *Perry Mason*? Do you really think Grant would do something so devious?"

"You never know," she said.

The tide was going out. It was another beautiful South Carolina day. There was so much blue sky it was amazing. The beach was empty, except for a couple strolling together, farther down the Island. We could see them throwing a stick to their dog and the dog running around, obviously having a wonderful time. Where else was there so much endless beauty and serenity?

The beach always gave something to me, something akin to checking the cosmic e-mail. I could talk to God on Sullivan's Island.

"Getting chilly, 'eah?" I said.

"Winter's coming," Maggie finally answered after her eyes scanned the entire beach.

" 'Eah, gone be in the fifties tonight. Time to turn on the furnace."

"Yep. Hey, do you remember the time we caught Daddy fooling around with his secretary?"

It wasn't exactly on the front row of my mind, but given her suspicion of Grant's behavior, I could see why she dredged it up. "Who could forget that?" I said.

"You think Momma ever knew?"

"Yeah, she knew. Livvie told me."

"But she never said anything to us. Amazing."

"That was her attempt at dignity in a war zone. You know, in my middle age, I'm starting to realize a lot of things about old MC that I never could understand before."

"Such as?"

I picked up a handful of sand and let the fine white particles run through my fingers. Looking out over the horizon, I spotted a cluster of shrimp boats, nets down. I thought for a moment about which thread to pull to begin unraveling our mother's story.

"Such as, nothing ever prepared her for the life she had. Life threw her one disaster after another. I'm not so sure I could've tolerated all she did. I probably would've run away from everyone."

"You don't mean that."

"I certainly do mean it. Maggie, look at her life. Six kids. That alone is justification to pickle your own liver. Can you imagine believing that using birth control would send you to hell for all of eternity? And she had her parents to contend with *and* Daddy. I don't know how she did it all, how she bought into it. I couldn't."

"I couldn't either. But she was from another time, another generation."

"Guilt, honey," I said. "Good old-fashioned Catholic guilt. Her parents spread it on her like mayonnaise on white bread, and then they stuffed it with bologna. And you know what else? Here's the big revelation coming."

"Okay, I'm ready."

"Even though Livvie made it possible for us to survive all the insanity, I grew up and committed the stupidest sin of all." Feeling dead serious, I stood up and walked a few paces away. "Come on, let's walk." I turned to pull her up and rolled up my pants legs to under my knees. I wanted to tell her things we had never discussed. We walked along the water's edge, the startling cold water of early November washing our bare feet.

"Maggie, I despised Daddy." My voice was low and strong.

"For good reason."

"You are always asking me why I can't let his death go. I think he was murdered." My voice rolled over the sound of the ocean. If the wind was right, half of the Island probably heard me. "All these years I have struggled to accept the heart attack story, but something in my guts tells me it ain't true."

"Susan, there was an investigation and an autopsy. The investigation proved nothing and the autopsy showed a heart attack."

"Daddy didn't die of a heart attack. I'm sure of it! He may have had one in the process of being run off the road, but I just know that his death was no accident. And the fight we all had with him didn't help."

"I don't know what you're talking about. What fight?"

"What fight? When I hit him with that branch!"

"I don't know what you're talking about. You hit who?"

"Daddy! Why can't you remember this?"

"I don't know."

Maggie had one of her classic psychological trauma blocks. The wind was picking up and the fine sand was swirling and blowing, stinging our feet and faces. I had other things to tell her about Daddy's death, but for the moment I was more concerned about her and Grant.

"Just don't do what I did, Maggie. Because of Daddy, I grew up with a frozen heart and married somebody who did *the same thing* to me that Daddy did to Momma."

"That's not unusual." she said.

"Look, you've been thinking some very bad stuff about Grant — that he's possibly, just possibly, screwing somebody else. I've had a lot of time to think — almost a year. When I first found out about Tom what did I do?"

"You kicked his butt out."

"Well, not exactly. He left. But I let out a blue rage of fury I didn't even know I had in me. In truth, I did to him what I always wanted Momma to do to Daddy. How's that for introspection? I was trying to get even for Momma! And what have you done about Grant?"

"Basically, ignored it so far."

"Right, you're doing exactly what *Momma* did."

"Yeah, but let's face facts, as long as we're being so honest. You're anti-men, and you've been gunning for them since you were a girl."

"You can think whatever you want, but that's not true. I was unprepared for the whole business of marriage, terrified of men, and frankly, my dear, so were you. We're getting a little off track."

"So where's the wisdom in this discussion?"

"The wisdom is that I couldn't believe that anyone would ever love me after the way Daddy treated Momma. Plain and simple. And when Tom betrayed me, as I always suspected he would — because in my mind, *that's what men did* — my anger outweighed my disappointment."

"What are you saying? That you never loved Tom? You loved Tom, you know you did."

"I'm not saying I didn't *think* I loved Tom, I'm saying I didn't know what love really was! How could I? Daddy was an abusive, unfaithful son of a bitch of a husband and a sadistic bastard from hell. How are you supposed to learn about healthy love relationships from that?"

"Good point."

"Here's the clincher. I didn't *miss* Tom when he left. That bothered me a lot, that I didn't miss him. But then I saw! How could I miss a love I couldn't feel? One that was never a full emotional investment? Oh sure, my pride was annihilated," I said. "But hurt pride is not the same thing as a broken heart. I get mad at him when he jerks me and Beth around about money and custody visits. But mad is different from the soul longing for reconciliation. Tom was nothing more than some psychological canvas on which I continually repainted my relationship with Daddy."

"Wait a minute, you're practicing psychiatry without a license now."

"Don't you see?" I insisted. "If you never invest that much of your heart in your marriage, you don't lose much when it comes to its inevitable end! It's like wading in the water instead of swimming!"

"Are you saying that you always knew your marriage with Tom would end?"

"No. I'm saying that I've only just realized what a fool I've been all my life."

"I need a glass of wine. It's the weekend. I can justify it. This is pretty heavy and I can't see how it's gonna help me figure out what to do about Grant." She pulled her jacket around her and zipped it.

"Look, forget the wine for a minute. I gotta go soon anyhow. Just think about this. Beth is *us* when *we* were young. I work so hard to keep her relationship with Tom functioning. You know why? Because I want desperately for her to have a father. Tom's no Prince Charming, to be sure, but he's not half as bad as Daddy was. Girls need fathers to love or it's hard as hell to love a husband. But, what about *me*? Will I ever let myself really love somebody? I mean, this is all assuming that I'm not too ancient to attract someone normal with a pulse, but let's say I do. What then? Wouldn't it be the finest tribute I could pay Momma if I lived my life with not just my mind but with my heart too? Wouldn't it somehow redeem her suffering?"

"I don't know. I think she really loved Stanley, don't you?"

"No way. Marriage of convenience. Period."

Stanley was our mother's second husband.

"Well, yeah, probably. Do you think that maybe I don't love Grant? Is that what you're thinking?"

"No. Of course not. I'm saying we should both really look at ourselves. If you want your marriage with Grant to work, then you gotta *really* love him. Talk to him! If I'd loved Tom with all my heart, it would've been an honest failure, if it was meant to fail."

"Having second thoughts? Good grief, Susan."

"Good Lord, no. But the guy taught me the most valuable lessons I've learned in twenty years. Maggie, if you can't *really love* somebody, you're only half alive. If you're only half invested, you can't lose too much. It's the dishonest method of dealing with fear."

"What fear?"

"Of being hurt."

"Do you think it's too late for Grant and I?"

"Grant and me."

She smiled at me and I warmed all over. Finally, she understood what I was saying. "Let's go back, Susan, I'm freezing."

"Maggie? All I'm saying is don't cheat yourself like I cheated myself. And I cheated Tom."

We walked back down the beach together and across the yard toward the Island Gamble. *Gamble. If you don't gamble, you can't win.* The house, the Island, every lesson of life worth learning was right there.

In my mind's eye, visualizing as Livvie had taught me to do, I could see MC standing up from a rocker on the front porch and smiling at all of us, her children, returning safely from the beach. I could feel her relief. She *had* loved us. With whatever was left, after life squeezed her dry, Momma had truly loved us.

Maggie reached over with her hand and completely goofed up my hair, which was already windblown into a thousand knots. "You, mussy, got you'self a busy little factory gone in there, now don't you, chile?"

"Shuh, ain't nothing, nothing in there a-tall, nothing but a mess of worms." I threw my arm around her shoulder.

It was unfair that trouble consumed you in landslides and understanding arrived with the miserly drip of a faucet.

Maggie stopped and picked up a small piece of driftwood. She turned it over, looking at it. "I could make a doorstop out of this," she said.

"What?" She was going to recycle the world. "Hey, Maggie?"

"What? Don't you think that if I stained and varnished this that it would be pretty? Look at the shape of it!"

"Nice. Listen. I found something weird on microfilm in the library archives."

"What?"

"A picture of old Fat Albert holding a fire hose on a bunch of black women and children back in 1963. It was a small civil rights march in Conway. Freedom Riders. The picture was from the *State* paper in Columbia."

"What would Fat Albert have been doing at a civil rights march in Conway? That's like a hundred miles from here."

"Exactly. He was also in charge of the investigation of Daddy's death, wasn't he?"

"I think so. I don't remember."

"All the facts are in the library. I know it. It's all

in the microfilm somewhere. I just have to keep digging."

"You're gonna drive yourself crazy and for what?"

"Peace of mind. I'd like to know that it wasn't me beating Daddy over the head that caused his heart attack. I'd like to know what really happened and I have this new theory about Fat Albert."

She stopped and looked at me with the most serious face I'd ever seen on her. She said, "Susan, I hate to see you doing this to yourself, but you know what? You just might be on to something. In those days men were capable of some pretty hideous things."

"That's right. Please, rack your brain. Do you remember anything else about Fat Albert?"

She took a deep breath and looked away from me. I followed her up the steps to the front porch. She put the driftwood on the floor in the sun to dry it out. We stood rubbing the sand from the bottoms of our feet and put our shoes back on.

"I remember this," she said, "Fat Albert came around the house to warn Daddy about something, didn't he?"

"God, yes, when was that? I remember it, but when? I'll have to ask one of our brothers."

"Save yourself the phone call. It's all coming back. Don't you remember him coming around the house and kicking us out of the kitchen so the grown-ups could talk? It was about the new school. Remember? That's when Daddy was having all that trouble?"

"Wait! I think you're right! God, I always thought Fat Albert was a creep."

"Well, not that it proves anything, but I distinctly remember the week before Daddy died. There were those gunshots through the house and all kinds of stress going on. Uncle Louis was hanging around all the time. Remember?"

"Fat Albert probably fired the shots himself."

"Probably."

"I have to think about it. It's so vague now. I just remember feeling guilty."

"Take my advice, get over it."

"You're right, I'm sure, but I have this thing about knowing the truth."

"Well, the holidays are coming. I think you need to have a little more fun and stop worrying so much. Hey! I have an idea," Maggie said suddenly.

"Not another blind date, please!"

"Nope, let's call Simon and invite him to come for Thanksgiving."

"Simon? My Simon?"

"Yeah, your Simon. I wonder if he still has a sports car?" Her eyes met mine. It was a double dare. "It's less than five hours to Atlanta if you push it a little. Simon could drive it with no sweat. He could even come with Henry if he comes."

"Okay," I said slowly. "I've been thinking about Simon, but I just wasn't ready, you know? And Thanksgiving is rough, Maggie. There's never been one that I don't relive what happened to Daddy."

14

THANKSGIVING 1963

I heard the solid clunk of a closing car door, but struggled to ignore it. My eyes were still shut as I hung in the hazy balance between waking and dreaming. What had I been dreaming? Were Timmy, Maggie, Henry and I all dancing together in a circle? Yes. Was it a celebration? Livvie was out in the yard happily digging a hole. What was she planting? It was pampas grass, already blooming. Enormous plumage. *She looked over to us. We each took a spear and paraded down Sullivan's Island.* Then the image was gone.

Outside, birds rustled through the bushes, singing, whistling and scavenging their morning meal of cassina berries and small bugs. Noisy things, I thought, gathering my quilt around my shoulders. I felt chilled. Slivers of daylight threaded their way through the edges of my eyelids. I was awake then and remembered it was Thanksgiving. I decided I might as well get up.

Knock! Knock! Knock! Knock! Knock! There was the distinct rapping of knuckles five times on the back screen door. The ill-fitted, slightly warped door complained in response to each whack.

What in the world? Below my window I could

just make out the color and model of Mr. Struthers's car, parked under the palmetto tree. A thick cloud of morning fog covered the yard. This can't be good, I thought. What time was it? I bumped my way down the hall to Maggie's room and shook her awake.

"Maggie! Get up! Mr. Struthers's here!"

"What?"

"Mr. Struthers!"

"What time is it?"

"Early!"

"Get Daddy! Or, go get Livvie!"

"You get Livvie! I'll get the door."

Barefooted and wearing just my pajamas, I hurried downstairs to the back porch. The fog was so dense, I couldn't see Mrs. Simpson's house next door. But I could see Mr. Struthers's unshaven face through the screen. He looked very old to me, with spurts of white whiskers among the black ones. Even in November, he wore sandals.

"Mornin' Susan." Mr. Struthers's voice was very somber. "Y'all awake? MC up yet?"

"No, sir," I said. "Come on in. Happy Thanksgiving!"

I offered the greeting hoping to cheer him. I looked at the clock. Five-forty-five. I heard Maggie's and Livvie's footsteps behind me. Then, no one moved. We all looked at Mr. Struthers. He was here to tell us something terrible. I knew it, like Livvie knew things.

"Yeah, God. Thanksgiving," he said. "Y'all bess go get y'all's momma. I called your Uncle Louis. He'll be 'eah in a minute. Let's make us some coffee. It's gonna be a long day."

"What's happened?" I said, feeling queasy. Mr. Struthers hadn't asked for Daddy. Just Momma.

"Go on, now. Get your momma up," he said, sidestepping my question politely.

"Lemme go fetch her," Livvie said. "Maggie, honey, put the coffeepot on."

Mr. Struthers looked so awful standing there in the kitchen. My throat grew lumps. Momma always said he was so handsome but it seemed like all he ever did was tell bad news and deal with people's troubles and every bit of it showed on his face. Being mayor wasn't all it was cracked up to be.

"Should I wake up Timmy and Henry?" I asked. This was about Daddy. He must never have come home last night. I knew then that Daddy was dead.

"No call for that yet. Let them sleep a little." He smiled at me.

Livvie came back in and took the orange juice from the refrigerator. The next thing I knew Aunt Carol and Uncle Louis were coming through the door. They said nothing to Maggie or Livvie or me, which was strange. Usually Uncle Louis at least would greet Livvie and all of us. The room was filled with adults whose anxious, labored breathing was contagious. Maggie and I exchanged knowing looks of anxiety, the fatal kind we learned about when Tipa died.

I began taking cups out of the cabinet. I found the creamer and filled it with milk. Maggie opened the plastic bag of bread and started making toast.

"Is MC up yet?" Uncle Louis asked.

"Be down in a minute," Mr. Struthers said.

Momma appeared in the doorway, a specter in a zip-front terry cloth robe and wild faded auburn hair. She took one look at Mr. Struthers's expression and began screaming.

"No!" She collapsed against the doorjamb and Uncle Louis grabbed her and put her in a chair. *"Oh, God! Please, no!"*

"I'll go call the doctor," Aunt Carol said, and disappeared.

Livvie stepped across the room between Maggie and me and looped an arm around each of us. We all turned to face the table. Mr. Struthers sat down next to Momma and took her hand.

"MC, this is the hardest thing I've ever had to do. Please, just listen. There's been a terrible accident. I'm so sorry. Hank's dead. His car must've gone out of control coming down the last span of the bridge and he went into the marsh. Could've been a heart attack or maybe it was the fog. Could've been the brakes or something. We don't know. There's most likely going to be an investigation to find out what happened. I'll try to handle most of that for you. But for now, you need to make some arrangements for him. The autopsy will begin as soon as possible today. I'll call the coroner's office to double-check, but I'm reasonably sure they'll release his body by tomorrow. I'm so sorry, MC, you know I am."

"Oh, dear God," Momma mumbled. She put her head down on the table and wept. "I can't take it. I can't."

Uncle Louis began to sob and Aunt Carol put her arms around him. He had really loved my daddy. Even Livvie cried. *"Oh, Lawd! Oh, Lawd!"* She searched her pockets for tissues. Maggie turned back to the toast she was making and her tears fell on the bread as she tried in vain to butter it, the knife tearing the bread instead. I put my arm around her. I couldn't make sense of it, the tragedy of it.

Daddy's dead, I said to myself, and I felt light-headed and dizzy. At least Timmy wouldn't get beaten anymore. But poor Henry would be heartbroken. Henry was Daddy's favorite. Well, at least he was nice to somebody.

Uncle Louis blew his nose, sat down on the other side of Momma and rubbed the top of her back.

"Now, MC, I don't want you to worry. Carol and I will be right here for you every step of the way. Oh, God, I'm so sorry. He was like a brother to me." He choked up again and then collected himself, clearing his throat. "Listen, we'll figure out what to do about money and everything, so don't think about that. I'm going over to the city this morning to check on Momma and I'll go to McAlister's and make all the arrangements. All right?"

Momma nodded her head and threw herself into his arms. My uncle began to cry again and Momma just wailed and wailed.

"You'll be alright," he said. "I swear, MC, you'll be alright. All the children too. Please. Let's get hold of ourselves. We've got to." He looked around the room. "Did anybody call the rectory yet? Father O'Brien needs to be called."

"No, I came straight 'eah from the police station," Mr. Struthers said. "The wrecker got the car out the marsh and it's over to the Phillips 66 station by the Cooper River Bridge." Mr. Struthers's answer had little to do with the question and I wasn't so sure I wanted all the details.

"I'll do it right now," Aunt Carol said, once again leaving the room, rubbing her eyes.

Livvie put her arm around me again and squeezed. Everyone was crying except me. I choked up then, but it was rage I felt and fear.

"Now what?" I asked. "Tell me. What's going to happen to us?"

I looked up at her and even Livvie, in all her wisdom, knew I was right. Daddy's death would mean an instantaneous and magnificent downslide for our family. Momma didn't work — she didn't even drive. Livvie hugged me so hard I thought she'd never let me go.

All I could manage was a series of deep sighs.

We'd be poor and fatherless orphans. Momma would go to pieces. Maggie and I would raise the twins. We wouldn't be able to afford Livvie anymore. That was the worst scenario I could imagine. I broke away from her and ran to my room.

I threw myself on the bed and considered running away, but, pathetically, I had nowhere to go. Finally, I started to cry. My tears burned. I heard my door open.

"Susan, please." Maggie was still crying. "Please talk to me."

I continued crying but eventually I rolled over and faced her. "What's the use of living, Maggie?" I asked. "If you can tell me what's the use, I'd give you anything."

"I don't know the answer to that and I don't know why Daddy's dead. I don't know. This is so awful, Susan. Please don't shut me out. You're all I've got!"

"No, she ain't." Livvie was in the doorway with two cups of coffee for us. Her face was dry and she had put on her apron. "Whether y'all likes it or not, y'all got me. Amen."

She handed us the coffee. Maggie took a sip. I took it but didn't want it.

"I don't drink this stuff, Livvie. Thanks anyway." I smelled it and put it to rest on my bedside table.

"It's a grown-up drink, 'eah?"

"Yeah, tastes bitter."

"Life's bitter. Gone, drink it. Y'all bess be growing up today. Y'all got little brothers and little sisters to take care of. People gone be coming like cattle to this 'eah house. Good thing I clean for the holiday. Least we don't have to worry none about that. Drink him, Susan, and both you girls 'eah me good. This is a terrible thing done happen to y'all, but that don't mean you ain't got nothing to do except wail and moan about the injustice of it all. Don't talk to me about injustice. Humph. This 'eah is sure enough bad news, but Gawd got His plan."

"Oh, come on, Livvie. Where was God when Daddy was beating the slop out of Timmy?"

"Susan!" Maggie said, shocked.

I was good and mad.

"You listen 'eah, Miss Susan, don't be disrespectful about Gawd to me!" Livvie said. "You ain't got no right! I don't know *why* these thing happen! They just do! Maybe Gawd think this family be better off with Mr. Hank gone! How do you like that? Maybe He need him in heaven for some kinda work. Or maybe the devil need him to sharpen pitchforks! I don't rightly know. You gots to be a woman, not a ugly-minded, angry chile! Just like when your granddaddy die, people gone be coming around with cake and ham and such. We ain't got no time for wallowing." She looked at us, and then she said more gently, "Now go on, wash your face and put on some clothes. Both of you! This day ain't over yet!"

I dressed, but wasn't aware of doing it, and went downstairs to figure things out. Timmy and Henry finally got up about seven. They wandered down to the kitchen and found all of us there except for Uncle Louis, who had left for the city. Momma was still at the table, head down.

"Momma?" Timmy said.

She lifted her grief-stricken face to him.

"Momma! What's wrong?" Henry said and they both just started crying.

"Sit down, boys," Aunt Carol said. "Your momma has something to tell y'all."

"Daddy. Your daddy's gone," Momma said. She choked up and started sobbing again. Rather than rise up and hug her boys, she put her head back down on the table.

"Where'd he go?" Henry asked.

"Dead," Momma said with difficulty, "car accident."

"Is this true?" Timmy asked.

"Daddy's *dead?*" Henry screamed. "You mean I'm never going to see him again?"

"Come on, son," Livvie said, "let's go for a walk on the porch, just us two."

Henry's crying could be heard across the water

in Charleston, I was sure of it. *Bam! Bam! Bam!*

"He's kicking the walls," Mr. Struthers said to no one in particular. "I'll go outside and see if I can help Livvie."

The fog distorted Henry's cries, sent them pulsating in all directions, until you couldn't tell if it was Henry or someone else crying. Or maybe an animal.

Timmy had been delivered. Henry and Momma felt they'd been robbed. Maggie and I had to be the responsible ones. My anger was like a bonfire.

The phone rang from the hallway. Maggie answered it. It was Uncle Louis. He wanted Aunt Carol. I heard Aunt Carol gasp and say, *"No!"* Instantly, I knew. Grandma Sophie was dead too.

The door slammed and I knew she had gone to the porch for Livvie and Mr. Struthers. Aunt Carol wasn't about to bring that news to Momma alone. She had enough spine to lift her skirt, and enough arrogance to stick her nose up to Livvie, but not enough to face my mother solo.

Timmy, who still sat silently at the table, whispered to me. "Grandma Sophie?"

I nodded my head and he shook his. I jabbed Maggie with my elbow. "Grandma Sophie bit the dust," I whispered.

Her shoulders lurched, she covered her mouth and ran to the bathroom. Timmy and I just stared at each other. I realized that during this entire morning of unbelievable bad news, Momma had not once tried to console any of us.

"Momma?" I said. "Do you know that Maggie's in the bathroom throwing up?" And there was no answer. "Come on, Timmy. Let's go get the twins.

Somebody needs to take care of them."

I looked out the window as a car door closed. The stick-'em doctor was coming up the steps. Momma looked up at me and a shallow line of discontent was drawn between us. I ignored her and left the room with Timmy.

"This is some day, huh, Susan?" Timmy said.

"Yeah. You okay? Shit! I can't believe Daddy's dead."

"Are you kidding me? This is the first break I've ever caught! I hope the son of a bitch is writhing in hell with a branding iron up his butt."

"Timmy! Don't let anybody else hear you say that!"

"Well, aren't you glad he's gone?"

"Yeah, I guess, in a way," I said. "But if he had a heart attack, I'd feel pretty guilty."

"Why? What do you think?"

"I don't know and, right now, I don't want to know."

We passed Mr. Struthers and Livvie in the hall. I pulled on her sweater.

"Grandma Sophie, right?" I asked.

"I'm sorry, Susan, but it's for true," she said, putting her arm around me.

"I knew it," I said.

"Come 'eah, Timmy."

She reached out for him and he shrugged his shoulders, wiggling out of her arm.

"I'm okay, Livvie, really. It's okay. We're gonna go see about the twins."

Timmy raced up the stairs and I stood with Livvie for a minute, then I heard Momma scream again and knew that Mr. Struthers had delivered the news. Livvie ran for the kitchen. I called to Henry and Aunt Carol through the screen door.

"We're out here!" Aunt Carol responded.

"Henry? You okay?" I said. I ignored her, letting the door slam. Henry was lying in the hammock, arms crossed, knees drawn up. Aunt Carol was standing beside him with a tissue pressed against her lips, while her left hand rocked the hammock slowly. She had on khaki pants and a starched blue shirt tucked in tight. Her belt and loafers matched and her hair was sprayed. I had thrown on something and everybody else was still in pajamas. I wondered how long she'd made Uncle Louis wait so that she could accessorize herself.

The sun was up now, burning through the fog over the eastern end of the Island. At least the day would be clear.

"Henry, answer me. Are you all right?"

"Guess so," he said.

"Henry, this is the worst day of our lives, no doubt about it. I love you, Henry. You know that, don't you?"

"Guess so," he said.

"Okay, wanna help me and Timmy? I mean, we all gotta pitch in today."

"Help you do what?" He looked up at me pitifully and my throat buckled.

"About a million things. Come on." I reached for him and he took my hand and stood up. I gave him a hug and he ran for the door.

"Timmy's upstairs," I called out.

He let the door slam. I thought to myself that we'd probably let it slam over and over today and Livvie would say nothing about it.

"You're a good sister, Susan," said Aunt Carol.
"Well, I try."
I leaned over the banister, wanting to tell her what I thought of her, what I had seen her do, blast her away. I fought to hold my tongue. We needed Uncle Louis and I didn't want to start more trouble than we already had.
"This is so incredible, so awful," she said. "How could God take y'all's grandmomma and daddy in one day? I just don't understand it."
"Me neither. Momma's a complete mess."
"I would be too."
"Guess we're all gonna have to get jobs."
"Uncle Louis will figure it out, don't you worry. You're still a little girl, Susan. You shouldn't have to worry about these things. I'm gonna go help your momma."
"Yeah, Dr. Whicket's here to give her a shot. She ought to be collapsing any second now."
She gave me an odd look. What I'd said had the distinctive ring of impudence to my aunt's ears. On the other hand, what she said had the ring of pure fantasy to me. Saying nothing more, she left me quietly, alone on the porch. Alone to think.
Not worry, Aunt Carol? I have an aching inside of me that could match the pain of any adult. How would I cope? Was it my fault? I wondered. Had I caused Grandma Sophie's stroke when she helped me to bed? Did the fight give Daddy a heart attack? Would Momma wake up one day and blame us? If he had a heart attack, were us kids responsible? Was it the Klan? Was it an accident? Would the police be here, asking questions?
I wondered what Mr. Struthers thought. Maybe

he thought Timmy, Maggie and I caused Daddy's death. If he were going to have us all put in jail, we'd know soon enough. But it would be hard to prove, I decided.

I started going down the list as I paced the floor. I'd encourage Timmy to shield Henry from the horrors of the funeral. Timmy would help. It wasn't Henry's fault that Daddy was dead or that Grandma Sophie had died. This could have a terrible effect on him, I thought, he could start wetting the bed or something. The twins would never know the difference, but Henry could suffer forever.

Timmy would eventually feel guilty about being glad that Daddy was dead. I'd get Maggie to keep an eye on Timmy. I wasn't exactly glad about Daddy, but sort of relieved to know he wouldn't be back. The last time I'd seen him he was screwing his secretary. And at least the beatings would stop.

Grandma Sophie, well, she was another case entirely. Eccentric. It was too bad she kicked the bucket, I thought, but, hell, she wasn't really living. Sitting in that room, stinking up the place, running us around to wait on her, eating the same thing every day, not talking.

I decided to go find Maggie. Maybe she could make me feel better. Timmy was heading for the kitchen to heat up bottles for Sophie Jr. and Allie.

"Thought you were gonna help me!" he said.

"Sorry, I'll be there in a minute. Promise. Just wanna check on Maggie."

"Okay."

"Be right back!" I called back as I ran up the stairs. The twins were crying and Henry was cooing to them like a daddy pigeon. Let him deal with it for a few minutes, it won't kill him, I thought. Opening Maggie's door, I stuck my head in. She was lying in bed on her side, her knees drawn up to her stomach.

"Hey, you okay?"

"Yeah, I just feel like throwing up every two seconds."

"You sick?"

"I don't think so. Nerves. Susan, come in. Talk to me."

"I told Timmy I'd help him with the twins. Gotta feed them, you know. You need anything?"

"Yeah, a new identity."

"Don't we all? I'll be right back as soon as they're fed."

In the twins' room, Timmy picked up Allie and sat in the rocker. I took a bottle, curled up with Sophie on the daybed, tested the milk on my arm and stuck the nipple in her mouth. She grabbed it, started sucking like a madwoman and looked up at me, gratefully. What did she think? That we'd let her starve to death?

I looked over at Henry, who was standing behind Timmy, making faces at Allie and poking her tummy with his finger. Allie giggled and spit out the nipple. I smiled and began to relax. We'd be all right, I thought, we'd make it through this.

I looked down at Sophie's eyelashes; she blinked as she drank and her lashes swept her cheeks. My two little baby sisters were precious. If I spent more time with them and less time trying to figure out the grown-ups, I'd be better off.

"Hey, Henry!" I said.

"What?"

"Wanna feed Sophie?"

"Sure!" He bounced on the bed and reached out for her. Carefully, I put her in his lap.

"Watch her head. And don't drop her. Babies don't bounce."

"I know, I know. Jeesch!" Henry rolled his eyes at me and I smiled.

"Hey, how's Maggie?" Timmy asked.

"Barfed her guts out but I think she's gonna live."

"Well, thank God for that!" Timmy said.

"Yeah, around here, you never know," I said, sliding off the bed. "I'm gonna look in on her again. Be careful!" I pointed my finger at Henry.

"Yes, Mother!" Henry teased.

"Don't worry, I'll watch him like a hawk," Timmy said.

"Be right back."

Walking down the hall to Maggie's room, I felt marginally restored. We children were inside a ring, living in our own circle, almost self-sufficient. We all loved each other, and each of us could depend on that. And we still had Livvie.

The reality of the funeral hit me again. I couldn't imagine what it would be like to have my father and my grandmother in caskets before my eyes. Maggie and I would figure out a plan to get through it. I opened her bedroom door again. She was gone. The bathroom door was closed. I put my ear next to it to listen. I could just barely hear her, gagging and coughing. I almost gagged myself. Poor Maggie. At last, I heard the water running in the sink.

"Hey! You need me?"

"No, I'm okay."

I opened the door anyway, barged in, and soaked a clean washcloth with cold water.

"Brush your teeth and go lie down. Put this on your head," I said.

"God, I feel awful. Thanks." She took the cloth and, hands shaking, she put toothpaste on her toothbrush.

"I'll bet. Think you have the flu or something? Your eyes are glassy."

"No. Just my stomach is so bad."

"Well, today's enough to make anybody sick."

"Yeah." She brushed her teeth while I waited, sitting on the side of the tub.

"I wonder how Momma is," I said.

"I went downstairs a little while ago. Would you believe she's sleeping in Sophie's bed?"

"Gross me out! You're kidding!"

"Nope, and Aunt Carol is in the kitchen with Livvie. I guess they're gonna be here for dinner."

"Some lousy Thanksgiving this is gonna be," I said.

She hit her toothbrush on the side of the sink a few times and put it back in the holder. She looked in the mirror and held back her hair. She swayed back and forth. "No lie. Speaking of lousy, I look green!"

"You'd better get back in bed. I guess the wake will be tomorrow or the day after. You'd better get well."

"I'd rather stay home, if it's okay with you." She stumbled toward her room and flopped down on her bed. I pulled her spread and sheet up over her, then laid the cloth across her forehead.

"Oh, no. I don't care if you have to wear a bucket

around your neck, you're coming. No way am I going through this without you."

"I'll be all right. Don't worry, I'll be better."

"Why don't you try to get a nap or something and I'll go change the twins. Then I'm gonna go help Livvie. Call me if you need anything."

I closed Maggie's door and went back to the twins' room.

Henry had Sophie up on his shoulder, hand poised to slap her back. Timmy had Allie on his shoulder, his hand extended in the same position.

"One, two, three!" *Slap!*

"Whurp!" Both babies belched like lumberjacks.

"Hey! We're having a burping contest! Listen to this!" Timmy said. "Come on, Sophie. Let one rip!"

Sophie made a huge noise, more like a sailor than a three-month-old baby. Timmy, Henry and I started laughing, loud and long. It was good to laugh.

"Gimme that child, Henry!"

Still laughing, he handed her over to me and I put her on the changing table.

"Ah, Susan! She's my champ!" Henry said.

"You should've heard Allie! 'Whurp!' " Timmy imitated.

We began laughing again.

"Uh-oh. She's wet and you know what else she did too. Yuck! Stinko! I'll put her in the crib. Come on, Henry, let's go watch the Macy's parade."

"Poop!" Henry shrieked. "She pooped!"

"Thanks a lot!" I said.

"Poop! The whole room stinks like poop! Pretty

soon the whole house is gonna smell like poop! You're gonna smell like poop!"

"Henry Hamilton! Hush your mouth! Mr. Struthers will hear you!"

"Who's going to make him hush?" Timmy winked at me.

Oh, my God. The tigers had been unleashed. I needed to talk to Livvie about the boys right away or they'd run around like wild bandits getting into trouble. Then I thought, So what? Let them run.

15

THANKSGIVING 1999

We left a message on Simon's answering machine. It was exhilarating to hear his voice. He sounded exactly the same as he always had, mellow and slightly amused. I hoped he would call us back. We left Maggie's number and mine.

The following Monday, Michelle Stoney called. The papers were finally ready. I went to her office that afternoon. My hand shook as I signed my name.

"Michelle, I can't thank you enough for everything you've done for Beth and me," I said.

I got choked up and she handed me a tissue. "I know this is hard," she said.

"Yeah, but it's the right thing. I know it is."

"I'll file them with the court next week and if it all goes smoothly, as I expect it will, it will be final within the year."

I put the pen down and blew my nose. We talked a little more, shook hands and said good-bye.

"Call me if you need anything, Susan. I mean it."

"Thank you. I will."

I drove myself home and took a long walk around the Battery wall on the harbor. Laps of water splashed the sides of the seawall. All the years with Tom crossed my mind in scenes, like a home video. How my life had changed! But it was all right. I felt good. I had another chance to rebuild my future and this time I'd do an honest job with my heart.

As soon as the ink was dry on our papers, Tom called. I guessed that we were both feeling kind of strange about the official end of our relationship. It was the first time I'd spoken to him since the hurricane. I wasn't angry with him any longer. In fact, once he agreed to the terms of our separation, I was grateful to him. My heart had forgiven him.

His voice sounded odd and when I asked him what was wrong he said, "Nothing. I just was wondering what you're doing for the holiday, that's all."

It seemed that Miss Natural High, his love goddess, had left him again. This time she was off for a trek to Nepal to find herself and to dig for crystals in the Himalayas. He knew I would find that hysterically funny and I thought he was telling me the story to make me laugh. He was.

"Stop, no more," I said, "my sides are killing me! This girl leaves you so often I can't keep track."

"Like you always said, I need a revolving door," he said. "So what's up?"

I told him I was cooking dinner for Maggie and her bunch.

"Well, the plan is to have Thanksgiving at my house and Christmas at hers. It's just us, although there was some noise about Henry and his gang coming from Atlanta. I don't know."

"Gosh, that sounds nice," he said. "Any special plans?"

"Just the usual troft frenzy — turkey, ham and the million mashed things we like. God, you'd think we can't chew, with all the creamed vegetables, right?"

"Yeah, it sounds wonderful." A long silence. Then he said, "Guess I'll just go out to Morrison's Cafeteria and eat with the Lonely Hearts Club."

"Oh, all right, you old pain in my behind. Do you want to join us?"

"I thought you'd never ask!"

He asked if he could bring anything and I said, "Yeah, bring enough wine to float the *Queen Livvie*."

Thanksgiving Day arrived and Simon still hadn't called. I told myself that he must've been out of town. Roger had sent me flowers. I debated throwing them in the garbage but put them on the coffee table instead. They were extraordinarily beautiful, too fabulous to waste. Every time I looked at them my feet itched.

Maggie, Grant and the boys arrived and Tom pulled up in the driveway at the same time. It took the males about twenty seconds to turn on the football game, grab beers, Cokes and potato chips and start making macho noises at the television. It took another two seconds for the females to suck our teeth in disgust and put on aprons.

Beth, Maggie and I were in the kitchen basting the bird and finding counter space for all the casseroles of vegetables.

"This holiday always reminds me of Livvie,"

Maggie said. "I sure do miss her."

"Yeah, Gawd, that's for true!" I said. "Lawd have mercy! That woman had us chopping *vegetubble,* 'eah? Chopping and such till we like to drop!"

"You sound just like her," Maggie said.

Beth giggled.

"You know, every year I make rutabagas in her honor and collard greens too. Remember how she used to get on us about how we picked collards? 'You gots to pull out every single vein and put some vinegar to the pot water or he gone stink up the whole house!' God, was she great or what?"

"The greatest," Maggie said. "She never gave up trying to teach you to cook, did she?"

"Poor woman, I was hopeless," I said.

"I got gypped not knowing her," Beth said.

"Yeah, but you got your momma, and that's just about the next best thing," Maggie said.

Everything was finally in a pot or an oven and Beth wanted to go see a friend down the block.

"I'll be back by three, come on, Mom! I swear!"

"Don't swear, and take a sweater. It's chilly. Dinner's at four."

I gave her a peck on the cheek and in a moment she was gone out the back door. Maggie and I watched her disappear around the side of the house.

"She's so grown up," Maggie said. "Where did the time go?"

"Seems like we ask that question more and more lately." I put the knives and the cutting boards in the sink and turned on the faucet, squirting liquid soap over the whole mess, scrubbing away.

"Sure does. Where's the butter? I'll nuke some more to baste the bird," Maggie said.

"Second shelf, in the cheese thing."

She found it, cut some squares into a bowl and covered them in plastic wrap. I heard the door close, followed by the programing beeps of my microwave oven, and I thought, here we were, the older ones now. It made me pause and reflect.

"So, what's up with Tom?" Maggie asked. "He seems so subdued."

"Oh, Maggie, who knows? He thinks he's coming back again, I guess, now that he and Miss Kama Sutra have broken up again."

"Well?"

"Oh, gimme a break. Our divorce is going through next summer, I hope. I talked with Michelle last week and she said it's on the books for then. I can't be with him anymore, you know? No spark!"

"Whoa. Well, if there's no fire to light, hang it up."

"We're practically like old war buddies or something at this point."

"That's the best thing if you can handle it," Maggie said. "You know, considering Beth."

"Yeah, definitely."

"Did he say why he and what's-her-face broke up?"

"She ran off somewhere, and I'm sure I'll hear the details before the day's over. He gets sentimental around the holidays."

"Most people do," she said.

"By the way, I have to tell you that writing this column is about the smartest thing I ever did that you told me to do, O Excellent Sister of Mine."

"Yeah, tell me what criminal act of genius I've committed this time."

"Well, it's just that all the things you've told me to do, I've done — and I really feel better about myself, you know?"

"Big sister is God. All-knowing, always right. How's the column going?"

"Well, I was gonna wait until dinner to announce it, but what the heck. Guess what?"

"Spill it!"

"It's being picked up by the *Atlanta Journal*!"

"Ha! I can't stand it! And do we earn a bit more in the deal?"

"Yes, we do! And the *Miami Herald*!"

"Oh, my God! Susan, this is so wonderful! I told you you were the best! Let's celebrate!"

She opened the refrigerator and pulled out a bottle of white wine. It was, after all, a holiday. We clinked our glasses and hugged.

"Well, I'm not the only licensed therapist in the family," she said. "I have to tell you about Grant and me."

"Tell it, sugar. Gimme the butter and I'll paint the turkey again."

" 'Eah, watch your fingers." She handed the hot dish to me. "Well, after that big speech you gave me the day we were on the beach —"

"What do you mean *speech?* Damn! This is hot!"

"It was a *good* speech, okay? I went home and thought about it for days and then I decided to do something I've never done with a man before."

"Suck his toes?"

"Jesus! Now you've got me cursing!" Maggie

said. “No! I came clean with him. I called him at the hospital and I said, ‘Grant? There are a few things we need to talk about so we know where we stand with each other. When are you coming home?’ ”

“Oh, God! Did he get nervous or what?”

“No, I don’t think he had time to. I took out a good bottle of wine, made spaghetti and salad with homemade croutons, strawberry shortcake, and sent the boys to their friends for the night. I had my hair done, charged three hundred dollars’ worth of Chanel cosmetics to the American Express card and bought an armload of flowers and some very sexy lingerie and mood music on tape at Victoria’s Secret. I perfumed myself, the bedroom, and changed the sheets. Then, I set the table with my best everything and lit every candle in the house. When he walked in I thought I’d have to give him oxygen! You should’ve seen his face!”

“Oh, my God. Talk slow. I want to remember this. I might need it someday.”

“Don’t write about it, okay?”

“Maggie, I’d never do that. I swear! Continue!”

“Okay. So! He said, ‘What’s all this?’ And, I said, ‘ ’Eah Grant, drink this and sit down. We have to talk.’ And he said, ‘What about?’ I took a big gulp of wine and let it roll! I said, ‘Grant? I thought for a long time that you were fooling around on me and I even thought I had proof. I was so paranoid I couldn’t stand it. I think a big part of this just might be my fault. I think that if we understood each other a little better we’d be a lot happier. What do you think?’ ”

“This is good. Tell me more!”

"Well, at first, he waffled all around, saying, 'Shoot, honey, I think we're the perfect couple!' but I held my ground. I said, 'Grant, listen 'eah. We're no better than hamsters on a wheel. You're running and I'm running. I'm so bogged down with committee meetings and carpooling and you're at work nine-tenths of the time. How can we be the perfect couple when we never see each other? Sure, we're nice enough to each other and we do all the right things on the surface, but there are things I've never even talked to you about. You must have secrets you'd love to share with someone. Dreams? I do.' "

"So what did he say?"

"Well, at first he just listened to me. I told him about things I'd never told him, about old Lucius and how he broke my heart, and about Daddy and how Daddy terrorized us all the time. I had never told Grant any of that stuff. You have to remember, he only knew Stanley."

"Right, that's right, God rest that sweet man's soul."

"Amen. Anyway, I told Grant I knew I hadn't been loving him right, and that, in fact, he hadn't been loving me right, but that it was probably because we didn't know what the other one really needed. You never knew his momma and daddy like I did," she said, "but they were pretty strict Baptists. When Grant converted to the Church, they almost died and never really considered us family after that. That really hurt him, but I was too afraid to say to him that he didn't have to convert at all! I thought that if we didn't go to church together we wouldn't really be a family. Is that dumb or what? Oh, God, Susan, we talked about so much stuff that we had bottled up for years! We stayed up all night."

"So what else happened? I mean, I was away at college and then when I came home I met Tom and that was that. You were living in Savannah and pregnant."

"That's right. I was going through the setting-up-the-parameters part of my marriage and didn't have a clue what it meant! I mean, all these years, Grant never knew all the secrets I carried. I was so ashamed that we were poor. I mean, we looked so unsophisticated next to his family. Ridiculous, right?"

"Not really. You had the same problem with Lucius's mother, remember? She wanted him to marry a debutante from Charleston, not a Catholic girl from Sullivan's Island. Remember?"

"Oh, dear Lord, you're right! I did! And who wound up coming back here and loving it when Grant decided to practice here? I did! God, isn't life funny?"

"It sure is. You can't get the Geechee out of the girl."

"True. Anyway, Grant and I spent a lot of time laughing at our stupidity and Grant swears he never meant to hold out on me. He thought I didn't care about the lining of his soul. I told him that I wanted to really and truly live for his love if he'd live for mine."

"So things have been good? Want some more wine?" I poured myself another glass.

"Nah, thanks, I'll wait for dinner. Yeah, things have been real good. I really love him, Susan. I love our family and I don't want to shortchange it. I just knew it was time to tell him my whole story. Like you said, if it heads south after that, it won't be because we didn't give it an honest shake."

"Damn, Maggie, this is great. I'm so proud of you. If I ever fall in love again, I'm gonna come clean too."

She threw her arm around my shoulder and gave me a good squeeze. The front door closed and I knew Beth was back. It was three o'clock on the nose and time to take the bird out of the oven and put the casseroles in. We fussed around some more and soon it was finally time to eat.

"Well, we'd better feed the Pilgrims before winter sets in," I said.

"I'll call everyone," Maggie said, leaving the room.

"Need any help?" Beth said and gave me a kiss on the cheek.

"Perfect timing, missy, go wash your hands."

We had enough food for a small battalion of starving soldiers, which turned out to be the correct amount, given the voracious appetites of Maggie's boys and the men. Maggie and I had cooked and baked for a week. As I looked over the pots and casseroles, I was almost embarrassed by the excess. But by the grace of God, I hadn't burned anything.

I lit the candles on the dining room table and thought to myself that it looked beautiful. My mixed collection of small antique bowls held sweet pickles, artichoke relish, mustard and mayonnaise. Maggie had brought over her straw cornucopia and filled it with flowers and skewered vegetables.

The table was set for the seven of us and I decided to put Grant and Tom at the ends. It might be the last time we celebrated a holiday with Tom and I felt a generous spirit.

"All right, everyone, let's sit down and bless the last Thanksgiving of the millennium," I said.

"Looks great, Aunt Susan," Bucky said.

"Thanks, honey. Tom, why don't you sit here? Would you like to say grace?"

We gathered around the table and bowed our heads.

"Bless us, O Lord," Tom prayed, "and these Thy gifts, which we are about to receive, through Thy bounty, and Christ our Lord."

"Amen," we responded together.

"And, Lord," he said, his voice quavering, "please bless and protect my family, especially my daughter and her mother, and all of us here today. Please let us live in peace. Amen."

"Amen," we said again.

Tom's eyes were filled with tears. I held on and was grateful when the talk and chatter of the holiday began. I lifted the tureen and began to fill the soup plates.

"Pass the biscuits, Grant," Maggie said. "Gosh, Susan, that soup smells so good!"

"It's divine and it should be. After all, you made it!"

"Not too much, Susan, I want to save myself for the turkey!" Tom said.

"Grace was so nice, Tom, thank you," I said.

"I meant it."

"I know you did," I said.

The meal began with a Lowcountry specialty —

oyster stew, which we had served every Thanksgiving I could remember. We had so many dishes of food that the buffet had to be set up on my kitchen island. Turkey, stuffing, giblet gravy, glazed ham, collard greens, creamed rutabagas, creamed beets in orange sauce, fresh peas and onions, corn pudding, string bean casserole, candied sweet potatoes, a huge green salad, homemade biscuits, pecan pie, pumpkin pie, mincemeat pie and a whipping cream pound cake with lemon sauce. Over the next hour, we got up and helped ourselves until we could eat no more.

No one talked about the Thanksgiving when Daddy and Sophie had died, thank the Lord. We had beaten that horse to death over the years. No, we just ate and laughed, and the house was filled with good spirit and outrageous lies about fishing trips and athletic accomplishments.

"Let's have dessert later," I said, finally.

"I'm so tired of chewing my jaw hurts," Grant said.

"Let's go in the living room for a little bit," Maggie said. "Beth, honey? Switch on the coffeemaker, okay?"

"Sure thing," Beth said.

I read somewhere that there's something in turkey that makes you sleepy. It must be true. Maggie's boys and Beth did all the dishes while I fell half-asleep on the couch in the living room. I could vaguely hear Grant, Tom and Maggie talking over the noise of a third football game on the television. I loved having them all in my house. My house now, but part of Tom would always be here.

Finally, the television was turned off and somebody pulled an afghan over me. I heard Beth saying good night, exchanging kisses and was relieved that my sister's family understood that I was too wiped to get up. After a while, my radar told me Tom was still in the house. I knew he was hanging around for something. I forced myself to get up, and sure enough, I found him in the kitchen talking to Beth.

"Dinner was great, Mom."

"Thanks, doodle. I'm just going to wash my face and try to revive myself. I'll be right back."

"Yeah, Susan, it was really a great dinner."

"Thanks. Stick around, I'll buy you a sandwich."

He smiled at me and we were friends at last.

Upstairs, all I wanted to do was get under the covers and close my eyes. I gave the comforter on my bed a pat and said, "I'll be back soon." My face needed powder and lipstick, which I applied after brushing my teeth. Somehow brushing my teeth always wakes me up.

Tom was in the living room waiting for me. "Beth went to the movies with her girlfriends," he said. "I told her it was okay."

"Sure, that's fine," I said. "Want some coffee? I have to wake up."

"Got any scotch?"

"Sure, help yourself," I said.

He followed me to the kitchen and filled a glass with ice and three fingers of alcohol. It was a very strong drink for Tom. I stirred the milk into my coffee and waited.

"Susan, I want to talk to you about something," he said. "Let's go in the living room."

"Sure," I said.

We sat on the couch and he took a giant gulp of his drink. "Susan, I don't know how to say this except to come right out and tell you the truth."

"Please."

"Karen and I are not really broken up," he said.

"You told me last week you were."

"Yeah, but I didn't tell you everything," he said. "We're just taking some time off."

"You don't have to tell me all this if you don't want to, you know. I mean, it's none of my business."

"I've changed my will," he said.

"Oh?"

"Yes. My estate is worth nearly two million dollars and I've made Beth the sole beneficiary. The money would be held in a trust with you as the guardian until she's thirty."

"Where on God's earth did you get two million dollars?"

"My parents left me a huge block of blue-chip stock that I never told you about."

Good grief, I thought, another minor secret of our marriage.

"Why are you telling me this now?" I asked.

"I have prostate cancer."

"Tom! Oh, my God! Oh, Tom, I'm so sorry!" I put my arms around him and he started to cry. Then I did too. I couldn't help it. "Come on, now, tell me everything," I said.

"It's why I told Beth she could go out. No one knows except Karen, and I had to tell somebody. . . ."

"When did you find this out?"

"About a month ago. I'm so worried I can't

begin to tell you."

"Of course you are. Look, darling, it's gonna be all right. Prostate cancer is common and they can get it out. We'll find you the best surgeon and you'll be fine!"

"I'm not having the operation," he said.

"Why not? Is it gone that far? Oh, my God!"

"No, no. It's in the beginning stages. It's because — look, *if* I have the surgery then there's a large chance that I can't ever have sex again."

I couldn't believe my ears.

"Tom, they've got that new pill."

"I know, but with the particular kind of cancer I've got, they don't think it will work for me."

"Tell me this again. I don't think I heard you correctly."

"It's why Karen left me. I was going to have the surgery but she said that if I do and I can't perform, then it's over between us forever. Sex is such a big thing to her and she's young, Susan. I can't expect her to spend the next fifty or sixty years of her life not ever having sex."

"Let's go back here a little bit. First of all, I can hardly believe this conversation. This is about you and your health and your life, for God's sake. You have a daughter, Tom. Would you miss seeing Beth get married, holding her children in your arms, all that can happen in your life for this self-centered little whore? Have you lost your mind?"

"I knew you'd see it this way."

"What is that supposed to mean? How else *should* I see it?"

"Look, Susan, this is something you can't possibly understand. You're a woman."

"That's right. I am. Not a horrible child like Ka—"

"Let me finish, okay?"

"Sorry. Go ahead."

"Even if I break up with Karen, who else would want a man who can't get it up?"

"You are really a damn fool. Who wants women with mastectomies? Who wants women with hysterectomies? I'll tell you. Real men, that's who."

"Yeah, you're probably right, but I can't imagine it . . . never making love to a woman again."

"Don't preach to me about the importance of having a sex life. I'm something of an expert in that area, and guess what? I've always found plenty to occupy my time and plenty of satisfaction in those things. And, as long as we're being so brutally honest with each other, there's a long list of what you can do when making love besides penetration, Tom. Books have been written about it. Lots of them."

"So what should I do?"

"Are you serious? You have the surgery, that's what. Plain and simple. Look, don't they have those prosthesis things, a pump or something to make it work? And they'll improve the pill!"

"I don't know about that stuff. I haven't gone that far yet. I just got the lab report and went home."

"Who's your doctor?"

"Some guy Grant sent me to. Youngworth, I think."

"Does Grant know?"

"No, I told you, just you and Karen."

"Well, Tom, I'm not running away to the Himalayas to hide from you."

"That's good. Thanks, Susan."

"Look, you may have broken my heart and I may have cried a river over it, but I'm not going to stand by and watch you throw your life away."

"I just don't know what I'm going to do."

He hung his head and wrung his hands. I felt so sorry for him. He was watching his life slip away and couldn't decide if it was worth saving. When he looked up at me, his eyes were tearing. From his breathing, I knew he was on the verge of weeping again and then the floodgates opened.

"Susan, tell me this. Do you still love me enough to let me come home? Will you take care of me? Would you do that?" Tears were streaming down his face.

"Tom, listen to me. There's a place in my heart that's gonna love you until the day I die, but I do not want to live with you as man and wife, even if you *didn't* have this terrifying problem. However, you are the father of my only child, and I will not abandon you if you need me. I will help you find the best doctors and see that you have the best care. That much I promise."

"I don't know what to do. I don't want to go through this alone."

"You won't."

"I have to think about it. I'm going back to my apartment now."

I stood up and gave him a hug.

"Call me tomorrow, okay?" I said.

"I will."

I looked at the door as it closed behind him. Through the window I watched him go through the gate and toward his car. It used to be *our* gate. You could see his terrible sadness in the back of his shoulders, the way he walked, the way he held himself. So much had changed. Another Thanksgiving and another disaster. My head was pounding and my heart raced. I didn't want Tom to die. The thought of it terrified me.

16

Operating in the Christmas Theater

1999

It was Wednesday afternoon, December first. Tom had seen an oncologist that day and I was waiting for him to call. We hadn't told Beth about Tom's cancer yet, but Tom had called Grant for advice, so then Maggie and Grant knew.

Beth and I were searching for Christmas ornaments up in the dark attic. A single bare lightbulb, with a pull chain of yarn, was the guardian that saved us from falling through the rafters. It was a favorite ritual, performed each year with the excitement of anticipating a birth. The birth of the Christ Child, of course, but the holidays also marked the end of one year and the birth of another. And this year had been extraordinary. Beth had transformed into a young woman and I too had begun a new life. And there was the rapid approach of the Millennium, which was sure to bring change to the world.

The ornaments in the boxes chronicled our

lives. Some were shaped like stars, teddy bears and balls that I had stitched together and decorated with sequins when Tom and I were first married. Cookie ornaments by the dozens that Beth and I had baked together and then shellacked. And every paper chain that Beth had ever made was somewhere in a box, wrapped with care in tissue paper.

Tom was very much on my mind as I carried the boxes down to the living room. It was going to be our first Christmas without him living in the house and now my heart was heavy with his illness.

I decided to move the couch and put the tree in front of the window. I had hoisted one end out about five feet when Beth came in with another load of decorations.

"Want to give me a hand here?" I said.

She put three boxes on the chair and gave me a small round of applause before coming to help.

"Very funny, wise guy," I said. "Let's push this over on that wall and move the chairs to the sides of the mirror."

"Okay. Momma? Do we have to use the fake tree this year?"

"Why not? It doesn't shed and it looks very real."

"I'd like just once in my life to smell a real tree, that's all," she said.

"You know what? You're right. Let's go get us a real tree! A big one!"

"What if it dies before Christmas?"

"It ain't gonna die, because you're in charge of watering it."

"Oh, great. Me and my big mouth."

"Come on. Get your jacket."

Small forests had sprung up overnight in front of the grocery stores. I drove west of the Ashley River and Beth was confused.

"Where are we going?" she asked.

"Kroger's."

"What? We, like, *never* shop there!"

"Well, because it's not so convenient, but, my dear child, the front of the store is in the shade. That's where they have the trees. It means they don't bake all day in the Lowcountry sun and we might get one that will last all month."

"God, Mom, you are, like, a total genius. You think of everything."

"Don't say . . ."

"Right. Sorry."

"Thank you."

All the streetlights had glittering wreaths hanging from them. Their red bows waved in the chilly breeze. The city was putting on its holiday finery, and I was getting excited about Christmas. Something inside told me that Tom would survive and that he'd be fine. I was going to worry, though, just in case. In my family's Catholic tradition, if you took good health for granted you risked terrible disease. So part of me ran a silent novena, pleading to all the saints for God's mercy for Tom, and the rest of me prepared for the holidays with a child's wide eyes. And here I was, about to open the wallet for a fresh tree when we have a perfectly good artificial one. That was an indication of the slight recklessness I was feeling.

"I'm really excited about Christmas, doodle," I said, "how 'bout you?"

"Yeah, I mean, I can't believe that everybody is really coming. It's going to be a blast!"

"Yeah, Uncle Henry and Uncle Timmy and their clans are coming to the Island. We have tons of shopping to do. They're staying through the Millennium too. What a party! What do you want from Santa this year?"

"Oh, the entire contents of the Gap would be good for starters. How about you?"

"Gosh, I don't know. Let's see. A Jaguar, a shopping spree that never ends and a face-lift. How's that?"

"You don't need a face-lift, Mom. You have a gorgeous face."

"Ah, my precious one, I see a Gap in your future!"

"So, Mom, what do you think about the Millennium? Do you think the world's coming to an end? A lot of kids at school say so."

"Beth, every day is the end of the world for someone. It's a sin to be superstitious. But I think it's going to be the wildest New Year's Eve of your entire life, and nothing's ending that I know of."

"Well, I suppose. We'll see."

We pulled into the parking lot and got out. Kroger's had hundreds of trees from which to choose. A teenage boy wearing a sweater over his apron was outside helping customers. We would surely try his patience before we finally decided on the perfect tree. He was cute — in spite of his acne — long and lanky. He flirted with Beth with no shame.

"So, where do you go to school?" he said to her, smiling like a Cheshire cat.

"Bishop England," she said, grinning back.

"Are you a cheerleader?"

"Well, I do it for the exercise. Most cheerleaders are, you know, *'Puh-leeeze!'* " she said with rolling eye drama and he started laughing.

"Yeah, airheads. Me, I play football."

"Whatever," Beth said, effectively blowing him off.

"I play tennis too."

"You do?" Now he had her attention. "For who?"

"Porter Gaud," he said.

"Do you know Jonathan Ashton?"

"Yep, whipped his butt about a million times. He's a jerk."

"Yeah, no kidding," she said. "I went out with him."

Now, technically that was a lie, but I didn't say anything. I just kept my mouth shut and looked at the Douglas firs.

"I'm Chris Stapleton," he said and shook her hand.

Nice manners, I thought and pulled a tree away from the wall.

"Beth Hayes," she answered.

"Excuse me, but do you think that you could hold this tree up for us?" I said.

"Sure, sorry." He cut the nylon cord from around the tree, hit the trunk on the sidewalk and the limbs flopped down. "Here we go. Whoa! This is a beauty."

He was right. I walked around it and he watched Beth follow me. A new puppy love was in bloom and I was a witness. It delighted me to see it. And it made me remember Simon again. He had never called. Maybe he was just not interested.

"Well. Beth, what do you think?" I asked. "Is this the tree of your dreams?"

"Yep, definitely," she said, and I knew she couldn't have cared less.

"We have to cut a hole in the ceiling to get this baby up, but hey, it wouldn't be the first hole in the house."

"Mom!" She turned to him (obviously I was ruining her life) and said, "We don't have *any* holes in our house."

"Okay, son, we'll take it," I said.

"Great. Just please take this tag inside to pay and I'll wrap it up for you. Where's your car?"

"Here, Beth, take the keys. She'll show you."

In that moment of excellent judgment, I left my daughter for a few minutes to give them the chance to swap phone numbers or whatever it is that they do swap these days. E-mail addresses? Beeper numbers? Cell phone numbers? Whatever. I was definitely getting mellower lately.

When we got home, together we hauled the tree from the car to the back porch, tripping and bumbling from the weight and the sheer size of it.

"She had to have a fresh tree," I said.

"Oh, don't be a Grinch, Mom."

"Sixty dollars." I was short of breath and cash.

"What? Sixty bucks for a stupid tree?"

"Hold on! Take it easy on the steps!"

"On the other hand," she said, "we're the only family I know that has a fake tree that sheds."

"Okay, okay. Go get the bucket and fill it with water."

We left the tree on the porch overnight to give it

a good drink. Decorating for the holidays had always been a family tradition, something that we did together. In the short passing of one year, all our traditions became things of the past — just memories. Now Beth and I would face what life had brought and find our way through the holiday together without Tom. It broke my heart a little, thinking how it would be so lonely without him. He was the one who always untangled the lights, swearing to heaven that this year, he'd put them away neatly. He'd string the lights on the tree while we supervised and he always made hot cocoa for us while we hung ornaments. Tom would direct us — "Too many big ones on top," he would say, or "Too many on the left." We'd laugh and tell him to put away the empty boxes and to leave the women to their work. But he never would leave us. Tom loved Christmas as much as any child.

Most years we would order Chinese food or a pizza and play old Perry Como music, singing along. We always played the Chipmunk Christmas album and imitated them, and then we'd dance like crazy to an old Christmas disco tape. And the evening never came to an end until the mistletoe was hung and we'd both kissed Beth. "I love Christmas," Beth would say as we tucked her in, "and I love you too." It was the guaranteed best night of the year for our family. Not Christmas morning, but the promise of what Christmas brought out in us as a family. But this year would be different, I thought, wondering how the old saying that "everything happens for the best" would apply this time. Tom's absence would be painful.

On Friday after work, I found a tree stand in the shed and somehow, between the two of us, Beth and I got the tree up. It was magnificent and the fragrance was heavenly. I had bought a wreath from the young one, as well as some garland, and Beth had promised to wire ribbon to it.

"So, Mom. I gave Chris my number. Do you think he'll call?"

"Definitely."

"Really?"

"Yep. Betcha a buck."

"If he doesn't call, I'll die."

"You won't die. Hand me the cord, will you? I have to anchor this thing. Do you remember the year —"

"That we didn't anchor the tree and the whole thing fell down in the middle of the night?"

"Yeah. Well, 'eah, hold this thing straight."

I hammered two slim nails in the corners of the windows and tied the cord to them. Then I crawled out from behind the tree and gave it a look.

"Rockefeller Center," I said. "It's perfect."

"Yeah, it's really beautiful," she said.

The phone rang and I thought she'd go out of her skin getting there. In the next moment I heard her practiced and breathy *"Hello?"* Marilyn Monroe lives. People who aren't raising a teenage daughter have no idea.

"Hi, Dad! What's up?" Pause. "Sure, she's right here."

She handed me the phone and I held my breath, hoping the news was good. "Tom?"

"Hi! Everything's okay. I just left Dr. Youngworth's office and he said that from the tests it looks like a pretty straightforward, just-beginning-stages case. He doesn't think the surgery should be too invasive. So that's good news."

"Very good news," I said.

"Yes, very good. So I'm scheduled for the operation next Monday. Can you come?"

"Of course. Hey — wanna give two damsels in distress a hand tonight?"

It took less than five minutes for him to arrive in the living room.

"You got the wrong side in the front," he said, kissing Beth and eyeballing the tree at the same time. "I can't believe you got a real tree."

"It's a year for miracles," I said.

"I hope you're right," he said.

Silence. Beth looked back and forth between us suspiciously. "What's going on?" she said.

"Anybody want hot cocoa?" Tom asked.

"Daddy needs to talk to you, Beth," I said. "Come on, let's fix it together."

"Wait," she said, "tell me now."

Tom put his hands on her shoulders and looked her square in the face. "Here's the poop," he said. "I have early-stage prostate cancer. I just found out. I'm having an operation and I'm going to be fine."

Beth's face became pleated with worry, and her eyes filled with tears as she searched his face for the rest of the story. "Are you telling me everything?"

"Yes, I am," he said.

He told her about his surgery, that the odds were ninety percent that it would be a breeze. She took it very well and said she'd pray for him.

"Now, let's get that hot chocolate going," I said. And we did.

By eleven-thirty, the tree was decorated and we were all very tired. We sat together in the living room with just the tree lights, listening to "White Christmas." We had stolen a night from our past. Not one unkind remark passed between us all evening. Knowing that Tom's surgery was but a few days away made me very nervous, but after his initial telling about it to Beth, we didn't discuss it again. Without saying so it was understood among us that the night we decorated the tree had to be free of stress. I suppose we had put Tom's health in the hands of someone higher.

When Tom left, I turned off the lights and after my closing-up-shop ritual, I finally climbed the stairs to go to bed. Beth was in my bed.

"Can I sleep with you tonight?"

"Sure, honey, just don't hog the covers," I said.

At last, I climbed under the covers next to her and turned out the light.

"Momma?"

"Mm-hm?"

"When you pray, do you pray to the Blessed Mother or to God?"

"Funny you should ask. I was just lining them all up for a special emergency meeting."

"What?"

"Honey, I pray to God, to Mary, to my poor old dead momma, to Livvie — I pray to everybody and everything that has ears."

"Did Livvie teach you to do that?"

"Yep, now just ask God to take care of Daddy. God listens to children's prayers first."

"Think so?"

"Know so." I threw my arm over her side. "Now, let's get some sleep, doodle."

Sunday night, Beth went to the movies with her new fellow, Chris. He had called that afternoon and I'd said, "Okay, go ahead, but be home by nine-thirty." As expected, she floated through the door on a cloud at ten minutes after ten. She looked so happy I didn't have the heart to reprimand her. I merely pointed to my wristwatch to deliver the message.

"I'm totally in love," she said and continued floating up the stairs to her room. "I gotta call Lucy. Guess what, Mom?"

"What?"

"He *loves* to shag! He does this awesome break step. He was showing me in the parking lot."

"At last, the perfect man," I said.

Monday morning Beth and I were at Roper Hospital by six. "Nothing is gonna happen to Daddy, is it, Momma?" she said.

"Don't worry, baby, Daddy's gonna be fine."

The purple hue of the early morning light and the damp air rolling in from the harbor sent a chill down my spine. We went right to Tom's room to let him know we were there. The sight of him in a hospital gown with an IV drip in his arm was frightening. His room was in darkness except for a night-light. And in the faint light, he looked small in the bed, vulnerable. When I put my hand on his arm, I realized that I was shaking. He was half-asleep, but opened his eyes.

"Hi," he said quietly, "glad you came."

I leaned over and gave him a kiss on the forehead. "Don't worry, we're gonna be right here waiting for you," I said.

"Hi, Daddy," Beth said. She took his hand in hers and squeezed it slightly, then leaned over him and kissed his cheek. "I love you," she said.

"They gave me a pill about an hour ago. I feel all kind of stupid in my head," he said.

"That's so you don't sit up on the operating table and give the doctor a litany of his liabilities," I said.

"Wiseacre," he said.

"Listen, you have nothing to worry about. They're double careful around here when they touch lawyers, you know."

My attempt at humor wasn't doing much to cheer any of us. He would go in whole and come out something less. We wouldn't know the outcome for hours. He took my hand and held it, drifting off again.

Soon the door opened and two orderlies came in and turned on the light, followed by a nurse and his doctor.

"Good morning, Mr. Hayes," the nurse said, "time to wake up for a few minutes." She took his temperature and checked his blood pressure, making notes on his chart.

"Good morning," the doctor said to me, "I'm David Youngworth."

We shook hands and I smiled at him. "I'm Susan Hayes. And this is our daughter, Beth."

"Right, right. Beth." He shook her hand as well. Then he said, "Okay, Mr. Hayes. Ready to roll?"

In one swift movement, the orderlies transferred

Tom to a gurney and held back the door to take him to surgery.

"Where are you going to be?" I asked.

"Third floor, operating room E. There's a waiting room there. We shouldn't be more than two hours. I'll come find you when we're finished, if you'd like," the doctor said.

"Yes, thanks," I said and went briefly to Tom's side before he was taken away.

Two hours crawled by and no word. Beth watched *Today* on television. I went back and forth between the newspaper, the television and the assortment of magazines on the table. We drank coffee and then Cokes — the real thing, sugar and all. I looked at my watch again. Ten minutes to nine.

"Should hear something soon," I said.

"Yeah, God, what's taking them so long?"

I didn't correct her language; I didn't even look at her face. People came to the waiting area and left. I continued my fretful prayers. *Dear God, please watch over Tom. His only child is standing here, filled with anxiety. I am too. She needs her daddy, God, please let him be all right.*

Then, I remembered that I hadn't called Beth's school to let them know she'd be absent. I reached down for my purse on the floor and found my change, but the phone in our area was in use.

"Be right back," I said, "gotta call school. You wait here for the doctor."

"Okay," she said.

The next phone was also being used and the next was broken. I asked at the nurse's station and was directed to the next wing of the hospital. By the time I made the call and found my way back, Dr. Youngworth was talking to Beth. She was nodding her head and saw me.

"Here's Momma," she said.

"Tom's going to be fine," he said. "I'm pretty certain that we got it all, but I'm concerned about the lymph nodes. That's why the procedure took a little longer than we thought it would. I biopsied them and as soon as I have the pathologist's report I'll know if he needs radiation as well. It's possible the cancer was slightly more advanced than we originally thought, but I don't think life-threatening. I was afraid about the nodes, but we never really know until we get inside the body."

"But he's okay?" I said.

"Oh, he did very well. He's in post-op recovery now. He'll be back in his room by around noon, as soon as he wakes up and his blood pressure has stabilized. He's going to sleep most of the day."

"Thank you, Dr. Youngworth," I said.

"You're welcome," he said. "He should be out of here in a couple of days. We can talk about his care and recovery routine tomorrow."

I watched him walk away and I hugged Beth. The doctor could've come to us and said almost anything and we would've stood there like mannequins, thanking him, tape-recording his words to play at a later time. Indeed, what he had said was that he suspected Tom's cancer was more serious than he had thought.

Beth and I went home for a few hours, had lunch and then went back to the hospital. We tiptoed into Tom's room, and he was there, sleeping like a stone. I closed the venetian blinds to keep the light at a minimum and sat down in the corner chair.

"I'm going to go get him some flowers," Beth whispered.

"Get me a Snickers and a bag of potato chips," I whispered back.

"Shame on you! No way!" She smiled and left.

Since our conversation with his doctor and our return to the hospital I had found the strength to compose myself. I couldn't see just dropping him off at his apartment with no one to see about his meals or to help him bathe. This was a situation that would have to be taken one step at a time. And he was a proud man — vain, in fact. He wouldn't burden me or anyone unless he was on death's doorstep.

Slowly, I told myself, go slowly and cautiously. No, first we had to get him back on his feet and then see what would be.

It was nearly six o'clock when he finally realized where he was. He smacked his lips, dehydrated from the anesthesia. I poured some water in a cup and put the straw to his lips.

"Hey, how do you feel?" I whispered.

He took a sip and opened his eyes. When he leaned up to take the cup, he winced in pain and fell back into his pillows.

"Take it easy," I said, "just take little sips. I'll help you sit." I pushed the buttons on the bed to raise his head and shoulders, and adjusted his pillows.

"Where's Beth?" he said.

"Down the hall, on the phone, no doubt. She's got a new boyfriend. Chris something."

"I'll kill the varmint," he said.

"No need to do that. His acne will most likely do

him in. Do you want me to release some pain medication? See? Just press this and you get drugs."

"I'm okay. Sleepy. How long have you been here? What did the doctor say?"

"He said that you're gonna be fine. That you might need some follow-up treatments, but that you're fine. You'll see him tomorrow morning."

It wasn't the complete truth, but I didn't have the heart to tell a man who had just come out of major surgery that he wasn't one hundred percent.

"Thank God. Susan, thanks. For being here and all. I mean it." He winced again.

"Hey, what are ex-wives for? Now, I'm going to drug you and then I'm going to let you get some rest." I squeezed the button, then his arm, and left him. His door sighed as it closed mechanically behind me.

On the second day after his surgery, Tom was up and walking. On the third day, he was released from the hospital. Beth and I had talked about it and we decided to bring him home to our house. As soon as he was feeling better, I emphasized, he would go back to his own place.

I was afraid I might fall back into living with him and that all the steps I'd taken to rebuild my life would vanish. I wanted him cared for but I didn't want to be used. No, I'd been used for the last time, if I could help it. Also, Tom's staying with us presented some legal complications. Under the laws of divorce in South Carolina, we had to live separately for one year to have our divorce finalized. If Michelle Stoney found out that Tom was under my roof, she'd be forced to refile or it would be fraud. I wasn't telling her and, under the circumstances, I didn't think any judge would hold our divorce up on that technicality. I said another novena for that.

I had rented a hospital bed and folded my dining room table away. He could sleep in there. He had been advised to avoid steps for a while. Getting him into the car was a bit of a struggle, but Grant was there to help.

"Come on, old boy, that's right, lean on me," Grant said.

"I feel like an old woman," Tom said.

"You are an old woman," Grant said. "Maybe you should lie down in the backseat."

"Good idea," Tom said.

"I'll roll the wheelchair back inside," Beth said.

"Okay, thanks. Tom, you okay?" I said.

"Yeah, okay, let's go," he said.

Grant closed Tom's door and held the passenger door open for Beth. He leaned in to speak to me.

"I'll follow you home," he said, "but I have to come back to do rounds."

"No problem, Grant. Thanks."

After we got Tom settled, Grant left and I gave Tom lunch. He sat up on a kitchen bar stool and fed himself a sliced chicken sandwich with lettuce and tomatoes, a handful of potato chips, two pickles and a Coke. This was not a dying man; this was a hungry man.

"Boy, am I glad to be out of that place," he said.

Over the next two days, we continued to plan for the holidays and our lives found a noninvasive routine together. Tom's recovery was extraordinary. After work at the library, I'd come home, make supper and go to work on my other job. While Tom and Beth did the dishes, I escaped upstairs. He watched television in the living room, Beth studied in my room and I wrote and laughed in her room. Tom seemed to be doing so well, Beth was happy and I was glad to have the chance to do something for him. His illness had given us all a lesson in compassion.

At the end of the week, he moved home to his apartment. We were both aware of the legal jeopardy that it posed to have him at home and it was really time for him to leave. He was fully mobile and getting antsy. Beth pouted a little when he left, but she understood.

I knew he had an appointment with Dr. Youngworth to go over his pathology report the following Monday. I expected to hear from him with an update. We were all feeling pretty relaxed, figuring that if it had been really bad news, we would have heard right away. Bad news traveling fast, and all that.

Monday evening he rang the doorbell.

"Hi!" I said. "How's it going? Want a beer?" I knew the moment I saw his face that something was wrong.

"Hi," he said and gave me a peck on the cheek. "Where's Beth?"

"I'll call her," I said.

Beth came running down the stairs and hugged him. I knew all at once why Tom had come over instead of calling. He could've been Marvin Struthers. There's a feeling of sliding down a chute into blackness that came over me before he told us what he had come to say.

"What's wrong?" Beth said.

"Why don't we all sit down," Tom said.

Beth sat next to me on the sofa. Tom stood in front of us.

"Beth, Susan, I have something to tell you that's very hard to find the right words for, so I'm just going to come right out with it. It seems that I'm very sick. My cancer spread into my lymph nodes and metastasized."

"How far?" I said.

"Daddy! What are you saying?"

"Honey, I'm saying I might not have a lot of time left."

Beth flew from the sofa to him and threw her arms around him, holding him tightly and screaming, *"No! No! No! Tell me it's a lie, Daddy! Tell me it's a lie!"*

"I wish it were a lie, Beth, believe me," Tom said, his voice cracking, his heart breaking.

"I can't lose you! I need you, Daddy! Daddy, I need you!"

Tom held her while she sobbed and I went to them, putting my arms around both of them. Tears rolled down our cheeks and mixed with each other's as we kissed Beth over and over. Beth cried so hard that she shook all over. Finally, she sank to the floor in despair. Tom knelt at her side and whispered to her.

"Please get up, baby," he said. "Please be brave for Daddy's sake. Please don't fall apart, I need you now. Please, Beth. I need you, honey."

When he said that he needed her, she looked up at him. "Oh, Daddy, please don't die," she begged, hugging him hard around the waist.

"Sweetheart, I don't want to die, you know that."

"There must be something they can do," I said. "Isn't there anything?"

"Some radical treatments, heavy radiation and chemo, some experimental stuff — a new medication that looks promising on laboratory mice," he said. "I mean, you can be sure that I'm gonna try everything on the planet."

"Oh, my God," I said. "Come on, Beth, let's get up, sweetheart. We've got to be brave for Daddy."

"Tom, you know we're gonna help," I said. "Whatever we can do, we will."

"I know, Susan. Thank God for you," he said. "Come on, Beth, let's try to pull ourselves together, okay?"

We lifted Beth from the floor and put her to bed. She continued to cry for three hours, nonstop. I cried with her. Tom sat by her and rubbed her back. Finally, she was quiet. When we were sure she was asleep Tom and I went into the living room.

"Tom, I'm so damn sorry. I'm so sorry," I said, and realized I was crying again.

He put his arms around me and gave me a squeeze. "Why are you sorry, Susan? It's not your fault. It's nobody's fault. Listen, why don't you help me plan whatever future I've got? Maybe there's someplace we can go, the three of us. A trip you always wanted to take?"

"Yeah, but Tom, what if you get sick? How would I care for you? How long do . . ."

"Do I have? Well, if that undertaker surgeon is right, about thirty years if I'm lucky. Six months if I'm not. Certainly enough time to put my affairs in order, which, by coincidence, I had already started doing."

"Six months or everything," I said. I was quiet for a few minutes. Six months was not a lot of time. If I could have had my father for six months, what would I have wanted? "Spend the time with Beth if you can. She needs all the good memories you can give her, no matter what happens. You know?"

"You're right. Well, my life's not a total loss. I had the good sense to marry you and have Beth."

"She's the undisputed love of my life, Tom. Thank you for giving her to me."

"She is mine too. You're welcome, but let's not get too maudlin. I feel fine, other than a little nausea now and then."

"I'll pray for you, Tom," I said.

"Thanks. I think I'm gonna need all the prayers I can get."

"You pray too, okay?"

"Are you kidding? Hey, cheer up, I'm still breathing."

He put his arms around me, my head touched his shoulder and he stroked my hair down the back of my head as though I was his child as well. When he left at last, I watched him back out of the driveway and listened until I could no longer hear his car in the distance.

Beth *was* the best thing in his life. She didn't know what heartache lay ahead for her, but I did. My grief for Tom and for her was magnified by the burden I had carried since the day my own father died.

It was midnight when I finally went to bed. I was under covers up to my shoulders. Everything was quiet. I barely made out the soft sound of Beth's footsteps coming to my room.

"You still awake?"

I said, "Sure, come on in."

She crawled in the bed next to me. The house was chilly, as the furnace had gone on the night cycle at ten o'clock.

"Think Dad's gonna be okay?"

I patted her leg with a reassuring hand. "Yes, somehow I do."

"Can I sleep with you tonight?"

"Sure, sweetheart. Now turn off the light and let's get some shut-eye."

In the darkness of my room, I listened to the rise and fall of her breathing. She curled in a fetal position on her side with her back to me, sleeping almost right away.

17

CHRISTMAS 1963

Momma's door opened without a sound and Livvie appeared there, her face somber. We watched and waited to hear what she would say. She said nothing. She passed me and her hand rested on my shoulder. Then she touched the shoulder or arm of Maggie and the boys. She'd arrived at our house an hour ago and she'd been in there ever since. It was the morning after the day our father had died. We thought Livvie was leaving us.

"Gone sweep the steps," she finally said, and we exhaled for the moment.

We got out the masking tape and came and went from the chairs around the kitchen table, moving in a wounded trance, corpses ourselves. The visiting neighbors, their hands outstretched, with generous offerings of fruited hams, bowls of potato salad and pound cakes. The hams were baked with secret glazes, the potato salads made with closely held recipes, the pound cakes, each egg beaten in by hand. But our throats were closed to food. In spite of their kindness, food was the last thing we wanted.

Our neighbors and friends were awkward and

uncomfortable, anxious to have their duty done. They said they were stunned, that they'd see us at the wake, that they were so sorry, that if they could do anything . . . but what could anyone do?

The wake broke all records for McAlister's funeral home. That's the main thing I remembered. Huge clumps of time were missing from my father and grandmother's wake and funeral and I guessed that was a blessing. But in my recollections were snippets of the events.

There were a ton of flowers. So many that I'd always hate gladiolus and carnations. Gladiolus never bloomed right. If the middle of the spear looked good, the tops were too tight. If the tops were in flower, the middles were on the wane. And carnations. Oh, Lord, I hated carnations. I knew the florists used them so much because they lasted a long time, but the smell of them was sickeningly sweet to me.

I remembered seeing Daddy in his casket at the funeral home and that was pretty terrible. He seemed far away, at the end of a foggy tunnel. His skin looked gray. Maybe I never went up to it, maybe I did.

On the day of the funeral Mass, Stella Maris Church was packed with people. And, the bells. Mr. Struthers rang the funeral bells slowly. The bells rang out from the tower and every dog on that end of the Island began to bark. My skin crawled. Reality began to sink in. This was the moment we would put the final blessing on them. They were gone.

We stood in a line outside the church as the two hearses were opened and the pallbearers removed the caskets. My knees started to knock and I couldn't swallow. We were to walk behind Momma, Maggie and I, then Timmy and Henry, following the bodies of our father and grandmother. Aunt Carol had arranged us and told us what to do. She and Livvie would follow with the twins.

We watched the caskets slide from the back like so much cargo. Lifeless. Still. Just the weight of our dead and their crates. They can't breathe in there, I thought ironically. Henry must've heard my thought and he began to sob. Then Timmy lost his composure, and began crying too. I grabbed Henry and rubbed his head, trying to console him. Maggie threw her arms around Timmy and I could see his back convulsing. Momma turned and saw us and her heart flipped over, finally realizing the enormity of our feelings. Unable to cope with us on any real level, she lifted the veil of her black hat and opened her purse.

"Come on, now," she said, rubbing our backs slightly and dispensing tissues, "your grandmomma and your daddy wouldn't want you to carry on. Let's try to put on a brave face now and show everyone how strong we are."

"My daddy's in that box, Momma!" Henry said, continuing to weep in my arms.

"Henry, you listen to me," I said, not knowing what I would say next. "This isn't a bravery contest! Daddy's in heaven. That's just his body. This is a terrible day. Just hang on to me! If you want to cry, go ahead."

His huge blue eyes searched mine and he felt I had given him something, I guessed, because he took some deep breaths, fell against me again and then stood back. I'd never forget the fury in him as he lashed out at Momma. *My daddy's in that box, Momma! My daddy's in that box, Momma!* I'd never forget his words. And his little eyebrows, they knitted together in worry and sadness. I wondered again what would become of us. We just had to hold on to each other, squeeze our eyes shut and soon it would be over.

The Mass was another blur in my memory. I only recalled the horrible maudlin songs of our choir. Even as we pulled away from the church in the funeral procession to the cemetery, I could hear the mournful music.

By the time we got home, I was so tired. I'd never been so tired. I just wanted to sleep. The house was still crawling with people, but I managed to slip away to my room, close the door, kick off my patent leather shoes and lie on the bed with all my clothes on. I pulled my quilt up around me. I should've recorded everything about the funeral in my journals, I should've checked on the twins. I should've been doing almost anything else, but I felt like I had turned to stone, sinking into my mattress. The window was opened just a little and the sheer curtains floated out like spirits on damp air.

I buried my father and my grandmother today, I thought. I should've felt worse about it than I did. That was the problem, I didn't feel anything much except tired.

I must've drifted off, because when I opened my eyes, it was night. I washed my face, splashing cold water in handfuls over my eyes and cheeks and, at last, went downstairs to the kitchen. Uncle Louis,

Aunt Carol, Momma and Maggie were talking, sitting around the table. I looked out the window over the sink. The yard was finally empty of the cars, except Uncle Louis's.

"We're just talking, Susan," Aunt Carol said. "Why don't you join us? Are you hungry, honey?"

"No, thanks, I don't have much of an appetite today."

She was oddly solicitous. I looked over to Momma. She had big poofy bags under her eyes, but for once, I didn't blame her for that. If I'd been her today, I probably would've torn out my hair. We had all become older overnight, I thought. Yesterday I hated my mother for not taking care of us, and today I sympathized with her. I poured myself a Coke and took a seat.

"I was just going over some options with y'all's momma, Susan," Uncle Louis said. "You know, honey, things are going to have to change around here."

"Daddy didn't have life insurance, Susan," Momma said.

"What does that mean?"

"In a nutshell, we're flat broke," Maggie said. "Flat out broke."

"Y'all're kidding, right?" I looked around at the faces of my family. Jeee-sus, when would the trouble end?

"Now, Maggie, don't go scaring your sister," Uncle Louis said. "We've all been through enough for one day. Honey," he said to me, "here's the truth. What money y'all have is what's left in your daddy's savings account and checking account. It's not much. Your momma can get a job. But if she does that, she can't earn very much because she never went to college. Then, too, who would take care of the twins and Henry? And by the time you subtract the cost of transportation and clothes and so forth, it doesn't make economic sense. So, if she's going to work, it would have to be something she could do at home. For one thing, I have a friend who's always looking for a bookkeeper."

"Louis, I don't know the first *thing* about bookkeeping!" Momma said, panicking.

"Well, then damn it all, MC, if not that, then something else! You are simply going to have to find a way to earn whatever you can! I'm sorry to say it so bluntly, but it's true!"

It was the first and only time I'd ever heard Uncle Louis curse, but I forgave it right away because I cussed my ass off all the time. Uncle Louis was usually in a good mood, Mr. Easygoing, but this situation would have stolen anybody's sense of humor.

"We'll see about that, Louis," she said.

"What? Do you think that I can take care of all of you?"

"I'm going to bed," Momma said in a low voice. "I need to *rest* a little."

She rose slowly from her chair and looked hard at Uncle Louis and Aunt Carol. She was pissed off to the gizzards. I understood. If our momma hadn't spent her life taking care of Uncle Louis's parents, she might have gone to college and wouldn't have been in this hopeless predicament today.

Uncle Louis refused to meet her eyes. He merely sighed, dropped his head and rubbed his ears and the back of his neck. He probably figured it wasn't his fault she was a girl.

After Momma left the room, Aunt Carol smiled, got up and investigated the contents of a cake cover, lifting it and inhaling. "Mmm! German chocolate cake! My favorite! Won't someone share a slice with me?"

By the next week, Uncle Louis had his plans for the survival of us Hamilton children and his sister. Uncle Louis was a pretty handy guy. If a sink backed up, Daddy would always call Uncle Louis. In five minutes he would be at the back door, next heard lecturing my father on what was a man worth who couldn't fix a sink? My father's voice would bounce all over the house, calling Uncle Louis a big old know-it-all smart-ass. Fifteen minutes later all the insults would be forgotten and they'd be drinking a beer together on the front porch, laughing and cutting up the fool.

Once our washing machine went crazy from being overloaded and danced across the kitchen floor. Daddy had to call Uncle Louis to help him move it back into place. Uncle Louis and Daddy laughed like crazy over that. In fact, it was Uncle Louis who actually did most of the building on the new bathroom for Livvie. If you needed supervision you called Daddy. If you needed something fixed or built, you called Uncle Louis.

Maggie, Timmy and I were washing supper dishes with Livvie when Uncle Louis showed up at the back door. Momma was sitting at the table sighing. He informed my mother that he was going to remodel the second and third floors of our house to rent the rooms since she was too lazy to get off her fat behind and go to work. Momma's face turned beet red.

"The house has no mortgage," he was saying, whatever that was, "so whatever you earn from rent can cover the cost of feeding your children and the maintenance on the house."

He would begin by building two bedrooms and one small bathroom on the back of our house. The boys would sleep in one and Maggie and I in the other. The twins would sleep in Sophie and Tipa's old room and Momma could stay where she was. He had talked to Marvin Struthers, he said, and Marvin had agreed to change the zoning for our house to allow four power meters, so our tenants would pay their own electric bills. Momma would have to calculate the cost of water into their rent, he said.

"I can't think about this," Momma finally said. "I'm going to put my *fat behind* in the bed. I need to rest."

Uncle Louis blew out a sigh, exasperated.

"I can help you," Timmy said.

"Good, son, I'll need your help."

"Sure! We can all help!" Maggie said.

"I ain't washing no more clothes and cleaning no more bathrooms! That's that!" Livvie said. "Probably gone lose my job anyhow, ain't that right, Mr. Louis?"

That horrible possibility hung in the air for a moment, scaring the breath out of me.

"You don't have to, Livvie. Don't worry about it," I said quickly, "I'll do that."

Uncle Louis looked at us and said, "I don't

know how my sister gave birth to all of y'all. She's so lucky and she doesn't even know it, 'eah?" He came across the room and put his hand on my shoulder. "Susan, you ain't gone be washing no laundry for nobody but your own family. You need to study. And Maggie? Don't worry about helping me with the building. It's man work. You just help your momma and sister take care of the little ones with Livvie. And Livvie, don't you worry. I'm paying your salary for now, 'eah? This family needs you now worse than ever!"

Saturday brought the sounds of hammers and power saws as Uncle Louis had arrived to put our butts back into gear. I climbed up to the cupola to observe. Five men, all friends of my father's from his construction business, showed up from nowhere to help. Uncle Louis shook their hands and slapped their backs as each one arrived. Mr. Struthers arrived with his toolbox. The hammering got so loud it made me want to scream. Then two black men rolled up in a broken-down pickup truck and the group became quiet.

"Did y'all know Hank?" I heard my Uncle Louis calling to them.

"Sure did. He tried to help our children with getting a new school! Miss Harriet told me what y'all was up to. Figured iffin he could build for us, we could build for him."

Oh, shit, I thought, here it comes. The papers were full of race trouble and the Island men weren't too keen on working alongside colored men.

"All right," Uncle Louis said, "thank you. Come join us. I'm Louis."

"Yes, sir, Mr. Louis, call me Sam. This is my friend Albert."

They all shook hands. The other men all shook their hands and I almost fell out of my perch. They might be rioting in Alabama, but on Sullivan's Island, things were okay. And I guessed my daddy had something to do with that.

Maggie found an after-school job on King Street in Charleston, Henry had a paper route and, by that afternoon, Timmy had blisters from the hammer. I resigned myself to running the family baby-sitting service, first for my baby sisters and then for other families on the Island. In one week, Uncle Louis and the men had framed the addition to our house. *Hammer! Hammer! Hammer!* The next thing you knew, it had a roof that matched the rest of the house. *Hammer! Hammer! Hammer!* The wiring went in and the walls were closed.

By the nineteenth of December, the Island Gamble had grown another appendage. She was looking downright mythological, like one of those eastern religion figures with all the arms. The two new bedrooms were far from finished, and they sure weren't decorated, but they were good enough to sleep in, according to Uncle Louis. And the bathroom? Well, the plumbing worked, but it wasn't exactly the bridal suite at the Waldorf Astoria, whatever the hell that was except a place we were always invited to move to when we complained.

Livvie's cousin Harriet had been there all day Sunday with her, moving us from our old rooms upstairs to the new addition on the back of our house. They moved up and down the steps, heads wrapped in kerchiefs, carrying on laughing like we weren't even there. But that's how Livvie always was when Harriet was there.

It was a good thing that somebody thought this move to the hinterlands of our house was funny. As far as I was concerned, it was a one-way, third-class trip to Siberia. There went my privacy and solitude. Maggie wasn't any happier about it than I was, but it would've been useless to complain. We would've looked bad, spoiled and self-centered. We would have had to endure an endless harangue on how it was worse in India, where children lived in the streets. But Maggie and I knew that somehow this new living space was different from our pipe dream to become roommates in college. This was like being cell mates. Change the diapers. Warm the bottles. Rock the babies. Gimme a break. I felt like a pack mule whose burden would never end. Just fourteen years old, with only a marginally celebrated birthday anyway, and who cared about me? Happiness? It was a dream from the movies. We had rooms to rent and we had to get them ready.

Aunt Carol and Uncle Louis came by that afternoon with a truckload of old furniture, old bed frames, chests of drawers, end tables and chairs. Their castoffs would furnish the rooms upstairs. Maggie and I were to repaint them. We got busy spreading newspaper on the floor of the boys' room, which — and this goes to show you that it's a man's world — was the largest. We chose a bed to paint that almost matched another chest and end table. Uncle Louis was down on one knee and, with a Spackle knife, he opened the cans of white paint for us, carefully laying their lids on the paper.

"Okay, now, y'all girls be careful," he said. "This is primer. Goes on first, nice and thin. When it dries, and I mean really dries, then you can put on the enamel. If it gets on the floor, wash it up right away with this stuff. Don't eat it, throw it or get it in your eyes. 'Eah me?"

"Yes, sir," I said and saluted him. He looked just like Sergeant Bilko from *The Phil Silvers Show.* "He thinks we're total morons," I whispered to Maggie when he left the room.

"Shhh! Just get busy. He's got a lot on his mind."

"Right." I picked up a paintbrush, dipped it in the can of primer and wiped it across the top of the table. "Where's Momma? Think she's still pissed off at Uncle Louis?"

"I don't know. Who cares?"

"Well, if my brother barged into my house and started hammering," I said, "even if it was a good idea, I'd kick his ass to Kalamazoo!"

"Yeah, big talk, gutter-mouth. Uncle Louis is right! She doesn't know how to *do* anything. At least I'm learning how to do *something.*"

"That's true. But she could be helping us, you know."

"Yeah, sure."

"Hey! Who brought you home last night? I saw you get out of a car up the street."

"Swear to God not to tell?" Maggie's eyes got all gooey.

"I swear on the cross! On the wounds of Christ! On the tears of the Mother Virgin! On the —"

"All right! Enough!" Maggie said. She lowered her voice until I could hardly hear her. "Lucius.

Lucius Pettigrew brought me home."

"Holy shit! Have you been, you know, going out with him?"

Lucius Pettigrew was the most gorgeous man in the sophomore class at Bishop England. Even I knew who he was. All the girls called him Luscious Lucius. He was from an old blue-blood family and had a reputation as a big-time make-out artist.

"Sort of. I mean, he has a car and picks me up from work. The most we've done is stop at the Piggy Park for a barbecue sandwich on the way home."

"What are you telling me, *the most we've done?* Are you hiding something?"

"Susan! Good grief! What do you think? That I sit around the corner and make out with him or something?" She was smiling from ear to ear and not the least bit embarrassed or ashamed. Mrs. Simpson had successfully spread her lewd influence like a virus. Or maybe it was in the genes, although the only slut in our family married in.

"Yeah, do you?" I was curious. Not interested for myself, you understand, just curious.

"Yeah, well, sometimes we *do.* So how do you like that?"

"Really?"

"Yeah, really."

"What's it like?" I asked. "Does he try to make you do it?"

"Susan! Where do you get these gross ideas? No! I mean, God, Susan, he tells me things and sometimes we just kiss or hug. *Do* it? You're cracked in the head, you know that?"

"Do you French-kiss?"

"Well, maybe. God, Susan, why are you asking me all these questions? It's pretty private, you know."

"Well, if I were you and I had a guy who looked like him, I'd at least want to see what it looks like."

"See what *what* looks like?"

"You know, his *you know* . . . I mean, his is probably gonna look as good as one could —"

"You are a total disgusting pig! That's about the last thing I want to see! Good God!"

"Sure. I'd say the same thing if I were you. Ha!"

"Well, you don't have to worry about seeing one. You look like such a slob, you'll never even get a date!"

"Well, you're so damn skinny, nothing but a bag of bones, I can't believe he wants to kiss you! And wait till his family finds out! They'll have a fit!"

"Shut up, Susan. Just shut up."

I shut up. We painted in silence. Ever since Maggie went to work in the city, things between us had started to change. She wore makeup all the time now and tweezed her eyebrows. She washed her hair every single morning. She even brushed her teeth about a thousand times a day.

Uncle Louis posted a sign for the rented rooms at the end of our driveway on the same day he stapled Christmas lights around our back door. I don't know what we did before staple guns. In our house they held up shades, lights, wires, you name it. Don't forget black electric tape! Whatever you couldn't staple, you could tape. But when Uncle Louis hammered that sign into the ground, I got a funny feeling. Maybe something exciting would happen. ROOMS TO RENT! DAY, WEEK, OR MONTH! INQUIRE WITHIN! CALL 744-0812.

Maybe a movie star or somebody famous would take a room to rent in our house and discover us. Who knew? I was standing there with Maggie, looking at it, reading it over and over.

"I hope Lucius doesn't see it," Maggie said.

"Why?"

"Because then he'll feel sorry for us and think we're poor."

"We *are* poor."

"No, we're not. We have enough and I have a job."

"Right." You have a job and live in dreamland, I thought. I have four children, a chain around my neck and I'm hoping movie stars are moving in. "Well," I said, "things could be worse."

Saturday, the twentieth of December, brought a knock at the back door. We were at the supper table, everybody except Maggie, who was probably parked up some dirt road with Lucius.

"I'll get it!" Timmy said. He jumped up and ran for the door.

"Hi!" I heard Timmy say. "Sure, come on in!"

"Thanks," said a male voice.

My momma stood up from the table, scraping the chair along the floor. Livvie turned around from the stove, Henry reached over for some more bread, and Timmy gave him a karate chop just for the hell of it.

"Hi! I saw your sign and I was wondering if there's still a room for rent?"

He smiled and he had lots of dimples. Deep ones. And brown eyes with gold flecks. Beautiful eyes, black lashes. His nose was sort of big, and his mouth was kind of wide. He made me nervous and

I didn't know why. He just kind of filled up the room. He was smart and funny and, boy, was he cute.

"Why, yes! Yes, we have rooms available!" Momma said. "What's your name, son?"

"Oh, sorry! I'm Simon Rifkin. I didn't mean to disturb your dinner, I was just riding by and saw the sign . . ."

"Oh! Don't worry! We were just finishing. Would you like some soup? Livvie made wonderful okra soup! She uses a ham bone to flavor it. Delicious! I'm Marie Catherine Hamilton, and these are my children, well, some of them, that is!"

"It's nice to meet you, Mrs. Hamilton."

He shook her hand and waved at us. He was wearing a navy blue windbreaker with a little yellow alligator on the top left side of it and khaki pants with a white shirt. I sat there like a tub of lard while Momma droned on. I'll bet he's over twenty-one, I thought.

"Why don't I show you the room and you can tell me something about yourself. My brother, Louis, says I should find out everything I can about somebody who wants to live in my house. I mean, after all, a lady has to be careful, don't you think so?"

"Yes, ma'am." He caught my eye and winked at me. It was a friendly wink, one that said to me that he knew Momma was gonna blab and blab and he'd take it with good humor. My neck got hotter and hotter. He wasn't that tall. No, probably only about five feet, nine inches. Why was I sweating? And why was I wearing this nasty old sweatshirt? Livvie looked at me and raised her eyebrows.

"What?" I said.

"Nothing, chile. Finish up your cornbread. Henry? You want some more?"

"Sure!"

She knew. She always knew. Henry held his bowl up to her and I fished a kernel of corn out of the bottom of my mine. Simon Rifkin. What kind of name was that? Who was this guy?

A few minutes later Momma led Simon into the room like a pet dog or something. "Now, will you have some soup with us, Simon?" she asked.

"No, no thanks. I gotta get back to the city."

"All right, next time. Well, then, it's all settled. You'll move in Monday?"

"Yes, ma'am. Nice meeting all of you! Well, see you then!"

The door slammed, Livvie jumped at the noise and I leapt to the window to watch him walk to his car. He had a little dark green British MGB convertible. Cool. He walked to it, zipping his jacket, opened the car door and looked up at the house. He saw me staring at him through the window. He waved at me and I waved back, blood rushing back to my face like a rocket.

"I have to call Louis!" Momma said. "A hundred dollars a month! This is wonderful!"

While washing the supper dishes we learned everything that Momma had found out about him.

"He's from where?" Livvie said.

"Michigan! Can you imagine? So far from home, poor boy. He's a student at the Medical University! A doctor! Anyway, his father is a doctor too, and he's divorced, and guess what?" She whispered, "He's Jewish!"

"Big deal," I said.

"Well, it could've been, Miss Smarty Pants. Your Uncle Louis wasn't too thrilled about that, because, you know, Jews are peculiar sometimes."

I just rolled my eyes. "Momma, Jesus was a Jew," I said.

"That's a lie and you know it! The Jews killed our Lord and that's why Uncle Louis was a little worried."

"Momma. The Romans killed Jesus," I said. "At least that's what it says in the Bible, if you can believe what you read these days."

"Well, no matter about that. It's just that, well, I don't want you to go discussing his religion with him or his daddy's divorce either. It's not polite and we don't want to be too nosy, do we?"

And she went on and on. I mean, here came the best-looking guy I'd ever seen in my whole life and my momma had to have something to say about his religion! Maybe she was afraid we'd stop going to Mass. Maybe she wanted to convert him so she could sit next to the Blessed Mother in heaven. They say that for every sinner you brought to wash away their heathen sins in the Catholic baptismal font of conversion, you got a guaranteed seat practically in the lap of the Blessed Mother, if and when you got to heaven.

"I told him that I had prayed every night to Saint Joseph," Momma was saying, "who is the patron saint of families, by the way, to send a nice person to live with us. I told him that so he'd know we're *Catholic*. Anyway, good old Saint Joseph came through! I have to remind myself to light a candle for him tomorrow. Such a reliable novena! Oh!

This is such *good* news! And, guess what else?" She whipped out a check for a hundred dollars from inside her blouse. "Deposit! Louis never said *anything* about deposit money! I thought of that *myself!* Ha! We have an extra hundred dollars now and Christmas is gonna be all right. What do y'all think? Should we get a turkey?"

I hadn't seen Momma so animated in years. She was really happy and it was catching.

"No more ham?" I said.

"I want a drumstick! Does he play ball?" Timmy asked.

"I don't know! You'll have to ask him!" she said.

"Can he fish?" Henry asked.

"I don't know that either! We'll have to find out!"

"Want to know what I think?" Livvie said.

"What?" Momma said.

"I think Gawd send this boy to take y'all's mind away from your own worry. He needs a family and y'all need something to set y'all sailing back to the land of the living! He's just the right thing! Yes, sir! He's a Gawdsend, sure enough."

Sunday after Mass, Maggie and I went with Uncle Louis and Aunt Carol over to Mount Pleasant to buy a Christmas tree. It was cold for a South Carolina day, but that added to our excitement about the holiday.

I was excited for another reason. One more day and Simon Rifkin would be sleeping under our roof. I had one short day to turn myself into a girl and, unfortunately, Maggie was the only person who could help me.

We lifted Christmas trees from their piles and

stood them up, debating their various shortcomings and assets.

"Too bare in the front," Maggie said.

"Top's crooked," I said. "Hey, Maggie? What do you think? Should I cut my hair?"

"I've got sap all over my hand. I hate that." She pulled another tree from the pile. "Yes, you should cut your hair. It looks like a rat's nest. You know I always tell you that if you're not willing to take care of long hair you shouldn't have it. And you live in a ponytail."

"Right, you do always say that. So now I'm thinking I might like to cut it. What do you think about a bubble cut?"

"And what then? You're gonna stick a little velvet bow in the front of your head like a birthday present? Spare me."

"No, I'm not gonna stick a little bow in the front of my head and look like a birthday present. I just think I need a hairstyle, you know?"

Maggie looked at me and narrowed her eyes. It was the first time in my life that I ever said anything about trying to improve my looks. She was the mad Dr. Frankenstein and I was her experiment.

"A little makeup wouldn't kill you either," she said, "clean up your pores, you know? It would make a big difference."

"Probably, but I don't know how to use it, you know?"

"I'll help you when we get home. I've got a drawer full of free samples. Let's get this tree and get out of here. I'm freezing. It must be forty degrees!"

"Done! You know what, Maggie?"
"What?"
"I'm getting sorta excited about Christmas, even though we're practically broke."
"Yeah, me too. Who cares?"
She put her arm around my shoulder and gave me a squeeze. I thanked God the old Maggie was back.
I sat on the kitchen stool in front of the bathroom mirror, staring at my face. She cut my hair straight off across the bottom at my shoulders with the same scissors we used to cut wrapping paper, coupons and everything else.
When she finally stopped yanking and measuring my hair, she combed globs of gel through it and rolled it on orange juice cans, sticking the clips almost through my scalp.
"Ouch! Maggie! Stop! You're killing me!"
"Pride knoweth no pain!"
"What the hell is that supposed to mean?"
"Grandma Sophie used to say it all the time when she saw me pulling my eyebrows with tears running down my face."
"Yeah, so?"
I was getting cranky and fidgety. Now that she had my whole head wrapped around her version of rollers, she taped my bangs to my forehead to give them a final trim.
"Hold still or you'll look like Moe! It means that vanity has a price. If you want to look good, don't complain about the process."
"Are you sure these cans are clean? I don't want bugs in my hair."
"You know what, Susan? You're skating on thin

ice. I'm doing this for you for nothing except an unselfish desire on my part to help you out and you are being a little pain in the butt. Plain and simple."

"Sorry."

She pulled the hair dryer out of the closet and spread the big hood over my head, tightening the strings. When she flipped it on, my head got as big as a basketball.

"Forty-five minutes! You'll be dry in forty-five minutes!"

I pulled my ears out of the hood.

"I'm not deaf! Do you have tweezers?"

"Do I have tweezers? Of course." She shook her head, completely exasperated with her nincompoop of a sorry-ass sister, as she fumbled around in her makeup case. "Here. Use this too. Brush your eyebrows toward your scalp and just pluck the hairs that aren't in the line."

I peered into the mirror and did as I was told. It hurt like all hell too.

"Jesus, Maggie! This is awful! I'm bleeding!"

"Give them to me! Who told you to pull out fifty hairs at the same time? You won't die from this."

The end result was rather stunning. I didn't look like my old self hardly at all, except that I was the same size. Of course, the wonders of elastic had rearranged some of that. Maggie had produced another invention of torture — a Maidenform bra.

"Put this on," she said.

"I'd rather eat glass," I said. A bra? No way.

"Put it on," she said. "I'll buy you some more next week."

The major change was my head, inside and out.

On the outside, my hair looked shiny and it swung when I turned my head. And it wasn't all kinky and fuzzy, thanks to the orange juice cans. The makeup that Maggie had finally decided was the right color for my skin covered my freckles and made my skin look smooth. A little mascara, a squirt of Estée Lauder Youth Dew and I felt like a big deal. I felt like Maggie's peer. She made me confess why I was doing this and she insisted that he'd fall right in love with me.

"He's about a zillion years old," I said.

"So what?" she said. "You look really beautiful."

Anyway, all this led me to believe that I *had* changed and I was ready for Simon to appear on the doorstep. At least that's what I told myself.

Nobody said much about my transformation. Livvie just smiled and nodded her head, Momma said, "Oh, you cut your hair," and Henry wouldn't have noticed anything different about me if his life depended on it. However, Timmy's eyes got big when I brought in a box of ornaments from the hall closet.

"So what's *this* supposed to mean?" he said.

"What's *what* supposed to mean?" I said, embarrassed to hell and back.

"I mean, you look, you know, grown up or something weird like that."

"Thanks a lot, Timmy."

"No, I mean, you look good, just different."

I wanted to slap him.

The day passed slowly. Bing Crosby crooned from the stereo. Momma was taking a nap. Livvie was making rum balls — and sands for us. We decorated the tree, unwrapping each ornament and remembering Daddy, Tipa and Grandma Sophie. Bad things happen in threes, we told ourselves, and we'd seen the three.

Christmas was a few days away, Simon was merely hours away and my ears thumped from waiting to hear him pull up in the backyard. I wanted to ride in that car of his in the worst way, but I'd sworn to Maggie that I'd be cool about it. Finally, I heard the motor turn in to our yard and stop. Maggie looked at me.

"He's here," I whispered to her.

"Yep," she whispered back, "he's here. Now what?"

"I don't know! Should I go out and offer to help him carry his stuff inside?"

"Don't you dare! He'll think you're a tomboy if you do that!"

"Right. Stupid idea! I'll just stay here and ask him if he wants to help decorate the tree!"

"Are you nuts? He's Jewish! Jews don't decorate Christmas trees!"

"Right! I'll just stay here and do nothing!"

"Right! Get a grip on yourself! Just play it cool and relax!"

"Right."

"What are y'all whispering about?" Timmy asked.

"Nothing," Maggie and I answered at the same time.

Simon Rifkin, arms filled with clothes on hangers, stuck his head in the living room to say hello. "Hi! Oh, wow! What a great tree!"

Timmy immediately stuck out his hand to him. "Hey! Welcome to the Island Gamble! I'm

Timmy, remember? And this is Maggie, my sister, and that's Henry over there making a mess. You probably don't recognize Susan. She had major work done on her head yesterday but, yep, that's her."

"Hi, Susan! Great haircut!"

"Thanks," I sputtered.

He turned to face Maggie and inhaled. I knew it. One look at her blond perfection and he was gone.

"I'm Margaret Hamilton, the eldest," she said coolly and offered her hand to him as though it were a rare orchid.

The family's ugly duckling seriously considered a double murder. There was no hope.

It would be our first Christmas without Daddy, Sophie and Tipa. It was very strange not to have them there, almost as strange as it had been having them. The silence was loud. The sweet smell of fresh air, offensive. The peace, painful. We had tried so hard to get past all our crying jags and our feelings of emptiness and guilt that we were almost used to the idea that they were gone to their great reward. With the preparations for Christmas Eve dinner and Midnight Mass came reminders of them everywhere. But no one spoke of them. Not one word.

For Momma the worst moments had come when she had to clean out their closets, or when bills came due. More and more often, she'd pour herself something in a dark red, double old-fashioned glass, pop a pill and set about the task. Me, I studied harder than ever so I just wouldn't think about it.

Maggie and I had set the table for our Christmas Eve feast of fried fish and hushpuppies. It looked festive with red candles in the polished brass candlesticks. Then we just cut some branches of pyracantha with red berries from the yard, flicked off the bugs and put them on the table around the candlesticks. The house smelled good. We got a big can of Johnson's Paste Wax from Uncle Louis last week and had waxed everything that resembled wood.

The gifts we had bought for each other were modest, but nobody cared about presents too much.

What to buy for Livvie had been a problem and we argued a lot about it, but finally we settled on a cardigan sweater. I wanted to buy her a white one so it would match everything, but no, Maggie said, it would get dirty. After a whole lot of bickering, we bought a red one, knowing she'd love a red sweater because it was exciting like she was.

The twins were all washed and dressed in red velvet dresses, courtesy of Aunt Carol's charge account at Condon's department store. Timmy and Henry had their hair plastered down with water and had on new sport coats, khakis and Top-Siders, thanks to Uncle Louis's charge account at Max's men's store. Maggie and I wore new pastel Villager sleeveless princess dresses with our initials monogrammed in the center of our chests. The matching cardigans waited on the hall chair. These were our gifts from Aunt Carol and Uncle Louis. Momma had on her standard black dress because she had refused to shop with Aunt Carol.

In any case, we appeared to be ready for Christmas.

We were all about to sit down to Christmas Eve dinner when Simon came down the steps. As always, Momma took on this instant new personality in his presence — the charming, effusive innkeeper. She fluffed her hair, sort of licked her lips and ran for the door. I quickly sucked in my stomach. Simon just had this *effect* on practically everyone.

"Simon!" Momma said. "We were just about to have dinner! Fried fish and hushpuppies with grits and salad! Won't you join us?"

"Is that what it is? I could smell it upstairs! Smells wonderful, but I don't want to intrude."

"Son, you couldn't intrude if you wanted to. Come join us!"

My face got hot, and I turned away to get another place setting from the silver chest, as Simon greeted everyone.

"Hey, Susan! Merry Christmas!"

"Thanks, you too!" I replied automatically. "Oh, Jesus! I mean, oh, God, Simon, I'm sorry."

"For what?"

"I mean, you know, saying Merry Christmas and, Jesus, I mean, oh, just forget it."

He was smirking at me and his brown eyes twinkled. I hated it when people smirked at me. God, he smelled good. One of his front teeth was a little crooked and I found myself concentrating on how close I'd be to his mouth if we were dancing.

"Susan, Susan, Susan. Don't worry so much."

"I'm not a worrier, really, I just . . ."

"Trip over your tongue occasionally?"

"No! I mean, it just came out, that's all."

"Gosh, you sure do have yourself a little spitfire temper, don'cha? Are you always this sensitive?"

"I am *not* sensitive! God! Men! Are you always this *exasperating?*"

"*Exasperating?* That's a pretty big word for you. How old *are* you?"

"I'll be fifteen in the fall, for your information."

"Pretty smart for a fourteen-year-old. Anybody ever tell you that?"

"Kiss off, doctor!"

He ruffled my hair. I punched him in the arm. He faked pain elaborately, staggering and wincing. I was in love. And, worst of all, he knew it.

After dinner Simon left to go over to the city to see some friends of his. I regained consciousness as his car pulled out of the driveway. Livvie and I were standing at the sink, washing dishes.

"You got it bad, 'eah, chile?"

"What?"

"Been bit by the love bug, that's all. Ain't fatal."

I groaned. How was it that I, who had been immune to boys all my life, suddenly found myself in this slippery quagmire? And how did Livvie always know what was going on with me? At least Timmy and Henry seemed not to have noticed. So far.

"What am I gonna do, Livvie?"

"Remember this feeling all your life, gal, 'cause it's true magic. Can't buy him, can't fake him. If the spark ain't there, the spark ain't there! Oh, chile, I was just about your age when I meet my Nelson." She stopped wiping the sink, her face softened, her eyes stared out into space and she shook her head, back and forth, exhaling.

"Oh, it was sweet, so sweet. Tall and skinny I was, all lanky like a filly. We done gone down to the church for a social, me and my momma. I don't know where my daddy was that night, but I remember being with my momma. There was a breeze, and the air smell like honeysuckle and pine all around. We could 'eah the music before we get in the churchyard. I remember being all excited because I was wearing stockings, might've been my first pair! Anyway, we get in the door and my momma go over to see some of she friends to say hello. I look across the room and there's my Nelson! He so fine looking! I finally get introduced to him somehow, I don't remember. Turns out he visiting some family, he from Charlotte, North Carolina. I think to myself that he's a city boy and he ain't gone find nothing about me to write home about. Well, we dance and dance and I can feel the *heat!* I ain't never feel like that before or since! Yeah, when love finds you, you can't hide, no sir. Gone getcha! Ha! He was ten years older than me."

"No kidding."

"Mizz Susan, you listen to ol' Livvie. Don't you worry none, when the time comes you can have him, iffin you want him. 'cause, honey? The woman pick the man. The man don't pick the woman. Remember that! Time ain't right quite yet."

"Time ain't right? How do I know when the time's right?"

"You'll know. That's all. Gone now, now gone get yourself ready for church, and ask Jesus to help you!"

We walked to Stella Maris Church for the main Christmas event for all the Catholic families on the Island. It was only five blocks, and it was nice going down the street with Momma pushing the double carriage. Maggie, my brothers and I followed in her trail, under the stars. The brilliant stars! Millions of them! There were no lights to speak of on the Island and the night was velvet. It was a perfect lesson in humility to walk to Mass on Christmas Eve under that sky. The night was cool enough to see your breath, but not cold enough for a coat. If it ever got that cold we would ride with Uncle Louis.

I enjoyed the walk, even though the lineup was short three people. Under the stars I could believe that they were up in heaven watching us, praying for us, asking God to help us. I hoped they were. I really didn't like to think about Daddy being in purgatory or hell.

We walked by Fort Moultrie and just beyond it, across the street, was Stella Maris. I'd always thought it was perfect, the old stucco over brick, painted white, weathered beige. The top had a dome of blue light. Stella Maris — star of the sea.

Uncle Louis and Aunt Carol had saved seats for us. Momma left the carriage by the door and we tiptoed up the aisle, genuflected, blessed ourselves, whispered Merry Christmas to them and finally settled ourselves on the hard wood of the pew. It was only ten-thirty; we had come early to hear the choir, but us kids made a sport out of giggling at the snoring and of silently imitating the sopranos, poking each other and snickering. Last year there would have been hell to pay if Daddy had caught us in our predictable sacrilegious antics, but this year we had the sympathy of the entire congregation. We had gone from being the "notorious Hamilton brood" to those "poor Hamilton children." Timmy and Henry figured that was license to get away with murder. And they did. When the soprano hit the high note in "O Holy Night," she sang *dee-vine* off key enough to break the stained glass. We all came undone; even Momma and Uncle Louis finally snickered in agreement. We got our money's worth of entertainment.

After church we stood outside, shivering then, while Momma tucked blankets around Sophie and Allie. People kissed our cheeks and wished us well, we said good night to Aunt Carol and Uncle Louis and finally began making our way back to the Island Gamble.

At the Island Gamble, Livvie was waiting on the back porch, the Christmas lights blinking all around her. She was waiting for Uncle Louis to drive her home. I hated to see her go at night, and tonight especially, but I knew she had to go be with her family. Then I remembered that we hadn't given her our present.

"Merry Christmas!" she called out to us as we crossed the yard.

"Merry Christmas to you too!" we sang out. "Merry Christmas, Livvie!"

Uncle Louis pulled up in the yard to take her home.

"Don't go yet, Livvie! We have something for you!" I said.

I ran in the house and back to the living room to get her present from under the tree. Running out, I saw that the kitchen was clean. I looked up at the clock above the refrigerator. One o'clock in the morning. Christmas morning.

"Merry Christmas, Livvie. This is from me, Maggie, Timmy and Henry."

"Thank you! I got something for y'all too but can't bring him till tomorrow! Y'all get some sleep now! It's late! Merry Christmas!"

"Merry Christmas!" we said, all together.

We watched her get in the backseat of Uncle Louis's car. Maybe Uncle Louis didn't want her to sit next to him. Was that it? I'd have to ask tomorrow. I'd ask Momma in the morning.

I heard a bicycle bell ringing and a horn tooting. I rolled over and looked at my alarm clock. Seven-thirty. The ringing and tooting continued. I put my pillow over my head.

I got up on my knees and looked out the window. Timmy and Henry were riding on new bicycles around the yard in their pajamas, cutting doughnuts and figure eights through the morning mist. Aunt Carol and Uncle Louis had their arms around each other and were obviously very pleased with themselves. They had made Christmas happen for the boys and for all of us, really.

"Look at them!" I said.

"They're having a ball!" Maggie said, now awake too.

"I love Christmas, don't you? I mean, this is kind of what it's all about, isn't it?"

"Yeah, it is."

The noise continued and soon the house

smelled of coffee brewing and bacon frying. My aunt and uncle left, threatening to return sometime around noon.

Momma had a huge bowl of pancake batter mixed up and she stood by the stove.

"Let's go open presents," I said, "we can feed the hordes later!"

"Good idea!" Momma said. "Call the boys!"

And we did. There was something for everyone. Crazy, fuzzy, purple bedroom slippers for me from Maggie, a secondhand red union suit with a drop back door for Maggie from Henry that he bought from the Army Navy store, an armful of comic books for Henry from Timmy and, of course, a turtle named Rufus went to Timmy from me. Momma had scraped up enough money to buy us all new sweaters, all of them cotton, crewneck pullovers, kelly green. My worst color. Well, it's the thought that counts. I put on the bedroom slippers and gave Maggie a kiss.

"They're great!" I said. "I'll wear them to church!"

"You will not!" Momma said, pretending to be horrified.

Maggie put on the union suit over her nightgown, unbuttoned the back flap and let it drop open. Henry started laughing.

"I'll wear it to the next dance at school!" she said.

"You'll get arrested for indecent exposure!" Momma said.

"You'll get *peeee-pneumonia* in your butt if you do!" Timmy said.

"Timmy!" Maggie said.

"Hey! We forgot the stockings!"

Furious competition ensued to see who'd get to them first. It didn't matter, because in true democratic style, they all contained the same things — a Hershey's bar, a pack of Juicy Fruit gum, a Sugar Daddy and a handful of Fire Balls. At the bottom of each one was a twenty-dollar bill. That was a fortune, in my mind. One by one, we all threw our arms around Momma and thanked her.

"Gosh! Where'd you get all the dough, Mom?" Timmy said.

"I'm rich!" Henry said.

"Thanks, Momma," Maggie and I said.

I realized then that she hadn't opened our gift so I reached under the tree and pulled out the big box, wrapped in green-and-red-striped paper, and handed it to her. She opened it, unfolded the tissue and pulled the robe from the box. It was pale blue quilted polyester with a front zipper. She stood in front of the big mirror and held it up to herself, smiling at her reflection. Half-dancing, she turned to us, waiting to be paid with her pleasure.

"It's beautiful," she said, "really beautiful." She choked back her emotions and we did the same.

"Let's go make pancakes!" Maggie said.

"Yeah, I'll help!" Timmy said.

"It's the most beautiful robe I've ever had," Momma said, "and I'm not just saying that. It really is. Thank you so much."

Experience told me that Momma was spiraling down again and it wouldn't be long before she was in the trouble zone. It was a good thing that Aunt Carol and Uncle Louis were coming back for dinner. Maybe they could slap a little sense into her.

It wasn't that I didn't care about how she was feeling, just that I wanted a Christmas without tears.

After breakfast, the turkey was in the oven and an old Perry Como-Bing Crosby movie was on the television. Momma had jammed the bird in the oven and gone to her room. We were on our own and had made it through the morning. Maggie and I set the table.

"Getting to be like déjà vu, isn't it?"

"Yep," she said. "This is good practice for when I'm Mrs. Pettigrew."

"Right. Mrs. Pettigrew. Right."

"He wants to get married after we graduate."

"You mean he wants to go all the way now," I mumbled.

"*What* did you say?"

"Nothing," I said.

Timmy and Henry came flying through the room, saving me from Maggie's wrath. If she wanted to screw Lucius Pettigrew and get knocked up, ruin her reputation and wreck her life, that was her business. It really was!

"I'm taking my bike out for a ride," Timmy said.

"Me too!" Henry chimed.

"Just be back soon, okay? Dinner's at two-thirty!" I said.

"Yeah, yeah," Timmy said, and slammed the screen door.

"Yeah, yeah," Henry echoed, slamming the door again.

Arms filled with plates for the table, I watched Timmy take off on his bike with Henry behind him. As soon as he got to the street, Timmy started riding with no hands.

Aunt Carol and Uncle Louis rolled in at one-thirty. "Where's your momma?" Uncle Louis asked.

"Taking a nap," Maggie said.

"Is she always lying up in the bed?"

"No," I lied, "she just tries to nap when the twins are napping. Gonna be a long day."

"Yeah, well, Carol, go tell her we're here."

There was no reason for me to fan the fire between my mother and uncle. He had started up picking on Momma right where Daddy had left off. At that stage of the game, I'd heard enough fighting to last me for the rest of my life.

"Do you want some coffee, Uncle Louis?"

I was so polite, even Maggie gave me the hairy eyeball. But what the hell, I figured, may as well be nice.

"Sure, honey. Thanks."

Christmas dinner, which we finally ate at four P.M., was really and truly delicious. I ate myself stupid and needed a nap in the worst way, especially after picking at the pumpkin piecrust. I love crust. I decided to lie down for a while. But then I saw Livvie roll up in the backyard in her nephew's car. She got out and went to the backseat for a big cardboard box. I went out to greet her.

"Got y'all something y'all need in this family!" she cried.

"What?" I yelled back.

"Come on see, chile, come on 'eah and see!" She put the box on the ground. A little pink nose stuck itself up over the edge. It was a fat little puppy with a red bow around his neck! I was wide-awake now.

"He name be Rascal! He 'eah to keep y'all company!"

"Oh, Livvie! He's so cute! Oh, thank you! Timmy! Henry! Maggie! Come see!" I was shrieking.

In an instant, they flew down the stairs and bent over the box. He was as cute as a button, part collie, part German shepherd and part Heinz. We let Henry lift him out and he tumbled and jumped and hopped all over the place. We played and laughed until I thought we'd get sick from it. Aunt Carol, Momma and Uncle Louis watched from the steps, Momma and Aunt Carol each with a twin on her hip.

Livvie stood by watching. "It's a good Christmas, 'eah, Miss MC?"

"Yes, Livvie, it's a fine Christmas after all."

18

SIMON

1999

On Friday, Tom came by to pick up Beth to do some Christmas shopping and have dinner. His color wasn't good but his mood was fine.

"Hi," I said, opening the door, "how are you feeling?"

"Not bad for a guy going through chemo," he said.

"Yuk, right?"

"Yeah," he said, "my hair's falling out, but thing's could be worse. I got a call from Youngworth this afternoon. I've been accepted into an experimental group through the Medical University — some new medication that allegedly makes tumors disappear."

"Tom that's truly wonderful," I said, suddenly chilled at the hope of a cure, "let me call Beth."

I climbed the steps to the second floor to get Beth and also a sweater for myself, thinking that we needed a miracle for Christmas. Just one little miracle, God, please. It's me, Susan Hamilton Hayes, God, I don't ask for much. Yeah, sure.

I told Beth that Tom was waiting for her, rummaged through my chest of drawers and threw a cardigan around my shoulders.

Downstairs I found them reading the *Post & Courier*. Beth was showing Tom my column.

"I knew it!" he said. "I saw this yesterday and said to myself, that's Susan or I'm a monkey's uncle!" He smiled at me. "You are one funny gal, you know."

"Thanks," I said.

" '. . . at my age, if I were sexually harassed, I'd send the guy flowers,' " Tom read. "Susan, don't you realize that every feminist group in America must be torching the *Post & Courier* right about now?"

"Read the rest of it, counselor," I said, "then you can work my gears."

"Okay, okay," he said, and continued reading it to the end. "Ah, now I get it. It's the unwanted advances that makes harassment into harassment, right?"

I took a small bow. "Thank you very much," I said.

"You should've been a lawyer, Susan," he said, "there's not enough humor in the courtroom."

"Yeah, right," I said. "See, even sexual harassment can be a riot, right? Everything is point of view."

"What made you decide to do this?" he asked.

"Your daughter and her mall habit," I said and Beth groaned.

"Susan, everything's gonna be all right," he said. "Give your momma a kiss, Beth. I'll have her back by nine."

"No problem," I said.

It has been one hell of a year, I thought to myself. But I was not unhappy with how life was playing itself out, with the exception of Tom's cancer. His twit girlfriend, Karen, was still in the picture. Even after everything she had put him through he was still seeing her. It seemed to me that their relationship at this point was more grounded in guilt than love — her feeling guilty for making him delay his surgery, and him seeing her to remind her that his state of health was her fault.

For once in my whole history with Tom, I finally felt that things were as they should be. I had come to the conclusion that Tom and I were better off living apart. And Michelle Stoney had been right to advise me to leave the divorce proceedings in place. That guaranteed consistent and necessary support. His health was the bigger picture at the moment and we were focused on that alone. If Tom's treatments didn't work I'd be a widow.

Christmas was right around the corner. We tried to be cheerful and not dwell on Tom's cancer too much. Maggie continued to plan the holiday for our family and Beth and I looked forward to seeing everyone and most especially to New Year's Eve. The Millennium. It was a time for profound thinking and serious resolutions. It was also a season for great parties.

The following week, I stopped by the *Post & Courier* and turned in another batch of essays that I'd been working on. I ran into Max Hall.

"Ah! Ms. Hayes!"

"Susan, please."

"Right! Susan! You've been on my mind. Glad I caught you. The missus and I are planning a small holiday party. Julia is dying to meet you and has been twisting my arm to ask you to come. Next Friday at our house. I'll drop an invitation in the mail and hope you'll join us."

"A Christmas party. What a wonderful idea," I said. "You know, Max, I could use a little fun in my life! Tell Julia that my calendar is embarrassingly open and that I'd love to come."

"Yeah, and you can bring someone too, if you'd like. Hey! Bring Jack!"

"Very funny," I said. Couldn't he just forget that one dumb remark?

As soon as I got home and hung up my jacket, the phone rang. Beth catapulted from the back porch in, it seemed, midair to grab it. It occurred to me that I should insist she try out for the track team and I made a mental note to do just that after Christmas.

I assumed it was for her because the phone didn't ring that much for me. I was wrong.

"For you, Mom!" she called.

"Who is it?"

"Dunno, some man," she called back.

I went to the kitchen phone and picked it up.

"Suz? Is that you?"

"Oh, God, this can only be one person," I said. It was Simon Rifkin.

"Yeah, it's me. So how are you?" he said.

"How am I? Let's see, well, I'm okay, actually. Yeah, I'm fine. How are your broken fingers?"

"What?"

"Well, I figure your fingers must've been broken or I would've heard from you."

"Go ahead, give me some heat. I'm an old man

now, you know. Have some respect for your elders."

"Right. So what's the deal, hotshot? I heard you were living in Atlanta doing germ warfare."

"Yeah, that's me. Dr. Germ. I love the little boogers. Love seeing them squirm."

"Yeah, you always did like to make things squirm."

"Yep, some things never change. Hey, by the way, I'm sorry that I missed your call about Thanksgiving. I was in Hawaii and then I went straight to Zurich to deliver a paper. I just got back last night. I swear to God, I don't even know what day it is much less what time zone. I would've loved to have spent the holiday with you guys, but I was gone."

"Good excuse. Okay, you're forgiven. God, it's so good to hear your voice, you old dog."

"Yeah, you too. So what's the deal with you? Still married to that asshole?"

"Actually, no. And you? Still married to your mail-order child bride?"

"No, it's a heart-wrencher. Fact is, the little witch up and left me for her personal trainer."

"So did you kill the bastard, or what?"

"The bitch. Her trainer was a woman," he said. "Helga the big mean Swede."

I burst out laughing and realized that Beth was staring at me like I had three heads.

"Oh, Simon. That's awful," I said. "I mean, it really is. Really."

"Yeah, really really. Oh well, I hope they're happy."

"Don't tell me. Let me guess," I said. "She said

you worked too much and she was lonely and she couldn't help herself."

"Exactly. The sins of the father and all that. So, you have a daughter, right?"

"Yep. Beth. She's gorgeous. She's fabulous. She's everything I never was." I took the phone into the laundry room and pulled the door closed.

"God on earth, she must be ugly and stupid."

"No, goofball, she's beautiful and brilliant!"

"So were you, Susan. Jesus, you sound exactly the same. Are you still the same?"

"No, I'm an old bag. I gained three hundred pounds, my teeth and hair fell out and I live in a bathrobe, taste-testing cookies for Nabisco. Why don't you come see for yourself? Maggie must have a floor you could sleep on or a hammock. Or a bed of nails or something." I hadn't had this much fun in twenty years.

"Great idea. I'll call her."

"God, I hate your guts for not calling me years sooner. I have missed you like you would not believe."

"Yeah," he said, "kiss my *bee-hind*. You could've called me too, you know."

"You're right. I stink. Listen, let me know when you're coming to town so I can polish my dentures."

"I will. Obviously, I need to rest up for this one."

"Yes, you do."

"Oh, you sound so grown up I can't believe it. What are you gonna do when I show up, Susan?"

"I'm gonna deal with you, Simon, like I should have twenty years ago, that's what."

"Thirty," he said.

"Whatever," I said. "I'm serious."

"Jesus, I'd better start taking my vitamins."

"And eating oysters."

"God, I'll be there tonight."

"Yeah, right. You can dress up like Santa and give me a thrill."

"My God forgives you for this endless diatribe of anti-Semitic remarks."

"My Lord forgives you for not accepting Him."

"The queen of retorts. Marry me."

"Marry you? Bump you, jerk. Call me more than once in twenty years and I'll consider it." I couldn't stop laughing and neither could he. We were literally screaming at each other. The creep still thrilled me. God, I loved him. I always had, I always would.

"Fine, big mouth," he said. "I'll call you next week, as soon as I get over my jet lag."

"Yeah, sure. I'll be holding my breath."

We hung up. My heart was dancing all over my chest. Beth opened the louvered door and saw me sitting cross-legged on top of the washing machine, hugging the remote phone.

"Oh, God, he is the funniest man on the earth," I said.

"Well, I *guess,* Mom! God! Was this somebody you love or somebody you hate? Just who the heck is Simon?"

It was time to come forward and tell her about Simon.

"He's this guy," I said, thinking that was good for an opener. "You want to make some tea or should I?"

"You're too wrecked. I'll do it," she said.

She filled the kettle with water and put it on the stove to boil. I finally climbed off the washing machine and replaced the phone in its cradle. I sat on a bar stool and watched her work. It was role reversal and it was about time.

"How about some cheese and crackers to go with it?" I said.

"If you'll tell me the truth, I'll give you food," she said.

"Simon was the undisputed love of my life at one time," I began. "He was also my stepbrother."

"Okay, start over. First of all, I knew that Grandpa Stanley had a son named Simon, but I never knew about this! Isn't that incest or something?"

"Oh, hell no."

"Gosh, Mom, you're cussing, like, wildly! I heard you say some very bad words on the phone with him." She was teasing me.

"Well, you don't know Simon. He could make a nun do the limbo at a church picnic."

"Yeah, right, so give me the skinny! Come on!"

"Okay, it was like this. Simon was a boarder in our house after Daddy died. I took one look at him and discovered that I was a woman. At first it was a mad crush, and then I really fell in love with him. Head over heels. Gone. Down the tunnel of love in a boat with no rudder."

"That bad, huh?"

"Yup."

"How old were you?"

"Fourteen. Almost fifteen."

"Fourteen! Good Lord! How old was he?"

"Twenty-one."

"Oh, no! You're kidding!"

"No, I am not kidding." I watched as she poured the water into a teapot with Constant Comment tea bags, sliced a lemon and dropped a piece into two empty cups while the bags brewed. "We used to sneak off to the beach and go for these long walks. It was the perfect romance."

"Did you ever kiss him?"

"Are you kidding me? I kissed him until his lips were frayed around the edges! He was the best kisser in the world. Or at least I thought so at the time, but what did I know? Not much, let me tell you!"

"Holy moly, I can't believe my mother walked the beach with some guy, kissing at fourteen years old! He was ancient!"

"I'm telling you this to let you know that I know what it feels like to be your age. But, Beth, I was probably indiscreet. I'm trying to teach you the value of discretion. Also, in my day, there was no AIDS, herpes or any of that stuff. And, you have to remember, we had no supervision. None. Momma was in a major fog, Daddy was dead and Livvie had her hands full."

I cut a piece of cheddar cheese and ate it with a Ritz cracker.

"Did you do it with him?"

"Oh, my God! I can't believe you'd ask me that! Of course not! Honey, I thought that sex sent you to hell forever! Plus, you could get pregnant! We never got close to anything like that. No, it was a lot of hand-holding and innocent kissing — okay, not so innocent — but never anything like the big one!"

"So what happened? I mean, how come you didn't marry him?"

"Well, for starters, his father married my mother and it was just too weird. I went off to school and he left the country to do his residency in Asia and I never saw him again. I met your father, fell in love with him and Simon married some Asian babe. Plus, he really was too old for me."

"I'd say so! If I came home with a twenty-one-year-old guy you'd lock me in my room!"

"Yeah, I sure would, but times were different then. People usually stopped short of the actual deed and took a cold shower or jumped in the ocean or something."

"So, are you gonna see him again?"

"I hope so, although I'm not sure my nervous system can take it. I'm pretty old for this stuff."

"You know what, Mom? You're not old and you should have a boyfriend. Hey! Whatever happened to that Roger guy?"

"Oh, Roger, well, he's around but he's not for me. Wrong chemistry."

"Oh. Well, who knows? Maybe you'll get back together with Simon!" The phone rang again and she said, "Maybe it's Chris!"

By Friday, the seventeenth, I was prepared for not one but three parties. A mountain of wrapped packages were under our tree and my closet had two great new outfits, courtesy of Kim the Make-over Wonder's advice. Beth and I had stopped in to see him out at the mall and when I told him I was going shopping for myself, he took me by the hand

and said, "Not without me, you're not." No one respected my fashion sense.

Kim had decided I looked better in brown than black. He forced me to buy a brown cashmere sweater with a short brown velvet skirt. It was true. I looked better in brown. Then he made me buy a red crepe tank dress and fake diamond cluster earrings. I felt stupid with my arms all naked and phony diamonds but he and Beth said I looked great.

I asked him to go to the *Post & Courier* party, explaining that it was business, and he accepted.

"Dear heavens, Susan," he said, "first of all, I'd go anywhere to get off the plantation, but a party with you in that red dress? I can't wait to see the girls scratch your eyes out! Of course I'll go, under one condition, however."

"What?"

"You must let me blow out your hair first. Just what have you done to my haircut?"

And Maggie and Grant had invited me to a big bash for the Medical University faculty on Saturday.

"Maybe you'll meet a doctor," she said.

"Maybe I'll see Roger," I said.

"Oh, Lord, don't worry about him, there'll be a million people there."

"Why should I worry? I'm not the pervert, he is."

And the library was having a cocktail party on Sunday night for employees and their families. It would give me a chance to dunk Mitchell Freemont in the punch bowl. Yes, indeed, the holiday season, the last one of the Millennium, was in full swing and I was ready for it all.

When Friday night arrived, I was ready to deck the halls. Kim rang the doorbell and found me dressed in the red dress with my hair in a towel.

"Don't you look like the most divine morsel!" he said.

"You look pretty deadly yourself," I said.

We exchanged elaborate air kisses on both cheeks.

"Fabulous tree!" he said. "Next year we should let my Jeremy do it for you. He's simply mad about old houses and decorating for Christmas! God, you still haven't met him! We have to have you out to the plantation!"

"I'd love it!" I said. "Want a glass of wine?"

"No, darling, but thank you. Gotta watch my waistline, you know."

He stood before the big mirror and admired himself. He wore a black Armani tuxedo that fitted him like an Italian glove. I couldn't help thinking how this man tickled my funny bone. He was more concerned about his appearance than any woman I'd ever met.

"Great mirror," he said.

"*Strange* mirror," I said. "Come on, gorgeous, let's dry my hair or we're gonna be late."

He made me change my pantyhose from sheer black to nude.

"Much sexier," he said.

"Now I feel really naked," I said.

"You look ravishing," he said, and brushed my hair back and then rolled the sides toward my face. I attached the earrings and they twinkled out from beneath my hair.

"Damn," I said, "I look good."

"Almost as good as I do! Ha! Let's go!"

We took my car to Max and Julia Hall's historic house on the lower end of King Street. A polite older man in a white jacket opened the door and took my coat. The house was decorated for the holidays from one end to the other. A chamber music ensemble was playing Vivaldi in the living room. A hundred or so people dressed in holiday finery roamed the rooms, talking, smiling and helping themselves to the hors d'oeuvres being passed by tuxedoed waiters on silver platters. I looked around for Max and saw him in the far corner of the dining room, engaged in a private conversion with another man.

"Well, what do you think?" I said to Kim.

"If the caviar's beluga, I'm staying all night. If they have weenies in pastry, we're out of here by nine."

"Guaranteed it's beluga," I said.

"Then you need a raise," he said.

"You're right!"

We wandered over to the bar and Kim got two glasses of champagne for us. "Dom," he said, "not too shabby."

We touched glasses and worked our way through the crowd toward the dining room. I didn't recognize anyone from the paper, but that wasn't surprising as I rarely went to the office except to drop off work. Everyone was smiling and I got a few good ogles from the older men. I smiled back at them, feeling pretty darn good.

"I saw that old man!" Kim said. "He positively leered at you! Shall I take him outside and challenge him to a duel?"

"Let's eat first. I'm starving," I said, smiling at Kim.

"Such a sensible girl you are," he said.

Everything was so beautiful that I didn't know where to look first. Julia Hall had placed full white poinsettias wrapped in gold foil on each step of her curved staircase in the center hall. Her dining room table had an exquisite centerpiece of white French tulips, long-stemmed white roses and corkscrew willow branches that had been spray-painted gold. The flowers were in a Chinese Export blue-and-white porcelain wine cooler that was probably worth a fortune.

At one end of the table, a chef was slicing filet mignon. Another chef sliced cold salmon at the other end. In between them were a pyramid of steaming baby lamb chops with a mint sauce for dipping, a platter of tiny pastrami sandwiches on rye bread and sliced turkey breast sandwiches in soft rolls.

"Try the lamb chops," I said to Kim, "they're yummy."

I was beginning to feel like an intruder since no one had greeted us, just as Max looked up and saw me.

"Susan! Hi! You made it!" he said, coming over to me.

"Max! I want you to meet someone," I said, and turned to Kim, who had his mouth filled with food. "This is Jack."

Kim narrowed his eyes at me, chewing madly and wiping his hands on a napkin.

"Jack, 'eah? Well, I've heard all about you!" He laughed like an old bear and shook Kim's hand up and down until I thought his arm would fly out of his shoulder socket. "Let me go find Julia! She'll want to meet you right away! I think she's in the kitchen fighting with the caterer. Some damn fool waiter was rude to a guest or something like that. Be right back!"

"Nice meeting you," Kim said to Max's back as he turned away. Then, turning to me, he said, "And who is Jack, may I ask?"

"Forget it. It wasn't that funny the first time. Have some pastrami."

We walked around the table to the seafood. Oysters on the half shell were in the center on a bed of ice with lobster claws on one side and a cascade of shrimp on the other. A silver chafing dish of hot crab dip and another of curried scallops flanked the whole affair.

"Lord," Kim said, "this could be a Park Avenue soiree!"

"What are you talking about? We had a million parties like this when I was growing up. This is how we do it in the Holy City, honey chile."

"You're a terrible little liar," he said, "and don't expect this when you come to Tara. Our finger food sits on a Ritz until we replace the roof. And why do they call Charleston the Holy City anyway?"

"Well, about a billion years ago, when Charleston was a newborn baby, they called her the Holy City because so many different religions were practiced by the original settlers. Religious persecution brought them here from Europe."

"Ah! And all this time I thought it was the potato famine," he said.

"That was later," I said, thinking that Kim may be eye candy but no Einstein. "Here comes Max."

"Here we are at last! Susan, this is Julia!" Max said, elbowing his way to us.

I shook her hand and thought, so this is Mrs. Max Hall! I should look so good when I'm her age. Her hair was swept up in a twist and her beautiful pearl earrings were surrounded by glittering diamonds. Real ones.

"Hello, Susan, welcome! I have just enjoyed your column so much!"

"Thank you," I said. "Your home is so beautiful and this is such a lovely party." How inane could I be? "I'd like you to meet my friend Kim."

"Hello," she said, "do I know you?"

"Now we know each other, Mrs. Hall," Kim said, taking her hand into both of his and holding them. "And what do you mean? What column?"

"Kim, dear man, don't you know who you're with?" Julia said.

"Well, I *thought* I did," he said.

"She's the Geechee Girl, son," Max said. "Yep, that column has brought us more mail than any other column in ten years. Going into syndication too. Didn't she tell you?"

" 'Geechee Girl Remembers'?" Kim said. "That's *you?*"

"Guilty," I said.

"Oh, my God! Wait until my Jeremy hears *this!* He reads every syllable to me on Thursdays at our breakfast table! It's cappuccino, granola and Geechee! Every Thursday!"

Julia was a very nice lady and her friends flattered me to no end. Before the night was over, Kim had won the heart and hair of every woman there. Most importantly, Max knew a man wasn't keeping me and that I still needed my job. All things considered, it was a successful night.

When we got home, Kim walked me to my door.

"Well, Susan, thanks for a wonderful night," he said. "Gorgeous house, gorgeous party."

"You are a character, do you know that?"

"I haven't had so much fun in eons," he said. "Old ladies love me. I can't wait to get the plaster out of their hair."

I was going to invite him in, but I'd had enough drama for one night.

"See ya, sweet cakes, thanks for coming with me," I said. Through the window, I watched the grace with which he moved, as he opened the door to his Jaguar and slid behind the wheel. He made me feel glamorous.

I arrived at the Sheraton Hotel for the party Grant and Maggie had invited me to and scanned the crowd for Roger Dodds. I saw him across the ballroom at the bar. I felt like starting trouble.

"Roger, Roger, Roger! How are you?" I said, looking very smart in my brown V-neck cashmere sweater and short skirt. Nude stockings, don't forget the nude stockings, and high heels. He was deceivingly conservative in his dark suit, white shirt and red foulard bow tie.

"Susan! What a nice surprise!"

He gave me a light kiss on the cheek and looked me up and down. Thank God my shoes have closed toes, I thought.

"Are you here with someone?" I said.

"No, I'm alone. God, you have great legs."

"Yes, I do. Thank you." The Rivieras were playing "Double Shot of My Baby's Love."

"Can I get you a drink?" he asked.

"Sure, a *cock-tail* would be great," I said.

"Feeling naughty, are we? White wine?"

"Thanks," I said, taking the glass.

"God, you're driving me crazy already," he said.

"Oh! There's Maggie and Grant! I have to go, Roger. Sorry. See you!"

"What, you're leaving me? Why?"

"I have a date," I lied, "and I have to go home. The truth is that I had a pedicure this afternoon. They scraped my feet just a little too close for these pumps. Then they massaged them with some oil that smells like coconut and fruit and they sting a little. They're very tender, Roger. Very pink, soft and tender."

"Come on, Susan, don't tell me this," he said.

"Yeah, I came with this guy who's a podiatrist. He says I need to get off my feet."

"Sounds like he wants to take you to bed and screw you."

"Gosh? Think so? Gee. That would be nice. Well, Merry Christmas, Roger."

I smiled at him and walked over to Grant and Maggie.

"Mission accomplished," I whispered to Maggie. "Great party, Grant, thanks for inviting me."

"You leaving already?" Grant said.

"Yeah, got a hot date with a young one," I said.

At home, my hot young one, Beth, and I curled up like two old friends on the couch and watched *It's a Wonderful Life* for the zillionth time. We shared popcorn, Cokes and tissues, saying the dialogue in perfect sync with the actors. We were perfectly content.

At the library party Mitchell Freemont told me with great sadness that he was taking a job in Spartanburg.

"When?" I said.

"In two weeks," he said. "I guess that's it for the two of us."

"Yeah, guess so, Mitchell."

There was no end to his arrogance. After he walked away I realized that his departure put me in line for his job, which if it happened would mean a substantial raise. I knew they'd have to interview other candidates but I put my name in the hat right away. It was a pretty boring party, but I used the time to lobby for Mitchell's position.

I called Maggie the next day to tell her the news.

"God, I hope you get his job," she said.

"Yeah, me too."

"By the way, what on earth did you say to Roger Dodds?"

"Nothing. Why?"

"He came over to Grant all befuddled and said you made him crazy."

"I can't imagine why," I said.

"You won't believe what Grant said."

"What?"

"Grant said to him, 'Well, Roger, my sister-in-law is the kind of gal that keeps you on your toes, isn't she?' I almost choked trying not to laugh."

"Good Lord."

On Monday, I woke up earlier than usual. I couldn't sleep. At six o'clock, I finally pulled on a bathrobe and went downstairs to make coffee. I had had the strangest dream the night before. I was alone in the backyard of the Island Gamble with Livvie. Livvie and I were hanging laundry on the clothesline. We had baskets of sheets, all of them white. She kept saying, "Look at these, Miss Susan! So many white sheets!" We just kept hanging them and hanging them and there was no end to them. They stretched the length of our yard and I knew that they would cover the entire length of the Island by the time we were done. The more I hung, the more there seemed to be. We used the old-fashioned wooden clothespins to attach them. "Keep hanging!" she called out to me. I was so tired in my dream — I just wanted to stop and rest for a while. But Livvie was so determined to hang them all that I kept working.

Sipping my mug of hot coffee I kept going over the dream in my head. What did it mean? Was it about work? Certainly it seemed like my work never ended. I knew that dreams had symbols but I didn't know much about them. What was all the white about? Peace? Purity? Who would use all those sheets? A hospital? Then it came to me. The Klan. Bingo!

I left my coffee mug on the counter and ran up the stairs as fast as I could. Beth was still sleeping and was out of school for the Christmas break. I opened her door.

"Beth? I'm going to the office; if you need me call me, okay?"

"Okay, Momma. What time is it?"
"Early. Go back to sleep."

By the time I showered and dressed and drove to the library, it was almost quarter of eight. Mitchell usually came in at eight. I waited, smoking and pacing, for his car to pull up in the parking lot. Finally he arrived.

"Good morning, Susan," he said, "early bird for a reason?"

"Yeah, I have something I want to look up."

He turned the keys, unlocking the door, and rattled the key chain at me.

"I understand you're interested in my job," he said.

"So is half of the world," I said.

"Well, good luck," he said, "I'll put a good word in for you."

"Thanks," I said, wondering what the price for that would be and then reprimanding myself for being so cynical and suspicious.

He went off to his office and I went right to the microfilm. I looked up Ku Klux Klan and found quite a few references. I went all through the newspaper clippings from 1963 and couldn't find what I was looking for and just as I was about to quit, I struck pay dirt. It was from the Columbia paper, a report about a Klan convention in some little town outside of Columbia. It showed a photograph of a group of white-robed Klan members. It was highly unusual to have a picture of them, as most of their meetings were held in secret. But there it was. Plain as the nose on my face. I wondered if the photographer was attacked by some of their goons.

In the picture the Klan members' heads were covered in hoods. I printed it and took it to the scanner copier to blow it up. I held my breath as I scanned the picture. The Grand Dragon was wearing *sandals* and the guy next to him wore *highly polished police-issue black shoes.* There was no mistaking their beer guts and there was no mistake about their identity. Marvin Struthers and Fat Albert. It was they who had done my daddy in. I knew I had finally found the truth.

I bit my fist and tears streamed down my face. The dark thoughts I had always carried regarding my feelings about Daddy began to reassemble after decades of anger. My heart broke; I was filled with regret — regret that I couldn't reconcile how a man who was such a bastard to the ones who loved and needed him most gave his very life for the Civil Rights movement. While I hated the way he had treated us, he had possessed strength in his character I'd never considered. He was a fighter. Like me. I was *like* him. He had never acknowledged that. Neither had I.

For years and years I had said in anger that I was glad he was dead. For the first time in my entire life I missed him. I felt the weight of sorrow in a way I had never known I could. I wanted to wail like a child. I wanted someone to tell me they would make it all right. There was no one who could have done that. I wanted to lie down on the floor and sleep. But I just stood there, my thoughts racing as I tried to sort out the pangs of despair I felt.

Maybe if he had lived he would have been proud of us. He would have seen me become a woman, a mother, a single parent. He would have seen how capable we had all become. How successful, how strong. Maybe we would have found peace with him.

I couldn't find it in my heart to blame him anymore. I just wished I had known him better. I wished he had known me. Maybe somehow through my recognition of his heroics he could feel that now. I prayed that wherever his spirit was, he knew I forgave him. And missed him. And, finally, that I was proud of him.

19

SCHOOL

1963

At home, I lived in diaper land. I could see myself raising my own sisters and eventually becoming Momma's nurse as she had been to her mother. It was the southern way. It was what was expected of girls. I guessed they thought Maggie could make a good marriage and I was so homely, I'd never find a husband.

My only hope was to somehow get to college, which seemed less and less likely. I'd probably wind up teaching public school, the plain girl's other option. I'd wear a big bun on my head, pencils sticking out of it, and kids would tape KICK ME notes to the back of my moth-eaten cardigan sweater. Just the thought of it was depressing. No, I'd figure another way out of my mother's prison.

I was very happy to go back to school after the holidays. School was the only routine in my life that made real sense to me, and it was time off from the house. Most people loved summer, but winter was my favorite time of year. The summer tourists were long gone and not due back for months. The silence of a walk along the shore with the spray of the ocean in my hair, on my face, let my mind travel. I could imagine myself to be Catherine searching for Heathcliff on the moors or, better yet, I could search for Simon in a place where I could be alone with him. I wanted to get past the silly banter and teasing that defined our conversations. I spent a lot of time thinking about him and his lips. The rest of my daydreaming involved refining various escape plans. At one point I considered taking a bus to Atlanta, pretending to have amnesia and throwing myself at the mercy of the biggest Catholic church I could find. But I knew my accent would betray me as a Lowcountry girl. One call to the bishop of Charleston and I'd be back home in no time. I was too young for enlisting in the army and not holy enough for early entrance to a convent — that was my most desperate plan. So I filled my days with school.

One morning in January, I was in class when Father O'Brien appeared again. We all jumped up from our desks and called out, "Good morning, Father," as good children with nice manners did. He wanted me to come to his office. *I hope nobody died* was my first thought, then I realized there weren't that many people *left* to die in my family, so it must be another reason. I immediately left my class, with all my classmates staring at me.

"How's your momma?" he said, closing the door and gesturing for me to sit in the big oak chair opposite his.

"Fine," I said, "everybody's fine."

"Good, good. I see they finished the investigation into your daddy's accident. That must be a relief to have that behind y'all."

"Yeah, it is, Father."

In fact, we were sick and tired of seeing Daddy's name in the paper and answering questions about his death. Fat Albert and the police department in Charleston had decided Daddy's death was not a conspiracy. They finally decided he had a heart attack and ran off the road. Because of all the trouble Daddy had when he was building the black school, they probably thought the Klan might have had something to do with it. So they poked around, asking the same dumb questions over and over again. Stuff like, Did he have any enemies? Excuse me, but my daddy was building a heated school for colored kids smack dab in the middle of the Civil Rights movement. He had more enemies than the Japs after Pearl Harbor. Starting with his own family and every bigot who ever heard of him.

Not that it would bring Daddy back to life, but I kept thinking they weren't exactly wearing themselves out with the investigation. Seemed like the newspaper articles asked more intelligent questions than the police did. It had been the biggest story the newspapers had had since the polio epidemic. I was just glad that Marvin Struthers hadn't blamed us for giving Daddy a heart attack.

"Well, that's not the reason I called you in here," Father O'Brien continued. "I wanted to talk to you about your school record."

"What did I do? Oh, my library books! I know they're overdue! Am I in trouble?"

"Heavens, no, child. In fact, you're doing surprisingly well, amazingly well. Bring the books back as soon as you can." He cleared his throat with a grown-up *ahem*. "Susan, every year the archdiocese of Charleston sends a student on scholarship to St. Anne's Academy in Columbia. Are you aware of that?"

"No, Father."

"Are you familiar with St. Anne's?"

"I thought it was a home for unwed mothers."

"No, honey, that's the Florence Crittenton Home. Not the same thing at all. St. Anne's is a privately funded Catholic girls' boarding school. Over ninety-five percent of their graduates finish college and go on to have careers, teaching or nursing or some other appropriate line of work for ladies."

"Oh."

"What's the matter?"

"I don't want to be a teacher or a nurse."

"Well, then, do you know what you'd like to do?"

"Yeah, I mean, yes." I was twisting in my seat. "I want to be a writer and live in Paris."

"I see. Well, there's no harm in having a dream, I always say."

"Right. So did the Brontë sisters and George Sand."

This caused a major clearing of his throat. "In any case, every year we hold a sort of competition for that scholarship to St. Anne's, and I'd like to submit your name as a candidate. Have you ever thought about going away to school?"

"No, Father. I mean, yes, I have, but I thought about going away to college, not high school."

"Of course, and you should've been thinking about that. Well, I suppose what I'm asking you is if you're interested? If you are, I can talk to your mother about it for you, if you'd like."

"Um, Father O'Brien, what are my chances of winning it?"

"Oh, I don't know, probably pretty good."

"Well, if it's all the same to you, why don't we see if I can win it and then we can talk to Momma about it. I mean, there's no point in putting another burden on her, you know, 'cause if I lose, then she's gonna feel bad and all."

"And she's been through enough?"

"Exactly. I mean, I'd also like to think about it a little. Like what would happen to the twins if I left? Can Momma handle it without me? I don't really know."

"I see." He reached into a folder and pulled out a brochure, handing it to me. "Have a look at this. It tells you all about the school. You have to wear uniforms, but they are included in the scholarship, as are all your books. Plus a stipend of fifty dollars a month goes to the winner for spending money. All medical bills are covered, in case you're ill or need glasses or something. All you have to do is maintain a B-plus average and you can stay for four years. It's an excellent program, Susan. I think you should give it serious thought."

"Oh, I will! Of course I will!"

"And, if you're worried about getting homesick, you can come home on weekends and, obviously, all the holidays."

"Right. I mean, thank you for thinking of me and everything. I really appreciate it. I'm sorry, it's just that I never thought about anything like this before and I'm not sure about Momma and all. You know?"

"Of course I do. But, I think let's try for it and if

you win, let me handle your momma, all right?"

"Okay."

"Fine."

"Father? Thank you. Thanks a lot. I really mean it."

"I know you do."

Something like this could change my life forever, I thought, it could be my ticket out.

I sat on the back steps that afternoon, tossing a stick for Rascal. I scratched him behind the ears every time he brought it back to me. I'd miss this little dog if I left, I thought. He was so eager to please and so grateful for attention. White seagulls swirled all around, squawking at each other.

I tried to imagine what it would be like to leave the Island and live in a dormitory with a bunch of girls. What if they were mean? What if they were all rich and stuck up? I could always come home if I hated it. What if it was a really hard school? What if I couldn't do the work there? Going to school in Columbia wasn't like school in Mount Pleasant, after all. Columbia was the capital of the state.

I heard the door close behind me.

"What are you doing, chile? Sitting 'eah playing with Rascal?"

I turned away from the afternoon sun and stared up at Livvie. "Oh, just thinking."

"Mm-hm. I thought I smell wood burning!"

"Yeah, that's me. Burning wood like a furnace out here."

"What's in your head, 'eah? Tell Livvie."

"Oh, I don't know, Livvie. Life is so confusing."

"Ain't that the truth!"

She folded her dress under herself and sat down

next to me. Rascal came bounding up the steps, jumped in her lap and started licking her all over her face.

"Get down, boy!" I said.

"Oh, that's all right. I don't mind him none. Better than getting bit."

"Yeah, that's for sure." I looked out across the yard to the sky and her eyes followed mine.

"So, you gone tell me what or do I have to sit 'eah till the supper done all burn up?"

"Livvie, if you had a chance to do something really big, would you do it?"

"Chile, I *am* doing something really big. I'm praising Gawd every day! Iffin that ain't big enough, then tell me what I should do!"

"No, that's not what I mean."

"Then spit it out, chile."

"Okay, Father O'Brien wants to enter me in a competition to win a scholarship to St. Anne's boarding school for girls in Columbia."

"Oh! Lawd have mercy! Your momma gone take a fit iffin you get it too, 'eah?"

"Exactly."

She thought for a minute. "This is a good school, I expect?"

"Yeah, look at this." I pulled the brochure from my pocket, unfolded it and showed it to her. It had pictures of smiling nuns and serious students working in a biology lab over microscopes, a picture of the dormitory rooms, a classroom photograph and a picture of the campus. She whistled through her teeth.

"Humph. All right now. Tell me how you feel in your heart."

"I'd love to go to a school like this. Who wouldn't? But I'm a little scared too."

"What you scared of?"

"Leaving everybody."

"They don't let you come home none?"

"Oh, sure, you can come home every weekend if you want to. But what if I don't fit in?"

"You raise your head up high, 'eah?"

"Yeah, you're right. I mean, this could be my only chance to get out of 'eah."

"Then, that's all she wrote. You ain't got no choice."

"What about Momma and the twins and Timmy and Henry?"

"Honey, don't fret none over y'all's momma. She gone do fine. Timmy and Henry gone get to go to college anyhow, 'cause your uncle gone see to that. Them twins is mine. Don't you worry none about them twins."

"Well, I gotta tell Father O'Brien something by tomorrow."

"Honey, Gawd's got a plan for you and it ain't about raising your momma's children for her. You needs to be in the world and maybe this is His way of helping you. Iffin it's Gawd's will, gone come to pass. Iffin it ain't, nothing you can do about him nohow."

"Well, we'll see. I might not even win it, you know. So don't say anything, okay?"

"Chile, my lips are sealed."

It was a beautiful Sullivan's Island afternoon and the sunset was beginning. Gosh, I thought, this morning I didn't even know St. Anne's existed, now I thought I might die if I didn't win the scholarship. How royally screwed up was that?

"Look at that sky," Livvie said.

"Uh-huh," I said.

"Ain't it marvelous?"

"Yeah, it's marvelous."

"No, chile o' mine, you ain't understanding what I'm telling you."

Her voice was so soft and loving, it was hard to keep my worries on my mind. "What do ya mean?"

"See them stars starting to twinkle? They's Gawd's diamonds. You 'eah me? And the night sky turning so blue? That's He sapphires for us. And see that streak of red across the horizon? They's a field of rubies. Whenever you feel troubled and poor in the spirit, just go look at the sunset and all Gawd's riches just be a-waiting for you."

"Yeah, sure, Livvie," I said.

"I ain't lying to you, chile. I is telling you for true."

I looked at the sky and it was full of riches, all you could want or spend. She put her arm around my shoulder, gave me a squeeze and then dropped it, taking my hand into her lap. My small white fingers were enfolded by her sturdy dark skin, her palms rosy, her nails deep ivory and thick. Her capable hands, roughened by years of hard work, her loving hands whose warmth radiated and soothed. She spoke to me as though deep sounds could penetrate my thick skull.

"Gone be all right, Susan. Everything gone be all right. Y'all gone see, by and by. You growing up, Maggie growing up, all y'all gone grow up. Trouble can't stop that, no sir. Gawd gone send help. He always does."

We glided toward Easter, me holding my tongue — I had given up swearing for Lent — and Timmy and Henry trying to behave. Livvie and Momma were doing spring-cleaning. I don't know what had come over Momma lately, but she had lost a lot of weight and the red glass was nowhere to be seen. She looked pretty good for someone her age, and as near as I could tell that was around forty-something. Momma never told how old she was. She said ladies never revealed their age. Well, if you were living right in the town where you grew up, didn't everybody know anyway?

One day Simon got a letter. It sat on the table by the stairs, waiting for him. I smelled it first to see if it was from a girl but the handwriting was a man's and I assumed it was from his father. It was.

Simon's father was coming to Charleston for a visit. Simon asked Momma if he could stay upstairs with him and Momma said, "Sure, why not?" He showed her a picture of his father, I guess to show her that he was normal or something. Apparently, he was divorced, which Simon said was for the best.

That was when the fun started. The life force flowed back into my momma. She started manicuring her nails again and wearing a girdle, even though she finally didn't need one. She got out her old Singer sewing machine and took her dresses in so they fit right, then, to our surprise, she hemmed them up to the top of her knees. She spent a lot of time in front of the big old mirror looking at herself. I'd never seen her act this way and it made me nervous.

She got on the phone to Aunt Carol and invited her and Uncle Louis to come for Easter dinner and then she invited the Struthers and a bunch of people who had cooked for her in our family's time of bereavement. Of course, she invited Simon and his father.

Simon's father was the head of surgery at the biggest hospital in Detroit. Bucks, honey. Lots of 'em. I knew my momma didn't want to be Mrs. Rooms for Rent for the rest of her life.

Finally, Good Friday rolled around. We were all going to Stations of the Cross that afternoon from twelve to three. Simon was bringing his father out to the beach later.

Momma had taken charge and she was formidable. The house was the cleanest it had ever been in my life. Momma had on a cornflower blue linen dress and jacket, one she had chosen deliberately because it matched her eyes. Her hair was all teased up and she smelled like perfume. She looked really pretty.

I just hoped it would all go all right because if it didn't she might die from embarrassment at having tried to snag him when she hadn't even laid eyes on him yet. I didn't think the fact that he was Jewish and divorced meant anything to her at all. She had somehow overlooked that.

Well, Simon's father didn't go home to Michigan until Tuesday — that is, the Tuesday of the second week after Easter. He promised to write to old MC every day. Seems the doctor caught a bad case of Magnolia fever. I even saw them kissing on the porch.

Things got dull mighty quick. Simon was

studying all the time, Maggie was working all the time and the rest of us had gone back to our old routines, except me. I'd been nursing a bad throat all week and had stayed home from school.

There was no question that Momma was mooning over Dr. Lips. She was walking around the house humming all the time and just waiting for Timmy or Henry to bring home the mail. When there was a love letter from Stan, she ran to her room with it and closed the door. I guess I couldn't blame her, it was just that she seemed a little desperate to me. Okay, that was not nice to say, but it was the truth.

When I finally felt well enough, I decided to catch up on my schoolwork. Being out of class for this long had given me terrible anxiety over all the assignments I had to do. I was looking for a pen to write a book report and every pen in the house either leaked globs of ink or was dry. I knew Momma had one in her stationery box and thought she wouldn't mind if I borrowed it, as long as I put it back.

The twins were napping, Livvie was ironing and the boys were I didn't know where. Momma was gone off someplace. I went into her room and opened her closet. I started digging around on her shelf above her dress rack, where she had all this stuff stacked up, and the whole blessed mountain came down on my head.

I started gathering everything up, her letters from Stanley and other thank-you notes she had received from the Easter dinner, and a long envelope caught my eye. For a minute it didn't register, but it was from St. Anne's school for girls. It was addressed to Momma. Okay, I shouldn't have opened it but my fate was right here in my hands and the next thing I knew I was reading it. *Dear Mrs. Hamilton, It is a great pleasure to advise you that your daughter, Susan Asalit Hamilton, has been accepted for the fall term with a full scholarship and all that entails.*

"Oh, my God!" I said. "I won the scholarship! I can't believe it!"

A flood of warmth came over me and in the next breath I looked at the date of the letter. It was a week old. Why hadn't she told me? Why hadn't Father O'Brien called me? Then my heart sank. She didn't want me to go. I knew it. Now what? I knew I had to confront her. I couldn't go without her permission.

I thought for a minute, trying to calm myself down enough to think my way through this while my brain was going a million miles an hour. First of all, did I really want to fight this battle? Yes, I did. I had to go. If I stayed here I'd never get to college. The only road to Paris went through Columbia. I had decided weeks ago that even if this school was overflowing with snobs I didn't care. I'd ignore them, get my diploma and get out. Four years was nothing. After what I'd endured in the last fourteen years, a bunch of bitchy schoolgirls looked like Cream of Wheat.

Okay, I said to myself, when she gets home, just ask her. Be calm and just ask her.

I was in the kitchen with Livvie setting the table for supper. I could hear Aunt Carol calling good-bye to her and Momma coming up the back stairs.

"Lawd, I'm so tired, I've got to go put my feet up!" She saw me and kissed me on the top of my head. "Hey, honey, how're you feeling? Throat still sore?"

"No, ma'am, I gargled with warm salt water all day." I was furious and she didn't even notice.

"That's a good girl. Hey, Livvie! What's for supper? Anybody call? Mail here?"

"Meat loaf and mashed potato and the mail on the hall table. Ain't nobody call."

"Nobody called, Momma."

"All right then, wake me in thirty minutes, will you? I just want to close my eyes for a few minutes."

"Sure," I said.

Livvie just went about her work, knowing I was stewing over something. She was waiting for me to tell her. *Chop, chop, chop.* The onions and bell pepper hit the bacon grease with a sizzle.

"Best to cook 'em a little before they go in the mix," she said.

"You need some saltines?"

"Yeah, crush up 'bout fifteen for me, 'eah?"

"Sure."

She put her knife down on the counter and turned to me. "All right, now. What's on that mind of yours? You gone tell me what's cooking or do I have to drag it out of you?"

"Livvie, you won't believe what happened." And I told her the story.

"Listen 'eah, Miss Susan," she said, "don't be gone on raising the devil about she not showing you this. Be real sweet. You gots to know your momma gone worry 'bout letting you go, 'eah?

Take her some of this tea I just make, with a cookie, and then you tell her. Then we see what."

"God, you are so smart, Livvie! You're right."

She handed me a glass of tea and two Oreos in a paper napkin. My mother had been resting for only a few minutes, so maybe she wouldn't be asleep yet. I knocked on her door.

"Come in," she said. She wasn't in her bed, but in the closet.

"Hi, Momma, I brought you some tea and a couple of cookies."

"Susan, have you been in my closet?"

"Yes, ma'am. I needed to borrow a pen for my homework . . ."

The look on her face was terrifying to me. I'd never seen her angry like this. I'd seen her upset and crying and depressed and drunk, but never angry. She stood outside the closet door and I was frozen to the floor by her bed.

"How many times do I have to tell you children not to go into my personal things?"

"Momma, I'm sorry, I didn't mean to pry, I just wanted a pen . . ."

"And I suppose you found the letter from St. Anne's?"

"Yes'm."

"And I guess you think you'll just be picking up and leaving me just like that?"

"I don't know, Momma, but . . ."

"But what? Do you realize how impossible it would be for me to get along without you?"

"That's not my problem," I whispered.

"What did you say?"

That's when I lost control of myself. I knew this

would happen, I just knew it. Everybody else could say that they'd step in to help me, or that surely she wouldn't hold me back, but here was the truth. I was on my own and, even if I lost, a few things needed to be said around here.

"I said that it's not my problem, that's what!"

"How dare you!"

"Because it's the truth! Instead of you being proud of me and getting excited for me, you hid this from me! How could you do that?"

"I wanted to think about it!"

"Look, Momma, it's not my job to raise your babies! It's not my fault you have so damn many kids! I'm going away to school this fall and you can't stop me!"

She got so frightened and she was so angry that she moved across the room before I could think of what was coming. She slapped me across the face with all her might. I stood there and said not one word more.

I ran from her room, out the front door, slamming it almost off the hinges. I went over the sand dunes to the beach. I needed to walk for a while, calm down and think things through.

It was low tide and there were football fields upon football fields of empty beach before me. It was warm enough to kick off my loafers and walk the water's edge. Tiny shells collapsed beneath my feet, breaking apart into millions of pieces. It felt good to break something.

An old palmetto log was up on the high ground in the white sand, near the dunes. I sat down on it and ran my fingers through my hair. The white sand was as fine as the kind in an hourglass. I let it sift through my fingers. Grains of sand, hours of my life, chances not taken, opportunities lost, lives finished, dreams never coming to life. Would Momma eventually come to her senses? Did she think she owned me?

My face stung where she had slapped me. I was so mad I didn't care if I ever saw her again. My head ached and my throat was raw. I should've taken a sweatshirt or a jacket, but I had had to escape and didn't think of that.

Pelicans and seagulls swooped all around, some of them walking near the water. Marsh hens dug their sharp beaks into the soft mud. The water was alive with dance and spirit, little waves swelling up, rolling in, layer on layer of them, stacked like steps, dissolving as the tide crept by inches toward me. The east wind was chilling.

I was so lost in thought, my head down in my hands, I never heard him or saw him coming, but I looked up and saw Simon standing before me.

"Hey, Suz, what's up?"

"Don't call me Suz."

"Okay, whatcha doing?"

"Thinking about life."

"Yeah? What about it?"

"It sucks."

"Yeah. Sometimes it does." His hair was blowing in the wind and while his humor was present in his teasing, the look on his face wasn't funny. He was serious. And he was the most beautiful man I'd ever seen. I realized that his being here was no coincidence. He sat down next to me.

"So, you know?" I asked.

"Yeah, Livvie told me. I figured I'd find you on the beach."

"How come?"

" 'Cause that's where Geechee girls go when they need to think. Sailors put their boat out, mountaineers climb, jocks throw a ball around, but Geechee girls, they have to go on down to the beach and stick their feet in the sand."

"How'd you get so smart?"

"Yankee schooling and just paying attention to what goes on around me. I thought you were sick."

"I'm better, almost."

"Good. Want to hear a story?"

"Sure."

"When I was about, oh, I don't know, fifteen or so, I came home and found my mother in the sack with another man just getting it on."

"What?"

"Yeah, and she made me swear not to tell my dad. I hated her for that, but I knew that if my father found out it would blow us apart. She bought me a car my next birthday. Soon after, I came home and found her in bed with somebody else. She apologized and all to me and tried to explain that she was just bored to tears with Dad. I didn't know that being bored made it okay to screw somebody else."

"So what did you do?"

"I told my dad."

"Why are you telling me this?"

"Hold on, let me finish. My mother called me a traitor, packed her bags and left."

"Good Lord, Simon. You weren't the traitor, she was!"

"Exactly." He looked at me, his brown eyes searching my blue ones. His face was so close to mine I thought I'd faint. I knew what he was telling me. I wasn't the only one in the world who'd ever been used by their parents.

"God, how could your mother do that to you?"

"Just because somebody's grown up doesn't mean that they can't be wrong."

"Boy, is that ever the truth!"

"Yeah." His breath smelled good. I looked at the outline of his lips. His top lip was almost a straight line, but his bottom lip was fuller and not as dark as the top one, or maybe it was shadow.

"What are you thinking about?" he asked.

I was thinking about reaching out and tracing the lines of his lips with my fingers, but I'd eat chopped glass before I'd admit it. So I lied.

"Your dad. Do you think your dad *is* boring?"

"Probably. My father is one hell of a surgeon, but he always feels a little stiff to me."

"Yeah, me too. My mother's crazy about him."

"Yeah, he's nuts about her too."

"My mother's really not a bad person, I guess. If I leave it *is* gonna make it harder for her. She slapped the hell out of me. Did Livvie tell you that?"

"She probably feels terrible about it."

"I know I do. It hurts like the devil." My voice cracked because my throat was so raw and then I coughed.

"I think she'll come to her senses. Here, you want my sweater? It's getting kind of chilly."

"Sure, thanks."

He pulled his navy crewneck over his head and

handed it to me inside out. He had on this light blue shirt underneath. I stood up to pull it over my head. I was having a terrible time getting the thing on gracefully. The arms were too long and the neck opening wrecked my ponytail. I turned into the wind to gather up my hair and he watched me.

"What the hell are you looking at?" I said.

"You, you little witch. How is it that you're only fourteen?"

"Can't help it. How is it you're so damn ancient?"

"I'm not *that* old. I'm also not your brother, not *yet* anyway."

I started getting nervous now. Was he gonna try something? Holy smokes!

"What do you mean *not yet?*"

"Listen, you don't know old Stanley. He set his cap on your momma the minute he laid eyes on her. Actually, come to think of it, they're perfect for each other. He needs to be needed after what my mom did to him and, boy, does she have needs! I mean, he just wants to have a family. He probably did spend too much time at the hospital, but his whole life is dedicated to helping people. Amazing, huh?"

"Well, practically Momma's whole life has been devoted to producing a population. It might be good for Timmy and Henry to have a man around here. With any luck, they won't have me come September."

"Do you really want to go to Columbia?"

"Yeah."

"I'll get Stanley to call your momma. Don't worry about it anymore. I'll get him to call her tonight."

"Thanks. You're great, Simon, you know that?"

"Thanks, Suz."

"*Please!* Don't call me that," I whined.

He was smiling now. I felt this funny feeling in the pit of my stomach. I knew he wanted to kiss me and I wished he'd just do it and get it over with so I wouldn't have to worry about it anymore.

"Simon?"

"Yeah?" he said. "You have great hair, do you know that?"

"My hair? Wait a minute, I was gonna ask you something. . . ."

He stood up. "The back of my sweater is all bunched up on you, lemme fix it."

"I forgot what I was gonna say. . . ."

"It doesn't matter. . . ." He put his arm around me to pull down the sweater, and his hand rested on my back, down by my waist. He looked in my eyes, probably realizing from the sheer terror on my face that nobody had ever kissed me before. I just looked at him, not sure of what to do, feeling pretty stupid with my arms hanging there like two loaves of Italian bread.

Finally, he decided to be the big winner of my virgin lips. He put his other hand on my face and over my ear and then around through my hair and sort of pulled me up to him. I thought, *Oh, God, this is it!* When his lips touched mine I just didn't know what to do. It was a little tiny kiss, I think, if you go by what's in the movies, and definitely not a sin, except that he was the wrong religion and a lot older than me. It felt wonderful.

Then he just put his arms around me and hugged me and we stood there on the empty beach, feeling the wind and watching the sky get dim. The tide washed around our feet. It was time to go home. I didn't want to go back. I wanted to stay here with him forever.

"Simon?"

"Hmm?"

"Don't you have a girlfriend?"

"She broke up with me. Got a letter yesterday."

"Gee. That's too bad. Do you think we could do that again?"

"Yes. A lot."

The next kiss wasn't so innocent. He seemed a little more excited and I know I was. Given the choice of being on a deserted beach and kissing the man of my dreams or going home, changing diapers and dealing with my lunatic mother, there was no choice to make. I had every intention of standing right there and kissing that man till I wore out his lips. Kissing him felt so good, I couldn't believe it.

"God, Simon," I said, in between what began to be of concern to my virtue.

"I could drink you," he whispered into my neck.

Men had power, girls didn't. I could have dug a hole, jumped in and buried myself alive and still not have accomplished what Stanley and Simon did in two phone calls. My momma was so stupid over Stanley Rifkin she would've jumped off the Cooper River Bridge if he'd asked her to. In this case, she agreed to let me go to St. Anne's and, in fact, became happy about it.

By May, she was bragging about my scholarship all over the Island like it was her idea in the first place. Like *she* had won it. I didn't care. People were like that.

I had another fish to fry. Simon. Simon and I would meet down the beach with some beer and potato chips and make out like two fools. We had gotten to the point of lying down together in the sand and I was about out of my mind from it.

One day, we were down by the end of the Island where no one ever goes. I walked down there on the beach and Simon took his car. We thought we were so smart. I was waiting for him.

"Hi!" I called.

"Hi!" he called back.

We weren't exactly the most poetic lovers in the world, but what we lacked in iambic pentameter we made up for in enthusiasm. I helped him unload his trunk. Simon had brought a six-pack of Budweiser and some Fritos. He pulled a blanket out of his car. Holding hands, we crossed the dunes and then spread his blanket to get a perfect view of the harbor. The tide was coming in.

"Want a beer?" He opened one and handed it to me before I could answer.

As usual, we drank about half of the can, sitting on the blanket, and then he turned to me.

The next thing I knew, we were kissing. We had graduated to him putting his hand under my shirt. I wondered if this would be the day that he felt my breasts. I was having a hard time deciding if I would let him, because it was supposed to be a sin, or I thought it was. The hotter the kissing got the more difficult it became to remember what I was allowed to do within the boundaries of impure acts.

We were kissing deeply now. He was lying on top of me, sort of pressing into my hips with a regular rhythm. I had a pretty good idea that this made him happy. And as long as he was happy he kept kissing me, so I let him rock and roll. He put his hand up my shirt and rubbed my back. The next thing I knew, he had unhooked my bra and his hands were all over me. I knew I should have stopped him and discussed this, but I just let him. It felt incredibly good and I couldn't think of a reason in the world to stop.

"Susan," he said in a voice like syrup.

"What?" I said.

"I love you, Susan, you know I do."

"I love you too, Simon."

I looked at him and his eyes were half closed. He was in another world and I wanted to go with him, wherever he was headed. He unbuttoned my blouse and started kissing my breasts. I felt a tingling so far down inside of me it took my breath away. He was scrambling all over me now and I began to feel this intensity for some kind of completion. I was breathing like a marathon runner after a race.

Slap! Slap! Slap!

"All right, you two, let's knock it off! Come on, son. Let the girl breathe."

I looked up right into the spit shine of police shoes. It was Fat Albert, the Island policeman, slapping his nightstick in the palm of his hand. We scrambled to make some order of ourselves, knowing we were in very deep shit.

"Miss Susan? How old are you now?" Fat Albert asked.

"Sixteen," I said, lying through my teeth.

"Mm-hm," Fat Albert said, adjusting his belt over his stomach. "And how about you, son? Got any identification?"

"Yes, sir, in my glove compartment," Simon said.

He and Fat Albert went over the sand dunes, and, after what seemed like an hour, Simon came back alone.

"What happened?"

"Well, he made a long list of our offenses. Drinking in public, drinking under age, corruption of a minor, you name it, we did it."

"And?"

Simon was folding up the blanket. I gathered the beer cans and put them back in the bag.

"And he said that if he ever caught us on his beach again, he'd arrest us."

"That's all?"

"Yep, we're two fools, free to go."

"Well, there's always the Isle of Palms," I said.

"That's what I love about you. You're out of your mind!"

And that's exactly what we were. Out of our minds and two fools. I mean, he couldn't even take me to the movies. I was too young to date! Well, maybe I wasn't really, but nobody in my class dated, and in my family you didn't date until everyone was sure you weren't convent material.

Simon was my first and only love. But I admitted to myself that Fat Albert showing up had probably been a blessing in disguise. I understood now why Maggie was so hot for Lucius. This make-out stuff was pretty fabulous fun, but dangerous too. I could just see both of us winding up pregnant. Good Lord.

May came and Dr. Send Her to School was coming for a weekend. When Momma and he weren't writing each other, they were calling each other. Momma may have been crazy but she was different, stronger. Suddenly she had opinions and she talked about things like a happy person, instead of one who lived on the edge of Armageddon. Love did that to you, I thought. She was sitting in the kitchen with Aunt Carol, talking about him. I was snapping five pounds of green beans on the back steps with Livvie. I guess they forgot we were there, like usual.

"What's wrong, Carol?" my momma asked.

"Oh, nothing. It's just that ever since Easter a person can't talk to you about anything except Stan. It's getting kind of boring to be around you, MC. I'm sorry to say that to you, but it's the truth."

Livvie and I looked at each other, smelling trouble.

"Jealous," I whispered to Livvie.

"Humph," she whispered back.

"Well, you don't have to be around me if you don't want to, Carol Asalit."

"What? Well, I never! Fine. That's fine with me! I'm going home to my husband, who appreciates me."

"My husband appreciated you too, I hear."

"Well! I never!" Silence for a moment, except for my aunt's gasping and clucking noises. "I don't need to stay here and be insulted and falsely accused this way!"

"If you don't behave — if you look so much as sideways at Stan — I'll tell my brother everything I know!"

"You! You think you're such a saint!"

"Ha! And you think you're the only woman in the world! You're getting old, Carol! Your varicose veins are showing and when you get angry all the little lines around your lips show."

"I am never stepping foot in this house again!"

"Fine!" my mother said. "Then I don't have to worry where your feet are during dinner!"

Holy moly, I thought, how did Momma know all this? And, more importantly, was that *my* momma talking like that?

I looked up at Livvie. She was a little sheepish. "I only told her about the feet after she tell me Miss Simpson tell she about the storm!"

Alice Simpson had spilled the beans on Aunt Carol and Daddy in their episode of "The Secret Storm." And Livvie had iced the cake! Good!

Aunt Carol slammed out the door and raced down the steps to her car, face red as a beet. Our dog ran barking behind her. She reached her foot out to kick him and he jumped away and then lunged at her. She tore out of the yard in reverse, the dust kicking up under her car. Rascal chased her, barking his brains out, until his voice tapered off in the distance. The back door opened again and Momma came out and stood on the steps. She looked down at us and smiled.

"Do Lawd, Miss MC, what bee got in your bonnet?" Livvie was grinning from ear to ear. So was I.

"No bee, Livvie, I'm just not afraid of her anymore. In fact, I've never felt quite so good. Lord! What a beautiful afternoon!"

"If it makes any difference to anybody around here," I said, "I never really liked her much and I ain't gone miss her!"

Momma looked at me as if she were surprised all at once to see me so much older. We started to laugh.

"Did you see her swishing her butt down the steps?" I said to Livvie and Momma.

"You should've seen her face when I told her I knew!" Momma said. "She makes me so mad, that woman! I hope she *does* tell Louis and then I can tell him what I know!"

"Yeah, Momma! You were great!"

"You know, I've been wanting to give that you-know-what a piece of my mind for twenty years!"

"Well, ya done good, Momma," I said. "Come on, let's take the twins for a walk."

And we did.

Livvie and I were sweeping the porch together. Dr. Divorced, Rich and Jewish was coming in soon to spend the Memorial Day weekend, and Momma wanted everything just so. The twins were in the playpen, gurgling like babies do. They played so well and hardly ever fussed unless they were tired or hungry. Of course, with all of us to play with them, they never lacked attention. They would have their first birthday soon.

Dr. Stanley Rifkin arrived in a red convertible rental car and parked in front of the house. I heard Simon coming down the steps to greet him.

Stanley got out and waved hello to us.

"Hi!" I said. "How was your flight?"

"Oh, just fine, Susan! Thank you for asking! Such a nice girl you are!"

"Jeesch," I said under my breath and Livvie giggled, knowing that this man got on my nerves. He wasn't like Simon, who was a wise guy like me. No, Simon's father was slow and deliberate, his manners from another time. Everything about his demeanor spoke of his intelligence. I just couldn't believe that a powerful, educated man like him would want to get mixed up with a crazy widow and her six children.

Livvie went to the door and held it open for him so he could put his luggage inside on the porch. It had *L*s and *V*s all over it. If he was supposed to have so much money, couldn't he have afforded his own initials?

"I'm glad you're both here," he said. "Oh. Simon, my boy! Come here, all of you. Got something I want to show you."

"Hey, Dad!" Simon kissed his father on the cheek.

Stanley was clearly nervous and excited. He dug around in his jacket pockets for something, eventually producing a little velvet box. He opened it for all of us to see. It was a beautiful, big, and I mean big, door knocker of a round white diamond ring. It could've been the night lights at the ball field. It had smaller, round rubies on either side. My jaw dropped. Simon's jaw dropped and Livvie started to laugh.

"Oh, Lawd have mercy! Lawd have mercy!" She was slapping her thighs and doing a little dance.

"Is this good?" Stanley asked, smiling widely. He pointed to Livvie. "Does this mean she approves?"

"Mr. Doctor? You don't need me to say it's okay, but I tell you what, you just what this family need! Yes, sir! You just the medicine they all need! Yeah, Gawd! That's the biggest diamond I ever did see! Wait till I tell Harriet 'bout this!"

"My brother!" I said and hugged Simon.

"My sister!" He laughed and hugged me back.

"Well, Miss Susan, I want to tell you this," Stanley said. "First, I'm going around to see Louis and ask for your mother's hand. With his approval and, of course, MC's, I'd like to marry your mother in the fall. Now, I want you to understand that I know I can't replace your father, you're too old for that. But, I *would* like to be your friend. If you ever need anything, you come to me, all right? And call me Stan. I always wanted a daughter, now I could have four! If Marie Catherine says yes, I swear I'll be the happiest man in the world!"

"Oh, Stan," I said, giving the old goat a good hug, "I'm so happy for both of you. I really mean it. Please make sure Aunt Carol gets a good look at the ring, okay?"

"I understand completely," he said and winked at me.

I had kissed the twins and everybody else twice or three times. Even though Momma was engaged and they could now afford Livvie, I was still very nervous about leaving. Everything would be different for Timmy, Henry and Maggie when Momma married Stanley Rifkin. But at least they would all have each other. I would be alone.

Maggie and I had had long talks, late at night, all summer long. I would miss her so much. She was considering breaking up with Lucius for the same reasons I had cooled things with Simon. Even though she was older than I was, she was beginning to realize that Lucius would never marry her. His mother and her Virginia Tidewater family would never accept a girl from Sullivan's Island, even though our family had fought in every war in America for the past two hundred years.

Simon and I were just friends by that point. Momma and Stanley getting engaged made our love feel too weird. Anyway, Simon had promised to write me and he was going to drive me to St. Anne's. I had given him a picture of myself that I had had taken at Furchgott's Studio in Charleston. I looked pretty good in the white cotton lace drape. I signed the back before I put it in a frame. *To the only man I'll ever really love, Susan.* I was counting on him never opening the frame and seeing it.

Timmy started to cry when he saw my bags all packed. Then Henry started to cry. I took care of that by kicking them in the shins as hard as I could.

"Remember that this is how life here can be," I said, "and write to me every week, okay? Look after Maggie and the twins and if they get into trouble, call me. Swear it."

We made pinky oaths and then we hugged. They would be all right and I would be home in three weeks for the wedding. They weren't getting rid of me quite yet. I scratched Rascal behind the ears.

The hardest person to leave was Livvie. She was waiting for me in the kitchen.

"So now what?" I said. "If it weren't for you, I'd

probably be going to jail instead of boarding school."

"That's true enough," she said.

"I can't tell you good-bye, Livvie."

"You never have to, Susan."

"What? What do you mean?"

"The mirror. Even when I gone to glory and my Nelson, I still come to you."

"Yeah, but Livvie, I can't see *anything* in that mirror."

"Someday you will. And don't you ever forget, this old colored woman loves this Geechee girl so."

"Oh, God, Livvie, and how I love you. I always will."

20

LOWCOUNTRY MAGIC

1999

"Maggie?" I was on the phone with my sister. "Guess what I found?"

I told her about the pictures of Fat Albert's and Marvin Struthers's feet in the photo at the Klan rally. She was stunned.

"Well, I'll be darned. It wasn't enough for old Marvin to be mayor? He had to be the Grand Dragon too?"

"I know. I mean, Maggie, it makes perfect sense. Albert probably ran Daddy off the road and Marvin Struthers and him probably pushed Daddy's car into the marsh. I have to think this all through and I'm sure if I kept digging I could find the evidence, but I swear I am so relieved just to know. No wonder Marvin headed up the investigation with Albert! No wonder no one was blamed! Pity that old Marvin and Albert have been fertilizer for years."

"You're right. I mean, what would you do with the proof anyway? Can't put a dead man in jail."

"Exactly. And it wouldn't be worth embarrassing their families."

"Yeah, but at the same time, it's good that you can finally put your mind to rest."

"Yeah. Maggie, did you ever think of Daddy as a hero?" We were quiet for a moment, numbed by the news and the suggestion that he was.

"Never even considered it. Until now, that is."

"God almighty. Life is so weird."

It was the Wednesday before Christmas. I had been working late at the library every day and at the same time trying to prepare for the holiday. We had been blessed with perfect springlike weather all week, which made gathering greens from the yard a very pleasant task. I had finally put the last of our decorations on the tree and around our house. I arranged some of the smaller branches of magnolia in a glass bowl in the middle of the dining room table, and put red glass balls on florist's sticks in between them. I polished the magnolia leaves with Wesson Oil — a trick Maggie taught me — and I thought you could part your hair in their reflection. Speaking of hair, I was pleased that I remembered to send a card to Kim. He was turning out to be a good friend and I was grateful to have him in my life. I needed someone besides Maggie and Beth.

I had hardly heard from Tom since he had left my house after his surgery except to discuss money and visitation, which led me to believe that Karen was firmly in his life. Occasionally, we'd discuss the treatments he was having and he seemed to be hanging on. I was relieved not to have him full-time to contend with. And speaking of money, by the grace of God, I was appointed as interim director of the library. The board planned to conduct the requisite search, but the board chairman and the search committee had assured me, privately, that they preferred to give Mitchell Freemont's job to me. They had cited the old Gullah maxim, Keep the evil that you know. That wasn't exactly the high praise I wanted to hear, but the raise in salary compensated for any personal slight I may have felt.

When I got home, Beth was bringing presents to the kitchen to wrap, having a wonderful time decorating packages that looked too pretty to open. She had used brown paper, twine twisted with gold metallic cord, and had sponged on stars with gold-toned paint. Thank God she has the Maggie gene for this, I thought.

"God, honey, don't you hate to give them away?" I said. "The wrapping is a present all on its own!"

"Yeah, it sort of is, huh? Well, you know, I have like a *ree-leey* good feeling about this holiday, I don't know why. I guess it's because I totally love my aunts and uncles and when they're here I finally get some girl cousins almost my age to talk to. Bucky and Mickey drive me up the wall."

"Familiarity breeds contempt."

"Whatever. So what did you get Dad for Christmas?"

"What?"

"Are y'all still gonna exchange gifts, or what?"

"Um, I don't think so." I popped open a Diet Pepsi and took a long drink.

"Oh. Well, I think he got you something."

"Like what? A gift certificate to the root canal

doctor? Want a sip?"

"Nope, no thanks. You'll see. He's stopping by in a few minutes."

"Like when were you gonna tell me this? I look totally disgusting!" I ran upstairs and brushed my hair, changed my shirt, put on some cologne. I was just brushing my teeth when he knocked at the door.

"Merry Christmas, Daddy!"

"Merry Christmas, princess! Where's your momma?"

"I'll be right down!" I called and thought, oh great, what if he wants to come to Maggie's with us for Christmas Eve?

But as soon as I said hello to him he made his announcement.

"I can only stay for a few minutes. Karen and I are going to Myrtle Beach to meet her parents and spend the holiday."

I saw Beth's face fall and so I stabbed him on her behalf.

"Well, I'm sure you'll have a lot in common with them. After all, they're your age and . . ."

"You don't have to say it, Susan, I get the drift," he said. "Look, I didn't come over here to discuss Karen's age. I came to bring you something for Christmas. I know you think I'm a jerk and that I don't care about you. This is to let you know that I do care and how proud I am of you."

He pointed to an enormous box and a smaller one.

"Gosh, thanks. Are they household appliances? Plugs aren't gifts, Tom."

We had always joked about our friends who

would give each other lawnmowers and blenders and toasters for Christmas and other important occasions. One sorry fellow we knew had a chainlink-fenced dog pen installed for his wife's fortieth birthday to hold *his* hunting dogs.

Anyway, it was the season of giving and I was caught empty-handed. Especially, given what he was going through with his cancer, I probably should've bought him something.

"It's got a plug, but, believe me, it's a gift. In fact, it's more than that. This is for your new side career or whatever you call it. I thought I'd try to do something to encourage you. You know, let you know that I really am in your corner."

"Holy smokes, Tom. I mean, thanks. I really mean that. Gosh."

I didn't know what to say. I sat down on the sofa and opened the smaller box first. It was a notebook computer. I almost fainted. "Tom! This is so fabulous! Honey, thank you! My God! Beth, look at this!"

"Daddy! It's awesome! Can I use it too, Mom?"

"You're welcome!" he said. "The other box has a color printer and all the cables and gadgets you need to recharge batteries and all that technical stuff that gives me a headache. But I'm sure you'll figure it out!"

I ignored Beth's question and realized that this was the final kiss from Tom. I no longer had to think about him wanting to come back. He didn't want to anymore, but he wanted to be friends and, given all we had been through, that was a minor miracle. I'd take it and be graceful about it.

"Daddy, I have something for you. I made it."

"Oh, princess, I almost forgot. This is for you. It's a Visa card for your clothes and whatever you want. You can charge up to three hundred dollars a month on it and I'll pay the bill. How's that?"

Beth started squealing and screaming. She threw her arms around Tom and I didn't blame her. I should do the same, I thought, these two gifts were unbelievable — one made my life easier and the other would keep me solvent. When Beth reached under the tree to search for Tom's gift, I patted the couch beside me.

"Come on, sit by me."

Like a good dog, he sat, obviously pleased with himself, as he should've been.

"Tom, thank you. This was so nice of you. I mean, this will make a lot of things easier for us and you knew that. Tom, really, I can't thank you enough."

"Susan, you and I have been through the wars together. I really want to try to make up for some of the colossally stupid things I've done."

I squeezed his hand and started choking up a little when I saw Beth's gift to him. She handed him a large, flat package. It had more gold and glitter than any of the others she had wrapped. It was, after all, for her daddy.

"Here, Daddy, this is for you. Merry Christmas," she said quietly.

Tom opened it slowly, remarking on the paper and how artistic she was. He made her laugh by asking her if it was a sports car or a stereo. We saw it was a scrapbook. She had made a title card for the front that read THE GOOD OLD DAYS. As we turned each page, we saw it was filled with photographs that chronicled our lives, all of them smiling and happy. Under each one, she had made a remark on a strip of paper to remind him what the event was. There was one from her first birthday party, me holding her, smiling, her face and dress covered in frosting. The caption read: *You and Momma didn't even mind that I made such a mess of things.*

That was just a little too close for comfort. I got confused and thought that she blamed herself for our divorce as I had blamed myself for my daddy's death. But we were the ones who had made the mess, not her. We were doing our best for her sake, and, in some way, for ourselves too.

Tom just pointed to the picture and said to her, "Remember how afraid you were of Big Bird?"

She said, "I remember you picking me up and putting me on your shoulders."

"Anybody want something to drink?" No one answered. "I'll be right back," I said.

In the kitchen, I poured a glass of water. Get a hold of yourself, Susan, I told myself, it's Christmas. People always get emotional during the holidays. You've had a tough year. A lot of changes, but good things too.

This was the relationship I wanted to fight for. This friendship. This relationship of Beth's with Tom. I could make it better for them. I realized that money had been one of the things that caused so much pain over the past months. Now that I would earn enough to provide a cushion, and now that Tom was stepping up to help a little more, we didn't have to fight about that anymore.

In an odd way, even though we were getting divorced, we were still a family. Always would be. We had too much shared history to ever give each other up completely. Somehow, I'd make Beth see that and understand it. If Tom and I didn't fight about anything, she'd have nothing to blame herself for.

I was leaning against the sink, my arms around myself, my jaw set square as it does when I'm deep in thought, when Tom appeared in the doorway.

"I gotta go, Susan. Merry Christmas. Give my best to Maggie and Grant and the boys, okay?"

"Tom! Of course I will. Hey, thanks again. I really mean it. I feel like things are working out better, don't you?"

"Yeah, if we want them to, they will."

"Well, they have to for Beth's sake. She loves us both so much."

"Susan, we all love each other so much."

"You feeling okay?" I asked.

"Yeah, I'm okay. The catheter's out and, well, I'll see what the future brings. Susan, well, I'll call you after the holiday and we'll talk."

"What? Is something wrong?"

"No. I swear. Everything's fine. A little tired and a lot nauseated, that's all. Now, you and Beth have a fabulous Christmas, okay? Give my best to Grant and Maggie and their boys."

"Okay, lover boy, your jail bait is probably wondering where you are. Tell her I send my greetings and don't drive like a maniac, okay? Be careful, you still have us to live for. Now get on outta here, before I insist on a conjugal visit."

"God, Susan, you are so great."

"That's true," I said as I opened the door for

him. "So are you. Hey, Tom, thanks, huh? For everything."

"You're welcome. You know, you could've bought me a bottle of aftershave."

"Oh, God, sorry, Tom. I was really insane that day."

"Well, it was a tough day." He smiled at me and we took a long look at each other. He gave me a peck on the cheek and turned to go. "Merry Christmas, Susan Hayes," he said over his shoulder.

"Merry Christmas to you, too, Tom Hayes."

Standing in the doorway, I watched him pull away in the twilight. I caught a burst of pine scent from our wreath, and the little white lights on our topiaries all came on with the timer. I wondered if he really was all right and what he had started to tell me that could wait until after Christmas. I decided not to dwell on it, thinking that he must be all right or he wouldn't be back with Karen. But he didn't look good.

It was almost Christmas and I couldn't wait to get to Maggie's house, out to the beach, to the Island Gamble, where we all belonged.

The next morning I cleaned up the kitchen, listening to the morning news, making a mental list of all we had to cram in the car to take to the beach. Timmy, Henry and their families were coming Christmas Day and staying for the whole week. The twins had sent their regrets again with some sorry-ass excuse. Beth had run out for a bag of coconut, marshmallows, a bottle of cherries and two cans of fruit cocktail. She was making ambrosia for her little cousins. They'd probably love it.

Now that I was a big-shot columnist and had this flood of money from my promotion, I decided to march myself into Berlin's and see what the chic were buying for the season. This beautiful and elegant woman, Nancee Rubin, took one look at me and said, "Want to see the most incredible sweater in the world?" Now, who could say no to that? She was right. Triple-ply cashmere, rust-colored, deep V-neck, long-sleeved tunic with slit sides. Then she pulled out a pair of rust velvet pants, narrow legs, flat front, side zip. When she held one on top of the other I knew they had my name all over them.

"You can get suede Gucci loafers in the same color at Bob Ellis," she said and laughed, knowing I was going to beg for "drive-thru" alterations.

They hemmed the pants while I bought the shoes. Gucci? I must have been losing my mind! Two pieces of clothes and I felt like a new woman. Wasn't that ridiculous? Merry Christmas to me, I said six hundred dollars later.

Finally, the car was packed to the hilt with gifts and our clothes for our Island holiday. Beth was taking out the last armload of gifts for my nieces and nephews and I was turning off all the lights. In the warmth of the Christmas tree's twinkling white lights, I took a good look at myself in my momma's big mirror. I look good in this color, I thought. I was older, yes, but still, I looked relieved, rested and happy. I was; that was all true. My head was in good shape.

Tom going back to Karen hadn't really bothered me all that much. I didn't care who he was with — I just wanted him to stay alive. No, I was doing just fine, but I wondered what my brothers would have to say about me helping Tom through his illness. Oh well, I thought, I could deal with them. It was a wiser woman who stared back at me, half-smiling, pleased with herself.

By the time we got to Maggie's, I was so far back in my memory that I half expected Rascal to come bounding up, barking and wagging his tail, to greet us. Instead, as I pulled in the driveway, I saw a yard filled with cars. North Carolina plates. That was Timmy! Georgia plates. That was Henry! All the lights were on. My brothers had come early and we were going to have a wonderful time. I could feel it.

Beth and I got out to raise the tailgate and unload the car. Beth went on ahead of me. Typically, I tried to carry too much and stumbled, packages going everywhere on the ground. I could hear shrieks of laughter and greetings as Beth entered the kitchen. The screen door slammed.

"Is this my sister? I can't believe my eyes! You look like one million. Net!" It was Henry, the tycoon of the family, coming down the stairs to greet me.

"Yeah, it's me, Brother Bucks! Gimme a kiss! They didn't get you for insider trading yet?"

"Why, you! I'm as pure as the driven snow, and damn grateful my office isn't wired!" He swung me around in the air in a huge circle.

"Put me down!" I screamed. "Help!"

The door swung open again. It was Timmy, the family psychologist (and boy, did we need one) coming down the steps. "Unhand her, you brute!" he yelled.

Finally, Henry put me down and the world was spinning.

"You're nuts! Oh! My head!"

Timmy was picking up my packages and Henry helped too. Henry, laughing to himself, went up the stairs with his arms filled.

"He's crazy," I said.

"Still crazy, to be accurate. You're nice to indulge his repressed childhood," Timmy said, in shrink-speak.

"Whatever! So how are you? God, it's good to see you, Timmy." I gave him a kiss on the cheek. "How's my sister-in-law and my nieces and nephews?"

"They're responding to treatment well," he said, deadpan.

"Very funny," I said. "Come on, there are a multitude of cocktails to be drunk!"

"Right! Think of all the poor sober people in China!"

I slammed the door of the car and, with a suitcase in each hand, struggled up the back steps.

The kitchen was crowded with my family, shrieking, pouring drinks and eating. I could hear Maggie in the dining room, shouting to Grant.

"Put on that Shannon Gibbons CD! For Lord's sake, Grant, if I hear Kenny Rogers one more time, I don't know what I'll do!"

A wave of pleasure swept through me. I was so happy to be here, with my brothers and my sister and all our offspring. I wandered into the living room and the Christmas tree stopped me dead in my tracks. Maggie had done it again. The tree was covered in varnished shells from the beach, popcorn and cranberry chains, red plaid satin bows and white lights. I was alone in the room and stood there for a few moments thinking about how everything Maggie touched became beautiful and glorified. I turned to see her standing beside me. Suddenly, I felt emotional.

"It's a beautiful tree," I said.

She threw her arm around my shoulder and squeezed me. "It's disposable. Just pull off the lights, that is, if they're still working by New Year's."

"How is it that you're so clever and I'm not?"

"But you are. This has been a rough year, Susan, but it's almost over. You know, you're surrounded by people who love you. You should always surround yourself with people who love you. Life's hard enough without fighting every battle all alone." She handed me a tissue from her pocket.

"I surrender," I said, wiping my eyes. "I'm fighting no one from this day forward."

"Okay, let's go have us a Geechee Christmas and to hell with the outside world."

And we did. We ate our traditional seafood dinner with riotous gusto, the noise level of the house at such a roar, I could almost see Fat Albert, dead for twenty years, coming to the house to arrest us all for disturbing the peace. We drank the six bottles of rare sauvignon blanc that Henry had brought from his cellar and we were cruising. We told Alice Simpson stories, Stanley Rifkin stories, Livvie stories. We teased each other to death.

We made the pilgrimage to Stella Maris together for Midnight Mass. The night was clear and crisp. The tide was out, so the sound of the ocean was like gentle background music.

Later, we had decaffeinated Irish coffee or night-caps, and hot chocolate with whipped cream for the children. We put the cups and glasses in the dishwasher and turned out all the lights. I went out for a look at the ocean. I just stood there thinking how lucky I was to have such a great family, how different from each other we all were but how we loved each other in spite of, and *because* of, our differences. Finally, I went inside and locked the front door. Grant and Maggie were long gone to bed and the boys and their families had turned in as well. The Island Gamble grew still and my head rested next to Beth's in an old double bed, under a quilt and two blankets.

"Hey, Beth? You sleeping?"

"What?"

"Hey, did Chris call you for Christmas?"

"He's a jerk," she said and began to snore softly. Beth's cold feet touched my legs and we curled up like two spoons. Mother and daughter. I prayed silently for us, for all my family, for Livvie, her Nelson, my momma and daddy, Tom and everyone else I could think of who crossed my mind. I prayed that Beth would learn how to handle men, but not too soon. I had not spent the night before Christmas at the Island Gamble in decades. I was astonished at how restful it was. The old Island Gamble had begun a new life with Maggie and Grant's family — a happy one. She had left the past behind and begun again welcoming us all home.

Christmas Day came and went, the morning spent making mountains of pancakes and many pots of coffee, opening presents and clearing away the wrapping paper and tissue. For the next few days, we simply enjoyed each other, taking long walks on the beach, cheating at cards and exaggerating family history.

The thirty-first of December dawned. Maggie and I were in the kitchen preparing for the picnic we'd planned for the eve of the new millennium. Even my macho brothers and their lazy wives helped to pack the coolers. One held shrimp, crab claws, turkey salad and ham salad sandwiches and the other was filled with wine, beer and sodas for the kids. We had bags filled with corn chips and salsa, cheese and crackers, grapes and apples, and the traditional chocolate, marshmallows and graham crackers for s'mores.

It was going to be spectacular. Special permits had been issued for bonfires to burn every hundred feet on every beach in Charleston County. It would be low tide at ten o'clock and the weather was clear and perfect.

Two huge barges had been anchored in the middle of the harbor for a massive fireworks display. And another two barges were positioned in the Ashley River for the other side of the peninsula.

Stella Maris had a special Mass planned for ten-thirty, giving us all enough time to attend Mass and not miss the fireworks. Then Stella Maris would join every Christian church in the world by ringing her bells for three hours. I showered and put on my rust pants and sweater, spraying myself liberally with Maggie's bottle of Allure. Maggie came in the room, all dressed for the festivities in black velvet pants and a red sweater embroidered with firecrackers, martini glasses and champagne bottles.

"Hey, you about ready? Grant's got the bonfire going on the beach and he wants us to watch it so he can change clothes," she said. "You look great!"

"Thanks! Sure, I'll be right there. Uh, Maggie, one thing."

"Sure, what?"

"Where on God's earth did you find that sweater?"

"Catalog. Like it?"

I just shook my head and said, "Yeah, I love it."

We walked to Stella Maris as we had done as children, the Hamilton parade of Island veterans, past the dark looming forts to our beautiful little church. Even my heathen brothers had decided to come.

"Who's on the altar?" Henry asked as we walked.

"You won't believe it," Maggie said. "Remember Ben Michaels?"

"The guy who ate thirty hot dogs on the Fourth of July? The pinball wizard? The shag king of the Isle of Palms?"

"Yep, same one. Went to Catholic University, became a priest, did ten years in the Amazon as a missionary and then the bishop gave him our parish," Maggie said.

"Holy shit," Henry said.

" 'Holy shit' is your uncle's idea of prayer," Timmy said to Beth.

"Don't make jokes," I said, "the guy's a brilliant priest. Stella Maris has over seven hundred families."

"Hold on, Susan," Henry said. "You still going to Mass?"

"Yeah, and lightning's gonna fry your bongee butt when you walk in the door," I said. *Bongee* is the Gullah term for the ridiculous or the stupid.

At ten-thirty we filed into Stella Maris and it took three pews to hold all of us. Over one hundred people couldn't even get in and had to watch the Mass on a TV monitor in the church hall next door. There were people in church whom I had no idea were even remotely religious.

Henry and Timmy probably hadn't even been to Mass since their children were baptized. The idea of voluntary attendance to church was beyond them now. Henry was so "of the world" and Timmy was so "out of the world" — searching for clarity of man's psyche. But, once we were gathered together as a family going to church together, we all got into it.

Father Michaels watched us file in and rolled his eyes at our numbers. He shook each family member's hand soundly, welcoming us. He was a tall man in his early fifties. His salt-and-pepper hair was beautiful and his paunch was an indication that the widows on Sullivan's Island saw to it that he never missed a meal. Every member of his flock knew he loved a good dinner. It was a small earthly indulgence for the man who guided the spiritual lives of so many.

We sang with the choir, off-key of course. Our ungodly sounds sent ripples of giggles through the children. There was the predictable snoring from some of the men who had been overserved at dinner and the occasional wail of a child.

Father Michaels's sermon was mercifully short. He had a reputation for three-minute homilies, tightly written, provocative and insightful. His words centered on the true meaning of Christianity. That it was all about love. Love of God, love of self, love of family, love of community. Love was a gift. He talked for a minute about compassion, and what constituted a gift, coming back again to his theme of love. In closing he wished us a future filled with hope and love. My heart began to ache for Tom and I prayed harder than I ever had for his recovery.

Father Michaels turned back to the altar to begin the second part of the Mass.

"Look!" an old man cried out. "The Virgin Mother is smiling!"

"Hush! Look!" an old woman called. "She's smiling at all of us!"

I looked up to the painted plaster statue of Mary, the Mother of Christ, over the altar. I had been in the midst of trying to cut a deal with my maker on Tom's behalf. I couldn't see anything unusual in the statue at all.

A small group of dazed old people began to make their way to the center aisle of the church. Their arms were raised and tears streamed down their faces. They appeared to be in a trance. As they approached the altar, Father Michaels, who was bewildered by the whole scene, stopped them short of coming on the altar. The church was so silent his whispering voice could be heard in the choir loft.

"Tell me what you see," Father Michaels said to the group.

"She's beautiful," the old man said, "she's smiling at me, at all of us."

Father Michaels turned again to face the statue. The altar boys shrugged their shoulders and looked too. I saw nothing. I looked at Beth, Maggie, Henry, Timmy and Grant. They shook their heads. Did we really expect the Blessed Mother to show herself to us? The notorious Hamilton clan? No way.

"Mother of God, pray for us!"

Father Michaels fell to his knees and began to say the Prayer Before the Rosary. There was a lot of rustling as women dug in their purses and men in their pockets for their rosaries. The entire church — including the Hamilton clan, rosary-less, slightly terrified and sinful — prayed with him.

We began the Joyful Mysteries, following Father Michaels's lead.

"Concentrate on the Annunciation," he said, "consider the humility with which Mary accepted the visitation of the Angel Gabriel and the role he told her she would play as the Mother of God."

Humility, I thought, there's precious little of that in me. *O Lord,* I prayed, *please teach me to be humble.* I held Beth's hand and we prayed together with the congregation.

"Hail Mary, full of grace."

We prayed the ten Hail Marys, one Lord's Prayer and one Glory Be. Then Father Michaels added another prayer.

"O my Jesus, forgive us our sins, save us from the fires of hell, take all souls to heaven, and help especially those most in need of your mercy," he said.

"Let's pray for Daddy, Beth," I whispered. "He's most in need of mercy right now."

She squeezed her eyes tight but the tears escaped anyway. I put my arm around her and choked back my own sobs. *Please, God, please make Tom better. Please. I don't want my daughter to lose her father as I lost mine. It just always hurt so much, not having my daddy. We never had a chance to make it right between us.*

Father Michaels began the second decade.

"Think of the visitation and concentrate on charity. The Blessed Mother visited her cousin Elizabeth before Jesus was born. Think of your charity toward your neighbors."

We began another string of ten Hail Marys. Our prayers were so devout you could feel an electric pulse in the crowd. Suddenly, Stella Maris was filled with bright white light and the unmistakable scent of roses. No one, not even I, could deny that that much had absolutely happened. It was a miracle, proof that God existed, at least it was enough for me. I held Beth's hand and we prayed together. As the rosary ended, Father Michaels began to distribute Communion. Every single person in the church lined up to receive it.

Finally, the Mass was ended.

"Go in peace to love and serve the Lord," Father Michaels said.

"Thanks be to God," the congregation roared.

The bright light faded and the smell of roses gradually dissipated into the thick musk smell of incense. Outside, people were crying tears of joy, exclaiming renewed faith. We gathered together, puzzled, sobered and confused. The church bells began to ring.

We began the walk home to see the fireworks, stunned by what we had witnessed.

"I don't know. Mass hallucination," Timmy said. "But I can't say I didn't see the change in light."

"Me either," Henry said. "Damn. I guess I'd better go to confession."

"I need a drink," Grant said. "That was the strangest thing I've ever seen."

"What do y'all expect?" I said. "This is the Lowcountry, after all."

"I brought a beautiful bottle of Corton Charlemagne," Henry said.

"Hey, Henry," Grant said, "no offense, bubba, but I don't think any chicken shit wine spodie odie is gonna do it. I need a real drink."

"Me too," Henry said, "the wine will keep."

"Me three," Timmy said.

It was near midnight. We decided to walk home along the beach. The sky was filled with stars and the moon hung over our shoulders. We passed bonfire after bonfire, wishing everyone well. The beach was filled with people and music played from portable stereos. I held Beth's hand, noting silently that it was now the same size as mine. I couldn't help but remember when it had been so tiny. How she had grown. I was filled with memories.

"I'm nearly a grown-up, Momma," Beth said. She seemed to be reading my mind.

"You'll always be my little girl," I said.

"Even when I'm old and you're old too?"

"You bet. I expect you to sit on my lap once a day for the rest of your life."

"Momma, what are we gonna do if Daddy

doesn't make it?" she asked.

I looked out at the ocean. I could feel her fear. I knew she worried that if she could lose him, she could lose me. She wasn't nearly grown and what was grown anyway?

There were things I needed to say to Beth and now was as good a time as any. I led her over to a sand dune and we climbed together to the top. A cold December breeze came up from nowhere and blew our hair back away from our faces. We looked at each other in the blue light of darkness. I put my hands on her shoulders and held them tight.

"Beth, listen to me. This is a night to remember. It's a turning point for you, and for everyone. You will remember what we did, who was here and everything that happened, like it was yesterday. For all of your life you'll remember."

"What are you talking about?"

"I'm gonna tell you something about your daddy. First of all, I think he's gonna make it. But if he doesn't, he's never gonna leave you, Beth. The people you love never leave you and as long as you love him, he'll live. I know this is true, as sure as you and I are here."

"Yeah, I know, but he won't really be here. He'll be gone. Your daddy left you, Livvie left you, your momma left. Momma, face it, when people die, they leave."

"No, they don't. It's that simple, Beth. If you want them, they come. I swear it."

She was quiet while her eyes searched my face. She saw me smiling and I knew she was reading my mind again. "The mirror, right?" she said.

"How did you know?"

"Momma, I've been talking to that mirror since forever!"

We burst out laughing, slapped high and low fives, and then hugged like a mother and child octopus. Laughing. Laughing. Laughter of hope, laughter of love.

"Beth, that weird old mirror is only one of many ways," I said. "I think prayer works, meditation works. Hell, honey, in fifty years they'll invent a telephone or something."

I hugged her with all my might. "You love your daddy and he'll never leave you. Of course, you'll have to find out a lot of things for yourself. Just don't wait too long to start. Life's precious."

"Yes. It is." There was no beebop in her tone now. "I'm gonna make you proud, Momma. Daddy too."

"You already do, baby. God, I love you so much."

From down the beach I saw Maggie and Henry coming toward us. There was a loud boom and the first fountain of fireworks burst against the sky. It was midnight and the dawn of the new millennium.

"Coming!" I grabbed Beth and we ran down the dune to them. "Hey! Who's watching our fire?"

"Oh, an old friend," Henry said.

We were about a hundred feet away from home when I saw the figure of a man throwing logs on our fire. He turned to face us.

"Hey, Suz!"

I'd have known that voice anywhere.

"Simon?" I said to Maggie, who nodded her head at me, smiling. "Simon!"

"Susan!" he called back.

I ran to him. He held out his arms and hugged me so hard I thought I'd break. His gorgeous curls were close-cropped and shot with silver. I was positively giddy.

"Just where have you been?" I said.

"Been busy. I heard you needed a friend." He was laughing at me.

"Boy, do I ever! Hey, you look pretty good for an octogenarian," I mumbled.

"I'm *not* an octogenarian."

I wiggled and pretended to resist his arms around me, but I was grinning from ear to ear. He burst out laughing again and then so did I. I didn't know how I'd missed him until I saw him again. He looked at me and I knew his lips were headed for mine, and then he kissed me.

"You make me feel like boneless chicken, boy," I said.

"You make me feel carbonated, girl," he said.

"You're one romantic son of a gun. Still got all your hair? Lemme see! Is this a rug?"

He swatted me on the backside and I jumped away.

I looked up and saw Maggie there with Grant, Beth and everyone.

"Happy New Year," we called out as we hugged and kissed each other.

"You have to be the one and only Simon," Beth said.

"My God, she's a screaming beauty," Simon said, winning Beth in one swoop.

"Just like my momma," she said.

"Yep, just like your momma."

If they thought so, it was fine with me.

The fireworks went on for over an hour, and the church bells continued ringing. The sky was filled with explosions of white, red, green — every color I could name. I couldn't stop looking at Simon. He held my hand and looked over at me every few minutes. My skin crawled with goose bumps.

"Let's go for a walk," he said, finally.

"Hey! Wait for me!" Beth said.

We reached out for her and held hands as we walked toward the end of the Island. It took no effort to fall in love all over again. As the fireworks boomed and burst we squealed and yelled together. When they finally ended, we rejoined the others, put out our bonfire and gave everyone something to carry inside.

"I have to get my suitcase out of the car," Simon said.

"I'll give you a hand," I said.

"By the way, how was church?"

"We got our money's worth," I said, thinking that when he heard the story, he'd say we were all a bunch of crackpots.

Beth went ahead of us with her cousins, but not before turning to me and giving me a wink.

"Great girl," Simon said.

"Yeah, thanks." I took a deep breath and walked around the side of the house with him. His car, with Georgia tags, was a new white Lexus.

"Cool car," I said.

"The seats fold down," he said.

"You, suh, are a lecherous pig," I said.

"Yeah, I am. Come here to me."

"What?"

He kissed me again, and I felt that old feeling in the pit of my stomach like I was going to sink. Livvie always said that when you met the man of your dreams, you would know. This was a bit like getting clobbered on the head. He pushed me against the car and leaned against me. When he kissed me for the third time, I knew he meant business.

"You still want me, don't you?" I said, laughing.

"Yeah, and this time I'm going to have you."

"Don't you think you should at least send a girl flowers first, Mister Big Shot Infectious Disease Doctor?"

"You're right. It was a most insensitive thing to say. I'll have to buy you a diamond bigger than the one old Stanley gave your mother," he said. "Susan, one way or another, Tom or no Tom, you're mine. Do you understand me?"

"Yes, I do."

"Well, as long as that's settled, let's get a beer," he said.

EPILOGUE

The Year 2000

I was taking down the Christmas decorations, trying to get my house back to normal. The tree had lasted well, but a shower of pine needles came down with each ornament I removed. The big gilt mirror reflected my movements. I wondered if anyone was watching me. I had the feeling someone was.

The holidays never passed without a deluge of memories about Livvie. I thought about the Thanksgiving that Daddy had died and how she brought us that mangy dog that we all loved. I thought about how she spoiled us as we wished someone would and how she had given me the courage to go away to school. I wondered if she could see us, if she'd be proud of us, Beth and me.

I thought about Livvie so hard and wanted her to see me so badly that I started getting emotional and felt a surge of tears rising, wishing I had a nickel for every tear I had shed in the past year.

The mirror became foggy. I wiped my eyes and stared again. There she was. I saw Livvie standing in front of me with a man, as clear as day. I began to shake all over with excitement. Livvie stood still and I realized it must be her husband whose arm she held so tightly. It was really Livvie and I was joyous. I whispered to them.

"Oh, my God! Happy New Year, Livvie! And you must be Nelson!"

He nodded his head, leaned in and kissed Livvie on the cheek. Her smile was pure happiness.

"Is this a dream?"

"No, chile, the sheets was a dream, but this is for real!"

"It was you! It was really you! You were trying to tell me about Mr. Struthers and Fat Albert! How did you know?"

"Chile, I'm in the place of knowing. Ain't no lies 'eah."

"Have you seen either one of them?"

"Can't rightly say, but I hear tell Mr. Marvin coming 'eah soon. He done his time to repent."

"And what about Fat Albert?"

"I think he done open up a barbecue place down south. Don't think he gone be 'eah. No, ain't got no room for poor old Albert."

"Hell? He's in hell?"

"Ain't never seen no hell, but if you ain't 'eah, you is there!"

"So you made it to paradise and you found Nelson! I'm so happy for you!" I couldn't think of what to say so I said, "Seen Momma lately?" Tears flowed down my cheeks in spite of my attempts to stop them.

Livvie shook her head, smiling. *"Don't fret about your momma. She fine."*

"Well, when you see her, tell her I asked about

her, okay? Tell her that I understand now. God, I miss you, Livvie, I love you, you know."

She smiled and nodded her head. In my mind I could hear her say, *"Me too, chile, me too! But I got my Nelson. What about you? You gone finally give your heart to Simon?"*

"Livvie, Tom's had cancer. Simon's back in Atlanta for now. Things have been pretty complicated! If you were 'eah with me, it would be so much easier! You'd tell me what to do."

"But, chile, ain't I 'eah now? Ain't I 'eah? Did you think I ever gone leave you? And don't you know what to do?"

"Yes, I know what to do. Give my trouble to the Lord, right?"

"That's right. And use that brain of yours!"

"What's gonna happen to Tom, Livvie? What can I do?"

"Say your prayers, girl. Prayers work miracles; don't you see that much yet?"

"You know, Livvie, I think I was as smart at thirteen as I was ever going to be. Seems like I haven't learned much at all."

"Now, why was you so smart at thirteen? 'Cause you had a situation to rise above! Ain't you back there again?"

"You mean the time's come to rise?"

"The time has come to rise up and take your place again. I love you, baby. Don't be afraid to love. Iffin you love Simon, don't be afraid. And don't worry about Tom."

"Buck up, right? Just go for it?" She nodded her head to me. I was laughing now through my tears, tears of joy, tears of relief. I could feel her starting to leave and I concentrated with all my might to hold her with me a moment longer. "I love you, Livvie, forever."

I was whispering to her. Love. It mystically transcended death. It healed hearts. It changed thoughts. And when you met it head-on, it gave you courage in return. I put my hand up to the mirror and she held hers to meet mine. The mirror was warm. I would have given anything to hold her hand, but the warmth was there. She faded away until she and Nelson were visible no more. Finally I saw just my own reflection.

Maybe the scent of roses, the bright light and the alleged vision of the Blessed Mother at Stella Maris had been a mass hallucination of some kind. I wasn't sure. Maybe seeing Livvie now had been some kind of desperate act of my unconscious. How could I judge? There was no question that Livvie had visited me in my dream. If she could come to me in a dream, then why couldn't she visit me through the mirror?

I had this sudden urge to turn and look all around me — to take it all in. The tree coming down, the table of photographs, the old armoire Tom and I had salvaged. Salvage. That was the order of the day for me — my cosmic marching orders.

I threw myself on the couch and lit a Marlboro Light, then put it out after the first puff, knowing I didn't need them anymore. Okay, I'd go to the drugstore and get the patch to help, just in case I felt weak. I couldn't help but laugh at myself and what had just occurred with Livvie's visit. I would pray like mad for Tom and get the whole family to do the same. Better yet, I'd get the whole congregation of Stella Maris to pray. And what of Simon? I already knew the answer to that. The energy I felt made me euphoric with hope. I knew everything was going to be all right. Yeah, even I — cynical Susan Hamilton Hayes — had to admit that just about anything was possible. At last, at long last, I could rest in the sweet arms of peace.

Author's Note

I could tell you real stories about my family and all the good people of Sullivan's Island and Charleston and go on and on. I could tell you about how, on the Island, from the last day of school in spring until the first day of school in fall, I knew no kids who wore shoes, just flip-flops that we bought at Miss Buddy's or Bert's for twenty-nine cents. And that any kid who owned Keds, especially if they were clean, was immediately branded an intruder from the outside world.

I could wax on about the summer days spent running free with my cousins — filling an empty coffee can with blackberries, wild plums and chainey briar (wild asparagus) and climbing the water towers — and how anyone with a bicycle of their own was obliged to tow kids who didn't have one. How we spied through the windows of summer renters and smoked stolen cigarettes under their houses in the winter and that our specialty was digging holes to China.

Once we did that at my Uncle Teddy's and then somebody — one of my Blanchard cousins, I think — got the brilliant idea to fill it up with water and make a swimming pool. The hose was devoured by the hole so, knowing Uncle Teddy would tell our father, we covered the whole mess with some planks of wood. Well, he must've gotten suspicious about the hose being pulled from across the yard to under the house. He went down there after supper. It was dark, he moved the boards, fell in the hole and got covered in mud. He beat our behinds with his brown leather slipper and told us to never tell Daddy. His version of a beating resembled the way Ella Wright — a.k.a. Miss Fuzz — who was my Livvie, plumped pillows. We hollered our heads off to make sure he thought it was enough and then we laughed about it for a million years.

If you ever meet my cousin Michael McInerny, he'll tell you the story about how he and his friends — I guess they must have been nine or ten — caught the biggest crabs on Sullivan's Island and sold them to all the mothers in his neighborhood. In later years he found out the reason the crabs were so large was that he was crabbing at the Island sewage pipe! What could the family do but give him full credit for pioneering recycling?

And what about the ghost stories? People would tell them at night on dark porches and scare themselves half to death. Of course, I would listen to them and snicker, thinking they should have a big mirror like ours. They would sleep with a light on for the rest of their lives! Yes, that part about the mirror is actually all true.

In the old days, there were lemonade stands and there still are today, and ball games of "half rubber," which is a Lowcountry version of stickball played with a broomstick and, you guessed it, a rubber ball cut in half. There were shag contests at Folly Pier, before it fell in the ocean, and sneaking into Big John's and the Merchant Seamen's Club with fake IDs to drink Singapore slings and beer when it was sweltering outside.

There were friends who went to Vietnam and others who fled to Canada. We burned our bras for women's rights in the same fires that made ashes of our brothers' draft cards. We argued civil rights until we were exhausted and then started over the next day. We rebelled against everything we thought was wrong. Good old boys grew long hair and traded beer drinking for pot smoking and Weejuns for sandals. And then, eventually, we buried our parents and became them, clinging to Lowcountry life with all the fervor of an Evangelical Revival, rather satisfied.

So many stories, too many to tell here. We don't live there now, but maybe someday that will change. Someday I'll have a home for my family on the Island.

Another time, we will shag, I'll teach you a little Gullah poem and we'll argue on how to make use of an entire ham. We will stroll down to the Sullivan's Island beach at dawn, talking hurricanes, tide tables and sand castles. You will spread your arms in the eastern wind and feel the sun rise in every one of your bones. Once the sand of Sullivan's Island gets in your shoes, your heart will ache to return. And return you will. You will be one of us. You won't mind being a little bit Geechee.

As the heat and light of day begin to rise and glow, I'll feed you a Lowcountry breakfast of warm salted air and, smiling, you will tell all these stories to your friends until you think they're your own. You will hum this music of so much magic forever. Yes, you will. 'Eah?

The employees of G.K. Hall hope you have enjoyed this Large Print book. All our Large Print titles are designed for easy reading, and all our books are made to last. Other G.K. Hall books are available at your library, through selected bookstores, or directly from us.

For information about titles, please call:

(800) 257-5157

To share your comments, please write:

Publisher
G.K. Hall & Co.
P.O. Box 159
Thorndike, ME 04986